# THE FUNERAL CRITIC

### RENALD IACOVELLI

STONE
TOWER
PRESS

Copyright © 2022 by Renald Iacovelli

Cover photograph: Foggy Landscape @ jplenim
(www.coolfreepix.com)

STONE
TOWER
PRESS

Stone Tower Press
New York, NY

ISBN: 978-0-9852181-9-5

*Printed in the United States of America*

# THE FUNERAL CRITIC

# CONTENTS

# I
## PRELIMINARIES

Let me begin by saying that the "Natural Burial" movement must be stopped! If I hear or read one more time about people who are dispensing with a proper funeral in order to plant their friends and relatives in the ground without a casket for the sake of "environmental friendliness";—just wrapping them in a sheet and plunking them into the dirt as though they were so many potato plants or pumpkin seeds;—if I hear or read about this one more time I am going to scream! Because it's just another indication of the coarsening of our society, of the degradation of the human being. And though the advocates of this degraded phenomenon like to present it in the wholesome aura of a "return to nature," I suspect that in ninety-nine cases out of a hundred the real motivation is cheapness. For let's face it: people are selfish. They want to spend their money on themselves. They'll splurge and even put themselves in debt to buy a big house, a new car, the latest computer or smartphone, but boy oh boy how they squawk about high prices when it comes to shelling out a few extra bucks to upgrade Mom's casket! Just deplorable! And I am not exaggerating. I've seen it for myself! I once had a neighbor—let's call him Beau (he was a handsome fellow)—who lived with a tippling uncle who passed away in his sleep after polishing off half a bottle of cheap Polish vodka. Beau knocked on my door early in the morning in a panic to tell me what had happened and to ask me what he should do. I told him to notify the police and then begin contacting funeral homes, which he did in just that order, and two days later he came back to me complaining about the expensiveness of funerals and saying he wasn't sure if he could afford one;—this from a man who had a well-paying job and had been living rent-free for years. I sought to help him out by contacting several funeral homes and getting prices on their various "packages," and I had found one within his means (he had told me how much he was "able" to spend) when he informed me that he had decided to forego a funeral altogether.

"What do you mean?" I asked,

"Oh, it's not necessary, they have other things now," he said.

"Like what?"

After an embarrassed clearing of his throat he told me he had gotten in touch through the Internet with a "green burial society" which had instructed him how to dispense with his uncle's body in a "dignified, no-frills service" for less than $200. I happened to be drinking some orange juice at the time and when he told me that I nearly choked. $200! I told him that he had to be joking. There were some meals in a restaurant, I said, which cost more than that. Was he really going to be such a cheapskate toward a relative whom he had lived with for the last ten years and supposedly loved or at least felt some affection for? I tried to argue him out of it, but to no avail. Less than a week later he informed me that his poor uncle's booze-pickled body had been "laid to rest" upstate in some horribly anonymous field abutting a soybean farm. The headstone was nothing more than a large rock, no bigger than a coffee mug, inscribed with his uncle's name and dates of birth and death. It was not even anchored in place, and two months later it was washed away by a nor'easter.

The fact that the headstone, or rather the inscribed rock, had been washed away was of no concern to Beau. He had been too fully indoctrinated in the propaganda of the natural burial movement, according to which there is something noble in the obliteration of all traces of one's life—in it being as whirled away, as forgotten, as the dust of the earth; an attitude which those in the movement, otherwise heathen through and through, love to justify by quoting the Bible passage "for dust thou art, and unto dust shalt thou return." But that passage was loony when it was written and is even more loony now. For how insulting and degrading to compare human beings, with all their hopes and dreams and struggles, to particles of dirt! If God himself were to come down from heaven and promulgate such a doctrine amid a fury of thunder and lightning I (unlike the scampering cowards around me) would stand up to Him, shake my fist in His face, and bellow back, "How dare you!"

—For consider what stamina, what bravery, what resilience are required to live even the average life. You enter the world a helpless quivering being, thrust into the light and cold, into a confusion of sights and sounds, of movements and colors and voices which shock the mind into cries of terror or overwhelm it into mute wonder;—then follow all those slow years of uncertainty and confusion, of learning how to speak, how to communicate, how to interpret gestures and tones of voice, of learning what is good and bad, of what is allowed and forbidden, of who you and the people around you are;—along the way enduring the sicknesses of early childhood, the colds and measles and chicken pox which cause one to spend so many nights feverish and sweating, coughing and crying;—and then, just when you have developed a little strength and a few certainties about life, just when you feel secure in your sense of the world, you are thrust out of it into the indentured slavery of schooling, whose ruthlessly rigid regimen will afflict you for the next fifteen or twenty years, forcing you to hateful studies, to sitting still and captive for countless hours as teachers pump information into your head though it were a bottomless slop bucket, even as the world outside, all sunlight and fresh air, beckons you to freedom and life;—always having to study more, to remember more, to pass the next test, to get ahead, to prove yourself over and over, even though you are only seven or ten or fifteen years old;—all the while pummeled with the anxieties common to childhood, such as whether or not you will gain the friendship of the popular kids, or win the approval of the pretty girl who has stolen your heart, and more frequently than not rebuffed by the former and scorned by the latter; —straining to maintain your composure, to hold up under an endless succession of demands and disappointments, and able to do so only because the hundred little emotional injuries already received have calloused your soul and made it a little more resistant to injury;—while you long for the day when there will be no more tiresome subjects to study, no more teachers to appease, no more tests to take, no more peers to contend with;—when the whole devilish business will be done with, and you will finally be "free";—only to find that freedom means leaving one set of problems for another just as bad, the mean teachers having become demanding bosses, the hateful studies having become the hateful job to which you are crucified by the fear of poverty; a job repetitive, alienating, calling up not the best in you but on the contrary smashing down whatever good in you there is, so that your mind is benumbed and your heart is broken, and from which the only respite are the weekends, which can never come fast enough and are too quickly over, or some yearly "vacation" consisting of a measly two weeks out of the whole year and which gives you only an illusion of freedom, is but an enticing sop to keep you trudging on the treadmill;—and sure enough you trudge on, hoping for change, hoping that next year will be better, happier, easier;—but it never is;—becoming, on the contrary, more difficult, more frustrating, more disillusioning, partly because in growing older you have less stamina to endure the physical demands made on you, and partly because experience has shown you how unlikely change is; and eventually you resign yourself to it all with the trite formula, "Well, that's the way it is for everyone," and find solace in that last refuge of the defeated, namely, in being "grateful for what you have," in "looking on the bright side of things";— till four or five decades have passed and you are left old, tired, sometimes sick, and stranded with the benumbing realization that time has run out and you are left standing on that cold, dark, miserable place at the brink of Eternity.

Good heavens! Who, after having endured the all this, as most of us do, doesn't deserve at least a decent funeral?

The problem is that most of the time what goes for a "decent funeral" never is. It means no more than a *traditional* funeral, which is *in*decent. For anxiety surrounds it, sorrow invests it, and after it is over the memory of it darkly dogs one's steps like a nightmare impossible to shake off. Insofar as almost everything about it is negative, it dishonors the dead and increases the misery of the living for whom it was meant to be (as the obscenely blithe phrase has it) a "part of the healing process." What is to account for the stark yet easily accepted discrepancy between intention and result?—between the reality and the charade? How is it that mature men and women, who would never allow themselves to be so taken advantage of in any other circumstance, blithely accept being bamboozled and abused in this one? The answer is that even worldly-wise people are kowtowed by the force of convention. Human beings are social animals, are born followers, with an instinctive need to be accepted into, to be part of, the herd. The essential humanity by which people are revolted by funerals is controverted and held in check by an indoctrination so early that it seems to be second nature. No wonder that misanthropes like to call people sheep.

—Nor was I, for a long time, any different. "Baa baa!" I said, along with everyone else, not only in the matter of funerals but in so many other things. For a long time nothing out of my mouth too but "Baa baa!" Baaing in school; baaing at play; baaing at the dinner table; baaing to get along, to obey, to be liked, to get ahead; baa baa baa baa!   Only—and here is the main thing—my color was decidedly *black*. I made the same sounds as everyone else, but these came from a somewhat different animal. I *sounded* the same: but I *was* not. And despite the anatomical sameness of the eyes of sheep white and black, those of the latter *do* see things somewhat differently;—a difference which was bound, sooner or later, to make itself apparent.

In my case they began to see things differently with the death of my paternal grandparents. They both lived into their nineties. They had Roman Catholic funeral services. The Catholic faith is notable for its pomp and panoply; thus there was no good reason why their funerals couldn't have been elevated by the diverting spectacles possible through their faith. Instead they were the typical horrors of doom and gloom. The church services were long and tedious, and for my grandmother's funeral music was provided by an organist and a two-bit local opera singer who belted out "Ave Maria" while making strange faces when she hit the high notes. At one point she "acted out" her rendition by extending her arms as though she were performing in a cabaret—which was bad form. In both services the officiating priests had about as much charisma as week-old bread, and their eulogies were mumbled messes. The funeral corteges on their way to the cemetery formed a long, slow, morose nuisance to other drivers. By the time most of the guests arrived at the gravesite they were so bored or depressed that they were ready to jump into the ground themselves.

But the worst parts of both events were the receptions. Somehow or other it had become the custom in that time and place to have it in the church building itself or in some annexed space—it was so long ago that I can't remember exactly where it was. At any rate it was a barren room outfitted with a couple of long tables covered in white paper by way of tablecloths and set with paper plates and plastic utensils. The food was cheap and starchy: pastas, potatoes, breads, rice dishes; and the culinary offense was topped off with bottles of soda and plastic party cups to drink out of. A children's birthday party would have had more nutritious and tastier fare.

Everyone tried to cheer up a little. Everyone tried to put the funeral and the burial in the past. There was light chatter and a burgeoning, if sometimes forced, sense that the worst was over, that we had all, as it were, weathered a storm and could breathe a little easier. Someone had brought her infant child, which she showed with overt pride, often holding it up, tickling it, cooing to it, so that its little arms and legs flailed in the air and a delightful smile lit up its cherubic face;—as though to show everyone that loss of the old generation was offset with the arrival of the new. Yet this attempt to emphasize the positive aspect of life was not successful because it was too little and too late as an anodyne to the negative atmosphere and emotions everyone had experienced for hours beforehand. There were easy conversations, there were occasional outbursts of laughter or good cheer, but they could not for more

than a few seconds disguise the sense of regret, almost of doom, which had descended on everyone
like a leaden veil.

In the following years I attended a few more
family funerals and they were all offensive.  And
then it occurred to me: Why *should* people have to
endure such things?  Are we manacled, in chains,
led forcibly before these outrageous spectacles of the
macabre?  Are we not the masters of our own fate?
Surely the first rule of individual life is self-preservation, a variation of which is avoiding exposure to
anything which would psychologically injure us—
and funerals certainly fell into that miserable category.  As I was by then eighteen years old, and not
easily forced to do anything I didn't want to do, I
made the decision: Never again!  I would never
again step into a funeral parlor.  And surely no one
could blame me for this any more than I could be
blamed for not wanting to stick my hand into fire.

How wrong I was!  What an uproar it caused!
"But she was your aunt!" or "But he was your uncle!" or "He was your cousin, for God's sake!"—such
were the formulas flung in reprimand at me, the at-
tempts to make me feel guilty and change my mind.
But by then I had seen the matter too clearly.  I
had thought it out too fully, knew what was what,
and was not about to be intimidated.  I shook my
head and said serenely, "Nope" or "Sorry" or, more
often, seeing the futility of answering, said nothing
at all.  If people didn't like my decision—too bad: it
was their problem, not mine.  I would not allow myself to be abused.

My aunt, whom I lived with growing up, was a
stickler for convention, and who, like so many

weak-willed or thoughtless people, derived her sense of self-esteem from how she was regarded by others, was appalled at my newfound conviction. She vainly tried to argue me out of it, regurgitating the reasons which she had unquestioningly imbibed since childhood. When she saw that none of her arguments had budged me an inch, and a few of them had even made me laugh with contempt, she drew her ace card:

"And what about me?" she asked. "Is that what you're going to do to me when I die?—huh? Not go to my funeral, either?"

"Exactly."

"Oh! How can you do that to me!" she said, horrified.

"It has nothing to do with you. It has to do with me."

"What? What is that supposed to mean?"

"I've told you a dozen times, I refuse to allow myself to be abused."

"What are you talking about, 'abused'? You don't want to see me put into the ground?"

"Thanks for the invitation, but I think I'll pass."

"But you can't 'pass'! Nobody gets to 'pass'! Are you out of your mind?"

"On the contrary, I'm very much in my mind and I'd like to stay there."

"But what about me! How do you think I'm going to feel if you're not at my funeral?"

"Now I know you're joking."

"I'm not joking! I'm serious! You have to be there. If you're not there it's a ... a terrible, terrible thing!"

"Why are you eager to see me tormented? That's

not very nice."

"You're supposed to be tormented! That's the whole point of a funeral!"

The poor dear woman: good in so many ways: honest, careful of my welfare, a good housekeeper, usually kind; but a born follower, and her powers of reasoning somewhat less than acute. In the end I assured her that I had only been "kidding around," and that I wouldn't miss her funeral for the world; which was of course a lie—but only a small one, only a little white one, very understandable, very forgivable, even somewhat admirable in light of the circumstances: in how much better it made her feel, and how little it cost me to say it. But costing me, some might say, my "integrity"? My dear friends, integrity doesn't amount to a hill of beans, and may rather amount to a mountain of dung, if it makes people more miserable than they need be—if it hurts rather than helps them. Adhesion to truth is a lovely ideal but if applied to every petty vicissi- tude and concern of life it sinks to a mean-spirited and degraded indifference to the wellbeing of others. I made my poor aunt as happy as I could while she was alive because she was incapable of understand- ing that once we are gone we are beyond all know- ing or caring about what is done by those who survive us. As it happened, I didn't attend her fu- neral and I'm pretty sure she wasn't aware of my absence.

My short and intense conversation with my aunt, recorded above, remained with me for years afterwards and was instrumental in my becoming a critic, for it helped me understand that people at- tended funerals mostly out of a grim sense of duty.

They hated, they loathed going to them, yet continued doing so as though they had been enchanted out of their own will, repeating to themselves the self-mesmerizing mantra, "It's the right thing to do … it's the right thing to do …"; or, if they had been close to the deceased, convincing themselves that their attendance would be part of their own "healing process"—even as the very thought of the ceremony intensified their sorrow.

This is why, in an ideal world, the family of the deceased are precisely the ones who should not attend the funeral. The saddest, hardest, most crushing day of their lives is often not the death of their loved one but the funeral service which shamelessly emphasizes and embellishes it. Instead of distracting their attention away from their loss, it plunges the hot blade of despair deeper into their hearts. Instead of guiding them to a peaceful shore, it casts them adrift onto endless seas of sorrow.

The problem with funerals—as I came to discover—was that they concentrated on death, which is inevitable and over which we have no control, rather than on life, which never more than after a death needs to be affirmed and celebrated. Thus the very basis and intention of the service were mistaken, and this was the less excusable because it was a matter of our choosing. Man (as Protagoras says) is the measure of all things; thus it is up to us to create or choose that which makes our lives better. Just because a maniac, or a group of maniacs, thousands of years ago, decided that funerals should be depressing and horrible in every way, does that mean that we have to do the same thing? Of course not! How utterly stupid to think so! It was time to relegate such life-poisoning attitudes to the dust heap of barbaric history! It was time to start afresh, and innocently and honestly accept as a first principle that it is always better to feel good than to feel bad, and that it not only behooves us to alleviate our distress and sadness at the passing of loved ones, but that we only truly honor their memory by doing so.

The first step in this reformation calls for the frank admission of our mortality. But people already know they are mortal? Yes; intellectually; but not emotionally, not morally. We all know we will die one day but for all that it seems a shadowy unreality. We usually think about it only when it happens to other people, and even then do not consider how each death we hear about brings us closer to our own. Day by day we go through the routine of our lives unaware that, every minute of it, we are being surveilled by death. It skulks around us at every hour of the day: while at our jobs, while watching television in our living rooms, while taking a shower, while eating in restaurants, while lying in bed asleep:—it lurks in the darkened corners or behind the curtains of our rooms, always peering out at us, noting our existence and awaiting the moment to strike—a stealthy, patient murderer stalking us from the moment of our birth. But just as exposing a stalker often shows him to be a puny, timid, ineffective character who resorts to surreptitiousness for want of courage to show himself outrightly, we are likely to find that in pulling death out of shadows and into the clear light of scrutiny, it is far less intimidating than we had supposed; in fact, the brighter the light we shine on it, the more it shows itself to be a bugaboo. We then find ourselves agreeing with Epicurus when he said that death has nothing to do with us, that between it and us there is an unbridgeable gulf, because so long as we exist, it cannot be, and when it comes, we do not exist. We rightly abhor the process of dying, for we are the embodiment of the will to life, but we should keep in mind that when our "moment" comes it will not be for us—we will not know it—but for those who survive us. They will mourn for us, or not; say good things about us, or not; remember us fondly or with a sneer of dislike; and as the world bustles along as it always has we will be a —————.

As funerals are, then, less for the dead than for the living, we must shift the focus away from the deceased (who in his physical condition must always be disagreeable) to the particulars of the ceremony, which can offer opportunities to create positive impressions for the benefit of the attendees. This objective can perhaps best be achieved by adopting the following notion:

*The funeral as a work of art.*

Like a fine painting, like a joyful piece of music, the service should elevate the spirit in a healthy, upward direction. But this is rarely the case owing to an industry which for too long has been a matter of commerce banking on convention. Today the great majority of funerals are provided by people who haven't a clue about alleviating the distress of others. For them that is a secondary consideration; the first one is to make a profit; and insofar this is the case they might as well have been lumber wholesalers or electronics merchants. Their advertisements "proudly" proclaim an eagerness to "assist families in their time of need" or to "be an integral part of the healing process"—but let the bereaved show up at their establishment without the proper, usually inordinate amount of cash required, and they are likely to have the door slammed in their faces.

In itself the profit motive is not blamable, since it is the engine behind the capitalism which, for all its shortcomings, has benefited the majority of mankind; but surely in this one instance the motive must be something more than a cold crude exchange of cash. In this one instance there really *does* have to be a genuine sympathy for others and, just as much, and perhaps more, an artistic sensibility. This is why 90% of funeral directors are not temperamentally suited to their profession: they are unprepared, or unwilling, to render the emotional assistance they pretend to offer.

Unfortunately this will not change till people in general do. We must come genuinely to believe what even to a child's mentality must seem obvious: that the well-being of the living always takes precedence over that of the dead, who are beyond needing or thinking anything. It is a fine thing to respect the dead, but it is a false, wicked, destructive thing when it is done at the expense of *dis*respecting the living. This is precisely the choice which confronts us in giving a funeral, and the rightness, the reasonableness of our choice will always depend on how much we value the light over the darkness, the good over the bad.

## II
## THE MAKING OF A CRITIC

Ihad long left home, moved to the city, and was living in an apartment building. I knew about forty of my "neighbors" by face, and four by name; which only goes to show you that if it's anonymity you're after, an apartment in a city will beat the most rural town every time. One of the people I knew by name was Mr. Beal, who lived down the hall from me. He was a chubby cheery fellow of fifty-two years old who lived with his wife and daughter. We ran into each other occasionally, saying hello and perhaps exchanging a few words about the weather. One day I learned that he had died: he had keeled over with a heart attack as he was driving into a fast-food restaurant for his daily triple cheeseburger. In the lobby of the building was posted a notice of his funeral, which was to be held at a funeral parlor two blocks away. It was supposed that many of the friendly acquaintances he had made in the building would want to attend the service, especially since it was so close by.

My grandparents' funerals had left such a strong and negative impression on me that on reading the notice of Mr. Beal's my first reaction was one of mild nausea. "Who would go to that?" I asked my-self. But a few hours later I had changed my mind, momentarily influenced by a sense of decency and showing respect for the deceased's widow and her daughter, whom I also knew and who were very sweet people. The proximity of the funeral parlor also inclined me to go, since it was only a five-minute walk away.

The funeral parlor, as the phrase goes, "served the community." Nearly everyone who died within two or three miles of it eventually wound up there because it was the only which the survivors, if they lived in the area, knew of. Its prices were suitable to the lower-middle class neighborhood in which it was situated. True to its type, it tried to recreate a "comfortable environment," a sense of home. One stepped into its foyer as though into someone's living room: the floor carpeted, padded armchairs and a couch, end tables with shaded lamps, and a few paintings of idyllic landscapes on the walls. But, also true to type, something about it undermined its attempt to put one at ease. It had a certain quiet yet odd atmosphere of the sort which characterizes the opening scenes of horror movies: everything looks as it should yet you know that behind the façade of hushed normality something terrible is lurking;—and your skin crawls. The first definitely strange thing you noticed was the doors: there were four or five or six all around—many more than in any living room you have known. The funeral director, dressed in a business suit, was there to greet attendees, asking them if they were here for So-and-so's funeral, and directing them to the open door of the visitation room. You entered it, and your skin crawled again.

In this instance the room was simple to the point of starkness. The walls were beige and undecorated. The ceiling was made of industrial tiles and inset with bright white lights. Rows of chairs were divided into left and right sections with, between them, a path—one might refer to it as the path of doom—leading to the front of the room. There the casket, lying on a bier, dominated that space like some terrible idol awaiting its sacrifice. A floral arrangement stood beside it. Behind it, set into the rear wall, was a stained-glass window without the symbolism of any particular religion but conveying a sense of spirituality by depicting a blue sky, white clouds, and rays of yellow descending from heaven.

The only things to be heard were sounds of one's own footsteps and the whimpers and sighs of the family members sitting in the front row. The widow and daughter stared at the open casket with eyes reddened from weeping. Their pale faces expressed unutterable woe over their loss and their fears for the future. I went up to them to offer my condolences, then turned to the casket and approached it.

The remains of the person there looked only vaguely, and not in a good way, like the man I had known. He was dressed, as he had never been in life, in a three-piece suit as though he were going to a business meeting. Rouge had been applied to his cheeks and red liner demarcated the outline of his lips, which were set perfectly horizontally in an expression of supreme indifference. His hair was dyed dark brown, combed severely back, and set with a gel, so that it looked like a strange plastic cap. A spotlight shone down on him and enhanced the inhuman oddness of his appearance into something downright grisly.

Perhaps half the grief the poor widow and her daughter felt came from having to endure the sight of their poor husband and father looking like a wax-work. Of course they had known that someone who was dead wasn't going to look the same way he did when he was alive: but *this* bad? He had been such an easy-going, good-humored fellow;—his face had been large, rosy, full of life and smiles;—and here he was looking like some ruthless tax collector who had been petrified and put on display;—a mean and miserable impostor!

I turned away with a shudder and took a seat in the middle of the room. For the next twenty minutes I watched as attendees intermittently trickled in, all with vaguely apprehensive faces, all dressed in black or dark colors, all going first to the family and offering their condolences, then stepping up to the deceased and gazing down on him. Depending on their tolerance for the ghastly, they stood there for either several seconds or a few minutes before turning around with expressions a little more blank and hopeless than they had come in with. They took seats among the rows of chairs and sat looking about as though they weren't sure what they ought to do next. And so we all sat there and waited.

Waited for what? For most of us, it was waiting for time to pass as quickly as possible, for the next half hour or hour to zip by so that the escape we were eager to make should not seem disrespectfully hasty. One of the many shortcomings of this funeral was its lack of a program. The guests didn't know what was to happen next. Certainly I was ready to leave as soon as I had offered my condolences to the family, and remained only because I

knew that to have walked out immediately afterwards would have been gauche. Some minutes later
another guest who took a seat next to mine, and saw
me looking at my watch, whispered to me that the
minister would be there "soon," though in fact it took
him another twenty minutes to show up. In the
meantime we all had to endure the carrying on of
the deceased's sister.

What a horrible woman! She had no respect for
anyone! She was, as her brother had been, short
and round, and was dressed in black from head to
foot, including the little hat pinned to her head. She
kept announcing herself (that is the only way to describe it) with a series of extravagant high-pitched
cries, which sounded like the inarticulate sounds of a
tortured animal. She approached the casket three
times, each time crying still more dramatically, and
one time raising her hands and calling out, "Artie!
Artie! Artie!"—her brother's name. Each time she
took her seat again at the front row she bent over,
coughing and spewing garbled words of distress,
among which we could all make out, "Oh no, oh no
no, ohhhhh noooo!"

She made the guests supremely uncomfortable.
They had come here to show their affection and support for the family, and rather than show appreciation for their effort with a dignified calm, she had, as
it were, thrown mud in their faces. I later learned
that she herself was a widow and lived alone. She
had probably been lonesome a long time and reck-
oned, consciously or not, that this was a perfect opportunity to satisfy the desire to be recognized and
fawned over. This was her "moment," and she was
determined to get as much out of it as she could. It

was cut short, however, when the Presbyterian minister arrived and the general attention shifted to him.

He was about thirty-five years old, of medium height, and rather nice-looking. When he entered the room he made directly for the widow and her daughter. He tenderly took their hands into his and expressed his heartfelt condolences. After exchanging a few whispered words with them he turned around and approached the open casket before which he stood in a pious attitude, his head bowed and his hands pressed together in prayer. When he turned back around he looked a little paler than when he had come into the room: apparently he had gotten a good look at the deceased, whose bad cosmetic work had appalled him. He quickly regained his composure, however, and gazed upon the attendees with an expression of subdued seriousness before beginning his eulogy and prayer service.

The first part of his performance was pleasant and effective: he spoke of the man, the congregationalist, he had known: of what a good father and husband he had been, of how he had donated to church events, of how he had always been eager to help those less fortunate than himself. But then he launched into things theological and spoke of the deceased's eternal "life" in heaven, of how he was there now, serenaded by the singing of the angels, joyously basking in golden glow of the Almighty, etc., etc., etc. This went on for fifteen minutes and was tiresome in the extreme. It was also insulting to most of his auditors. For they were not children, after all. They were adults, the products of a scientific, computerized age. They were also urbanites, their minds sharpened to the hard practicalities, and hardened to the sharp realities, of urban life. They could not but regard all this talk of another life in the clouds as so much hocus-pocus, ridiculous in all ways and as unbecoming in them to believe as it was for the grown man before them to speak. One could see by the way they sometimes glanced at one another that they were thinking, "Is this guy serious?" Only respect for the family prevented them from making overtly sour faces.

After the eulogy we guests were apparently expected to continue sitting there and bear the burden of the oppressive atmosphere, perhaps again approach the casket and get another horrifying eyeful of its occupant. There were no instructions about where the burial was to be. still more disturbing was the lack of information about any reception. I already sensed there would be none because the widow and her daughter had probably spent their last dime in paying for the funeral parlor and cemetery plot. The thought that I was to endure all this doom and gloom, and then be sent home, a psychological wreck and hungry to boot, began to tell on my nerves. I felt again that old sense of resentment at having allowed myself to be duped and abused. Becoming fidgety, then panicky, I couldn't bear the place any longer and, ignoring everyone who looked at me questioningly or disapprovingly, got up and walked out, no sooner stepping outside the building and into the bright light of day than feeling immense relief as though just escaped from a prison.

For the rest of the day I was appalled at the funeral and the small, or rather no, consideration given to the guests. It was clear that nothing had changed about funerals since the last one I had attended. They were as miserable as ever. I grumbled to myself about how my conscience, my desire to do the right thing, had once again resulted in a net loss to my own quality of life. A little later I considered the larger picture and how the same thing goes on all around the world every day. With an average of 60 million people dying every year, even if only two thirds of them get "proper," that is to say, miserable funerals, and only twenty persons attended each one, that still works out some 8 *billion* people in a decade who had been abused and often scarred for life. It's not an exaggeration! Do the math! Such is the world of misery created by unthinking convention!

Such an egregious state of affairs cried out for change. But who could effect it? It would take an extraordinary personality. He would have to be able to see through to the core of the matter. He would have to be brave and steady against intimidation, given the stubborn nature of custom, and the way it has evolved into a sacred cow. He would have to have a supernal view of social evolution, enabling him to see the consequences of actions not merely in terms of months or years but of centuries and millennia. He would have to be something of a philosopher, able to tease out whatever unfounded or mythic influences had shaped some of the most dearly-held social standards. He would have to have a very high sense of the rightness of his mission. He would have to be a patriot, wanting the best for his country; and more than this he would have to be a philanthropist, wanting the best for mankind. He would have to have extraordinary powers of expression to convey his ideas clearly and persuasively to a public averse to what he had to say. He would have to be charismatic, able to capture attention and earn respect: an aura of excitement, perhaps of some danger, would have to surround his person so that men, in his presence, would be intimidated into deference, and women would feel an immediate, overpowering, animal attraction.

—Of course in all this I am talking about myself. All of this was a very big bill, and I saw that I was the only one able to fill it. Nor should this surprise anyone. For the very quality which enables one to perceive a problem is precisely part of the ability to solve it. It was clear to me that the distressing nature of funerals was owing to their doom and gloom. The component parts which composed this disgusting situation had to be identified, exposed, and dragged out into the open; every element had to be pondered and measured in its effect on the human spirit: from the venue, to the casket, to the officiating clergy, to the guests;—everything! People had to know precisely what they were doing wrong and how to correct it. And the standard of measurement would be how well or ill these component parts contributed to, or retarded, the "healing process." Where they lived up to that standard and actually made people feel better rather than worse, they would be commended and held out as models for emulation; but where they didn't (and I knew already that most of them *wouldn't*) they would be called out as injurious frauds, and denounced with the scathing vitriol they deserved.

Achieving this objective would require wide expe-

rience with funerals.    I would have to attend
dozens, perhaps hundreds of them to gain insight
into why they were so bad and how to make them
better.  How ironic it was that I, who detested them
so much, would have to expose myself to them consistently!  But there was no way around it.  It was
a sacrifice which had to be made for the greater
good, in the same way that a surgeon must learn to
ignore the revolting process of cutting open the body
in order to save life.

Every day I went online and scanned the obituaries of local news outlets for funerals to attend.  I
had no apprehension that in attending them I
would be detected as an outsider, as a stranger who
was there for purely professional reasons.   There
was usually something in the obituary to give me a
handle on how I would introduce myself:  a home
address was sufficient information for me to pose as
a neighbor, or the name of a school or business to
give me the plausible cover of an old school chum or
colleague. After all, even those closest to us do not
know all the people from our past. I also discovered
that my presence, far from arousing suspicion, was
usually regarded with gratitude, for at such times
the survivors are in no skeptical mood and are just
grateful that people have come to pay their respects.

And yet at first it wasn't easy for me to attend
these services.  My sensitiveness, my empathy for
other people's suffering, undermined my critical capacity.  The grief of the survivors, their tears, their
whimpers, their bowed figures, their heartbreak beyond comforting, caused my own eyes to well up
and compromised my ability to analyze my sur-

roundings.  But if the work of a critic is to have any value, it must be objective.  No matter how much time or energy it took, I *had* to detach myself emotionally from the moment.  The conviction of the importance of my work goaded me to the extraordinary efforts needed to achieve this.  Each time I felt some sadness or pity rise up within me I would pounce on it like a ferocious lion, tamping, stomping it down, tearing it apart, suppressing it utterly; commanding myself, "Not now!  Pay attention!"  My heroic perseverance paid off.  In only a few months I reached the point where I might have attended the funeral of a whole family who had been wiped out at once, and while those around me were weeping and wailing and tearing out their hair, I could have stood there without batting an eye.

There was always so much to consider that it was impossible for me to remember everything and I had to rely on notes.  I carried a palm-sized spiral-bound notebook in the breast pocket of my jacket and, once I had taken a seat, would discreetly extract it and jot down my observations in a kind of improvised shorthand.  Sometimes I did this so quickly that it was even hard for me to decipher them.  For instance, here are a few entries from one of the first funerals I attended in a critical capacity:

> "... casket, budg. [budget] model ... too dark: black, nav. blue?... off-color art. [artificial] gold plating on trim ..."
>
> " ... deceased's left nostril ... chafed? feeding tube? .. tie not straight ... hair too dark, unsuitable, d.? [dyed?] ... looks unhappy ..."
>
> "... flowers too bright ... artificial ... "
>
> " ... window slightly open ...  traffic noise from outside ... 'La Bamba'!"

" ... candles—dim, odd flicker ... fake? Bat. [battery] powered?"

" ... Wife's clothes, disgraceful ... black, dowdy ... Target? Infamy!..."

" ... daughter, eighteen or nineteen, pretty ... nice blouse lc [ow-cut], those legs! ..."

" ... 'pastor,' face vulgar, dull-eyed ... eulogy overdone ... d deg. [divinity degree] online? ..."

" ... fd [funeral director], eyes bleared ... hung over? Just walked past me ... JW [Johnny Walker]?"

In the months following I would dispense with a notebook and carry a small digital recorder in my jacket breast pocket. What with its sensitive microphone set on high and facing upward, it captured my whispered observations. It also had the benefit of picking up any ambient noise, which helped bring back the service to my mind still more clearly. If a family member started carrying on, there was no question about it: the proof was right there, for anyone to hear, and no one could tell me I was exaggerating unseemly behavior. It also picked up any conversations I had with other guests whose tones of voice conveyed whole pages of the impression the funeral was leaving on them; which by the way was usually not a good one.

Immediately after the service and any reception, I would go home to write a first draft of the review while my impressions were still fresh in my mind, grinding out fifteen or twenty pages in two to three hours of steady writing. Later however I merely sketched out my ideas and over the next several days fleshed them out;—a method that was slower and sometimes frustrating because it lacked the concinnity found in prose dashed off under the impulse of first inspiration, but which had the benefit of additional thoughtfulness, which is probably more important in critical or polemical work.

In my first year as a professional critic I wrote ten reviews. The shortest was five thousand words long; the longest extended to twenty thousand. I was often surprised at my own facility: my fingers fluttered over my keyboard with the speed of hummingbirds' wings. Though I necessarily had to say some harsh things about the families in question, I always changed their names to protect their identity. Even so there was the possibility of their recognizing themselves. Did that possibility give me pause? Yes; but only a very *slight* pause. Even if they happened to come upon my review, even if they recognized themselves and became distraught, I would not have been too remorseful because the greater good had been served. Offending a few people now and then is a small price to pay for preventing hundreds of thousands of people emotional trauma in the future.

One can write a dozen reviews a day but they can't have any influence unless they are available to the public, unless they are published. I tried to interest a few local newspapers in them. That was unsuccessful so I sent them to national newspapers and magazines, hoping that the editors of those larger organizations would be more sophisticated and see the importance of my work. But my submissions were always rejected, coming back to me—if at all—with a polite form letter saying, in effect, thanks but no thanks. Sometimes the editor sent along a note, which was almost always snide and a few examples of which I am including here in order to document the kinds of obstacles my trailblazing work had to

overcome. Out of the goodness of my heart I am obscuring the names of these publications in order to
spare their reputations:

> Dear Sir:
> Thank you for submitting your work, "Goodbye to
> Gordon Gayle" to *The — Post*. However, we do not
> print "funeral reviews." In fact, we have never heard
> of such a thing and don't know where you got the idea.
> But it is not a good one. You seem to have some small
> ability as a writer. We suggest you might want to put
> it to better use.
> Yours, The Editor.

> Dear Sir:
> Thank you for giving *The New — Times* an
> opportunity to review your submission for the
> weekend "Leisure" section. However, we do not
> believe that regularly attending funerals is (as you
> state in your peculiar piece) the "surest way to take
> the moral pulse of the nation." That is preposterous.
> Sincerely, The Editor.

> Dear Sir:
> Your article entitled "Leslie Harper's Last
> Hurrah" is returned herewith. Though your piece was
> unique, we did not feel it would be appropriate for
> *Modern — Guide*, which is a *bridal and wedding* (!)
> magazine.
> Yours, The Editor.

I suspect these editors really rejected my work
because they recognized that it would expose their
own obituaries for the hasty, thoughtless, hack journalism they were. My enlightened perspective also
challenged long-held beliefs and values, and perhaps editors thought that this would upset too
many of their readers and cause a backlash. If so

they had forgotten that a large role of journalism is to scrutinize the status quo, to bring to light any questionable aspects of customs universally accepted, not to be the bulwark, mouthpiece, and protector of any "correctness," political or otherwise. But in an age when people are so dreadfully insecure about their self-worth, virtue signaling becomes the order of the day; and though it must, in time, undermine a society and reverse civilization itself—what matters that, so long as you can show others how "good" you are?

Then I tried the book publishers. I was more optimistic about their publishing my work because, unlike periodical publications, they were less likely to be concerned with public opinion and might welcome something "controversial" for its sales potential. By that time I had accumulated some fifteen reviews of which the best four or five might make for a nice volume of some 250 pages. Over the course of six months I approached at least two dozen publishers. Once again my bright anticipations were dashed by rejection notes of the pro-forma kind—the kind that are printed by the thousands and included with the unsolicited material which is no sooner taken in hand than slipped back into the stamped, self-addressed envelope with which it came, and returned, unread, to the author.

There comes a point at which even the most fiery determination is bound to be snuffed out when continually dumped on by the waters of indifference. That would have been the case with me but for the fact that I regarded my work as a kind of sacred mission. It's easy to discourage someone from doing what he dislikes; very hard, when he's doing something he loves; and impossible when he knows it fulfills a higher purpose.

Now, when no one will give you a platform to express your views your only alternative is to create your own. It will not be as extensive as one ready-made; it will not have the same prestige; it may carry the stigma of being self-initiated, and be attacked on account of it; but it will be a means without which one would never be heard of at all. Fortunately we live in an age when the Internet makes it possible for an individual to side-step conventional channels and bring his message directly to the public. Thus I created my own website, "Betterfunerals.com." After my first reviews were online, I emailed funeral parlors in the United States, Canada, Europe, and Australia, sending them a link to my site and asking that if they found it informative or useful they might want to spread the word about it to people in their industry.

How overwhelming and gratifying the response! Within six months I had over 4,000 subscribers. My readers were not only funeral directors but also casket and headstone manufacturers, florists who specialized in funerary arrangements, hearse drivers, cemetery groundskeepers, clergymen—in short, anyone who had anything to do with funerals. Many wrote to tell me how pleased they were to come across sentiments that mirrored their own but which they had never publicly expressed for fear of ridicule or professional retribution. Clergymen were particularly ardent on this head: they regarded their funeral duties as the miserable low-points of their careers. As one enlightened Catholic priest put it: "I had dedicated my life to God to bring light and hope to people, and instead there I am, at regular intervals, leading or partaking of a service in which everything is dark, dreary, and hopeless. Our Lord offers us the joy of eternal life, so the faithful should be, if anything, deliriously happy; or if not *deliriously* happy—I admit that might be a bit much—at least fairly content, and not sitting there with long pusses on their faces as though this is really the *end*. Either they don't believe in Our Lord's message of eternal life as much as they say they do, or I've done a pretty bad job of explaining what our faith is all about. I have sent a link to your site to my archbishop."

My most enthusiastic supporters are funeral directors, who constitute more than three quarters of my subscribers. I have come to know many of them and have discovered that they share common characteristics (not the least of which is knowing a good review when they read it). As a class they are largely misrepresented and misunderstood. Their reputation as lumbering, lugubrious, unapproachable, and creepily intimidating people is undeserved and owing to their demeanor during funerals, which is usually respectfully somber. But let me assure the reader that they assume this character because they believe— rightly—that it is expected of them. Their real character tends to be just the opposite. They tend to be outgoing, cheerful, and even a little silly. Coming so often face-to-face with the impermanence of life, they value it more than most people, and are quick to indulge in love, laughter, and light. They like to have a good time. They have a wonderful sense of humor. They often know a lot of jokes and riddles. After the last guest has left their funeral parlor they are likely to throw off their mask of unsmiling seriousness and become their old cheerful selves again, exchanging lighthearted banter with friends or colleagues, or making plans for a dinner date or even an evening of dancing. It may be hard to believe but often enough the slow, sedate, and apparently humorless fellow who stood about quietly while a funeral was in progress is, six or seven hours later, tearing up the dance floor at some trendy nightclub.

This is not to say that all my readers are fans. One can never work toward social reform without stirring up some resentment, especially among those for whom such change results in loss of business or insults their sense of self-worth by bringing home to them the errors of their longstanding beliefs. I have been called a lot of bad names and been sent some nasty emails. They are usually from people who have just given or attended a funeral, and who take it as a personal insult to read in my reviews the kinds of errors they are responsible for or have come away from. No doubt they are shocked to find that in doing "the right thing" they were in fact doing the wrongest thing possible. I made them feel bad—I showed them how appalled they should be at their behavior; and of course they don't like that. Some of them have threatened to find out where I live and assault me. Believe me, there are a lot of unstable people out there! I delete these messages as soon as soon as they come in.

A few so-called "journalists" have also attacked me from a professional standpoint. They say I am not a "real" critic because none of my reviews have appeared in mainstream publications. One can only remind these cackling cavilers that the value of a review lies in the quality of its contents, not on the extent of its publication or even on the reputation of its platform. Others have sneered that my reviews are just so much rigmarole: a blithe assemblage of groundless dicta, desultory observations, and mean-spirited attacks on people at a vulnerable time and who therefore ought to be regarded with only sympathy and indulgence. Well, in the first place, rigmarole can have a lot of charm and excitement—if you don't believe it, read Saintsbury's critique of De Quincey. And in the second place, what they disparage as my desultoriness is really a vigorous expansiveness, a refreshing spontaneity, which is the life's blood, the beating heart, of good prose. I admit it! I am not your everyday reviewer! I don't follow an AP style guide! I am not a two-bit lackey of *The New York Times* toeing the ideological line! I don't serve up paragraphs two short sentences long, the mental equivalent of infant's pap spoon-fed to readers with the attention span of turtles! And as for the criticism that my work is inhumane—that objection, when you examine it, only confirms why my work is so necessary and valuable. It's because people *are* so vulnerable at funerals that's it's about time someone was looking out for their welfare and calling out those practices which are so injurious to them. Forgive me for trying to make the world a better place!

No, the objections to my work only go to prove that those who make them don't know what they're talking about. But why should this surprise anyone? These so-called critics never see into anything. They concern themselves with appearances, reporting on the externals, giving opinions based on "experience," to be sure, but *thoughtless* experience. As for original ideas, they have none. More often than not their re-views are often chosen for them by editors whose primary concern is to meet the expectations of readers whom it would be bad business to "offend." Not to offend! That has become the main thing! That is the new standard in American letters, indeed in American thought. Never offend! Show how good you are and be nice to everyone! The problem is that this has been taken to the self-destructive extreme. Is someone a scoundrel? Don't say so!—it might offend him, and only goes to show how intolerant you are of those who are different from yourself. No, no, you must be large-minded enough, tolerant enough, *good* enough to accept even scoundrels; perhaps them most of all because they aren't responsible for being scoundrels. Something in their past, something which they had no control over, perhaps society itself, of which you're a part, and therefore you yourself, turned them into the scoundrels they are! But everyone else lived in the same society, some in even more difficult circumstances, yet didn't wind up a scoundrel? That you could even say such a thing only goes to show how heartless, how short-sighted, how ignorant, how mean-spirited you are! Shame on you! You are not a good person at all! Shut up! Be Quiet! Don't you dare utter another peep! We will not allow you to utter another peep!

—And so it is that a flabby sentimentalism, mating with mass personal insecurity desperate to assure itself and others of its worthiness, results in the acceptance of things which in a former and more reasonable age would have been seen as contributing to social decline and amounting in fact to a kind of insane suicide. This same kind of thought-lessness softens and degrades every other aspect of intellectual life, which is why the works of those in-fected by it are totally worthless, making a big, pub-lisher-funded, heavily-advertised splash when they appear, tempting the vacuously curious to buy them up for a while only to—throw them into a trash a while afterwards.

This same superficiality is responsible for the at-tacks against my work. People who are eager to prove how "good" they are express their "shock" that I would apply to a funeral the same principles of good taste which are applied to everything else; as though it were not here *especially* where good taste was important! This again only goes to prove that my critics *don't* care about other people's welfare but only, in their stupid insecurity, about being thought well of.

Are my criticisms sometimes harsh? I don't deny it. I may have a habit of mincing my words for the sake of euphony, but that doesn't detract from the vigor of the message. And you have to crack a few eggs to make an omelet. You have to be willing to risk the anger of people who foolishly take pride in their heritage, pride in their upbringing, above all pride in their "respectability." They need a few good hard shakes, a few sharp tonic slaps (all figuratively, of course), to rouse them out of their trance of com-placent acceptance of the atrocious. This accounts for my sometimes ad hominem attacks: not because I dislike the persons in question—I don't even know them!—but because anyone who can be satisfied with a funeral in which everything, from start to finish, is dark and depressing, is full of wail and woe, and so antagonistic to light and life, is too obtuse to be convinced of their errors by gentle or roundabout persuasion, and need to be *shoved* into more conscientious behavior.

I am already making some people's lives better. My influence is not yet extensive but it is making its way slowly and surely. There are now probably more funeral directors who know about my work than who don't, and the more conscientious of them have begun implementing my ideas. But even if my work had made only *one* funeral a little better, I would still have taken pride in knowing that because of my work some poor grieving wretch had found the peace and comfort he would otherwise have been deprived of. Save one life, an old religious text tells us, and you save the world: likewise might it be said that easing the distress of one person is a reduction in overall misery;—no small accomplishment.

# III
## BASIC PRINCIPLES

People who have just had a death in the family will often resort to the neighborhood funeral home whose director will escort them into his office and, with an appropriately sympathetic manner, present them with several "options." These are often package deals which seem opportunely affordable, but what the distraught shopper doesn't understand is that corners have been deeply cut. Whenever someone offers you a "complete service" which includes everything from embalming, the "casket of your choice," flowers, and the best room in their establishment, and all for $1699.99—you can be sure you're talking to a shark in a business suit. He is banking on your aggrieved naiveté. He is counting on your having no more common sense than people who rush into a department store on account of a heavily advertised, "Once a Year" white sale, even though there are better bargains elsewhere and at all times. When you break down and examine the offering into its parts, and examine these, you see that what you thought was such a good deal really isn't.

For instance a lot of "budget" caskets are not even of secondary quality. Look on the bottom of them (as I have) and it's likely you'll find a label, "Made in China." Do you think that's real wood?

It's not. It's particle board with a vinyl veneer. Do you think those are brass fittings? Not a chance. They're made of steel, and spray-painted. Those moldings running along the bottom and which look so neatly machined are in fact separate pieces made of plastic, and glued on and varnished over. You got a bargain by paying $700 for that casket? On the contrary, you were exploited, robbed, bamboozled, because the well-dressed con artist who assured you it was a "quality product" on which he would probably lose money was in fact making a 100% profit.

And that is only the beginning of the robbery. What about those arrangements of "fresh" flowers? Half the time they're smaller than they looked in the pictures, and most of the time they're not so fresh. Most likely they have been recycled from previous funerals, no sooner removed from one than set up in another. Some of them have gone through half a dozen in a day. I know of one funeral home that mixes fresh and artificial flowers in order to cut down still further on this expense. As for the lovely marble vases they are displayed in, they never saw a quarry: they are not marble but plaster, painted in such a way to resemble the real thing.

Do you want music? That's going to cost extra. Do you want different seating? Be prepared to take out your wallet again. Do you have particular ideas about how the casket is to be presented, or are uncomfortable with the aura of the visitation room and want to suggest changes which will made it a little less sinister? Be prepared to pay through the nose. For all those changes are (as you will be told) "special requests" which take time to accommodate, but which really just interrupt the factory-like flow of services which keep the establishment operating at the most profitable pace.

No, package deals are to be avoided at all costs. They probably could never have become so popular but for the fact that people who have just suffered a loss are too distressed to care about the particulars of the service. Their only concern is that it should be "respectable." This is why one never ought to make funeral arrangements immediately after a loved one has died. Indeed the rule of thumb is: Never wait till you *need* a funeral. Never contact or walk into a funeral parlor in the midst of one's grief! Certainly never do so in tears or with any visible signs of anguish, since then you might as well hang around your neck a sign saying, "Sucker here!" Whenever possible, do your shopping early! At the first sign of a loved one's illness, even if it doesn't seem serious, even if it seems to be nothing more than a bad cold or flu, one ought to be contacting as many funeral parlors as possible. If the death is sudden one must exercise some restraint and wait for a while—two days is an absolute minimum—so that one's shock has a chance to subside and one can more wisely choose options. For there *are* bargains out there. Especially in cities where there is a lot of competition the industry has seen some creative marketing in recent years: there are coupons, holiday sales, and senior citizen discounts, with savings of up to 20%;—a generous amount when one considers the overall high cost. These deals are sometimes co-incident so that when combined they offer still greater savings. Depending on the local death rate, one might also be able to negotiate a lower price with establishments which are hurting for business.

You need to visit the funeral parlor, to walk through it, to absorb and assess its ambience; and your main, your only consideration should be, "How does this place make me feel?" The layout, furnishings, lighting, and colors of the place should engender positive feelings. If on stepping over the threshold your first impression is of dark heaviness, you need to follow your instincts, turn around, and head for the proverbial hills. Never—ever—go against your gut instinct in this matter. Remember that you best honor the deceased when you want the best for your family and friends.

Unfortunately too many of these businesses have been in existence "for generations" and consequently were built at a time when consideration for the psychological welfare of the survivors was of secondary importance. In those days it was considered enough to provide a place where people could weep and wail to their broken hearts' content. The only thing that then mattered was whether or not the room was silent and subdued enough not to distract people from their sorrow, and that part of "the healing process" was to let them wallow in, and make no attempt to alleviate, their misery. It can never be pointed out too often how perverse that notion is: how something so clearly contrary to common sense was and too often still is accepted as a matter of course by people who would be mortified to find themselves so gullible in any other matter.

Much of the influence of a funeral is determined by the way it *looks*, that is to say, by the architecture of the building in which it takes place, the types of furnishings there, and the surrounding color schemes. The first two factors are inherent to the establishment and unchangeable, but one may have a great deal to say about the colors used in the service. In everything from the casket, to the flowers, to any number of miscellaneous decorations, colors should be selected to promote positive energy. The following may serve as a general guide for colors to avoid or use.

*Black.* Nowhere is the perversity of custom more apparent than in this color, or rather lack of color, which has become the standard for funerals even though its psychological influence is irretrievably negative. Our adverse reaction to it comes from the most primitive, most deeply-rooted, and therefore most human parts of our psyche, namely, our fear of the dark—of things unseen and potentially dangerous. It always summons up a sense of the ominous; it makes us uneasy and depressed. Whenever you see a lot of it at a funeral you can be sure the family are vulgar conventionalists who never gave a thought to how it might affect their guests. Nor should it be regarded as appropriate for mourning clothes. For what could be more intimidating than to walk into a room where everyone, from the youngest child to the oldest granny, is dressed in black? It sends a shiver down your spine—as though you were suddenly in the midst of some Satanic ritual where dark forces, where all that is hateful and hurtful, is appealed to and celebrated. No! Black should be forbidden at funerals! Instead nothing darker than navy blue should be used, and guests should be encouraged to accent their clothing (which may be formal) in a way which brings a little brightness, a little good cheer, into the place.  Thus the men may or may not wear suits, though sports jackets and casual slacks are a lot less stuffy; and their ties should be variation of staid reds, blues, purples, and so forth.  Older women might want to wear formal dress ornamented with fashion jewelry or accessorized with items in pastel colors.  Attractive young ladies with good figures should be encouraged to wear low-cut blouses and short skirts—especially if they have fine legs.

*Brown.*  This is in the same unacceptable category as black.  It is too negative in its connotations to be used much in a service.  It *may* be effectively combined with yellow, gold, taupe, slate gray, coral, and garnet, but even so great care must be taken that the particular depth of brown works well with those colors.  Generally speaking, one should avoid it unless guided by professional opinion.

*Gray.*  This is as problematic as it is potentially advantageous; it depends on its hue.  Dark gray, like black or brown, should be avoided as too negative.  A medium gray is acceptable in moderation.  A light gray however is almost always in good taste because its bright neutrality has a way of "opening up" a visitation room, giving small or moderately-sized areas an impression of spaciousness. It is also a perfect background for most colors, even bold ones: when used in drapes or carpeting it can be flecked or streaked with bright oranges, reds, blues, and greens, which will convey a sense of youthful vigor or sportiness.

*Blue.*  This color is so universally liked that it is hard to go wrong with it.  It is a favorite color of men.  Its connotations of sea and sky make it suitable for the funerals of specific individuals, namely, for surfers, divers, fishermen, merchant marines, navy seamen, oceanographers and ocean engineers, for the builders of dams and the diggers of wells, and generally for those whose penchant or profession led to a life spent in or near the oceans; also for pilots, astronomers, astrologers, meteorologists, speculators of the fantastic, imaginers of the impossible, dreamy-eyed idlers, and generally all those whose eyes were perpetually turned "upward and outward." Its darker hues are appropriate for mourning clothes since they sufficiently imply a sense loss without sinking to the oppressiveness of black.

*Turquoise.* There is something magical about this color. It is blue, yet not blue; green, yet not green: a blend of the air and the vegetable-fruitful earth, of the glowing, transparent aerial and the opaque, tangible terrestrial; the chromatic epitome of the earth itself. Therefore more than blue, more than green, it is emblematic of the earth, which should be called (if only for the sake of poetic license) the turquoise planet. This color is said to be applicable to friendly and clear-minded personalities: therefore, let it be used in the funerals of those who made friends easily and had a lot of them, and to those who were skeptical-philosophical.

*Red.* This is a hard color to use on account of its contradictions. As it is the color of blood, of the substance most closely associated with life, it has come to epitomize the extremes of consciousness: from hatred and violence to the tenderest love and self-sacrifice. It may designate the boldness of a bloody conqueror as well as the romantic passion of a swooning swain: a merciless and murderous fury as well as the tenderest pangs of a longing heart: the gore-dyed sword as well as bouquets of roses bestowed on Valentine's Day. Its prominence in a funeral can easily become melodramatic and gaudy. If a survivor wishes to use it as a symbol of affection for the deceased, wearing a small and simple red flower or ribbon is acceptable, as well as a few red blossoms in floral arrangements, but anything more than this should be avoided

*Purple.* Some may be inclined to use this color in funerals to intimate the "royal" (i.e., elevated, honorable, praiseworthy) character of the deceased. But its association with royalty is so specific and longstanding that its use for commoners is likely only to remind family and guests that, whatever the qualities of the deceased were, a royal lineage was not one of them. No, this color should only be used for kings, queens, and their immediate families; also for the Catholic clergy, where it has a history of use in liturgical accoutrements. For the public it may be used sparingly in floral arrangements where, especially against white blossoms, it adds a vibrant and exotic charm.

*Green.* One might think this is appropriate in the funerals of those who had a penchant for nature, for campers, hikers, botanists, geologists, and various sports enthusiasts, since it is the color of fields and forests, of the great outdoors. Unfortunately this color has been hijacked by the environmentalist movement, which has brought us, in addition to the outrage of "natural burials," such culinary delights as dried seaweed and salted beetles. If there is ever a state founded for hypocrites, this would assuredly be the color of its flag since the loudest and most publicly vocal advocates of a "green lifestyle" are wealthy celebrities who fly hither and yon in jets, own large carbon-producing homes, and indulge in every imaginable luxury produced by pollution-spewing factories even as they reprimand the rest of the world for not doing more to "protect the environment." It may also be used in cases where it connotes national pride, as among the Irish, or for statesmen whose national flags are mostly green, such as those of Macau or Mauritania.

*Gold.* This color is so closely associated with the actual element and its intimation of wealth and luxury that it carries a connotation of worldliness and, by way of extension, of greed. One is likely to see it used profusely just where it is most inappropriate to do so: in the funerals of the wealthy, where it has an air of vulgar braggadocio, and in those of the poor and middle class, where it is bound to be seen as a ridiculous affectation. In both cases the result is the opposite of the one intended. This color is most properly used in the funerals of leaders of countries or of major religious sects, since here it suggests the majesty of church or state. Tastefully restrained gold accents are acceptable in the decor of the funeral parlor and in various parts of the casket. It may also be used to good effect in the color of ribbons laced throughout floral arrangements, especially among light-colored blossoms.

*Orange* is innocent and suitable for children. It is the color of plastic toys, of clowns and balloons, of birthdays and birthday presents wrapped in colorful papers, of pumpkins and Halloween and wearing costumes and eating candy. Yet on account of its association with autumn, of the vital summer declining into its fainting opposite, it also hints at the cyclic nature of life, making it—when used in restraint—appropriate also for the services of older individuals.

*Pink.* This color, as a subdued variation of red, may be said to bespeak the warm but steady state of mind when engaged in the creative process; therefore it ought to have a prominent, though by no means *pre*dominant, place in the funerals of musicians, poets, painters, and artists generally. "But what if the deceased hated pink?" He should have it anyway, first because he won't be around to complain about it, and second because one cannot count on artists to know themselves. Let us rely on Socrates for this when he says, "I realized that it was not wisdom that enabled poets to write their poetry, but a kind of instinct or inspiration, such as you find in seers and prophets who deliver all their sublime messages without knowing in the least what they mean." Our respect for the final wishes of the deceased should never outweigh the honor of their memory. And so pink these people shall have, whether they wanted it or not.

*Yellow.* This is the cheerfullest color. It is emblematic of smiles and laughter, of cloudless days, of spring, summer, and early autumn, of bright futures and aspiring dreams, of all things fresh and happy. Ultimately it represents the sun, the giver of warmth, light, and life. Though it seems too much of it would be unacceptable the fact is that on account of its rare usage it takes on the character of an exciting novelty, and this makes it acceptable and enjoyable for the funeral service. In its paler hues it is the correct alternative to white. It is also a proper alternative to the color gold, which should be avoided for reasons already mentioned.

*White.* Oddly enough white is as problematical as black, though for the opposite reason of its connotation of purity and goodness. For the fact is that no one is worthy of unadulterated commendation. At funerals mourners tend to relate how "good" the deceased was; go on and on about him, ad nauseam; when in fact, like everyone else, he had his shortcomings—his baseless prejudices, his avarice, his envies, his moments of embarrassing meanness. Look closely enough into the life of a saint, and you'll find a few sins; and if there are angels, their wings are likely to have a smutch or two. And so pure white should never be used for an adult, since no one reaches maturity without having done some dirt. This includes the clergy. This also includes very young children, for even a toddler can tell a fib. Its only appropriate use is for infants, but even there it should probably be avoided lest it be taken for a pathetic indulgence on the part of the parents whose fondness for their child blinded them even to its unclean bodily functions. White should be confined to the color of casket bedding, floral arrangements, and (sparingly) attire on the part of the survivors and guests.

At least a dozen other common colors are not mentioned here, but they may be said to share the basic implications of those basic colors which are. Pastels, for instance, have the same effects of their bolder counterparts though to a lesser degree; they are also easier to use in combinations.

When dealing with color, it is necessary to consider the cognate issue of lighting, in particular its color temperature. The "natural light" option which boast of replicating sunlight, while providing for the most accurate colors (at least insofar as they would be seen outside), is fatiguing and even bothersome indoors. One often finds it in the "recessed" lighting so popular these days: one can scarcely look up at it without feeling one's eyeballs painfully pierced. That kind of lighting is appropriate in a dental office or a commercial kitchen, not in a home and still less in a visitation room! There the lighting should be much softer, in the cozy sub-2500 Kelvin range.

Of all the articles in a funeral, the casket is of course primary and may be said to be the focal point of the service. It therefore behooves the family to ensure they are getting best quality and style they can afford. The adage that you "get what you pay for" is never truer than here. Beautiful caskets are expensive, which is why most people can no more afford them than they can afford fine paintings or sculptures. People who have the regular costs of living, who have to pay rent or mortgages, health insurance premiums, their children's college tuition, and so forth, are likely to regard spending a lot of money on a casket as wasteful, especially because they figure it is going to be buried anyway. But that is always the wrong, and vulgar, way to look at it. Instead they should consider that they are buying something that they will not need more than once or twice in a lifetime, and which will have a profound effect on the event. When a casket is plain or shabby, when nothing about it is inspiring, everything else, no matter how good, is bound to be compromised. Why mince words? A cheap casket is *always* gauche, and its tawdry touch has a way of spoiling every other aspect of the service.

The problem is that most cheap caskets are mass-produced, their component parts sawed and stamped out by machine, and bolted or welded together on a production line. Their "designs" are as cold and lifeless as the bodies they are intended to contain. On the other hand a fine casket entails some handcraftsmanship. A machine may provide the bulk materials for it, the planks, the metal hardware for hinges or other mechanical parts, but skilled workers assemble it, decorate it, turn it into something wonderful to behold. There are manufacturers (several of whom will be mentioned later) who are devoted to producing really impressive and lovely products, but which are not generally known outside the industry, and which it has been part of my mission to acquaint the public with.

Nevertheless it is possible to buy a mainstream casket which won't result in a social catastrophe so long as one observes a few guidelines. First, black is to be avoided. A big black hunk of a rectangle dominating the front of a visitation room is an absolute eyesore. It is a loathsome presence which all but shouts doom and gloom. Preferable are light woods such as ash, birch, oak, or poplar, and their surfaces should be highly polished so as to reflect light, which always has a cheering, positive effect. For the same reason all metal fittings, such as hinges, corner guards, or brackets through which the lifting arms are placed, should be plated with highly-polished silver, gold, or chromium. It should be decorated with interesting details, preferably from nature, such as leaves or vines or innocuous animals, and its major structural components, such as corners and top or bottom moldings, should reflect the best models for columns, architraves, and plinths. Remember that the more artistic these are, the more they engage the intellect and heart of the viewer, and shoo away unhappy thoughts.

No one should buy a casket based on how it looks in a catalog. Such images have been digitally enhanced. The buyer must insist on seeing the product in person. Would he do less with regard to any other high-priced item? If buying a car, for instance, would he trust the salesman who showed him its picture and assured him it was a great vehicle? Not at all; he would insist on seeing it, walking around it, on looking under the hood, on kicking the tires; he would want to take it for a test drive. Likewise in shopping for a casket one should "try before you buy." Reputable funerals directors will be happy to accommodate customers who want to test it for fit and comfort. It's important not to be shy and to hop right in. For even an expensive product from a reputable manufacturer may be less comfortable than it looks. How often does the bedding of a casket look plush but in fact barely pads over the protrusion of some underlying bolt or brace, which grinds into the back or leg? If you couldn't sleep comfortably in it for a single night, why would you want to stick your loved one into it for all eternity? The obvious retort is: "He won't know it." But you will, and that is the whole point.

The bier, on which the casket is placed, is one of the most overlooked items in funeral arrangement. It should never be left plain, the less so when it is a simple, table-like structure consisting of legs and a shelf. In most cases the funeral director will have the good sense to cover it, usually with a cloth decorated with religious symbols. But this only provides minimal decoration and never sufficiently distracts attention from eyesore of the casket plopped on top of it. And yet an artful dressing of the bier is one of the most effective and least costly ways to snazz up a service. For instance silk or satin fabrics, in lustrous colors, may be draped over it, arranged in such a way as to fall around it in abundant, luxurious, gorgeous folds. Before these might be hung strings or pendants of gems, of which it is entirely proper for them to be imitations made of crystal or glass so long as they are highly polished. The sparkle of topaz and amethyst, the glitter of citrine and beryl, the blue fires on the surface of the sapphire, and the quieter flames within the heart of the opal—all would add a touch of enchantment to the service by appealing to the basic human joy taken in refractive color. Of course discretion needs to be used here since and too many colors and too much sparkle is bound to be gaudy.

Floral arrangements should be large, bright, and colorful. Lilies should be avoided because despite their whiteness they have become too closely associated with the traditional funeral and consequently tainted with a connotation of dreary sadness. Preferable are gladioli, carnations, chrysanthemums, roses, or some intermixture of those interspersed with ferns, ribbons, bows, or other decorations. Consideration must always be given to the decor among which they will be placed. How many times are red roses, for instance, placed directly on a brown casket, or blue carnations set before maroon, etc.? Color clashes like these are hard to ignore and make one uneasy; in really bad cases they can actually make one feel a little sick. Even when the deceased has had a "favorite color," this should not be a factor in choosing floral arrangements unless it conduces to the overall chromatic harmony of the service.

Whenever possible *exotic* flowers, though more costly, should be used because their sometimes startlingly unusual shapes and colors guarantee an interesting distraction to the service. I offer the following as good examples:

1. The passion flower (*Passiflora incarnata*, blue variety). This vine-borne flower ranges from South America up to the southern United States. Poor examples of it look as one might expect a wildflower to look: curious, but stunted and asymmetrical. But its best cultivars are marvels of color and delicacy, having a backdrop of mint-green sepals above which hovers a circular corona of fine and sometimes wavy filaments colored deep purple at their base and lightening outwardly to blue, or with distinct bands of blue, white, and brown, and having at their center a cluster stigmas, anthers, and ovaries in bright primary colors. It is no wonder that the passion flower has gained aficionados who have gone so far as to create a "society" dedicated to its preservation and cultivation;—though they have not (so far as I know) taken the next logical step in promoting its use for funerals, where it would certainly have the effect of arousing a positive admiration.

2. The pincushion protea (*Leucospermum*, various colors). It is South Africa's national flower but is also native to Swaziland, Zimbabwe, and Mozambique; thus it hails from the remotest jungles of the world. Like so many exotic flowers it looks at first a little unreal; in this case, as though created from

plastic because its hundred fine-spun styles are so perfectly concentric and, at their outward edges, turned inward at so precisely common an angle. A dozen pincushion flowers of various colors and gathered would form an astonishing bouquet. Their strategic placement throughout a visitation room would be a sure and welcome distraction to family and guests.

3. The scarlet banksia (*Banksia coccinea*, red, yellow, orange varieties). If you could go back millions of years to the Cretaceous period, when the world was wet and warm, and dinosaurs roamed the land, you would have found vegetation much different from what it is today. The trees would have looked like spindly palms trying to touch the humid sky, while the vegetation beneath them, thick-stemmed and thick-leaved, would hide in their umbrageous depths all manner of strange insects and beasts. And amid all that dark deep greenery, so full of the fragrance of leaf and loam, and so full of secrets and dangers, one might have come upon flowers no less astonishing for their elementary evolution. In shape they might have been basic, consisting of a few colorful petals at the topmost parts of their plants, or hanging bell- or ball-shaped from branches. The scarlet banksia would have fit in with that prehistoric scenery. In the compact ovality of its shape, in its tight aggregation of blossoms, in the way it offers itself to the world above the otherwise spiky protective leaves of its plant—it has the look, it gives one the feeling, of primordial nature.

4. The bat flower (*Tacca chantrieri*, purple coloration only). This flower is native to Thailand, Malaysia, and southern China, and more than any

other—perhaps more than anything else in the veg-
etable kingdom—looks as though it might be some
kind of animal, what with its several long, spindly,
leg-like appendages (so like the legs of a spider or a
crab), and its stamens which look like the supporting tentacles of a crustacean's curious eyes. It certainly looks like something sensible of its
surroundings and might, at a human's touch, pull
back in fear, or, at a harsh word, tremble in apprehension. Its usual black coloration is inappropriate
for use in a funeral, but its lighter shade of purple
has a soft velvety quality which enhances its fantastic shape. If set amid light-colored stargazers or
carnations, its almost alien presence would be sure
to distract even the most grief-stricken family members.

5. The jade vine (*Strongylodon macrobotrys*),
from the Philippines, is among the few flowers naturally turquoise—a color which, as discussed above,
has itself a peculiar attraction. Their large, up-curl-
ing flowers can grow up to a foot in length. They
have become rare and endangered on account of
their decreasing rain forest habitat and the diffi-
culty in propagating them artificially, since in the
wild they are pollinated by bats which hang upside
down into them and tongue their nectar. It is not
likely that they could be acquired in the West or
even in Asia by anyone without the means and determination to procure them. But Filipinos might
be supposed to have freer access to them, and they
would do well to place a few of these hanging blossoms on either side of the entrance to the visitation
room, where, as a pleasant surprise to entrants,
they would help set the right tone to the ceremony.

6. And finally we come to the simple, sweet, completely honest lotus (*Nelumbo nucifera*, white, yellow, and pink varieties). A water plant, it grows in unclear or muddy waters of rivers or ponds, and opens its petals to the world with charming naiveté, with a simple, chaste, classic beauty. No wonder that in Asian cultures, but also as far back as ancient Egypt, it was reverenced as symbolizing Life: arising from the invisible depths—its buds implying the first stirring of vitality—its bloom suggesting the full vigor of adult strength and consciousness—its withering away a metaphor for the inevitable decline and dissolution of the individual back into the ineffable Mystery which gave rise to it;—a dissolution only seeming, however, since in time other buds (like other lives) arise from the depths, come up into the light of day, and bloom all over again, just as wonderfully. Thus the lotus bespeaks immortality. It is best displayed singly or two blossoms at a time set in plain glass bowls or vases with a minimum of greenery. Unfortunately its philosophical connotations are subtle and not likely to have much of an effect on coarse sensibilities; in that case, one of the more striking flowers mentioned above should be used to help distract families from impolite exhibitions of grief.

The comfortableness of the seating is an important but often overlooked element of funerals. The wooden pews in churches are usually uncomfortable for more than twenty minutes; the family ought to request or provide cushions for themselves and guests. As for funeral parlors, many of them in the "budget" category unabashedly use folding metal chairs, which make the place look like a bingo hall.

Their hard surfaces bite into one's bottom and thighs and one has constantly to change position. Anyone who has taken pains to look his best, to wear a fine suit or dress for the occasion, will be doubly annoyed because the hard steel or wooden seats cause creases in one's clothing. A minimum of one-inch, preferably cloth-covered padding should be on all seating. Places of the better sort will provide armchairs or even couches in which guests can lean back, cross their legs, stretch out their arms, and take in the ceremony at their complete ease.

Silence at a funeral is another common faux pas. Far from "showing respect," it mars the service by making obvious any sniffles, whimpers, or sighs on the part of family members or guests. Sometimes the silence is so complete that one can hear one's own breathing, which gives one a sense of claustrophobic entrapment and makes guests anxious, restive, and eager to leave. Instead there should be music, soft enough to allow close conversation but loud enough to drown out any sounds of mourning on the other side of the room. Nor should this music be too slow and lachrymose. It should consist of pleasant and expansive airs—melodies dreamy, soothing, floating—which will encourage a distant, contemplative, but by no means depressed state of mind. It should always be present from the opening to the close of the service, even during any prayers or eulogies, though it may be lowered in volume for the sake of making the speaker more audible.

Another overlooked aspect of a funeral is the scent of air itself. At their best, funeral parlors have no particular smell, but one can sometimes detect the odors of furniture polish, floor waxes, upholstery, and (if nothing else) the dry-cleaned clothes of those who have gathered for the service. Not one of these things is positive. Instead the air should be suffused with pleasant fragrances, such as those of fruits like peaches and oranges, or of herbs like mint and lemongrass, or even with the forestry smell of pine (especially suitable during Christmastime). There should be as much *fresh* air as possible. If the weather is fine, or even a little cool, any windows should be open and any curtains drawn aside. True, outside sounds might sometimes be heard a bit too loudly, but so long as these are not continuous they should not be a problem. The distant beeping of car horns, the chirping of birds, the soughing of trees in the wind, people talking, children laughing—they are all grateful distractions and reminders of the light and life going on without.

As for viewings, some people think they are always in bad taste—and in too many cases that is true. The main factor in making this decision should be the appearance of the deceased. Does he look good or not? Was he the victim of a horrible and violent accident which disfigured him, of some wasting disease which left him skeletal, or was his death so sudden and unexpected that nothing about him looks different and he seems to be taking a nap? In general people never look as good dead as they do alive. But the objective should never be to make them look "good," since this often means no more than giving them a lifelike complexion and setting their features into an expression of bland contentment. Instead they should look as much like themselves as possible, an effort having been made to allow their personalities to show through.  Thus if someone was a complainer, a martinet, hard-hearted and selfish creature, it is inappropriate for his face to be worked up into an expression of angelic sweetness— no, not even for the sake of creating a final "good impression," since this will only the opposite effect of reminding everyone just what a creep he was.  In such cases a *neutral* expression is appropriate.  On the other hand it would be inappropriate to see someone who was, say, free-spirited and cheerful, loving and hopeful, lying in his casket with a puss on his face as though he had been a grumpy old scrooge.  In that case everyone rightfully feels that a mistake has been made, that the funeral home hasn't done a good job.  In short, it takes a real artist, and a humanist, to be a good mortuary cos-metologist, and unfortunately too many people go into this field without the required talent or sensi-bility, and just slap on makeup with the heavy hand of a mason applying plaster with a trowel. The result is a horrible, zombie-like appearance which is just another cause of distress to family and guests.

On the other hand a bad final showing cannot always be attributed to bad cosmetology. The prede-ceased himself has a certain responsibility on his final appearance.  For instance, a heavy person who receives a terminal diagnosis has a certain responsi-bility to do all he can to get himself into shape.  He should start eating right and going to the gym.  If he is too weak for physical exertion, he can still be careful of his diet and keep away from rich foods to help shed a few unsightly pounds.  It may be owing to our Western notion of "fat and jolly," but nothing seems more out of place, more odd and disconcerting, than an obese corpse. We cannot help wondering how someone who had such a robust appetite could be dead. Indeed we can't help thinking that at any moment he's going to pop up with a grin and inform us that we're all part of a practical joke. This disturbing dichotomy is almost always the result of selfishness: people who learn they have only a few months or years to live often abandon the discipline by which they watched their weight and start cramming their faces with every goody in sight—with cakes, cookies, candy, ice cream, pizza, pudding, pies, etc. They blow up like balloons as though there were no tomorrow. —Which there may not be for *them*: but what about the rest of us? Family and friends who hadn't seen them for a long time are shocked to see what happened to them. Out of embarrassment the immediate family is likely to attribute the weight gain to illness or the side-effects of a failed medical treatment.

The attire of the deceased is also important, for clothes not only make the man but also what's left of him. Too often, especially among the lower classes, he is dressed in something a family member found hanging in his closet, perhaps some cheap suit picked up at JCPenney and which he hadn't worn for twenty years. This is unacceptable. Even people on a budget ought to understand that the fine appearance of their loved one can make up for a lot of shortcomings in other areas. A fine suit for men, or, in the case of women, a lovely gown with a touch of jewelry, can go a long way toward making up for even an inexpensive casket. But professional uniforms, unless in the case of someone with a distinguished military career, should be avoided. Too often celebrated singers, dancers, or movie stars are dressed in the glittery, flashy costumes which distinguished them in the public eye, and which tend to detract from the dignity of the service. No one is going to take seriously a funeral in which someone who might have made his living as, say, a clown, is lying in his casket wearing a puffy orange wig and a big red rubber nose. That may be an extreme example, but it has happened, and it is deplorable. No, simple yet elegant attire is always the best choice.

As a funeral is a social event, the number of the guests affects its character. While there can never be too many people (provided the family has the means to afford the reception afterwards), there can be too few. Under fifteen or so persons always makes the affair seem a little straggling or forced, and seems to speak ill of the deceased. A large crowd does not however necessarily reflect on his good character or the affection felt for him, especially in the case of large extended families. For hypocrisy is never more apparent than at funerals. Many of those who come dressed in black and wearing long faces had not seen or even thought of the deceased for years before learning of his death. Only then did they think about paying their respects. A fine "respect" that is! That the survivors do not generally resent this hollow expression of regard is owing to their own sorrow, which makes them incapable or unwilling to analyze the motives of others; and so they docilely attribute the attendance of people they haven't seen in a decade to a longstanding, if seldom shown, affection, rather than to—what it really is—a guilty conscience over actual indifference.   But make no mistake about it: anyone who hasn't seen the deceased in a couple of years, or called him at least once in the last year, has no business attending his funeral.   In that case a sympathy card should suffice, or nothing at all.

Then there is the behavior of the family.  It is incumbent on them to set the right tone.  The excessive emotionalism they often display was the subject of a recent poll on my website.  Of the respondents, 73% said that they regarded such displays as stressful and the main reason for opting out of funerals, while only 48% regarded them as "understandable." In the same poll a full 91% said that they would not want such behavior to mar their own funerals.  This goes to show that despite a lifetime of inculcation about what is "normal" behavior at such a time, most people resent it as impolite.  Instead the family should conduct themselves with *dignified acceptance.* All crying, whimpering, sniffling, sighing, or any other kind of carrying on is to be held in check.  *A funeral is not the place for tears!*  As it never coincides with the day of death, there has been time to absorb the shock of the event and come to some terms with one's grief.  Certainly for an adult the worst of this should be over within the first two or three days.  Granted, everyone is different and some people, no matter how hard they try, will not be able to compose themselves in that amount of time, in which case they should have the decency to absent themselves from the room till they have gotten control of themselves.  In accepting condolences they should be quietly gracious, and if they have planned a reception (as they ought to have done) it is at such a time that they should express the hope that their guests will attend it.

If it is important for the family to show restraint, how much more so for the guests! There is absolutely no reason for any of them to appear to be more upset than those who were closest to the deceased. How many times have I seen people show up for the funeral of an acquaintance they haven't visited or talked to for years, and then start bawling their eyes out as though their own children had been strangled in front of them? Who can take them seriously? Either they are mentally disturbed or—as is more likely the case—making a show of grief for the sake of disguising the indifference which kept them comfortably out of touch with the deceased. Their sighs, sniffles, and tears are an act, a way of making others think better of them, a way of saying, "See, I really *am* sorry!" But you can bet that as soon as they get home they tear off their clothes, get into something more comfortable, turn on the TV to watch a sitcom, and hope they don't have to go through "that" again for a long time.

While good funerals should never be rushed, bad ones can't be over soon enough. They seem to drone on forever, much to the emotional detriment of the family and the discomfort of the guests. Thus the general rule of thumb is that a funeral should not exceed forty-five minutes. It is also important that a schedule be created and adhered to. It is boorish to specify the start of the service only for it to start much later and leave one's guests waiting uncomfortably till, say, a minister arrives or the eulogies begin. Any minister contracted for the event should be there at the stated start of the service and begin his ministrations no more than fifteen minutes afterwards.

Eulogies fall into three categories or styles:  the lightly casual, the soberly familiar, and the imposingly formal.  The value of the first lies principally in its attempt to lighten the atmosphere of the service. It consists in happy reminiscences of the deceased, in reminding the listeners of his love and family and friends, of the sweet or funny things he said or did, or depicting him as a kind and good-humored person whom it was a pleasure to be around.  This style should be delivered in an easy, wistful, sometimes sadly smiling manner.  It should also be delivered by a distant family member or a minister—someone less likely to be affected by the death and who therefore can be counted on to speak without any disturbing accesses of sorrow.

The second style, the soberly familiar, may be regarded as the norm.  It is more serious in its tone and is usually delivered by close family members who (this is a regrettable fact needing to be exposed) speak with the intention of stirring up tears and lamentations. They think that they best honor their dearly departed by making everyone as miserable as possible.  These people have no shame.  They will bawl their eyes out as they stutter and gasp through their little speeches, rudely and crudely indifferent to the stress their lack of self-control is having on family and friends.  A good funeral director, or minister closely involved in the service, will always vet the state of mind of speakers before allowing them to address the room, and dissuade them from doing so if they do not appear to be in complete control of their faculties.

The third style of eulogy, the imposingly formal, is the most difficult to do well because it requires literary finesse and an appropriately sophisticated delivery. It also requires an audience capable of appreciating it. A composition in which each word has been carefully weighed, in which lofty spiritual or philosophical sentiments have been neatly captured by exact diction, in which language has been wielded like a conductor's baton so as to summon up just the right sentiment here, just the particular thought there—it would all be wasted on the typical funeral audience, which is distracted by sorrow or otherwise too psychologically impaired to appreciate that kind of skill. It is most appropriate for anniversary memorial services—those which take place years after the actual funeral. By that time the attendees have long since resumed their normal lives and are clear-headed enough to find pleasure in a well-turned phrase.

Eulogizing should never take more than fifteen minutes, and above all should be *honest*. How many funerals are marred with a long, tiresome succession of eulogies in which first the minister, then several relatives, then a few friends, take turns standing in front of the room, pull out pieces of paper on which they have written whole speeches, and drone on and on to a captive audience about what a gem, what marvel, what a gift to the world the deceased was! In this way I have heard shoe salesmen, journalists, stockbrokers, janitors, television newscasters, and college professors talked up as though they had created the polio vaccine—it really is too ridiculous for words! Any funeral director worth his salt will insist on previewing the eulogies and suggest shortening long ones and excising all preposterously exaggerated accolades.

Often the service precedes the burial, and family and guests are expected to attend it: but this is always a mistake. The burial should never be publicly attended. There is no emotional satisfaction to be gotten out of it. It is too much a mechanical process involving load, opposing force, and leverage. The sight and sounds of several workmen huffing and puffing as they lower a bulky casket into the earth is at best embarrassing, and sight of this is also likely to make family members break out into new unseemly exhibitions of grief just when they had started to behave themselves. Instead the deceased should be discreetly whisked away to his final resting place while the family and guests proceed directly to the relief of the reception.

The importance of a good reception cannot be overemphasized. As the last event of the day, as the epitome of the social nature of the service itself, it should leave a completely positive impression. This is where lower- and middle-class families should spend most of their money. A poor or mediocre funeral service can in some measure be made up for by a good reception; but a poor reception has a way of undermining everything preceding it, no matter how well-planned or opulent. Guests who have strained every nerve to get through a service, who have sat in uncomfortable chairs for hours at a time staring at some cheap black casket, who have tamped down their nausea to approach its ghastly occupant, who have endured the disturbing weeping and wailing of family members, and the droning eulogies of clergy or guests; who have, in short, endured hours of the unseemly, the unsightly, the unnerving—don't they deserve a break? What's more, they know they do, and when they don't get it they feel taken advantage of and are bound to think a lot less of the family or even of the deceased himself.

The reception venue should present a calm and cheering atmosphere. This can be either in a restaurant, in a catering hall, or in someone's home which has been specially prepared for the occasion. The food should be of good quality, plentiful, and attractively presented. Family members should here be careful to repress any emotional displays for the sake of their guests. No one is going to be able to enjoy his meal if, only a few feet away, someone is bawling her eyes out. Family members who feel a bout of grief coming on should politely excuse themselves, repair to some distant room or closet, and there turn on the faucets, not showing themselves again till the reservoir is drained.

As for those families who do not provide a reception, what can be said of them? They are social morons—Yahoos who don't understand the first thing about living in society. They might as well have been raised by wolves. Even financial hardship cannot excuse them since it doesn't cost more than a few dollars to provide *something*, even if it's only coffee and cookies which they themselves have to hand out.

Then there is the matter of the headstone. For the average person it is the most important element of everything having to do with one's demise because it remains the only proof of one's *individual* existence. Some smart aleck will probably tell me that this isn't so—that one continues to live on in one's children and that they are, as living, breathing, thinking beings, the best memorial one could have. But I said of one's individual existence—not the mere continuation of one's surname. In fact the notion of you yourself living on in your descendants is a lot of baloney. You need only ask yourself about your grandparents' grandparents. Do you know anything about their lives? Eh? *Anything?* Of course not! Even those who have preceded you in so short a time are forgotten, expunged, banished to the eternal night of oblivion.

still others will say, "One's deeds remain." That assertion is even more ludicrous than the one about living on in one's posterity. In the great majority of cases people's deeds are no real consequence even while they are alive, let alone after they're dead. The world is a busy place. It hasn't time for any but the genuinely meaningful, for that which influences people at large, which changes their minds or behavior; and the rarity of that is appalling. Consider that some 100 billion people have lived on earth: how many of those have gained a place in the memory of posterity? Relatively not even a handful, not even a thimbleful. The deeds of most people, like their words, like themselves, vanish into nothingness.

Thus the headstone is all-important, due to the enduring nature of its material. Unfortunately people who are shameless in providing a depressing funeral or a shabby reception are no more conscientious or tasteful in choosing a headstone. Stroll through any modern cemetery and what do you see? Row upon row of short, squat, square slabs of granite, all so similar that trying to find the grave of one's loved one becomes as difficult as finding one's car in a crowded parking lot.  Properly speaking they are not headstones at all but only *markers*: an indication—a sign—a scratch or rather scar on the world—indicating where the remains of someone lie, and which in their aggregate turn what might have been a pretty landscape into an extensive eyesore.

There was a time when people knew better.  In the 19th and early 20th centuries headstones were large, fanciful, and ornate.  They had intricate yet deep and therefore long-lasting engravings.  They were works of art.  It took time and talent to create them.  Even families of moderate means extended themselves financially to provide a fine headstone and would have blushed for shame at the thought of plopping down over their loved one a block of granite no larger or more distinguished than what might be found at a construction site.  True, tastes change, and there is something to be said for simplicity of design, but there is a difference between lovely sleekness and an uninspiring plainness settled for only because it is cheaper.

There are several styles of headstone which ought never to be considered.  The first are those extra-wide types which are meant to contain the names and dates of both husband and wife.  The problem with these is that spouses rarely die close in time to each other, especially when they are, say, under the age of 50.  Thus they remain unfinished—with one name and set of dates missing—for years if not decades; and often enough permanently.  For as time goes by the surviving husband or wife realizes that he or she really *can* live without the deceased spouse, and indeed has already moved on to someone who is even more lovable.

Also to be avoided are those which feature an etched picture of the deceased. These came on the marketplace in the 1990s, and they were then, and are now, and will forever be, in bad taste. They are an offensive imposition on the public. People who visit the grave of a loved one should not have to see the crusty old mug of your aunt, uncle, brother, sister, mother, or father looking back at them! And it *is* their crusty old mug that's always shown: never what they looked like when they were young and strong and smooth and attractive, but only of how they looked in later years when they were old and wrinkled and feeble and ugly. Cemeteries should outlaw them.

As for mausoleums, they are not, in these expensive times, within the financial reach of most people. Anything affordable to a middle or even upper-middle class family will almost certainly be small and cheaply constructed. Even in what might be called their public heyday (again we look back to the late 19th and early 20th century) they were not especially attractive, and when iron bars had to be added to their stained glass windows to prevent vandalism, they looked more like miniature jails than anything else. But even if a family is wealthy and can afford something grand, they should avoid a mausoleum. For no matter how large or grand the architecture, no matter how spacious or garden-like its surroundings, one never forgets its unthinkable purpose. There is hardly a prettier dome than that of Les Invalides, and the Taj Mahal rises gloriously from its facing prospect: yet we know the dome of the former overspreads a crypt with corruption at its heart, and the spires of the latter, though reaching heaven-ward poetically, are but four points of a compass hemming in a nauseous core.

No, burial is always the proper way of sending off our loved ones because it ensures and fortifies a sense of separation between the living and the dead. The grave may be only six or ten feet deep but it's as though the whole earth were set between them and us—as though we existed in two different worlds. This contrariety, this sense of barrier or distance, hastens the healing process. A funeral director once told me about a young man whose burial took place in Pennsylvania and whose reception was right across the border in Ohio. It was a separation of only fifteen miles yet it had a profoundly positive effect on the survivors, so much so that the deceased's own parents who, that morning, were emotionally devastated, were able at the reception to get drunk and dance a tango.

As for cremation, it is to be avoided because it undermines this sense of separation. Burn up people in a crematorium, send them up a flue into the atmosphere, and they are—where? Nowhere in particular. They are floating endlessly around the world. They have been turned into restless, eternally wandering particles. One year they may be pressed against the palms of some South Pacific atoll, in another swirling round the tops of the Himalayas, and yet in another scudding before biting Arctic winds;—in the most distant, opposite, inconceivable places! They are the equivalents of the homeless of the dead. That is not a comforting thought for any family which prides itself on respectable stability.

Finally we come to one of the more controversial (but to my mind exciting) developments in the funeral industry, namely, the "living funeral." This is a funeral given "in advance" for someone who is still alive and wants to be able to experience his own service. As odd as it may sound, it has much to recommend it. It is a healthy step forward in our acceptance of mortality, and in lessening the blow to family and friends when the real event occurs. Hardly anyone comes away from such a service without considering that the next time So-and-so "dies" he will actually be dead. They will be a lot less likely to mar whatever ceremony takes place by carrying on, since they have already, as it were, gone through it. The family may even decide to forego a funeral altogether and lay their loved one to rest in a quick, private interment, thus curtailing all unpleasantness and better ensuring good memories.

A living funeral can also help us put our relationships into a more accurate perspective. Let's say, for instance, there is someone who is old, tired, penniless, friendless, etc.;—some poor soul who thinks he might as well be dead because he has nothing to live for and no one cares about him. He arranges his own funeral and, lo and behold, the service is attended by dozens of people whose affection he never suspected! That is bound to be a heartening surprise, to raise his self-esteem, to brighten the rest of his days. On the other hand suppose someone with a busy social life, who has dozens of "friends," whose home is often filled with people who drop by to talk, to drink, to have dinner—suppose he finds himself lying all afternoon in a casket in an empty room? What could be more disappointing, even shocking?

Yet it will be a salutary shock: it will reveal the falseness of the avowals of loyalty or love which he had been foolish enough to believe, and afterwards he will choose his friends more carefully. If he is wealthy it will also give him the opportunity to amend his will according to the reality of his relationships.

But perhaps the best thing about living funerals is that their receptions are bound to be more satisfying. People are more likely to enjoy themselves when they are not burdened with the consciousness of an actual death. They have better appetites, they feel freer to enjoy their meals, to chat and laugh, and even to start dancing if there is music. Best of all, the "deceased" can be present to partake of the festivities—though he should keep a low profile, be seated in some out-of-the-way place, and guests should be instructed to act and talk as though he weren't there in order to maintain the illusion of his eternal absence.

Finally, and strange as it might sound coming from me, not everyone should have a funeral. Some causes of death are so horrendous that not even most artistic presentations would be capable of distracting people's thoughts away from them. Among these are: attacks by grizzly bears, lions, tigers, sharks, and other ferocious animals; consumption by cannibals, or insects; decapitation, or multiple and simultaneous loss of several limbs; quick-frying by ultra-high electrical voltage; nuclear or other powerful explosions involving mass numbers of casualties; fiery destruction while being launched into space (as may happen to astronauts); falling into live volcanos; falling into vats of molten metal; falling into

vats of molten glass; falling into car shredders; falling from heights over 12,000 feet (for instance, due
to parachute failure while skydiving); and obliteration in high-speed airliner crashes.  One might also
include multiple lightning strikes, being swept away
by tsunamis, or being trapped in boats or shipped
capsized by rogue waves and sent to the bottom of
the sea.  In most of these cases there is very little, if
anything, left of the deceased and therefore a casket
is dispensed with, which removes from the service a
possibly elevating element; or, when it is retained, it
is only for symbolic purpose and is empty, which
adds a note of falsehood.

Scoundrels should also be denied funerals.  There
is a certain small percentage of the population which
is composed of bad seeds.  Even in their earliest
years they exhibited the malignant and violent behavior which leads them to committing cruel or murderous crimes.  These dregs of the earth deserve no
ceremony on their demise.  They only deserve to be
swept off the face of the earth as soon as possible.
You may know a healthy society by how quickly it
*does* sweep them off the face of the earth, and a sick
society by how much it tolerates their existence: and
you may know a moribund society—one well on the
way do disintegration—by how it coddles or otherwise makes excuses for their behavior, and imposes
on the public, including the family and friends of
their victims, a charge to keep them alive and in
good health!  Can anything be more sickeningly
backward than *that?*  It is the ultimate injustice because it is state-sanctified insult added to injury.
Again, such a disgusting state of affairs could never
have come about but as a result of mass insecurity

imposed upon by flabby sentimentalism: of people so uncertain of their worth, so desperate to thought "good," that they will ignore logic, abandon the most obvious sense of right and wrong, and delight in their feeling of superiority even as they leap into self-destruction!

It should be clear then that a funeral should only be given to someone who has died relatively intact and wasn't a scourge to society.

# IV
## A FEW REVIEWS

In an attempt to make my reviews more mainstream, I initially wrote them in a conversational tone, sometimes going so far as to liven up a passage with some racy slang; thinking that this would add a light-hearted *frisson* which would make my work more appealing. But I quickly came to see that this was not the right way to go about them. First of all, writing in that way was inconsistent with my character, which is essentially serious and contemplative, and second of all it was unsuitable to the subject, which ought always to be treated with respectful gravity. Besides, slang, though colorful, is often vague. Describing a casket as "crappy," a grieving relative as "a mess," or a funeral director as "creepy" doesn't express the precise nature of the shortcoming or offensiveness, which really needs to be spelled out. I did however appropriate one element of popular reviews into mine, namely, a rating system of the kind usually applied to hotels or restaurants; but instead of using five stars, I used five coffins. Thus a tedious, depressing, and life-poisoning service was reprimanded with a rating of ▮▯▯▯▯, while one which honors the deceased and survivors with an attractive, inspiring, completely positive presentation was praised with a rating of ▮▮▮▮▮.

As might be expected, good ratings are as infrequent as bad ones are common. Over three-quarters of funerals never get beyond ♥♥⬜⬜. This was especially true in the beginning of my reviewing career when I was attending mostly lower- and middle-class funerals—which I mention not out of snobbery but simply as a fact, since people in this socio-economic group tend to adhere strictly to the conventional practices of sending off their loved ones, and almost always make a depressing mess of it.

One of the first funerals I attended in a professional capacity was for a certain Laurie Loring of New Haven, Connecticut. She was a nurse who was crossing a street when she was struck by an ambulance racing its way to an emergency room. And yet that was the least ironic part of her death. still more disturbing (but also instructive) was that she had intended to retire the very next day, having waited till then when she would turn sixty-seven and receive higher Social Security benefits. She hardly needed the money. She had made a very good living as a nurse, and her husband, who had predeceased her by eight years, had left her a small fortune. She owned a large house in a good part of town, owned various expensive stocks, and had otherwise lived frugally and saved her money. She was easily worth several million dollars.

Nurse Loring's three daughters had made the funeral arrangements, and theirs was a case of distress taken advantage of. They had gone to the first funeral home they had come upon and had been too distraught to think about anything other than providing a "proper" service. The old fogey of

a funeral director had been but too willing to accommodate them.  And so with nothing but concern for
propriety on the one side, and ensuring a good profit
margin on the other, there emerged a service in
which everything was calculated to intensify misery
as much as possible.

I knew I was in for a disappointment as soon as I
walked into the funeral home.  It had been around
for a hundred years and hadn't been redecorated in
decades.  One often finds this problem in the establishments run by old funeral directors, just as one
finds it in the homes of old people generally: they are
comfortable with the style of furnishings and color
schemes they have had for decades and which were
popular in their youth.  They forget how, when they
were young, they looked askance on the fashions of
the preceding generation, and the styles they cling to
are in turn frowned upon by those younger than
themselves.    In this case the interior looked like a
worn throwback to the 1970s.  The main room was
filled with an avocado-green couch and the burnt-or-
ange chairs, their colors now faded and in some
places stained.  Lamps with bellying ceramic bases
stood on tables and threw out light from beneath
shades which, once white, had turned beige.  Drapes
hung over the windows and reached to a carpet with
bold geometrical figures now faded to dull, brownish
pastels.  On the walls hung the usual sad excuses for
artwork:   landscape paintings set in large bulky
frames meant to give them a sense of artistic gravity.  If someone had cared to check for dust he probably would have found plenty of it on the tops of the
window sills or on the upper surface of a projecting
molding which ran around the room just under the

ceiling.

The funeral director fit right in with his establishment. In his sixties, slender, tall, white-haired, chalky-faced, serious-looking, somewhat slouching, he was as subdued and lugubrious in a way that most of his colleagues affect only for sake of conveying a sense of sympathy for their clients' loss. I don't think he had cracked a smile since 2012. It may be that he was distracted by financial difficulties. Mortality rates for New Haven in the year of Nurse Loring's death were unusually low, so perhaps he was worried about the slowdown in business. At any rate he was not gracious in his welcome but stood glumly at the door and in a monotone directed people to the visitation room.

This was as unappealing as the rest of the establishment. It had off-white walls, dark tiled floors, and rows of chairs which, though made of wood and padded, were armless, stiffly uncomfortable, and looked like the kind found in fast-food restaurants. The drop ceiling consisted of large tiles interpolated with air ducts and small round spotlights shining down a dazzling white light. Four incandescent lamps stood in the corners of the room and they were turned on, but their low wattage bulbs barely illuminated their shades and consequently could not temper the general harsh lighting. There were no windows. Arrangements of yellow carnations were set upon tripods on either side of the casket.

The casket itself was a cheap import probably made in China but possibly in Vietnam or Cambodia. Typical of its kind it was all shine and shoddiness. Made of particle board, fake wood ornamentation, and pressed steel fittings, it was a nasty contraption thrown together with glue and a few screws. A band of rosettes running along the bottom proved to be made of injection-molded plastic—I know because I made a point of running my fingers along it. The bedding was covered in a cotton fabric which had been treated with a chemical (probably toxic) to feel as smooth as silk, and it was so thin that, at certain angles, one saw the wood shavings with which it was stuffed. The pillow was small, hard, and uncomfortable.

People entered the room hesitantly, their pace faltering a little when they stepped across the threshold: they saw that this was everything they had expected and dreaded. Nevertheless they went through with what they thought to be their duty; valiantly, at the cost of their own well-being, they stepped forth, offered their sympathy to family members, then approached the deceased (with what inward shuddering can be imagined), standing there a few minutes before turning around to find a seat in the room, walking calmly when they wanted to run.

Nurse Laurie herself was not looking her best. When hit by the ambulance she had flown some twenty feet before landing on her forehead, from which much of the skin had been scraped away. A talented mortuary cosmetologist would have finessed this problem into something perfectly acceptable and perhaps hardly noticeable, but she had been worked on by a talentless hack, perhaps by the funeral director himself. Some kind of membrane should have covered her injury but only makeup had been used, and it was so thick, so caked on, that it looked like a coating of plaster. Her attire was atrocious: a plain, long, gray dress whose frilly collar was buttoned up tight around her neck and made her look like a spinster schoolmarm. Also she was chubby and had been squeezed into the narrow casket: her shoulders were pressed together and gave her a shrinking pose as though she were embarrassed to be there.

But by far the worst part of the funeral was conduct of the family. It was shameful, inexcusable! The three daughters, who were accompanied by their husbands, cried profusely and loudly. Sometimes they fell into a rhythm in which they cried and coughed and gagged all at once. More than once several guests seemed about to get up out of their seats as though they would rush to their aid and offer a Heimlich maneuver. At one point they stood up and huddled around one another, and, what with their long black hair and long black dresses, reminded me of the witches in *Macbeth*. The deceased's sister and two brothers were also carrying on, though they probably would have been able to contain themselves if they were not egged on by the distressing sights and sounds of the daughters.

When they managed to rein in their hysteria for a few minutes, the family would look over the room and see how many guests had arrived. Their eyes would rove over the mostly empty seats, and surprise at the sparse attendance would momentarily quell their grief. Apparently their mother had had a great many friends and acquaintances and they were expecting a big crowd but no more than a couple of dozen persons had shown up. I have since come to understand that sparse attendance is not unusual in the funerals of old people. When one's

generation begins dying off, which means that the
generation before it has almost entirely passed away,
one has attended so many funerals, has been exposed so many times to their withering negativity,
that out of a belated (but for that reason more vehe-
ment) sense of self-preservation we forswear them all
with a final, "That's enough for me!" Moreover by
the time we have aged into our fifties, we have
reached the antithesis of our teenage years insofar
as our concern about what other people think of us:
whereas back then we sought everyone's favor, and
felt bad about not getting it, we now reject anyone
who doesn't think as highly of ourselves as we do.
We are also wary of whatever doesn't redound to our
comfort and security.  Consequently we see that
"paying our respects" to the dead does nothing for
them and only harms us, and brush off the criticism
of our selfishness as indifferently as we might brush
specks of dandruff off our shoulders.  We know what
we are about: we have lived too long—have struggled
too long—not to.

Thus the old friends and acquaintances of Laurie
Loring had undoubtedly been saddened to hear of
her death, wished her family well, and had perhaps
said a prayer for her soul;—but they felt themselves
to be at a time of life beyond the point of making
disagreeable exertions.

As for the old people who did show up, they were
the unwilling victims of a convention they could not
shake off no matter how much they had come to understand its toxic nature.  There were about six of
them.  Slow, gray, tired, they let themselves down
heavily into their seats and remained there, motion-
less, looking as gloomy as the Pit.  Sooner or later

they all went up to the casket, dutifully stood before it a minute or two, then turned to the family to offer their condolences. They returned to their seats with disgust written all over their faces. Three of them left after twenty minutes or so, satisfied that they had done their duty, that they had "shown their faces." Of the three who stayed one of them nodded off during the minister's prayer and eulogy.

In part those who stuck it out did so because, as pensioners on a fixed income and increasingly unable to meet living expenses, they hoped to enjoy a free meal at the reception. One can imagine their dismay when they were presented with what was referred to as "light refreshments." It was held in the home of one of the daughters and consisted of a buffet of cheap food, of starchy, pickled, canned stuff beside which had been laid out the "desserts" of cookies, cupcakes, and hard candies. Not only the old folks but everyone was disappointed. People exchanged condemnatory glances at one another or shook their heads in dismay. If this had been any other event they would have overtly called out the food for what it was—third-rate—but consideration for the family kept their tongues from wagging.

I happened to be sitting beside an old fellow in his seventies who walked slowly with a cane. Coming to the funeral had been an especial effort for him. He had not gone to the cemetery—that would have been too much for him—but he had driven to where the reception was held, no doubt hoping to relax a little and have something to eat before he drove back home. Like everyone else he scoffed at the offerings but unlike everyone else he could not refrain from expressing his contempt. He sat holding a plastic plate filled with macaroni salad and at one point lifted up a forkful of it, showing it to me and asking in a low, displeased voice, "What the heck is that supposed to be?"

I knew what he was getting at: the insulting paltriness of the thing. Half out of embarrassment for the family, and half to assuage his own disappointment, I acted as though I didn't know what he meant and told him it was macaroni salad.

"That's not what I mean!" he grumbled, lowering his plate to his knees. Now outright resentfully he said, "This is ridiculous!"

"Yes," I admitted, under my breath, "it does seem a bit thin."

"We've been here for hours," he grumbled, meaning the funeral as a whole, "and this is what they give us?— macaroni?"

"Well, at least the coffee is good," I said, though even that was only fair.

In the end he ate the macaroni salad, also partook of some potatoes and pickles, but sat there for the next forty-five minutes grumpily silent. Perhaps he resolved never to attend another funeral. But my sense of him was that he *would* go to other funerals—would not be able to help himself—because he could not cast off those cultural prepossessions which he had absorbed in his youth and which, though belied by the experience of a lifetime, remained with him as strongly as ever. In this respect I felt sorry for him.

Nurse Loring's children placed over her grave a headstone which reminded me of a low ottoman: it was about six inches in height, perfectly square, and its flat, matte, upward-facing surface was engraved with her birth and death dates and the trite words, "Beloved Mother."

When one considers that Nurse Loring left her considerable assets to her children, there was no excuse for the cheap, dark, depressing funeral they had given her, nor for the horrible, stingy reception afterwards (really, macaroni salad and pickles!), nor for the indifferent headstone with which they capped it all off. The funeral earned only ▮▯▯▯▯.

Two weeks later I attended the funeral of "Dirk Talbot." I put his name in skeptical quotation marks because though it was used in his obituary and even on his headstone, it was not his real name, which was Daniel Talbowitz. He came from a Jewish family and had changed his name for the sake of pursuing an acting career. An Internet search reveals that he appeared in such "indie" gems as *Anomalous Occurrences*, in which a woman disappears into a wall and is never heard from again, and *Crank It Up*, about a bus driver who pulls off a heist at the company he is working for, only for the stolen safe to be bobby-trapped, blow off his arm when he tries to open it, and leave him disabled for the rest of his life. He also acted in regional theater.

I only chose to go to this funeral because Dirk had come from a *secular* Jewish family. If he had been of the Orthodox version I would have kept away. For I had attended an Orthodox Jewish funeral before and it was a wretched disappointment. The Jews are admirable for many things, for their tenacity in the face of a hostile world, for their intelligence, for their humor, for the ease with which they assimilate into and enrich foreign cultures, but the funeral practices of their Orthodox are totally unacceptable. They don't embalm their dead and bury them within twenty-four hours. How is anyone supposed to plan a good funeral in so little time? It's hard enough to arrange it even when one has a week's notice. This hurry to get rid of the dead undoubtedly arose from a prudent concern for hygiene: five thousand years ago a hot Middle Eastern day was sure to induce in the deceased certain unpleasant transformations offensive to the nostrils and toxic to health, so it made good sense to stick him in a hole and cover him up as soon as possible. But that was then and this is now. My dear Jewish friends! We have come a long way in five thousand years! We have something new now: it's called refrigeration. Even if you don't like the idea of embalming, you can still stick your loved ones into a refrigerator and they can keep for weeks, even for months if frozen. I would respectfully ask you to reconsider what in the modern world is an unnecessary and really undignified haste.

The obituary didn't mention the cause of Dirk's death and I only found out about it because my exquisite sense of hearing enabled me to eavesdrop on a conversation between two persons four seats away from me. "Yes," somebody said, "it's always a terrible thing when someone kills himself." If Dirk had been famous the manner of his suicide would have been exposed by some "investigative journalist"; but he had been anonymous and the details of his end had been known only to himself and his closest family or associates. The only way I could have found out was if I had asked the family, and that would have been gauche.

Kudos to the temple in which the ceremony was held. It was a new building with modern architecture, and the space containing the service was spacious, bright, and colorful with stained glass windows representing in angular and rather cubistic design various scenes from the Old Testament. The seating consisted of padded pews and was fairly comfortable, though probably not for more than an hour at a time. At the front of the great room was the closed casket. It was too dark and too plain, having only a raised lip or edge around the top panels, and reminded me of a cigar box.

The conduct of the family sitting in the first row was reprehensible. And yet that was not entirely their fault. This was not an Orthodox funeral but there was still a sense of urgency to get Dirk out of the way as soon as possible; consequently the family had not had enough days to absorb the shock of their loss. The large family included parents, two sisters, three brothers, various aunts and uncles, and a dozen cousins. All of them were dressed in black and all of them were crying. A rabbi led the prayers in Hebrew, which he *sang*. His voice was horrible, and he had no right to be *singing* anything, let alone prayers. At one point he uttered something that drew a response from the guests; suddenly everyone around me repeated something in that mysterious ancient language. This happened several times, and each time it happened I had the strange and unsettling sensation of finding myself in the midst of some secret society. Fortunately the service only lasted about twenty minutes, and the family and guests shuffled out of the great room to go outside to their cars and accompany the body to the cemetery.

Having been dismayed by the drab casket, the unseemly behavior of the family, and the rabbi's singing, the last thing I wanted to do was to go to the cemetery where the family was sure to carry on even more. I only went because I didn't yet know where the reception was to be held. Sure enough at the gravesite several members of the family broke down into loud quivering wails, especially as the casket was lowered into the earth, while the rabbi, covered in a prayer shawl, stood before this unseemly spectacle and, holding a prayer book, regaled us with more of his nauseating frog-like vocalizations. There happened to be a crow cawing in a nearby tree, and even *it* sounded better than he did.

It is a part of Jewish custom that members of the immediate family should throw onto the casket a shovelful of earth. Undoubtedly this is intended to symbolize their own acceptance of their loss, and so help them along in their healing. But it is hard to fathom the depths of sadism on the part of the maniac who thought this one up. For it can only have the opposite effect of plunging the blade of grief deeper into broken hearts. By expecting people to perform an act which highlights their loss more keenly than ever only further burdens spirits already fainting under insupportable loads of sorrow; is a cruel practice to be accounted for only by that perverse streak in humankind which has led it to embrace or sanctify customs or beliefs which make life harder rather than easier.

The reception was held at the house of one of Dirk's brothers, Jonah, who, as it turned out, was an identical twin. Thus even though the casket had been closed during the ceremony I got a good look, as it were, at the deceased. He was tall, thin, dark, and handsome, with a slightly cleft chin, a noble profile, and a shock of thick straight hair—no wonder Dirk had thought he had a chance at success in an industry in which good looks count for a lot. When I told Jonah I knew his brother from having acted with him in summer stock in Maine (information provided in the obituary), he warmly shook my hand, thanked me for coming, and bade me relax and have "something to eat."

There was a lot of good food and liquor set out in both the dining room and the large kitchen. The house was crowded with people most of whom were relatives of various degrees of separation. They stood or sat holding plates piled high with food and eating and talking, usually in good humor. On the face of it the reception seemed laudatory but it rested on an invidious basis: according to custom it was to last for seven days. Now I am the first one in the world to promote and admire good receptions, but to expect of a family, which has just suffered a loss, to keep up a running buffet for a whole week is a barbaric imposition on their grief. No doubt the custom was well-intentioned as a way to coax mourners as soon as possible away from sad thoughts, but its only real effect is to increase distress by forcing people to be sociable at a time when all they want to do, and all they should have to do, is mourn in private.

When I factored all these things into Dirk Talbot's funeral I could not, despite the plentiful and good food at the reception (not to mention a few pretty girls), give it more than ▐▌◌◌◌. Perhaps it was unfair of me to rate it before I had a chance to see the headstone, but this was not to be set in place—again as a matter of custom—till a year later, and I was not about to wait that long before writing the review.  Besides, it probably wouldn't have made much of a difference.  Any family kowtowing to a custom which flies in the face of common sense, which lays down more rather than fewer responsibilities on people already emotionally devastated, and intensifies their grief by setting up barriers to its expression and release:—such people cannot not be expected to choose a fine headstone.  Vulgar is vulgar from start to finish.

I move on to a funeral only somewhat better, at least insofar as the conduct of the family and guests are concerned.  It was John Jason Sweete, or "J.J. Sweete," as he had been commonly referred to.  He was the last of an expiring breed: an editor for a local daily newspaper: a gruff, cigar-chomping man who every morning barged his way into his office, read copy, lambasted his staff for real or imagined slacking, and generally was the angry soul of a publication expiring beneath the irresistible pressure of digitization.  His drive and manner had enabled him to have some success from the '70s to the '90s, but he was a dinosaur by the early 2000s, and had neither the will nor the energy to take his publication in a new direction.  He had been retired from business and living mostly on Social Security when he died at 79.

His name was ironic because he was a nasty man, so much so that even his ex-wife and none of his seven children showed up for the funeral.  It was given by an aged sister who probably felt forced into it out of a sense of maintaining family respectability but who clearly thought the whole thing a nuisance. She sat at the front row with a puss on her face. Beside her sat her husband and a few relatives. There wasn't a moist eye among them.

The same was true of the guests, of which there were less than twenty. Most of them were old men over 60. They looked as though they had come to pay their respects for the sake of diverting their boredom. Most of them sat with mild, indifferent, sometimes merely curious expressions. Most of them were, as I later learned, journalists who had written for Sweete's newspaper. They had moved on to other, sometimes large news organizations, and after "distinguished" (i.e., totally forgettable) careers had retired and done nothing, which it would have been better for the state of journalism for them to have done from the first.

The funeral was characterized by its pro forma respectability. There was a casket, there were flowers, there were mourners in black clothes, there was the appropriate hushed atmosphere, and a eulogizing minister. Only, every one of these elements had been satisfied in the most cheap and convenient way. The casket was a plain, black, imported atrocity from a low-cost factory in Asia; the flower arrangements were small and set in plastic pots; the minister had not known Mr. Sweete and made his appearance at the (paid) request of his sister. For fifteen minutes he eulogized the deceased with generic praise interpolated with clichés about the afterlife. Everyone sat politely and played his expected part in the ridiculous charade.

But there *was* one bright side to the otherwise

tawdry service: there were no teary eyes, no gagging coughs, no faint, struggling, grief-stricken voices;— none of those distressing exhibitions of grief which so often mar and increase the general misery of a funeral. And this should be a lesson to everyone. A funeral may be tedious, its accoutrements cheap, a great part of the reason behind it a vulgar concern for maintaining respectability: yet so long as the family can maintain their composure, and set their guests at ease by ensuring a dignified tone to the service, they have gone a long way to making up for material shortcomings.

After the service the guests were expected to attend the interment at the cemetery and then go their separate ways. I was appalled to learn there would be no reception. A member of the family informed me that the elder sister, the one with the puss on her face who was paying for everything, had thought it would "not be appropriate." She probably meant that a reception is in some measure a celebration of the life of the deceased, and in this case there was nothing to celebrate but only to forget about as soon as possible. She had a point: but only a small one, and she had lost sight of the bigger, truer picture. For a reception is really for the living, for the guests; it is a token of thanks for their presence and a chance for them to relax from the unpleasantness of the foregoing service. It is the most basic politeness to have one. The sister should have wanted it if only for the sake of the respectability she had been so concerned about in the first place.

I am sure that many of the guests were as disappointed, and left as famished, as I was. I was so hungry that on my way home I stopped into the first place which sold food. Certainly when I had started out for the funeral earlier in the day I didn't think I'd wind up in the parking lot of a 7-Eleven chowing down on a bag of chips and a cherry Slurpee. Outrageous! I was determined to pan the Sweete funeral in every way possible.

Fortunately for my reputation I never write when I'm in a bad mood. I started the review a couple of days later after referring to my recorded notes and didn't finish it till I had had a chance to see the headstone, which was pretty bad: small, thin, ill-polished, its engraving so superficial that it looked as though it had been scratched out with a nail. It wouldn't have surprised me to learn that it too was an Asian import. A dozen hot summers, a dozen freezing winters, and it would begin to crack and crumble; and in fifty years it was sure to look like one of those gray, forlorn, tilted slabs of stone sometimes seen in old graveyards, and from which Time has effaced the name it was meant to memorialize into an indecipherable shadow.

The Sweete funeral earned ▮▮▯▯▯, and even that was being generous.

# V
## MAKING A LIVING

It should be obvious that I don't make a living as a critic. Outside of the funeral industry most people aren't too keen on reading funeral reviews, and for a critic to make a living he has to have a fairly large audience which can be capitalized on. I make a living by the ordinary job I have had for the last fifteen years—as a high school guidance counselor.

My job requires a Master's Degree in "Education" (a bit of psychology here, bit of administrative understanding there), but the only real requirement is common sense and a month's experience with how a particular school does things. In keeping with the (by now) completely corporatized educational system, so is my job essentially corporate in nature. Just take a look at my job description:

- Maintaining and organizing university listings with the aim of creating a flexible yet dynamic database to be continually appraised for its applicability and efficacy in meeting talent-oriented objectives

- Developing omni-channel strategies to interface with key contacts at appropriate institutions of higher education with the intention of expanding and consolidating career planning opportunities

- Accumulating, prioritizing, and communicating key admissions updates to students and consulting with them regarding college-specific challenges and helping them to develop interviewing strategies

- Collaborating with teaching staff to ensure any non-academic challenges to students are addressed in the context of helping to ensure a supportive intracurricular and extracurricular environment

Now, as much as one might be inclined to attribute this addled, bloated, circuitous verbiage to some kind of brain damage on the part of its writer, let me assure the reader that it came from a person who was, if anything, regarded as intelligent and competent, and who was probably hired for his or her position based on his or her "education." Which goes to prove my point about education having become a corporate enterprise, since this is exactly the kind of language which comes out of "corporate culture," which is to say, no culture at all. Those who are a part of it recognize, if only in some vague way, the simple-minded nature of their employments, which is why, in describing them, they resort to the fuzzy, superfluous, important-sounding language of corporate-speak. It is the language of morons trying to convince themselves and others that they are not engaged in moronic pursuits.

I always recognized this and consequently in applying for jobs always spun out my academic qualifications and experience into mountains of magnificent woolliness. Sure enough, my application impressed someone in my school district's Human Resources department and I was scheduled to be interviewed by the then principal of the high school in need of a new guidance counselor. She was a pleasant but corporately empty-headed woman (she might have worked for the State Department) who told me how impressed she had been by my "extensive qualifications and experience." In fact I had only worked at two other schools for a total of five years. I got the job.

My students are a cross section of the community in which the school is located: most of them are lower-middle-class, with a sprinkling of affluent outliers. (You can always tell which ones come from money because their parents buy them cars as soon as they get their driver's licenses.) Their energy, their enthusiasm for their future, is always attractive and stimulating. A lot of them have grand plans for themselves; they are sure their lives are going to be different, better, more exciting than that of their parents; and they have a spot of contempt for the generation which produced them. But fifteen or twenty years from now, when they are ensconced in workaday jobs and responsible for their own families, they will find that they have succeeded precisely to their parents' places; and will consider it a sign of their maturity to have accepted it. Then they will give themselves a dozen reasons why they could never have fulfilled the high expectations of their youth, though the real reason is that they were, after all, quite unexceptionable and therefore only suited to an average life.

Working with young people invariably has its wry surprises. This year two of them stood in my mind as remarkable for their charming naiveté or dismaying foolishness.

One of them was Catherine, a pretty, vivacious seventeen-year-old. She was mature for her age—I couldn't help noticing that she already had a nice figure. She was also lucky. Unlike most of her peers, whose families couldn't afford to pay for their room and board at some distant college, she came from money (her father owned a trucking company) and intended to go to college out of state. She brought to her consultation with me brochures of the schools she had requested information from. They were filled with big glossy pictures of beautiful old buildings and shady green lawns on which young people sat about, open books in their laps, smiling and laughing as though one of them had just told a joke. She came to me with her first, second, and third choices—one in Virginia, one in Georgia, one in California. The one she had her heart set on was located among charming mountain scenery and was not far from a large town described as having a "vibrant nightlife"—that is to say (I wasn't so old that I couldn't read between the lines), having several bars at which she could get drunk with handsome boys and dance on tables. And who can blame her? She was young and wanted to have fun, and if you're not going to have it when you're young, when will you?

We went over her academic performance—it was average—and discussed what she wanted to do for a living. She said she wanted to be a "marine biologist." She had settled on this career because she loved dolphins and whales and wanted to "help" them. She had never been within two-hundred miles of a dolphin or whale but she still loved them.

We spent several minutes discussing the job opportunities in that field, which were nearly non-existent. What if she couldn't find work after graduation? I suggested she might want to have something else to fall back on. She bristled at the idea that she might not become a marine biologist, but at my prompting to think of something else she answered ... "an archaeologist." Hers was a case of having watched too many movies and having too much money.

At the opposite end of the spectrum was Rory. He was a tall, lanky boy whose dull eyes and basic vocabulary disclosed a sluggish mind. He had passed from one grade to the next by the skin of his teeth. He told me had been "thinking" about "going into law." It took all of two minutes to find out that he had no interest in law or much of anything else outside of cars and girls, and it was his pushy parents' idea to turn him into a lawyer. One often finds this behavior among poor parents: having been traumatized by poverty, they are determined that their children shall have a better, more affluent life, and bully them into lucrative professions for which they have no aptitude. Rory would have done a lot better for himself going into a trade. He probably would have made a first-rate mechanic, and made a lot of money doing it. But my job is not to dissuade youngsters from pursuing their objectives, even when these aren't their own. The best I could do for him in this way was to remind him that law required a lot of study which would be intolerable to anyone who wasn't genuinely interested in it.

Strange as it may seem I rather put more than less hope in students like Rory, for it is within the *ab ovo* nature of youth that sometimes the most remarkable qualities lie dormant in those who seem least promising. It is true that a young person who is an impossible dolt is likely to stay that way; but this is not *always* the case. The best things often take time to develop. It may take ten or twenty years before some exceptional ability in a young person manifests itself. History is full of "dull" students who later went on to remarkable achievements. Take me, for instance! Who would have thought, to see me in my high school or college days, that one day I'd be reviewing funerals? Who could have imagined that such a sweet, quiet, charming, handsome, but by no means academically advanced boy, would one day see into the self-destructive errors of generations and, exhibiting the rarest critical gifts, attempt to correct them for the sake of bettering the lives of all people? You can never predict something like that because there has yet to occur the maturity of the personality in question and the circumstances which will elicit its unexpected response.

I also assist students with any personal problems they might have. In fact not many of them come to me for this. They may have problems but they also have their pride, and they're not going to disclose their private and potentially embarrassing struggles to someone who, they are sure, can't possibly relate to their much younger lives. Nevertheless sometimes they do come to me after the death of a best friend or a parent. A teacher will notify me of a change in their behavior, for instance skipping classes, or no longer completing assignments, or becoming generally silent and withdrawn. Almost all the severe cases of this "emotional blunting" (as it is known in psychology) can be traced back to the trauma of their loss and—even more—to the worse trauma of the funeral which followed. In such cases my counseling consists of trying to supplant their negative memories and emotions with expectations of their bright and happy future. I also try to convince them—gently, and in a way which does not attribute blame to anyone in their family (where of course much of the blame lies)—that the funeral they attended was probably mishandled and unnecessarily emphasized negative emotions.

Another one of my responsibilities is "monitoring duty." The staff in my school take turns standing in the hallway in the morning while students are entering the building and getting ready to attend their first classes. My turn is every other Wednesday morning. I stand there for about an hour, leaning against a wall with my arms crossed; smiling, looking kindly, saying hello or good morning when I'm accosted, but on the whole silent, observant. I often find myself feeling sorry for the kids. What a horrible thing it is to have to spend one's whole childhood going to school! Children could never endure it were they not so adaptable to harsh conditions. There is hardly an intelligent adult who would be willing to live over his life if he also had to repeat school. Of course I recognize its necessity: the disparateness of personalities must be brought into some sort of common line, must be molded into a similar shape if the cogs of the society are to turn smoothly and a new generation is to replace the older. But as in all things, here too nothing is gained but at the expense of something else, and it may be that for every ten thousand good little boys and girls who grow up into productive and upstanding citizens we have irremediably crushed or stunted rare abilities which, had they been recognized and cultivated in a way advantageous to their peculiar types, might have resulted in real contributions to civilization.  But recognizing them would require people in some measure *akin* to them, and our corporatized educational system is nearly infallible in weeding out those who are.

I spend most of my time in my office located at the end of a hallway in the administrative part of the building.  It is small but private.  There is only one window, which looks outside and has an opaque shade which can be pulled down.  I generally keep the door closed and locked.  I also keep plenty of papers scattered over my desk to keep up the pretense of being constantly busy, should anyone walk in on me.  That's especially important on those cold, gray, rainy days when it is hard for me to get up in the morning and I need a little more sleep, since then I can lock my door, adjust my padded office chair all the way back, put my feet up on my desk, and take a snooze.  I never sleep deeply.  If someone knocks on my door I'm up in a second and call out, "One moment please!"

And how do I like my job?  Well, I was never enthusiastic about it, and have come to loathe it.  Beware of finding your true vocation!  Every occupation thereafter is bound to seem a waste of your time.  I never get up on a weekday morning and begin the routine of getting ready for work than a pall of despair falls over me because, once again, I will be unable to attend a funeral or work on a review.  Someone might tell me, "But you are only at work for eight hours a day. Surely that leaves you plenty of time to do your reviews." Anyone who would tell me this—may I ask what planet you are living on? Because on *this* one there are only twenty-four hours in a day. What about all the time you need to take care of yourself, to shower, to dress, to eat, to commute, then to relax a little, plus the eight hours needed for a good night's sleep? Factor all that in and you're left with a measly four or five hours to do with as you will; and if you push yourself to utilize them, consistently, down to the minute, day after day;—how exhausting, how demoralizing it becomes!

No one in the school knows about my critical work. I know better than to tell any of my colleagues about it. One might think that the teachers among them would be interested in my reviews if only from an intellectual, a literary standpoint; but not a chance! They would consider it as too outré, as somehow unbecoming in someone who works in academe, as I learned when, on hinting at the subject to Mr. Porter, an English teacher, he looked at me as though it were the most absurd thing he had ever heard of.

The fact is that my colleagues aren't very bright, and when measured against any really high intellectual standard operate only on the tertiary, quaternary, quinary, senary (take it down however many levels you want) plane. —Which is a pity because Mr. Porter might at least have been able to point out any overtly bad grammar or diction in my reviews. No, I realized it was best to keep mum about the matter lest one of my "friends" rat me out to the principal.

The principal is Maurice Peckle.   Never did a man have an apter name because his carries the intimation of the smallness of his mind and body. How he became the principal of a high school, how he could possibly have gained a position of authority over others, is a mystery till one accepts that the public schools are extensions of the corporatized State.  People in his position are recruited by career functionaries as unimaginatively dutiful as themselves.  Thus they choose people who have done everything "by the book," though of course the personality which has strictly adhered to rules and precedent is precisely the one from which nothing extraordinary is to be expected.

Sure enough, everything about Peckle is uninspiring.   Picture a man forty years old, wearing three-piece suits with ties always too thickly knotted, going about with an air of hurried busyness, brusquely asking questions or giving orders, dashing off ten emails in a single morning about the first things that pop into his otherwise empty head, and always on the lookout for how to inject himself into other peoples' business.  His pathological need to be a boss is precisely what should have disqualified him from being one.  In him this surely comes from a Napoleon complex, since he stands 5' 5" tall in his thick-soled shoes.  He micromanages every inch of the school because in this way he can assure himself that even though other men and women are at least two inches taller than he is, he can directly affect their lives in a way which they cannot affect his.  But there is more to it even than that. The man has no outside interests or pastimes.  The whole of his Lilliputian mind is consumed by school administration. It may be that he sometimes perceives the superficiality of his life, which would go a long way to explaining his "busyness": for it's better to exhaust oneself in ultimately meaningless trifles than to look inward and face a harrowing wasteland.

He is always scheduling after-school meetings which he insists the staff attend. He loves to hear himself talk. He struts back and forth in front of the room and bloviates about various "projects" and "initiatives" for the school. He might have informed us of all this in an email of five or six lines, but that wouldn't take up enough of his time, so he makes a production out of it: shows us charts, graphs, pages of bullet-pointed PowerPoint presentations he has spent hours creating. When his back is turned we roll our eyes at one another, silently asking, "Doesn't this guy have a life?"

—Which is the whole point: he doesn't. But *I* do. I have funerals to get to. I have reviews to write, and I don't have enough time as it is. Thus I was always engaged in a fretful balancing-act between my critical work and my counseling job, allocating the absolute minimum number of hours to the latter. I took off as many days as possible, claiming illness or some pressing personal issue. Pernicious Peckle harassed me about my frequent absences, saying that they indicated a "lack of motivation"—about which he could not have been more right. Once, after demanding my more consistent attendance, he scheduled another one of his dopey meetings. It could not have come at a more inopportune time, since it was to take place on the very day when I had planned to attend a promising funeral. Of course there was no question about which one I would go to. My only concern was that he would regard my absence as an outright display of contempt or rebellion. I had to come up with an excuse which would, to his satisfaction, remove the element of my volition.

It occurred to me that the only excuse he would possibly accept was that of illness, and even then he would have to be able to confirm it. Thus the day before his meeting I ordered sushi for lunch. I made a display of it to a few people in the office and casually mentioned that it "didn't smell right." A few hours later I began complaining of stomach pains and, with a hand pressed against my stomach and making a sour face, passed before the secretaries at the front office on my way to the Men's Room, telling them there had been something "wrong" with the food I had eaten. A little later I mussed up my hair, splashed some bottled water on my face, and again assuming a sickly expression and again went out to the secretaries and told them I wasn't feeling well—was warm, sweaty, a little dizzy, and was leaving work early.

The next morning at ten o'clock I texted Peckle and told him that I was sick with food poisoning. I told him I had tossed and turned all night, had been in a high fever, at times was delirious, and now my head was spinning, my tongue was swollen, my eyes were red, and rashes had erupted all over my body. I was weak, exhausted, could barely stand up. It was a medical emergency! I would "probably" drive myself to the hospital if things didn't get better. At any rate it was impossible for me to come into work. Half hour later he texted me back and ordered me to call him, "ASAP."

I had no intention of doing so.  I didn't have time. The funeral was to take place at one o'clock in the afternoon, and I still had to dress and drive a good hour to Providence, Rhode Island.

I was particularly interested in attending this funeral because it was for a funeral director.  Mason Stretcher had for fifty years been the owner and director of Willow Gardens Memorial Chapel, and it seemed to me that if anyone had known what made for a good funeral, he, with all his experience, would have known, and planned accordingly.  But his case only proved the adage that some people never learn. He had probably never found anything wrong with the conventional services he had offered, and one could only shake one's head regretfully at the tens of thousands of people he must have made, over his long career, absolutely miserable.

In the first place Willow Gardens Memorial Chapel was a gross failure of interior design.  Out of some mistaken notion that its interior should match its rather pretty name, the walls of that room had murals of weeping willows, painted mostly in dark greens, grays, and browns.  It looked like a swamp and made one think of Gothic landscapes, of crypts and cobwebs, of hauntings and harrowing spirits; it set exactly the wrong intimidating tone.  The furniture was sturdy-looking but unstylish, and looked as though it belonged in some stodgy law office.

The visitation room was somewhat better; at least it was brighter and cleaner.  It was a large space filled with twenty rows of folding chairs.  The floor of blue and gray tiles shone with a high gloss, and the walls and ceiling gleamed white.  It was a neutral room and depended on the accoutrements of the service to lend it character.  In this case that was a problem because the casket was nothing to speak of. It might have been one of the better models from his own establishment, but it was still atrociously all black, with little ornamentation, and its fittings and lifting bar were clearly stainless steel, which gave it a second-rate industrial look.  The flower arrangements on either side were small and oddly profuse of daisies;—possibly owing to what had been a "good deal" on a quantity purchase. The Stretcher family and their guests were undistinguished.  All were dressed in black and vapidly correct in their polite silence.  As much as I rail against family members or guests acting inappropriately at a funeral—crying too loudly or otherwise carrying on— there is, on the other hand, and which also is not acceptable, a simple-minded *abstraction* from the service, a dull-minded, long-suffering patience for the thing to be over so that everyone can get back to his routine. In a word, the guests were not alert. Also there was not a pretty woman in sight.

Mr. Stretcher himself had left the planet at the age of 84.  He had been helping to escort others on the way to their celestial journey up till a week to his own departure.  One of the guests later informed me that he had been eating in a restaurant and had just been served a piping hot shepherd's pie when he fell into it, face-first—the result of a massive stroke.  Now he was lying in a proper suit, with a white carnation stuck into his lapel. He was expressionless, his mouth set in an almost exactly straight line, so that were it not for his pallor one might have thought him still alive but hypnotized.

Though the funeral took place in Mr. Stretcher's

establishment, another funeral director, Mr. Toggle, of Golden Fields Manor, had been contracted by the family to arrange the service. Apparently the two men had known each other. They were about the same age, the same height, and shared the same white hair parted on the side. They looked enough like each other to have been brothers. Mr. Toggle's behavior was crisply attentive to the details of the service. Most of the time he was standing in the foyer to escort guests into the visitation room, into which, however, he repeatedly ventured, standing at the back of it with his hands clasped before him; monitoring the guests, the family, and the minister and two family members who delivered eulogies.

When the service was over he announced where the burial was to take place and invited all to attend. I buttonholed him as the guests were leaving to go to their cars and asked him about the location of the reception. It was to be held in an annex to a nearby church.

Having only had a cup of coffee before leaving home, I was hungry by the time the funeral ended. I skipped the burial and headed straight to the church annex where the reception was to be held. People charged with setting up the tables for the event had only just finished doing so and were now laying out the food. The sight of it made me sigh. Bowls of cold pasta, trays of potato dishes, large containers of green salad, bread and rolls, neatly tiled cold cuts, and various condiments;—cheap, cheap, cheap. Alongside these dishes were trays of those pretty but tasteless bakery-style cookies. It's a big warning sign whenever you see the sweets and desserts laid out at the same time with the main dishes. It all but screams, "That's all there is, folks! Don't expect anything else!"

It took another forty-five minutes before the first guests arrived and I could start getting at the food. I made a couple of sandwiches with rolls and the leanest of the cold cuts, a few slices of tomato, and some mustard. I also helped myself to a few pickles (they were soggy), and some of the green salad, for which there was a woefully inadequate selection of dressing—just ranch or oil and vinegar. As for drinks, there was no whiskey, no wine, and no beer; only soda, coffee, and tea.

The people I sat with had nothing but good things to say of Mr. Stretcher, though their professions of admiration were unenthusiastic and rather pro forma, as though it were incumbent on them to speak well of the dead, no matter what they might think to the contrary.

Also I met several members of the Stretcher family: his oldest and younger sons, and their wives and a few of their children. The oldest son asked me how I had known his father and I told him he had assisted me with a funeral for a beloved uncle of mine. "Your father knew exactly what do," I said, "and provided our family with a lovely service. When I heard he had passed, I just had to come to pay my respects. He was such a good man—he helped so many people—he will be missed so much! I also remember him telling me how proud he was of his children, and looking at you and your family I can see why!"

I always find it a good idea to pile it on thick like this: everyone likes to be patted on the back, and it's some guarantee that any suspicions about my presence will be outweighed by gratitude for compliments. Sure enough Mr. Stretcher's son beamed with approval at my kind words and thanked me for coming.

It was a disappointing funeral and earned only ▐▌◌◌◌, in part because of the drab service but mostly because of the inadequate reception. It also proved to me once again that long experience in a profession does not guarantee of a real understanding of it: that those who are *in* it, even for a lifetime, are not necessarily masters *of* it. This may serve as an adage for a lot of other fields, and is the reason why we ought never to be impressed by someone on account of his title or apparent credentials. By their deeds you shall know them.

Later that evening, after I had been home for about an hour, I thought about the excuse I had given piddling Peckle for missing his meeting. He hadn't left a message on my phone but he must have been angry. It didn't surprise me therefore when I entered my office the next morning and he called me, saying he would like to "have a word" with me in his office.

When I got there he was behind his desk with his hands folded before him. His demeanor was determined. Apparently he had made up his mind about something, and it did not bode well for me.

"Take a seat," he said.

"I don't mind standing," I said, and glanced at my watch as though to show him that I didn't have time to waste.

He stood up at his desk and at once reprimanded me for missing yesterday's meeting. He reminded me that it was the fifth one this year that I missed—

the *fifth*. "That is not acceptable," he said.

"I had food poisoning," I said. "If you don't believe me, ask Janet or Margaret"—the secretaries. "They saw how sick I was."

He looked at me skeptically before asking, "Did you go to a hospital?"

"I stuck it out at home."

As though he had caught me in a lie, he smiled snidely and said only, "Oh, good for you! Glad to see it wasn't as severe as you made out."

"It *was* as severe as I made out. I was too weak to go anywhere—including a hospital."

You could see how he was on the verge of lashing out at me, only holding back because he knew I'd retort just as vigorously. The last thing a puny Peckle wants to see or hear is behavior which proves that others don't share his high estimation of himself. Instead, with something of an edge in his voice, he intoned:

"I should not have to remind you that participation in meetings is key for the smooth operation of our school. It's important for us all to be on the same page concerning events and procedures."

"Why is that?"

"Why is what?"

"Why is it important that we all be on the same page?"

"What do you mean, 'Why is it important'? Why do you think!"

"That's just it: I don't think it is."

"What!"

"My job is to counsel students. To do that I don't need to know about a lot of things that are discussed in the meetings. At the last one I attended you spent a half hour talking about construction that might or might not take place next year in the building, and another half hour about rallies scheduled for the football or basketball teams—which I may add is a waste of everyone's time."

"Is that right?" he sneered.

"It's exactly right."

"Rallies help build school spirit!"

—Which ridiculous, immature, really simple-minded comment and concept was not even worthy of words and for which I expressed my contempt with only a, "Pfuh!"

"Are you going to argue with me about that?" he asked.

"I'm not going to argue. I would only observe that your notion of 'school spirit,' insofar as it glamorizes the school's sports teams, in effect honors a foolish facility for throwing and running after balls. That is not going to help the kids get on in life. Instead I would suggest selecting the most academically gifted or artistically creative students, and having rallies for *them*. At least you'd be encouraging the kinds of effort that will help the kids make a living or conduce to their personal fulfillment."

"Is that right?" he asked, sarcastically.

"That is exactly right. It is also, now that I come to think of it, a wonderful idea. If you like you can take it and claim it as yours."

"Thanks but I don't need your ideas! And that has nothing to do with what we were talking about—your repeated absence at meetings. It's important for every member of the staff to attend. Do I make myself clear?"

"Very."

"Good!"

He picked up a piece of paper from his desk and handed it for me, saying, "Please read this."

It was a document he had written, the invention of his twisted mind, in which he had listed all the meetings I had missed, why my attendance at them had been imperative, and how he had repeatedly warned me about missing them. Such instances of "noncompliance" with "school policy" were "unacceptable" and any further infraction would be "grounds for dismissal." At the bottom of the document were areas for our signatures, and he had already signed his. I put the document down on his desk, stepped back, and said only:

"Alright."

"Alright what?"

"I've read it."

"You need to sign that."

"My signature would imply that I agree with its contents. I don't."

"If you don't sign it, I will have to let you go."

"You'll excuse me, then. I have to call my lawyer; then I'm going to call the School Board."

I turned around and had just reached the door when he called out, "Wait a minute!" And when I turned back to him: "What do you mean, a lawyer! What has a lawyer got to do with this?"

"I'm going to sue this school, and I'm going to sue you, and maybe even the School Board for illegal termination. You can't fire someone for getting sick."

"But I'm not *firing* you," pusillanimous Peckle said. "This is just a warning."

"I don't sign 'warnings.' You seem to forget something"—it seemed to me that now would be a good time to pull out my ace card—"I'm a *professional!* I expect to be treated in a professional manner and to work in a professional environment!"

I was just posing: I didn't believe what I was saying. But I knew that *he* did. There is no word which exercises more of an influence on dim-witted corporate mentalities than "professional," which, while it has valid applications (such as my critical work), is least applicable to what *they* do. That is why they cling to it so jealously, why it has a fascinating, a talismanic power over them: they want so much to believe that their duties require exceptional skills, that their capacities are more than average. In arrogating that title to myself in my confrontation with presumptuous Peckle, I thus took up a shield especially effective in deflecting his kind of haughty aggression. You could almost see him physically shrinking back.

"I'm just saying," he finally said, "that you need to be more conscientious about school affairs. That's all I'm saying. Maybe I did ... overreact a little."

I pressed my advantage with:

"I prefer getting emails about the meetings. It's the only way I can really absorb all the information because I can go over them as many times as I want."

"Really? Well ... maybe in your case that would be better."

"It definitely would be."

There was no goodbye, no word of thanks on my part, no real apology on his; and it seemed I had managed both to excuse myself from all further meetings as well as to indemnify myself against any attempt he might make on my livelihood.

Thereafter we didn't even recognize each other. We would pass each other in the halls and look straight ahead as though the other didn't exist.

Not able to force me to attend his idiotic metings, pestiferous Peckle tried to make my life miserable in another way. One morning I received an email from him saying he wanted my reports "to more extensively reflect all aspects of the counseling interaction between concerned parties," and he had the nerve to send me a "template" for the reports themselves: five pages filled with boxes to tick, with the multiple answers to choose from, and with blank sections to be written into. The man must have totally lost his mind if he thought I was going to waste my time following his over-complicated and cockamamie instructions. Then it occurred to me that that was probably his plan: he was going to use my refusal to cooperate as another proof of my insubordination and have me fired. I dashed off an email—there's nothing like an email to keep a record—telling him why his template was unnecessary, an inefficient use of my time, and of no benefit to my students—throwing in the "my students" to make it clear that their welfare was my first concern. I sent the email at 11:45 AM. He was in my office before 12, his face red, his eyes glaring.

"That report format stays the way it is!" he said.

"It's not practical," I replied, calmly. "It would detract too much from the time I need to spend with my students."

"You have plenty of time for them!"

"Actually, I don't. And, as I mentioned to you in my email, your format is inefficient."

"I'll be the judge of that!"

He raised his voice; so I raised mine:

"Excuse me, but I think I know what my job is about better than you do! I'm a professional with a degree in Educational Psychology!"

Once more the magical word, combined with that other magical word, "degree," undermined his aggression toward me, leaving him to look at me unsure of what to do or say next. But his evil disposition had only been checked, not eliminated. Perhaps he also understood that my credentials were not necessarily pertinent to the matter at hand.

"We'll see about that," he said, or rather threatened, and left my office.

His implied threat would have intimidated me but for two things: my dedication to my critical work—which comes before everything else—and my membership in the teachers union, which, as pushy Peckle knows very well, indemnifies me against his threats. He is a foolish man, a silly man, a little man; but even he understands that if he fired me I'd haul him before the Union faster than a snake can slide down a greased waterspout, and the last thing he wants is to be exposed for the kind of petty tyrant he is. Nevertheless I was somewhat worried that he was stupid enough to disregard what was in his best interest and pursue some sort of "disciplinary action" against me. But just then luck smiled upon me.

The next Monday morning I went to work to learn that putrid Peckle had gotten into a car accident over the weekend. A pickup truck had smashed into the driver's side of his car, obliterating that whole side of it. He had incurred broken bones and a concussion. He was in serious but stable condition in the hospital where he would be for at least the next month. He would make a recovery but he would be gone for the rest of the school year.

For me it was as though someone had opened all the doors and windows in a stuffy room and let in some fresh autumn air. While the rest of the staff were congregating in little excited clusters to swap expressions of concern over the fate of their boss, I was sitting in my office, leaning back in my chair with my feet up on my desk and drinking a cup of coffee, smiling from ear to ear. I remember listening to music that morning. What was it? Jazz? Rock and roll? I forget....

Not that I wished pulverized Peckle serious harm. I felt bad for his having to undergo physical pain and perhaps coming away from his accident with permanent physical limitations. I didn't relish the idea that his next few months would be uncomfortable. But while his broken bones mended, while his concussion healed, he would not be able to make my life more difficult.

Nor was I the only one who felt this way. Even those who had not disliked our principal felt the change for the better on account of his absence. There was a lighter, freer, happier atmosphere in the building. Big Brother was no longer around to keep his prying eyes on everyone. And as so often happens when a boss is absent, things went along just fine without him, and those who worked under him realized what an oppressive superfluity he had been all along.

Later in the week one of the teachers took it into her dizzy head to buy a gigantic get-well card for him. She sent it around to everyone to sign along with a request for money so that she might buy him some flowers and a fruit basket. The staff signatures, subscribing expressions of affection or hopes for a "speedy recovery," nauseated me for their hypocrisy. Not only did I not sign the card but I dropped a contumelious nickel into the donation envelope. A day later Mrs. Dizzy enthusiastically approached and said in a chipper chirping voice:

"Hey there! I noticed that you didn't sign the card yet! Want to sign it now?"

"Nope," I said, with a plaster smile.

"Oh!" She looked surprised and watched me in anticipation as though she expected me to explain myself. When I didn't, she said slowly, "Okaayyy," and walked away. At that moment she probably figured out who gave the nickel.

The removal of pesky Peckle's interference in my life could not have happened at a more opportune time, for soon there were to be a lot more funerals to review.

# VI
## WINDFALL

A new infectious disease had appeared. At first it was thought to be no worse than a flu; then, as the weeks passed, as more people were infected, and the mortality rate rose, its real danger was recognized. It had come from China, and there were two theories about its origin. Some said it was the result of nefarious experimentation with viruses in a laboratory and that the artificial, malignant strain had escaped; others said that it had jumped from wild animals to human beings from one of the "wet markets" in that country—places where animals are butchered as though they are no more sensible than dried sticks. My own feeling was that it was probably from the latter, and that even if proved to be otherwise, the latter had a lot more to do with it than would ever be recognized. The Chinese have the least empathy for the suffering of other creatures. To detail some of the inhumane practices they blithely engage in with animals would turn the stomach and provoke the outrage of anyone who wasn't a scoundrel. But such cruelties cannot go on forever without consequences. For there is a law of compensation or equilibrium in the universe by which every action provokes an equal or opposite reaction, however immediate or far into the future. And so whether

the origin of the virus was artificial or natural—
whether it originated in a test tube, or was exhaled
in the last expiring yelp of a tortured dog—it was
nevertheless the vehicle of retribution on behalf of
an abused animal world.

The theory, and probably the reality, was that at
first the virus had infected a single person, a re-
searcher transferring a solution from one test tube to
another, or a butcher indifferently stabbing or stran-
gling to death some terrified struggling creature. It
was conjectured that this person had breathed in the
virus, where it had begun replicating in his lungs by
the thousands or millions, and so made every breath
he exhaled spread the disease. Thus when he
stopped to talk and laugh with friends, he infected
them; when he hugged or kissed his children, he
passed along the germ to them; and when he rubbed
his eyes or mouth, everything he touched afterwards
became a vector of contagion, infecting dozens of others, who in turn infected dozens more; and so the
disease rose exponentially, first through the city
where it had started, then throughout the region,
then throughout the country.

And then throughout the world. Some of those
who had contracted the disease were travelers.
Some felt a little feverish even as they got on their
airplanes, thinking they might be coming down with
a cold. They took their seats among a hundred other
closely-packed passengers, and breathed and talked
and coughed—spewing the virus into the enclosed atmosphere. In this way the disease came out of
China and permeated Asia and entered into Europe
and the Americas. It was spread by businessmen
who greeted colleagues with a handshake in London

or attended meetings in New York, by students who went to see the sights in Italy or France, by aunts and uncles, mothers and fathers, who went to visit relatives in San Francisco or Brazil.

The world had been launched into a pandemic which would get worse in the months to come.

The funeral industry had a field day. Even those funeral parlors closest to me—small places, with reputations not the best—began getting a lot more business, and busily took survivors to the satanic cleaners, tumbling them round and round in intensified sorrow and feeding them through mangles of grief till their last bit of misery, and in some cases their last bit of cash, was wrung out of them. At such a time never was a critic like myself needed more! I rose to the occasion. I worked harder than ever, going to three, four, even five funerals a week. I would get up early in the morning in order to work on a review, and even work on it while on the job (a few stealthy sentences or paragraphs at a time); then go home and work on it again, either before or after attending another funeral. How exhausting it was! Yet how satisfying! I foresaw myself coming into a personal golden age of prolific creativity, producing longer, more incisive, better reviews than ever.

Was I worried about becoming a victim of the disease? Only slightly. Despite the exponential rates of infection, the number of those who had gotten sick were very low relative to the general population, and most of them did not have serious symptoms. I also recognized the random nature of the thing: the virus could hang in the air for hours and therefore might enter my lungs any minute of the day, or it might be carried far out of my way by some antic breeze to infect another or die out in the rays of the sun.  It seemed unreasonable to let the fear of contracting what would mostly likely be a mild illness stop me from exercising the critical talents for which my whole life had been a preparation. When looked at in that way, there was really no question about what I would do.

Most of the funerals were closed-casket affairs for fear that an exposed body would be a health hazard, which is why my reviews during this time less frequently addressed cosmetological failures or successes.  They were also sparsely attended.  People were afraid of entering a room with others from whom they might contract the airborne disease. Even people who had been popular during their lifetimes, who had had many friends or who had held political or high corporate office—even their funerals were limited mostly to immediate family members. For me an added frustration were the surgical masks everyone began wearing and which made it hard to see what the guests looked like.  I had to guess hard—to fill in the blanks, as it were—to see who the pretty young ladies might be.

Nevertheless some of my best reviews were written during this time, enabling me to provide the public with a lot of examples of what to avoid.  The funerals for Messrs. Olsen, Bergato, Fillmore, and Dugold, and for Mmes. McCormack, Ellwood, and Roona were characterized by some of the worst caskets, the worst visitation room décors, and the worst floral arrangements imaginable.  The families routinely misbehaved, and at the Dugold funeral the deceased's father, who was in his seventies, fainted and had to be carried out, causing commotion and distress among the guests. (That incident prompted me to write the essay, "Totally Unacceptable," which dealt with that kind of outlandish behavior.) The best of the receptions were only moderately good and vitiated by a nervous fear of ingesting something more dangerous than ravioli or fried chicken. In all cases the headstones were mediocre, and one of them—for Mrs. Roona—was downright disgusting for its puniness when one considered that her husband was a retired surgeon who must have been sitting on a bundle. They all received ratings between ♦♦◌◌ and ♦♦♦◌◌.

With so much new content available on my website, Betterfunerals.com, its popularity increased. One week I had as many as five thousand visitors! Sometimes I thought that half the funeral directors in the country must be checking in for the latest reviews. But once again not all my readers were thrilled with my work. Sprinkled among the sugar of kudos and compliments were the inevitable bitter grains of mean-spirited comments posted by clearly unstable people. Strange as it might sound, these unhinged reactions did not disturb me because I recognized them as the *strong* effect my work was having on some people. Anyone who was dashing off curses or threats to a stranger was clearly deeply affected by what he had read, and I could only hope he was sharing the cause of his upset with others. For a social reformer can hardly be expected to have any effect unless his work is recognized, and, insofar as it isn't, even bad publicity is good publicity.

This prolific trend might have continued and increased for as long as the pandemic lasted and still longer were it not that my attention was soon to be diverted.

# VII
## LOVE AND THE CRITIC

As a bachelor, as a man who has yet to find Miss Right, it sometimes happens that I come across a single young lady who happens to be at the funeral parlor, at the church service, or at the gravesite, whom I am attracted to and to whom I am tempted to make an overture for a date. Most of my dates or relationships over the last few years were women I met at funerals.

Now before anyone leans back and sneers, he should keep in mind a few things. The first one is that I am very discreet. It's not as though I run up to the first pretty girl I see and ask, "What are you doing this Saturday night?" Like every other guest I introduce myself and, if she is related to the deceased, express my condolences. Only after we have had a chance to talk a bit, only after I think we might be compatible, do I suggest we might want to get together sometime to explore our common interests.

You have to be a special kind of man to be able to pick up—I mean, *meet*—a woman at a funeral. You have to have a refined social sense combined with an expert use of language: the ability to phrase delicately a transition between contrary sentiments, to express heartfelt sympathy with one minute only to allude to the cheerful possibilities of

romance in the next. You have to know how to assure the bereaved of brighter days to come, and to
overcome any disinclinations she might have to take
steps in that direction. The average Joe is incapable
of this. He would botch the whole thing with a
coarsely direct proposition and come off as an offensive boor. At best he would use the same tired old
pickup lines that he's used in a hundred other
places, and which would be doubly offensive here.
Granted, sometimes even my skill is insufficient to
the purpose, and the object of my interest reacts to
me in a way less than positive, but at least my at-
tempts are graceful.

But a funeral is not the time or place to "meet"
someone? To think so would be to misunderstand
the nature of Love, which knows no boundaries. It
can bloom anywhere—even in front of a casket. And
there is even something wonderfully right about
that. For what is romance, what is love between
men and women, but the first tentative steps toward
the procreation of the next generation?—no less than
the overcoming of death? It is a ray of light and
hope shining through the gloom and doom, the promise of a better, brighter tomorrow. Meeting someone
at a funeral is also a lot more civilized than trying to
do so in a loud crowded bar where half the people
are too drunk to know what they are doing or saying, or meeting at work where professional consider-
ations are likely to discourage a relationship.
Granted, women attending a funeral never expect to
be asked out on a date, and some of them (usually
the ones who aren't too bright) become offended by
it, but on the whole they are rather pleased than
otherwise because it is such a pleasant contrast to

the depressing tenor of the day.

It is the more acceptable in my case because reviewing funerals is my true vocation, and it's natural for people to meet in their line of work. If I had been a police dispatcher, a store manager, a dentist, a real estate agent, and met a woman on the job, no one would think twice about it; but the moment you disclose that you met someone at a funeral, even though being there is a part of *your* job, you are judged by an entirely different standard. Is that fair?

Shall I admit that I once made an overture to the widow of the deceased? Believe me, that was not my intention when I stepped into the funeral parlor. But then I couldn't have expected her to be so attractive. Her features were ideal: the wide, large eyes, the high cheekbones, the pert nose, and slender, bow-like lips;—it was all so ideal, so perfect. And what a body!—tall, stately, and curvy, all at once and in all the right places. Her husband, a boiler repairman, had been killed when some sort of furnace he had been working on blew up. (Obviously it was a closed-casket funeral.) She was the more devastated by her loss because she had been married only a year. She sat in the front row with her parents and siblings, looking pale and washed out as though she had been struggling for days against a hurricane. She had hardly eaten in the previous week and had lost weight so that she looked particularly good in her tight-fitting dress, which thankfully was not full length and showed off something of her long smooth legs. I went up to her to offer my condolences and was taken aback by her flawless complexion. I couldn't help staring at her as I fumbled out my sympathies and held her hand—how soft it was!—a few moments more than I should have.    When I went back to my seat my heart—I swear it—was beating a little faster.

It was love at first sight. Does that sound childish, foolish? Yet it happens to me all the time.    I have seen people—I have come across faces—I have even heard voices—in which there was something, an expression or an intonation, which pierced me to the core and roused up in me a blind yet overpowering affection.    Here was an instance of that.    I didn't take my eyes off her, though from my seat I could see only the back of her head or her profile when she turned to one of the persons seated beside her.    My hope was that she would turn around so that I might catch her eye with a direct and intense stare which would let her know of my interest in her; but she didn't.    My next opportunity to see her full-face came at the gravesite, but naturally I couldn't make any overtures to her there; besides, she had begun to cry.

Poor woman, how sad she was!    Sorrow bowed her head, which was so lovely that it ought always to have been held high, if only as a favor to the world.    Yet, despite her anguish, she was luckier than she knew.    Because her husband had died when they were both young and she was in love with him, she would have for the rest of her life someone to idolize, a proof of the reality of ideal affection; and this would be a source of strength and hope to her in years to come when, after each failed relationship, she would still believe it was possible to find a "soul mate."    If she was very lucky she would cling to this belief far beyond the point where most people abandon it as a fantasy, and would never allow herself to be convinced, no matter how much experience showed her otherwise, that the breathless attraction which sometimes brings two people together is but an illusion, a ruse of nature for the sake of achieving physical ends, which, once met, and especially if they are met repeatedly, lift from between them the veil through which their shortcomings are disguised or softened, and they see each other for the flawed, less-lovable creatures they are.

—Which is strange observation to make for someone who claims to have fallen in love "at first sight"? Logically, yes; emotionally, not at all. Illusions may be baseless, but so long as they last they are lovely and enrich our lives. And who in the end has a better life? The clear-eyed one who sees the ugly realities everywhere and is miserable from morning till night, or the one who exists in a dreamworld of beautiful fantasies and goes about starry-eyed and smiling?

Fortunately she was more composed at the reception, which was quite good. It was held in a restaurant unexpectedly upscale (who knew boiler repairmen made so much money?) where fifteen tables, each surrounded by six or seven chairs, were set aside for the guests. I had the grilled salmon with green beans and Brussels sprouts, and a delightful semi-sweet cabernet. To my right some cousin or other of the deceased kept babbling on to me about what a wonderful man he had been, to all of which I agreed, enthusiastically, though my attention was really focused on his widow. She sat several tables away but was in clear line of sight. Her family surrounded her like a phalanx of guards:

her sister, her brother, and her and her late husband's parents. At one point she looked in my direction and I caught her attention, smiling and nodding
at her. She nodded slightly at me—and my heart
went pitter-patter.

I kept her in view, hoping and waiting for the opportunity when she would get up and walk about so
that I might meet her again. She finally rose from
her table and went to the ladies' room, which was located through adjacent hall. Knowing she would
have to come out of it the same way she had gone in,
I position just outside it. A large, tree-like, potted
fern stood there, its tall stalks curving gracefully upward then downward in a kind of waterfall of greenery, and I nestled among them for camouflage. In
about five minutes she came out, putting a tissue to
her eyes, which were a little red and watery. Apparently she had excused herself from her table for the
sake of giving way in private to a bout of tears.
How conscientious of her!

The possible inappropriateness of making an
overture to a woman who had just been crying for
the loss of her husband was not lost on me, but the
opportunity might not come again and so it was
worth taking a chance. I stepped forward as casually as possible as though I had just happened to be
walking by, and accosted her with a simple, "Hello."

She stopped abruptly, a little startled at my sudden appearance, but after a second said, "Hello."

I introduced myself to her, saying I had been a
friend of her husband's some years ago and, on hearing of his passing, had come to pay my respects.
Then I gently guided the conversation to my real
purpose. How sad it was, I said, whenever someone

we loved passed away. It was one of the great shocks of life which we all went through sooner or later. Yet even in the midst of our sorrow we should keep in mind that our departed loved ones would not want to see us in distress, and we honored their memories most by resuming our lives as soon possible. Did she agree with me about that? Suppressing a sniffle, she responded, "I suppose so." I resumed: Yes, we owed it as much to them as to ourselves to resume doing the things that made us happy. One of the things that made me happy was a restaurant called the Star & Anchor in Bridgeport. Had she ever heard of it? No? It was a lovely place. It was part of a marina and from June through August the removable walls were taken down to afford a panoramic view of the boats and wharves. The food was delicious and they served a frosted Blue Hawaiian with just the right balance of sweet and sour. Their old fashioneds were very good too. Nothing was more delightful than to dine there on a summer's afternoon, eating, talking, and sipping one's drink while looking out on the water glimmering beneath a serenely setting sun. It was so peaceful—so relaxing—so conducive to contemplation. I hadn't been there for at least a year and wanted to go again; in fact, was thinking of going this coming Saturday and—perhaps she would like to accompany me? For both of us it would be a pleasant few hours on a weekend afternoon.

She had heard me out without expression  till the moment I suggested that she accompany me to the Star & Anchor. Then something in her manner changed. The glistening, patient, kindly, lovely eyes squinted a little as something in them hardened. Her lips tightened and her whole body stiffened somewhat. She said, "Oh ... oh ..."—and looked about her as though for help. She seemed about to say something else but only shook her head, once, and said under her breath again, "Oh!"—and walked off quickly.

She returned to her table and continually looked over to me, each time more angrily. At one point she leaned in to man sitting beside her and whispered something, obviously about me. Whatever she said could not have been flattering because he looked at me hostilely. He seemed to be an inch away from getting up and approaching me. If he did so he was sure to come over to me and interrogate me about my identity and presence at the funeral, so I decided that now might be a good time to hightail it out of there.

Believe it or not but he followed me out to the parking lot. I had just gotten into my car when I saw him walking toward me. I started the engine, put the car in gear, and began pulling away. At the same time he raised a hand in a gesture for me to stop, shouting, "Hey, you!" I beeped the horn and waved as though in friendly leave-taking, stepped on the gas, and swerved around him. For a second it looked as though he were going to jump on the hood, but he didn't and I zoomed away. For the next mile I kept looking out of my rearview mirror, half expecting to see him following me, but he never did.

I didn't hold the pretty widow's behavior against her. She had been under a great deal of stress and wasn't thinking clearly, since otherwise she would have seen that I was a fellow of good parts and intentions who only wanted to get to know her better.

Nor did I let her behavior color my review of the funeral. I make it a point not to let my personal feelings about a person's behavior in a single or even in a few instances color my view of them as a whole, still less of their handiwork. The mark of a real critic is just this impartiality.

A month later I returned to the cemetery where her husband was buried to view his headstone. I was pleased to find that it was not of the double-wide variety grieving spouses too often choose. Perhaps her family had talked her out of it, or perhaps she had realized she was still young and so bound to meet another man she could fall in love with and whom she might even consider the truer love of her life. Whatever the reason, the headstone was for a single person, engraved with only with her husband's name and dates. A few bits of fancy scroll-work decorated its top but on the whole it was rather plain and predictable—nothing one would want to look at twice or take a picture of.

In the end the funeral received a rating of ♦♦♦◊◊. I would have given it ♦♦♦♦◊ but for the outrageous behavior of the barbarian who came running after me in the parking lot.

A funeral which took place several weeks later offered me another opportunity for romance, this time more successfully. Several factors aligned to make this possible.

First, the accoutrements for the funeral were well done, which put me into a good mood. The visitation room had been done up in the deceased's favorite colors: lilac and rose. These vivid colors complemented each other and brought an unexpected vivacity to the venue. The casket was lovely: off-white with a gold trim, its metal stamped or embossed with stylish wavy lines along the bottom. Bowers of flowers surrounded it: lilacs and roses which perfumed the air. Second, the behavior of the family and the guests was admirable. There were a few tears, but not many. None of the middle-aged children or adult grandchildren cried. In the front row in the room they sat quietly and with smiling and appreciative nods accepted the condolences of family and friends. It probably could not have been otherwise, considering that the deceased had reached the age of 104, had been able-bodied and clear-headed to the very end, and had died in her sleep. She had had a good long life and had gone out of it with painless unconsciousness;—so there was little to be sad about. She also looked good for her age: she could have passed for 85. Dressed in white and pink, with a high frilly collar above which her tiny face seemed to express a satisfied acceptance, she lay holding a quaint bouquet of flowers from her own garden. Third, the eulogies were short, sweet, and spoken not only dry-eyed but also with a subdued sense of joy. Lastly, there was no trip to the cemetery. The family had decided to let this happen unwitnessed out of a healthy instinct to save themselves and their guests and unsightly experience. The reception was held some two miles away from the funeral parlor in the home of one of the daughters.

Generally speaking I dislike attending receptions in private homes because it increases the risk of someone finding out I'm an outsider, what with the close setting, the common recognition of family members and friends, and the greater ease of access by which people can come up to oneself and begin a long and perhaps inquisitive conversation. My cover story for attending this funeral was that I had lived across the street from the deceased when she had lived in Middletown, Connecticut, twenty years before—a detail mentioned in the obituary.

The prettiest of the granddaughters—the one I had been keeping my eye on from the first—happened to be sitting by herself on a couch. I was standing in the middle of the rather crowded room, holding a plate of food and trying to eat while talking to a fellow who was an insurance salesman and trying to sell me a policy. I excused myself from him and casually sat beside the object of my interest, smiling in an excusing kind of way as I did so, then introducing myself with my real first name and expressing my condolences on her loss.

Her name was Jessica. She had brown, shoulder-length hair and an open, friendly face. She wore a simple pantsuit, which unfortunately was all black but tight enough to show off her tall, shapely figure. She spent the first few minutes talking about what a nice woman her grandmother had been and what a wonderful life she had had, then told me a little about herself. She wasn't from Connecticut but lived in northern Pennsylvania, about ten miles above Scranton, where she was the manager of a clothing store. She had been married once several years earlier for about nine months. She had no children but she owned a St. Bernard. When I expressed my enthusiasm for those dogs and dogs generally, she warmed up to me, mentioning that her ex-husband hadn't liked dogs—which she could never understand in anyone. She wasn't drinking anything and I proposed getting her something, a glass of wine perhaps, and she said, "I don't usually drink, but okay, maybe half a glass, thank you"—which let me know that she was interested in me.

She had been close to her grandmother but like everyone else she recognized that the ancient lady had had a good long life. I believe that was part of the reason she was so responsive to my overtures. Another part (I have no doubt about this) was because she was 32 years old and still unmarried. Whatever the reason, she didn't think it out of place when, after we had been talking a good hour and I couldn't eat another bite, I suggested that "one day" we might get together to "talk some more." That would be nice, she said, and gave me her phone number.

That she lived some distance from me, in Pennsylvania, was a sticking point—but not much of one, since she lived in the easternmost part of the state, about an hour's drive from my location. She lived in a ranch style house surrounded by four acres of ground. The first time I showed up at her place I brought a bouquet of flowers, which she accepted enthusiastically and with a hug of appreciation. Her huge dog, Wally, stood at the door behind her, looking around her legs at me and vaguely wagging his tail, not sure what to make of me. She introduced me to him and he could tell by the sound of her voice that he was supposed to accept me; and he warmed up to me within minutes.

We went out on two dates before she spent a weekend at my place. She brought Wally with her, as she would continue to do. The dog and I got along very well. He was always jumping on me, always wanted to lick and play with me. This made her like me even more, and she would say, "I've never seen my dog take to anyone the way he does to you!" Her satisfaction at this was not unlike that of a single mother who sees her child express affection for the boyfriend she has another reason to hope will become her husband.

We had no sooner spent a weekend together than we called each other every day, and sometimes twice a day if only for a few minutes. We were going through what might be called the consolidating phase of a relationship when two persons make it clear to each other, and perhaps to themselves, that they are "together";—a happy, satisfying time which gives rise to fine fantasies of a long happy life together. And indeed the first few weeks of our relationship were so pleasant that visions of domestic happiness often floated across my mind. I saw us buying a house together, living together, even marrying. She would have her business to run and I would have my reviews to write. I had not yet told her about my critical work, holding off till we knew each other a little better. It was my hope however that one day she might help me with it: for instance, reading penultimate drafts, or giving me her opinions about funerals we had attended together.

She liked to cook and entertain. She often invited one of two of her many friends over to her place for dinner on a Saturday or Sunday night. They were pleasant evenings but I never felt entirely comfortable at them. There is always an element of show, of performance, in a social setting, and these dinners required of me an effort I preferred not to make, the less so because as a part of my critical career I already often had to assume a persona. I didn't want to have to make similar efforts on, as it were, my own time. Surely one of the points of forming a close relationship with another person is that while in their company one can be as free and easy as when one is by oneself. But these get-togethers with her friends, of which she must have had dozens, made her happy and so I accepted them as one of her minor, tolerable quirks.

Her domesticity was charming and reliable, but she took too much pride in it. Cooking well, keeping a clean home, and managing domestic economy efficiently are admirable traits but they hardly rise to the level of rare abilities. More impressive to me was her relationship with Wally. She loved that animal more than she loved anything else. She probably loved him more than me. Far from making me jealous, or making me think her foolish, it raised her a lot in my estimation. For there is a lot to be said for people who can detect in other creatures the same principle of life which exists in themselves: it represents not only a fine evolution of the understanding but also an essential kindness.

And Jessica was kind. She wouldn't have unnecessarily hurt a fly. She was soft-spoken and never said a harsh word. Indeed she was averse from "bad" language, which she flinched from as from a threatening bee.

"Don't you ever curse?" I asked her.

"I'd have to be pretty angry to curse," she said. And she couldn't remember the last time she had been so angry.

She didn't read or listen to music, and had no interest in art or politics. She was blissfully unaware of what was going on in the world because she made a point of not watching or reading the news because it was "always bad." When she was not working as the manager of a clothing store she spent her time learning new recipes, watching movies, or taking care of her dog. Her satisfaction with the easily accessible and everyday was yet another testament to her sweetness of temperament. She embodied the best characteristics of her sex: she was sweet, sympathetic, demure, patient, complaisant—a *real* woman; as opposed to the hard-headed, hardhearted, militaristic, even military version of womankind which has for some unfathomable reason has become a bizarre ideal. Perhaps she was not intelligent in the conventional sense of the word—but so what? Intelligence should never be a criterion in the choice of our friends or lovers: in them we want and need only one thing: a good heart.

She was also an optimist and liked to think the best of persons and things. This positive attitude was essentially consonant with my view that we ought always to do what enhances and enriches life rather than what detracts from it. This encouraged me to think she would approve of my critical work, and I was on the verge of disclosing it to her when she said something which warned me that she might not be amenable to it after all. She complained to me that a lot of people at her grandmother's funeral had not seemed to be "very affected" by it. She had expected people to be a lot sadder, to be crying a lot more and showing their sorrow. I answered that, if anything, that was a good thing because it had made the event less upsetting for her and everyone else. But she shook her head and said regretfully that in some ways it hadn't "seemed" like a funeral at all. She sounded as though she had been cheated out of something. But the real clincher came when several weeks later we visited her grandmother's grave to look at the tombstone. It was horrible, an insult, just another puny, inelegant square of granite nearly indistinguishable from the hundreds around it. Yet after Jessica had placed some flowers before it, she stood up, regarded it for a few sad moments, and sighed:

"It's such a *nice* headstone, isn't it?"

I smiled faintly and tightly—unable to bring myself even to nod.

You have to accept what you can't change in those whom you would have a relationship with. You have to remind yourself that nobody's perfect—yourself included and perhaps especially. You have to take stock of what is good and bad about them, and in your mind, or even literally when you are by yourself and with pen and paper, create a ledger with one column headed "Positives," another headed "Negatives," and as honestly as possible mark down the good or bad points, then sum them up at the bottom, and see whether the greater number is for or against. After one such careful analysis I had to admit that Jessica had a lot more in her favor than otherwise.

For almost two months everything was going pretty well between us. The only slight hitches occurred when Jessica would call me while I was attending a funeral, at which time of course I couldn't talk on the phone and would call her back. She would question me about my whereabouts and be satisfied with my excuses of having taken a nap or gone for a walk without having taken my phone with me.

It's just when you think everything's going to work out—when you think you've finally met someone you like and think you might have a future with—that a wrench is flung into the mix. It happened one Friday evening while we were having dinner. She had made Fettucine Alfredo, roasted vegetables, and an apple pie for dessert. As usual it was a delicious meal. The well-behaved Wally lay on the floor a few feet away, sometimes watching us at the table, sometimes extending his head on his forepaws and sleepily closing his eyes. We were talking about nothing in particular when she turned the conversation to my past relationships. Never before had she asked me about my dating life, and it undoubtedly came up now because she had called me a few times during the week and I hadn't answered her calls because I had been attending funerals and couldn't talk, though I had called her back later. She had probably become suspicious that I was out with another woman. And so now she asked me:

"Where do you usually meet women?"

"Well, I don't meet them anymore. I'm going out with you, now."

She smiled at that; she appreciated it, seemed relieved by it; but she pressed, "Well, where did you *used* to meet them?"

"Oh ... anywhere. You know ... just going about and seeing someone I like and saying hello."

"That's pretty brave, isn't it?"

"Well, I never did it to just anyone. I had to think they were interested in me too, or could be."

"Did you think I was interested in you?"

"I was hoping so."

She smiled and said, "I sure wasn't expecting to meet anyone at a funeral!"

"Just goes to show you, you can meet someone anywhere."

She nodded and seemed to accept my reasoning, but only because it pertained to her now. If, before meeting me, she had heard it of anyone else, she would have thought it strange. And recalling where we had met, she shook her head sadly and said:

"My poor grandmother. She was such a lovely woman. You would have liked her."

"It's nice that you have good memories of her."

She looked away nostalgically for a moment, thinking of her past, and said, "Everyone liked her and she liked everyone. Well ... *nearly* everyone. She didn't get along with my ex."

"Your husband?"

She nodded, yes.

"Why not?"

She shrugged. "Different personalities. Nothing in common. Not that they hated each other or anything like that. They just didn't talk."

She had never spoken to me about her husband of almost a year, and I had never asked her any questions about him, first because I wasn't particularly interested in what had happened between them, and second because I knew that sooner or later she would tell me all about it. Now was apparently that time. She had met him, she said, when she had gone to an accounting company in Scranton to have her taxes done. He was the accountant assigned to her. They had sat together in his cubicle, he asking her questions about her finances, she answering; their conversation becoming more personally interested as the minutes passed.

"Was it love at first sight?" I asked, smiling.

She shook her head and said, "No. But he seemed like a nice guy at the time. He asked me if I was seeing anyone, and when I said no he asked me out on a date. And I said yes. And six months later I was Mrs. Peckle."

"You were *who?*"

I must have looked as though I had seen a ghost. I must have sounded that way too, because there was a distinct rise in my voice so that even Wally, who was lying on the floor nearby, perked up his head and looked at me a little more attentively.

"Mrs. Peckle. Why?"

"That's ... such an unusual name!"

"Yeah, I guess so. I don't know. Do you think so?"

I could only nod, and gulp.

"Well, it doesn't matter. It was a mistake. Looking back on it, I don't know why I ever married him. We were so different. And aside from everything else, he was way too short for me."

"Oh my God," I said.

"What?"

"I can't believe it!"

"Can't believe what?"

"I can't believe ..."—really, I was speechless, I was stupefied, I even felt a little nauseated. "I can't believe ... you would go out with ... someone so short."

"What do you mean, 'so short'?  How do you know how short he was?"

"I don't ... I mean ... was he?"

She nodded yes and frowned as though she could hardly believe it herself.  "Pretty short.  He came up to here on me," she said, raising a horizontal, close-fingered hand to her neck.  "But I didn't hold that against him.  And he was nice to me at first."

"What did he look like, this guy?"

—For I had to be certain we were talking about the same person.  It seemed to me impossible that there could be more than one poisonous Peckle living on the East Coast of the United States.  But I had to be sure.  The more she described him, the more I realized that her Peckle was my Peckle, and I sat there in a kind of staring stupor, struggling to maintain a composed, pleasant, merely curious demeanor.

She told me all about the marriage.  After the glow of the honeymoon had worn off, he began to show his true colors, first asking her to do things for him, then making demands on her.  He had "definite" ideas about what he expected of her.  "Once he even wrote up a list of what he called my 'duties.'  He even told me how much time things should take.  He was such a control freak!  Can you imagine?"

"Somehow I think I can."

"Well, after about a year, I had enough of that.  We were fighting all the time.  And you know what?  I should have known.  Really, I should have.  Because he didn't like my dog.  And when someone doesn't like dogs, that's always a bad sign—like somebody not liking kids.  But at the time I figured, you know, everyone's entitled to his opinions, and it's not like he ever told me to get rid of him. Anyway, he just kept making too many demands on me, and we started fighting a lot, and I couldn't take it anymore, so we just ended it. You look a little pale ... are you all right?"

"I'm fine. Just ... is it a little warm in here?"

"You think so? I feel fine."

"I'll be all right. Maybe it's just the hot food."

"Drink something!" she said, nodding to my beer.

I took a swig of it—a swig long enough to finish off the whole bottle. Jessica smiled at this and said, "Wow, you must be thirsty! I'll get you another one." She got up and went to the refrigerator, took out and opened another cold bottle of beer, and placed it before me with, "There you go, sweetie."

She liked me so much; and I liked her, so much. But this thing—this new thing—this revelation—this sudden blot—this unexpected, shocking, initially incredible disclosure:—how was I supposed to absorb it, to ignore it, in the light of my detestation of anything, however remotely, having to do with pathetic Peckle? To think that she had married him, that she had been embraced by his insect arms, that her lips had been touched by his insect mandibles;—it was (oufa!) too horrible to contemplate; it made me grimace, it turned my stomach. A shiver went through me as I sat there. Poor woman! At first I pitied her for having gone through the trauma of marrying such a creature. She must have endured a lot of psychological abuse. Then I wondered how she could have made such a terrible mistake. Perhaps she had been lonesome when she met Peckle, and her eagerness for a boyfriend or a husband had blinded her to his faults, which in a more objective state of mind she would have seen at once as glaring. One couldn't blame her for that. But one would have thought that after a week or two she would have seen him for the creep he was and run for the hills. That she had instead remained Mrs. Peckle, for a whole year, sloshing about in the Peckle puddle, among all that Peckle putridity, astonished me. On the other hand no wonder she was so pleased at meeting and getting to know me. She must have thought (and she was right) that with me she had hit the relationship jackpot.

What I had not foreseen was the degree to which having a relationship would impinge on my critical career. I was still working at the high school and attending and reviewing funerals in my spare time. Now some of that time had to be apportioned out to Jessica. Whereas I used to go to two funerals a week, I was now lucky if I could get to one, and sometimes I couldn't even do that—a drastic reduction which aroused in me a nervous sense of dereliction of duty. I rationalized this by thinking that even if I could produce a review every couple of weeks, it would add up in the course of the year to some twenty-five reviews, which wasn't bad.

We had been seeing each other for a little over a month when, on coming to spend time at my place, she began bringing a small suitcase filled with clothes, which found their way into my closets. "I might as well leave them here," she would say, "this way I don't have to carry them next time." But the next time she would bring and leave more things, among them several pairs of shoes, various cosmetics, bottles of shampoo, a hair dryer, and even favorite food items which she stuffed into my kitchen cabinets or refrigerator.

None of this bothered me; on the contrary I regarded it as a charming affirmation of our relationship. But she still didn't know about my critical work and that sometimes gave me pause. Would she have the largeness of mind to take an interest in it, to understand the importance of it? Would she appreciate the fact that my ambition went far and away above my elementary job as a high school guidance counselor? I tried to feel her out on the subject one evening as we were having dinner. A perfect opportunity presented itself when she mentioned—as occasionally she did—her surprise at having met someone at a funeral.

"Tell me something," I asked her, "what do you think about funerals generally?"

"What do you mean, 'generally'?"

"I mean generally... what do you think about them?"

"I don't, usually. What kind of question is that?"

"Don't you think it's odd that most people don't think about them? I mean, they're so common, sooner or later everyone goes to them, and they're inevitable for oneself."

"Okay, but why would I 'think' about them? There are more pleasant things to think about."

"That's just it. They're *so* unpleasant. Don't you think that might be a mistake?"

She shook her head a little and said, "I'm not following you."

"What if I told you that we've got it all wrong about funerals? That we should look at them in a different way."

"Oh, yeah?  What way is that?"

"In a way less … negative."

She smiled and said somewhat snidely, "So what do you want people to do, jump for joy?"

"I don't say 'jump for joy,' but just be more mature about it."

She shook her head a little again, and said, "I don't follow you."

"Don't you think it's immature and unnecessary, the way some people act at funerals?  All that crying and stuff?"

"Well, what do you want people to do?  They're sad, they're hurt.  What do you expect them to do?"

"But don't you think," I pressed, "that it would be great if they tried to look on the bright side of things."

She laughed and said, "What's the bright side of things at a funeral?"

"Well, that's just it.  Usually there isn't one.  But maybe there *should* be."

She reached out to me, her hand in a fist, and with her knuckles gently tapped at my forehead, saying, "Honey, why don't you give that noggin of yours a rest?  You've been thinking too much."

The way she discounted my questions and implications as too ridiculous for serious consideration did not exactly give me a better opinion of her.  She was a lot more conventional than I had thought her.  Yet my disappointment didn't substantially reduce my affection for her.  I was confident that in time, with a few more conversations, I could bring her round to a more enlightened point of view.

And then the second wrench came flying into the works.

It happened that on a Tuesday following a week-end spent in Pennsylvania with Jessica, I attended a funeral for a Wall Street banking executive whom the pandemic had taken out. The service took place in Danbury. I was sitting in the third row and had noticed that among the members of the family was a young woman in her late twenties or early thirties who was wearing high heels and a long dark dress which, however, was close-fitting enough to show off her nice figure. At one point she went up to the casket to pay her respects, but on turning around and returning to her seat her expression was not so much grief-stricken as it was impatient and even a little resentful, as though she had been imposed upon. She herself was probably not even aware of this expression. But I saw it, and understood the reason for it: she had been revolted by the cosmetological work done on the deceased. It was indeed the work of an amateur or a talentless hack, a fumbling attempt to make someone who had died at 86 and after an extended illness look like a ruddy, healthy man of 40 or 50. His hair had been dyed and was so evenly dark that it looked as though his head had been dunked into a vat of shoe polish, and the makeup on his face was so thickly applied that in hiding most of his wrinkles it turned his face into a chalky mask.

The reception was held in the large house of the deceased's younger brother. It had an "open living space" design with no divider between the living and dining rooms; consequently there was plenty of space to hold the forty persons who showed up. Unfortunately by the time I got there all the seats around the dining room table, where most of the good food was, had been taken. Seating generally was insufficient because some people had to sit in the kitchen. There was coffee and plenty of soft drinks, but the only adult beverage was wine—and not very good wine at that.

About forty minutes into the reception two persons who had been sitting at the dining room got up to leave. I wasted no time in taking one of their seats—and just in time, too, because the fried chicken was almost gone. Whoever had planned the event had not ordered ample food for the number of the guests, another miscalculation which cost a half coffin in the rating.

I had just helped myself to three of the five remaining pieces of chicken when the person beside me, and whose back was turned to me as she spoke to someone to her left, turned back toward the table and revealed herself to be the woman I had noticed at the service. She said hello to me and we introduced ourselves.

Her name was Nicole. She was not beautiful in the high glamorous sense of the word, but she was cute and her smile was attractive. But even more attractive was her intelligence. It was apparent in the way she spoke: beautifully, the words sparkling out of her lips and keeping articulate pace with the ideas forming, combining, and recombining in a mind whose synapses must have been firing like a flurry of fireworks. Her face was as animated as her speech; by turns she laughed, pouted, smiled, frowned. She looked about her constantly, taking in everything, everyone; assessing, calculating, deciding; absorbing and putting into some personal context every sight and sound. By comparison those around her seemed only half awake, half alive, or drugged into stupid indifference.

As we talked she sometimes looked at me with an unsettling objectivity, the way a scientist might look into a microscope to assess the magnified organism under her gaze, only to smile with satisfaction, with some pride, as though she had found out some hidden thing which had escaped others' notice. There were times when I thought she suspected me of crashing the event, but then it was clear she had accepted my story of having been a brokerage client of the deceased when she said it was nice of me to have gone out of my way to pay my last respects to him.

She clearly liked me. She smiled at me a lot in that admiring, half-hopeful way some people have when they meet someone whom they think they might have a relationship with. But I didn't feel it would be appropriate to make any overture toward her when I was already seeing someone else. As it happened, it was Nicole who made the overture to me. When I sensed she was going in that direction, and in order to spare her any embarrassment, I mentioned to her that for the last several weeks I had been dating someone. The information didn't faze her in the least; if anything, it seemed to encourage her; and the unexpected and honest selfishness of her response was itself strangely attractive.

"For how many weeks?" she asked.

"About eight."

"Oh, that's nothing. So you're dating someone. That's nice. But it's just dating. Right?"

"I don't know. Is it?"

"Of course it is, you silly person!" she said.

She reached out and put a hand behind my neck and gave it a little squeeze. She didn't take her hand away but rather let it slide across my shoulder, slip down onto my arm, glide along my forearm, and reach my hand, which she tapped as though to say, "There!" And she continued:

"Don't you know what dating is? It's just going with someone to see if you like them. That's all. It doesn't mean you're going to *marry* them. This girl you're seeing, are you going to marry her?"

"Well ... I don't know."

"That's a 'no,' " she said, definitively and frowning at me as though she were disappointed in my not knowing my own mind. "If you were going to marry her you'd know it by now."

"After only eight weeks?"

"Absolutely. And you know it as well as I do. Don't you?"

I didn't know what to say, so I didn't say anything.

"How old are you, anyway? It sounds like you've got some old-fashioned ideas!"

She spent the next five minutes coaxing me out of my old-fashioned ideas. She made a lot of good points, chief among which was the necessity of going out with "a lot" of people in order to increase the chance of finding the "right one." So many people, she said, made the mistake of thinking that they had found partners for life simply because they liked them. Wasn't that absurd? One could *like* a hundred people, but that didn't mean they were all equally suitable for a long-lasting relationship. No wonder the divorce rate was so high! And it seemed to her—she asked me to excuse her if I thought she was getting a little personal—it seemed to her that I was on the path to making the same mistake.

She wouldn't have said any of this, especially the *way* she said it, if she wasn't attracted to me. She repeatedly nudged me with her elbow in order to make physical contact. When she or I said anything the least bit witty or funny she would laugh and incline toward me, lowering her head almost to the point where it rested on my arm. She wanted me to know how much she liked me, and it was hard to resist the appeal of such behavior. In this respect she ought to be a guide to women who have been led to believe that acting indifferently toward a man makes them alluring. Young and immature men may find coyness a challenge, but maturity regards it as a foolish affectation, and forthright expressions of interest far more attractive. Nicole showed that she liked me and made me feel good. Even Jessica didn't have this ability to the same exuberant extent.

After an hour and a half I had seen enough of the reception to judge it fairly. Besides, all the chicken was gone, and some fat guy on the other side of the table had cleaned up all the potato salad before I could get my hands on it. I excused myself to my tablemates and told Nicole that it had been very nice talking with her but it was time for me to go.

"Maybe," she said, before I got up to leave, "we could get together sometime, under better circumstances." She took a pen out of her pocketbook and wrote her phone number on a napkin, folding it discreetly and handing it to me. "You can call me any time. I'd love to talk more."

"Sure, that would be nice," I said. I put the numbered napkin into my jacket pocket but I had no intention of calling her.

Jessica called me while I had been at the reception, but I had turned off my phone. She left a message on my answering service. I called her back that evening and told her I had gone out to dinner. She asked where. I told her, "A restaurant." She asked, "Which one?" I returned, "Why does it matter?" She said she was just "curious"—but she clearly suspected me of something less innocent than eating. I laughed off her curiosity and shifted the conversation to seeing her over the weekend, saying:

"Shall I come to your place?"

"No, no, I'll go to yours."

"But you were here for the last two weekends."

"So what? I like being there."

"But you have a nicer yard. Maybe we could have a barbecue or something."

"Some other time. I'll be at your place at ten."

"That's kind of early, isn't it?"

"I get up early these days."

She arrived promptly at ten o'clock on Saturday morning, greeted me with a kiss, and stepped inside my house looking about with unwonted interest as though she were looking for something. She exhibited the same peculiarity throughout the day. When she went into the bathroom I could hear her opening and closing the medicine cabinet.

We did the usual things that weekend—and I felt to a greater degree the usual impatience to be at my work. While the stockbroker's funeral was still fresh in my mind, I wanted to write the review. Unable to do so I tried composing it in my head, which sometimes distracted me from Jessica's conversation. At one such point she said:

"Helloooo!"

"What?"

"I just asked you a question."

"What's the question?"

"Well, you tell *me!* I just asked it!"

"I'm sorry ... I was thinking of something. What was it?"

"I said, how would you like to have dinner next week with Tom and Toni"—two of her many friends whom we had dined with before.

"Uh ... maybe we could just stay by ourselves this time."

"What's wrong, don't you like my friends?"

"It's not that I don't like them, it's that—I'll be honest with you—I'm not interested in them."

"Why not? They're very nice."

"They *are* nice. But I'm still not interested."

"Well maybe if you saw them more often and got to know them you *would* be interested. They happen to be very interesting people. Tom is a very bright guy—he's a software engineer"—ho-hum—"and Toni has a degree in history"—which is why she was working for a car rental agency? "And what about Carol and Simone? They like you a lot. And you haven't even met Jenny and Max yet. They're very interesting people."

"You have a lot of friends," I remarked, not without a note of exasperation in my voice.

"Yes, I do. I *like* having a lot of friends. I'm not like you—no friends at all."

"I could have as many friends as you do if I wanted them."

"So why don't you?"

"Because I'm too busy."

She laughed; she had expected any number of excuses, but not that one. "Busy with *what?*" she asked. "What're you, the Head of General Motors or something?"

Nothing better could have shown me the unattractive side of her conventionalism than such a remark, which tried to diminish me by contrasting me against—of all people!—the executive of a car company. She hadn't the sense to understand that such a person, in the larger scheme of things and ultimately, was a total nonentity. Such a person would never improve the way funerals were given, could not hope to have a tenth of that kind of influence in advancing society and civilization. Granted, she didn't know that I reviewed funerals, but she knew that people wrote great books, composed wonderful music, produced amazing paintings, thought up life-enhancing philosophies: yet rather choose one of them as a standard of excellence she had chosen a glorified office worker. And then I reminded myself that she had agreed to become Mrs. Peckle. That was more than just the "mistake" she had said it was: it was in keeping with her lack of discrimination and idealism.

She began calling me a lot more. She called me at my office in school, she called me while I was commuting from work, she called me in the evenings. When I was at a funeral with my phone turned off, she left messages like this: "Helloooo ... where aaar-rrre youuu? I need to talk to you so call me back as soon as possible!" Or like this: "Just calling to say hi. Are you there? No? Hello? This is the second time

I'm trying to call you!" Or like this, "Hmmm ... now where oh where could you be?" Though the tone of her voice was affectionate it had an accusatory edge. I usually called back the next day, expecting she would—as she did—interrogate me as to my whereabouts. I would tell her that I had just gone out for a walk or worked late at school.

"So why didn't you call me back as soon as you got the message?"

"I'm calling you now."

"Hmmpf!"

A couple of weeks later, when she and Wally spent the weekend at my place, she suggested we might move in together "to save expenses." She said she wouldn't mind living in Connecticut, that for a while she could rent her house and get another job. And just think, I would get to see her and Wally every day! I politely declined, saying we were both too set in our ways to make such a fundamental change, and that living apart was the best insurance for a harmonious relationship. That was true, though it was not my only reason, which was that living with her would put yet more demands on my time, too much of which, already, had been detracted from my critical work. At first she was only disappointed by my declining her offer: she looked away and shrugged. But in a few more moments she seemed to take it as a personal insult, for she looked at me a little angrily and said:

"You know, you really need to start thinking about changing your life around."

"Why do you say that?"

"Because your life is a mess."

I laughed and said, "How so?"

"Because you're not going anywhere. You have no direction. You're just floating in the wind. I mean, what are you *doing* with your life?"

Ah, Jessica!

"You might want to start thinking about growing up—*prontissimo*," she added.

Now, quite aside from the silly misuse of the foreign superlative, what irritated me most about her response was its frank expression of discontent with me based again on superficial notions of propriety. She was dissatisfied with me for living in a way somewhat different from the way most people lived theirs—and this without knowing the most important fact about me. It had begun to dawn on me—and her latest remarks had accelerated the emergent and revealing light—that she was not the type to understand either the value of funeral reviews or respect the sacrifices entailed in writing them. She had no sense of, no respect for, ambition except in its most fleeting, everyday manifestations. She was less concerned about what a man was (again, had she not been Mrs. Peckle?) than on the constancy of his companionship. She was, poor thing, a lonesome person. That was piteous and sympathetic, but also cast another unflattering light on herself, since lonesomeness depends as much on who we are as on whom we're with. Her neediness was not one of her better qualities, and was increasingly dominating all the others.

I recalled what Nicole had told me about the nature of dating, how it was meant to be exploratory and not a compact between two persons for a lifelong commitment. A woman who held such views was certainly in line with my own feelings about the matter.   I wanted to see her and talk to her again about that—about a lot of things.   The napkin on which she had written her phone number was still in the jacket I had worn to the funeral at which we had met.   I took it out and, not without some guilty hesitation, called her.

She was happy to hear from me.   She said she had been hoping I would call and asked what had taken me so long.   I told her I had just been "busy."

"Busy with that other girl, right?" she asked, and she laughed as though my relationship Jessica was some silly thing that had nothing to do with her.

"Busy with a lot of things," I said.

She did not refer to Jessica again and we talked for the next hour easily and enjoyably; there was no undercurrent of complaint or blame which had begun to strain my conversations with Jessica.   Nicole was lighthearted and often funny.   Her quick mind seized on opportunities to make witticisms or irreverent comments at which we both laughed.   She made me feel as though I had known her for years, an ability which is as much the hallmark of a good conversationalist as it should be a warning to those susceptible of its charms that appearance may not correspond to reality.

She suggested that we go out for a cup of coffee or a drink, and said she would be available Thursday or Friday night, or on the weekend.   It would be easy to see her because she lived only fifteen miles away from me.

"Friday night would be good for me," I said, because I had a funeral to attend on Thursday and Jessica was supposed to come over on Saturday.

"That'll work for me too," she said.

We met at a bar in her neighborhood. It nestled between a laundromat and a grocery store. A large hand-written sign, taped onto its impenetrably dark front window, proclaimed "You must be over 21 to enter these premises!" Behind its bulky wooden door loomed a dim, cozy, relaxing space with a long bar at the front and tables visible in the darkness beyond. She had gotten there before I did and was sitting at the bar before a barely-sipped vodka and tonic. When I stepped inside she got off her seat, stood up, and, when I reached her, greeted me with a great hug and a kiss on the cheek;—a delightful greeting.

She was more attractive than I had remembered her. She had put on more makeup than she had for the funeral; her eyes seemed larger, darker, more enticing; her lashes were longer. She wore tight jeans, high heels, and a blouse unbuttoned almost halfway down.

There are some people who, like Nicole, only drink when socializing, celebrating, or as an anodynic last resort to emotional distress. My observation has been that at such times they make up for their abstinence with an unhealthy overindulgence. Nicole polished off two vodka and tonics in forty minutes—for her an unprecedented amount; in part because she said she was "feeling good," and in part because she lived close enough to the bar to walk home. At any rate she got a little tipsy, was sometimes silly, and was even more fun than usual.

Unlike Jessica, who increasingly had been telling me of all the things which bothered her (including myself), Nicole only related the things she liked.

She liked to go swimming, to go to farmers markets, and to try ethnic foods. She liked Christmastime with its decorated trees and wreathes smelling of pine, and the magic of its glitter and twinkling lights. She liked the long nights of winter and looking through the windows to see the snow fall in the darkness, and she liked the long warm days of summer and how they came to a languid end with the sound of crickets and a sky all pink or orange from the setting sun. She liked her house; she liked her job; she wanted to see the world; she had a hundred plans for herself.

"And what about you?" she asked. "What do you like to do? Do you like your job?"

"I hate my job."

"*Hate* it?" She seemed surprised by the extreme note. "Well then you need to change it."

I shook my head, no, and said, "I don't mind hating it because I can hate it from a distance. It doesn't define me."

"What *does* define you?"

"Other things."

"Which are?"

"I'll be specific without being specific: I want to change peoples' attitude."

"About?"

"About life—in all its stages."

She smiled and leaned back and said, "I don't know what that means but it sure *sounds* impressive!" She smiled at me conspiratorially, narrowed her eyes at me, and leaned in and whispered playfully, "Are you some kind of revolutionary or something?"

—Which made me laugh a little: her question

was so much more acute than she knew!

"Maybe," I said.

"But you don't want to say in what way."

"Isn't a little mystery good?"

"I agree 100%.  It keeps things interesting.  But tell me, that girl you're going out with—does *she* know you're a revolutionary?"

"Oh, she thinks I'm a lot of things—but I don't think that's one of them."

"Hmm," she said, raising her brows and looking away.  "Doesn't sound like you two are living in paradise."

I only raised a hand in a gesture of uncertainty.

"I'll bet she's not very nice," Nicole said, then.

"Oh, no, she *is* very nice."

"But ...?"

Again, I only raised a hand for a second and put it down.

"Where did you meet her, anyway?"

"I met her at someone's funeral."

Nicole blinked a few times.  "Wait a minute.  You met *her* at a funeral too?"

"It just happened that way.  It's ... a coincidence."

"I'll say!"  She sipped her drink a few times, considering the coincidence; and apparently reconciling herself to it—concluding that, after all, it was within the realm of possibility.  Then she said:

"Well, it can't possibly last.  I think you should end it now and cut your losses.  This way you won't feel so guilty when we go out again."

"How do you know I feel guilty?  And how do you know we're going out again?"

"I know you feel guilty because you're not as outgoing as you were when I met you.  And as for going out with me again, you'll do that too because you like me."

We stayed at the bar for almost three hours, during which time I nursed a single beer and a glass of seltzer because I had to drive. It was almost eleven o'clock before we left and I drove Nicole home.

We were strangely quiet on our way to her house. We were both reflecting on the pleasant time we had spent in the bar and wondered when we would see each other again. When we stopped before her door she turned to me and said, "Thanks. I had a great time." She leaned toward me and kissed me on the cheek, then turned around, got out of the car, shut the door, and stood there for a moment, a little bent over, looking at me. She waved with a smile and said, "See you soon!" I watched her, not without a sense of loss, as she walked to her house and disappeared inside.

I knew that the few hours we had spent together might be the first step in a longer, closer relationship, and the anticipation of it was already vitiated with a sense of danger, rather the way one might feel on starting a hike into a beautiful countryside which, however, is said to contain landmines. Maybe, I told myself, it wasn't such a good idea to see her again. I resolved that I wouldn't, unless it were as a friend; and even then I would make no effort in that way.

It was she however who called me the next day and told me what a grand time she had had the night before. She spoke as though we had gone on some rare adventure rather than merely sat talking for three hours. Hearing the enthusiasm and affection in her voice, I knew I had to nip in the bud any extravagant expectations she might have for us and which were so impossible for me in my current circumstances. I told her that I thought she was a wonderful woman, that she had a wonderful personality and that I had enjoyed spending time with her, but that it might not be in our best interest to see each other because I was, as she knew, already seeing someone else. She brushed off my concern as though it were as insignificant as an observation on the weather. And it was she who said:

"Well, we can be friends, can't we?"

Her reply was so unexpectedly welcome that I couldn't help but respond enthusiastically with, "Of course we can!"

"Great! So, *friend*," she said, "what are you doing next week?"

Our second meeting was as pleasant as the first, perhaps more so since we were both more comfortable with each other. She drank just as much; was just as silly; just as affectionate. We laughed a lot. She mentioned Jessica once, saying, "What do you think she would say if she knew you and I were friends?"

"I'm sure she wouldn't mind. After all ... we're just friends."

She laughed with a gleam in her eye which—as much as any such gleam could—fulfilled the conspiratorial office of a hard wink. For some time afterwards she would agree with a smile and a nod, or confirm with an outright expression of concurrence, any reference I made to the relaxed and noncommittal nature of our relationship. But either she didn't know her own mind or (which was more likely the case) she had decided that for now the pretense of keeping our relationship on a cool footing was the best way of ensuring the much closer relationship she was aiming for.

I should have known that she was not looking for a "friend"—not even a friend who provided certain benefits; an arrangement which women are not generally eager for. But at the time I thought she was one of the wonderful exceptions to the rule. That she might be so occurred to me the next time we met at a local restaurant. She looked better than ever. She greeted me with the warmest hug and a kiss smack on the lips. She wore a very short skirt, very high heels, and a very sheer blouse which kept distracting me from my eggplant Parmigiana. When the waiter took away our plates, she asked:

"Guess what I bought this week?"

"I have no idea."

"But *guess!*" she insisted, smiling, her eyes sparkling; and looking at me with a knowing expression as though I had to know what it was.

"I don't know. New shoes?"

She laughed. "Silly! No. It's something *you* like."

"Something *I* like?"

She nodded fervently a few times, holding her wine glass just beneath her lips.

"I have no idea. What do I like?"

"Don't you remember what you told me? About what you wanted to get?"

I was lost. I shrugged my shoulders.

"The Old Kentucky Eight Year!" she announced.

It took a few moments for me to recall that a

week before I had mentioned wanting to buy a bottle of that very good, very expensive, and very hard-to-find rye whiskey.  I could understand why I would want it but why would she?  She didn't like whiskey. It was obvious she had bought it for me.  She had ordered it over the Internet at what was undoubt-edly a premium price.

"After dinner we'll go to my place and try it," she said, enthusiastically.  "We'll see if it lives up to the hype."

"Oh, Nicole, I don't know.  I can't drink and drive."

"You're not going to drink *a lot,*" she said, shak-ing her head as though it were preposterous in me to think she would allow such a thing.  "Just a *little* taste.  A teeny-tiny one.  Just to see if it's as good as they say it is.  Then take it home with you."

"Well ... maybe just a tiny sip."

"Of course!"

It was the first time I had been to her house.  It was spacious because uncluttered, very clean and neat, and a faint smell of the perfume she had worn at dinner hung in the air.  She brought out the bot-tle of rye and presented it to me as though she were presenting an award, cradling it from the bottom in her left hand while with her right tilting it back somewhat by the neck.  Insofar as bottles went it was attractive for its sturdy and utilitarian plain-ness:  an inverted U with a glass bottom half an inch thick, and a straight, short neck into which the corked cap was visible beneath the green sealing band laid over it crosswise.  The green and white la-bel, in an Old Western type font, proudly proclaimed its name and, beneath this, in smaller typeface, the information that it came from an "original Colonial recipe, made with the purest Kentucky spring water and charcoal-filtered for unparalleled smoothness." Its color bespoke the care of its creation and aging: it was a luscious amber—as the rivers in Paradise, according to Milton, are. I pulled out the cork and brought the bottle to my nose and smelled its contents: lovely, lovely: burnt sugar, oak, a hint of pepper, a hint of vanilla—cardamon (perhaps), and the tiniest bit of lemon zest or orange peel.

"Oh my," I said, "that's very nice."

"Let's try it!" Nicole said, taking the bottle from me and going into the kitchen.

"Nicole, I have to drive."

"Don't worry! I'm just going to give you a little!"

I followed her into the kitchen. I expected her to put a little of the rye in a teaspoon for me to taste. Instead she opened a cabinet and took out two tumblers into which she placed ice cubes and started making drinks. I asked her what she was doing, but she didn't answer, only flashed a smile at me, and continued. Into two small glasses she placed a couple of ice cubes, poured in some rye, added a caramelized simple syrup, a dash of orange and Angostura bitters, and, for garnish, two wide swaths of lemon and orange peel. She swirled my drink a few times before handing it to me and said, "There you are! A nice old fashioned. Try it!"

"I'm not going to drink all that."

"Just try it," she said, putting it into my hand.

I tried it. It was delicious—it was like candy—it was superb.

"Oh my goodness," I said.

"Told you," she said.

"But I can't drink all this."

"You don't have to." She took up her glass and said, "Let's go back into the living room."

I intended to take no more than two or three sips more and then leave. But as we talked, and the quarter hour lengthened into a half, and that approached the next hour, two thoughts occurred to me: first, that it would be a sin to take only a few sips of such a good and expensive whiskey and throw the rest away, and second that I was drinking it so slowly that it was not bound to affect me much. My mistake in this matter is mostly owing to Old Kentucky Eight Year, which, though bottled at a 100 proof, is as smooth as silk, and so rich, so fragrant, so delicious in an old fashioned, and so cheerful in its influence, that it seduced me away from my usual good sense.

Nicole sat beside me, turned toward me with her crossed legs touching mine. I couldn't help noticing that her blouse was even sheerer than it had seemed in the restaurant. I had consciously to keep my eyes on hers as we spoke. When she laughed she leaned in toward me; as she did when smiling, or speaking, or listening to me. In fact she was *always* leaning in toward me in an engagingly confidential way. When I had finished my drink, I set it down on an end table and told her I had to be going. She looked at me closely for a moment before saying:

"That might not be a good idea."

"Why not?"

She shook her head at me gravely. "You'd better not drive. I think that drink affected you more than you realize."

"Really?"

She nodded and said, "Yes, I think you might be just a *liiiittle* tipsy, so you definitely can't drive. Listen, why don't you just relax? What's the rush? Just have another drink, and you can sleep here tonight on the couch. Besides," she said, lifting her glass, "these really are good, aren't they? Might as well really enjoy them and have one more."

"Oh, Nicole, I don't know—"

"Shush!" she said, getting up while reaching out and lightly pushing on my chest as though to make sure I sat back, "you stay right there. You're not going anywhere. You can't drive, and neither can I, and that's that. And we're having such a nice time just hanging out—aren't we? Here," she said, taking up my glass, "I'll make you a fresh one. Hang tight!"

She sailed away into the kitchen and came back a few minutes later with a second drink for me, but not for herself, saying that she still hadn't finished her first one. She plopped down on the couch close beside me, nudging into me with a wiggle of her shoulders and saying, "This is so nice and cozy, isn't it?"

I don't remember at what point Nicole told me that I would not sleep well on the couch and offered me other accommodations which would be perfectly acceptable because we were "friends." Nor do I remember (though she later insisted on it) the alacrity with which I accepted her offer. What I *do* know was that the next day, as we sat before each other drinking our morning coffee, our relationship was on a footing different from the one on which it had begun. If I was largely silent, if I didn't say much, if I was even eager to get out of there, it was because I knew we had crossed a threshold which I had specifically let her know I didn't want to cross.

Would it be an exaggeration to say that she took advantage of me?  I believe she did.  Nicole was a master manipulator, and poor me—I was so naïve and innocent!  And Nicole could pursue her program more unreservedly because she believed, as she was henceforth to try to convince me, that my relationship with Jessica wasn't real, wasn't serious; that it was only a kind of play-acting, a charade between two persons who *thought* they had found the right person in each other, though anyone on the outside— for instance, herself—could see that they hadn't and that they were indeed totally incompatible.

But that morning on my way home my biggest worry was how this situation complicated my relationship with Jessica.  I had intended to tell her about Nicole, saying she was just a friend, which would have been an accurate description indemnifying me against any jealousy Jessica might feel.  But now that was not possible.  I knew that a single instance of what is usually associated with something more than friendship between two persons does not *necessarily* imply anything more than that, but I doubted that Jessica would share that enlightened view.  She would see it as a grand betrayal.  She would be terribly hurt by it.  She would probably be too angry to sympathize with my having been taken advantage of.  She would only see one side of the matter—the side in which I stood in the glare of intentional and unforgivable wrongdoing.

It seemed to me best to say nothing about it, even to consider it as never having happened.  Who knew but that it had been a flash in the pan—a mistake never to be repeated? It would be very foolish to risk a relationship for the sake of what in the end was a one-time lapse of good judgment, and I was determined that the next time I spoke with Nicole I would suggest that we not see each other again.

I turned on my phone when I got home and of course there was a message awaiting me from Jessica, who had called the night before. She happily asked where I was and said to call her back. I sighed at the thought of doing so. She would want to know where I had been, and I would have to make up an excuse; which happened to be that I had gone to sleep early because I had been so tired.

"You've been tired a lot lately," she said. "Maybe you need vitamins or something."

"Maybe."

We made plans for the week, to which I happily assented, though my pleasure arose less from the prospect of seeing her again than from the relief that she had not questioned me further about my whereabouts the night before. But that did not mean she wasn't going to. The next day when she arrived at my house one of the first things she said was:

"So why were you so tired the other day?"

"I just was."

"What time did you go to sleep?"

"About eight-thirty or so."

She considered a moment before saying, "How come? You usually don't' go to sleep till twelve or one."

I just shrugged and nodded in agreement. But her questions made me uneasy: she would not have asked them, especially a day later, if she had not been uneasy about my whereabouts. On some level she must have suspected that I had told a little fib.

How many little fibs does it take to make up a great big one? It depends on how little the fibs are: if they're very little, if they're teeny-tiny, no larger, say, than the hundredth part of a grain of sand, or some infinitesimal fraction of a hair's breadth, then one could conceivably tell them all day long and they still would not add up to a pinch's worth. One also has to consider the nature of the person they are told to. If someone is excitable and incapable of putting things into perspective, then of course she is going to react out of all proportion to what are in fact the tiniest peccadilloes. Knowing that Jessica fitted into that category I decided not to mention anything to her about Nicole, whom I had decided not to see again except on strictly platonic terms.

She called me a few days after I had stayed the night at her place and told me she wanted to see me again. I told her it was probably not a good idea. She laughed off my concern. She assured me that what had happened between us was "nothing, nothing!"—that it was I who was making a big deal out of it. "Listen, it doesn't matter to me one way or the other," she breezily continued. "You can do whatever you want. But we *do* have a good time together, don't we? We can still be friends, can't we? So let's go out for dinner or something this week." And when again I hesitated: "Oh, c'mon, stop being silly! There's a restaurant I want to try out. I'll even treat you, how's that sound? You can't pass up something like that, can you?" Even as I protested that I couldn't agree to meet her there she told me to write down its name and the time for our meeting there, adding that she would be there and it wouldn't be nice at all if I stood her up.

So I went. What was I supposed to do? At the very least it would give me an opportunity to set the record straight with her regarding the merely cordial footing our relationship had to assume. I was going to tell her that at most we could only be friends, that what had happened between us had been owing to a slip of better judgment on both our parts, but that we were both adults and mature enough, practical enough, to put it behind us and resume a simple friendship. And I did say so much. But as though I hadn't said a word of it, Nicole responded by referring to Jessica with:

"*She's* the one you need to stop seeing. You're wasting your time with her. I would suggest that the next time you talk to her, you tell her it's over."

"Oh really!" I wondered at her presumption as well as despaired at it: she had so clearly ignored everything I just told her.

"Of course," she said easily. "She's not the right one for you. Why do you think we're here together now?"—and she tilted her head with a knowing smile as though she expected the only answer possible.

"Nicole, I'm here because you said you wanted to talk to me."

"Okay, but that's the only reason you're here."

"I love the way you always think you know me better than I know myself."

"I do."

"No you don't."

"I know one thing: you're not interested in her.

Not really. Maybe once you were, but not now, not in the same way. You know what else I think?"

"I'm sure you'll tell me."

"I think you don't want to admit you made a mistake. I mean in going out with her. But you know what the bigger mistake is?—to hold on to someone you're not feeling the same for anymore. And it's selling yourself short, and it's not fair for the other person."

Amazing how she could transform whatever devotion I had for Jessica into something I ought to be ashamed of.

As I have said, Nicole was a master manipulator. She had a talent for convincing you that she knew better than you did and inclining you to see things her way. She would listen sympathetically to your concerns or objections, then explain why they were unfounded, looking at you with a smile or giving a contemptuous wave of her hand as though you, poor worrywart, had no idea of the mountains you were making out of molehills. In this way, before dinner was over, she had alleviated my concerns about any future relationship we might have. She took one of my hands and petted it as though it were the head of sick puppy. "Let's go back to my place," she said.

"I don't think that would be a good idea."

"I do. I have to talk to you about something else."

"What? We can talk here."

"We really can't," she said, looking about as though the place were full of eavesdroppers. "C'mon. I don't want to stay here."

At her place she worked on my sympathy, appealed to my better nature, exploited my willingness to think the best of others, and the upshot of the evening was that she made me a martini and—took advantage of me again.  The next morning she was breezily enthusiastic about having done so.  She laughed off my concerns and told me how there could now be no doubt in my mind that we were meant to be together.  She repeated that my relationship with Jessica wasn't an "issue" because it wasn't real.

"Tell her goodbye this week and get it over with," Nicole told me, when we parted a few hours later.

Later that day it occurred to me that she might be right.  Perhaps she did know me better than I knew myself.  The proof is always in the pudding: I couldn't have been taken advantage of, and two times at that, unless there had been something *to be* taken advantage of.  Undoubtedly I liked Nicole more than I had supposed, but that didn't mean (and this was the crux of my dilemma) that I liked Jessica any less.  In fact my time with Nicole brought home to me how much I liked Jessica also.  They were so different; they had such opposite but equally attractive qualities.  Nicole was adventurous, vibrantly atypical, perhaps a little reckless; the kind of person who, if you got stuck with her at the edge of the world with danger at your backs, would encourage you to jump with her off some seaside cliff into the waters below.  On the other hand Jessica was a lot safer, more thoughtful, much more patient, more reliably sweet.  From her one could not expect sudden leaps of any kind, and her safe equanimity appealed to me as some becalming influence to the sometimes stressful demands of my critical work.  But of course I couldn't see both of them at the same time.  That wouldn't have been fair to either one of them, and it wouldn't have been fair to me.  The weekends Jessica and I spent together had already cut into the time I should have been attending funerals, and now at least two of my weekdays were being commandeered by Nicole  What was I supposed to do?

My decision rested ultimately on the answer to this question:  Which one of them would be a help and support to me as a critic?  In particular, which one of them would  genuinely, and not merely out of some sentimental impulse to be "nice" or "supportive," enter into the spirit of my work and even, if necessary, be willing to make sacrifices for it?  I couldn't see Jessica doing so, especially when I recalled how, on my broaching the topic, she had regarded it as a ridiculous attempt at humor.  True, I had never said anything about it to Nicole, but surely the same personality which didn't think twice about liquoring up a guy and taking advantage of him was not going to be intimidated by a new form of social criticism, no matter how unusual it might strike her at first.  Yes, Nicole was the one for me.

For a whole day I obsessed over how to tell Jessica it was over between us.  I phrased and rephrased the words to be used, the tone and manner in which to deliver them;—the objective of it all being to make the breakup as gentle as possible.  I had it all planned.  I would ask her to sit down and, still standing, would tell her I had something important to say.  I would begin by showering her with compliments, telling her what a fine person she was, how she was the sweetest, kindest, most affectionate woman any man could hope to know. Despite all that (I would continue, with a regretful demeanor) I had begun to recognize that I was not feeling for her the kind of all-consuming affection which she had a right to expect from me, and which was necessary to bind two persons together in the kind of lifetime commitment they had hoped to find in each other. No one was sorrier for this than I was. She had to understand that it wasn't my fault, nor hers; that "fault" had nothing to do with it; that it all came down to what one could or couldn't feel, and was thus beyond one's control.... Yes, it would be a good, a heartfelt speech, ending with half a dozen apologies. She would see how difficult it was for me to say such things, and with any luck would feel sorrier for me than she did for herself.

When, that Saturday morning, I heard her pulling into my driveway, I went to the door to let her in. I watched as she got out of her car, saying, to Wally, who bounded after her, "C'mon boy!" As she came my way I steeled myself for what I had to tell her.

But she ruined everything! As soon as she reached me she flung her arms around my neck, kissed me, and exclaimed "I missed you so much!" How was I supposed to tell her I wanted to break up with her after that? The incongruity between her effusive affection, and my rather helpless returning of it, followed by my declaration of wanting to leave her, would have seemed even to me like some kind of cruel joke. At any rate, this was not the right time.

The problem became that there never *was* a right time. Week after week passed, and each time

I saw her with the intention of ending our relationship she would say or do something—tell me again
that she loved me, or look at me in an adoring doe-
eyed way—which melted my resolve.

There was also Wally to consider. I had really
come to like that dog. The feeling was mutual, since
he jumped on me the moment he saw me and hardly
ever left my side. He even preferred staying with
me whenever his owner walked away; she had to call
him, several times and emphatically, to come to her,
upon which, before heeding her summons, he would
look at me almost apologetically as though to say,
"I'm so sorry, but if I don't listen to her I'll get in
trouble!" Poor thing—wouldn't he miss me?

Nicole noted my tardiness in breaking up with
Jessica. At first she was confident that it was only a
matter of time before I did so, prodding me with,
"C'mon already!  Tell her and get it over with!"
Then her patience and encouragement hardened into
irritation. As though to hurry along the process, she
started speaking negatively of Jessica. It didn't matter that she had never met her; she knew, she said,
her "type"—and it wasn't a good one. I had probably
mentioned things about Jessica which annoyed me,
little suspecting how aggressively Nicole would latch
onto them, blow them out of all proportion, and try
to turn them to her account. For instance when she
told me that Jessica was "inconsiderate."

"Why do you say that?"

"You told me yourself:  she keeps pushing her
friends on you."

"I don't think she 'pushes' them on me. She just
has a lot of friends and when she makes dinner she
invites them."

"But you told her you don't like that."

"I told her I preferred eating by ourselves."

"But she keeps having her friends over. So what does that tell you about her? I'll tell you what it tells you: she's selfish!"

I shrugged and said, "It's not a big deal."

"But you should make a big deal! Because if she's going be selfish about this, she's going be selfish about everything else. Just wait! You'll see!"

And another time:

"She's too old for you anyway."

"What do you mean, 'too old'? She's younger than I am."

"Yeah, but she's an old lady up here," she said, tapping her head.

"Why do you say that?"

"Didn't you tell me once that she knits?"

"Did I?"—at the time, I couldn't remember having said any such thing. Only later did I recall having mentioned that Jessica had knitted a sweater for herself.

"Yes, you did. And that's what old ladies do: they sit on their rocking chairs and knit. And why would anyone go through all that trouble when you can buy something for thirty bucks? She's obviously not too bright. She's probably already a little senile."

She increasingly took these jabs at Jessica, which at first amused me but then made me a little sad because they were so clearly made in dislike of someone she didn't know and who deserved to be spoken better of. Nicole's attitude was also ironic because in any other circumstance she and Jessica would probably have been great friends. They were both good people. They both had good hearts. The differences in their personalities—Jessica's homey simplicity and conservatism, Nicole's reckless adventurism—might in many respects have complemented each other. I knew too that Nicole's execrations of Jessica were just so many expressions of frustration at my inability to separate from her.

Jessica didn't know about Nicole, at least not for sure, but she was becoming suspicious as increasingly it became harder for her to get through to me by phone, since I always turned mine off when I was with Nicole. When I called her back she would want to know where I had been. My excuses were endless: I had gone to sleep early, or had had a headache and didn't feel like talking, or was working on something for school and didn't want to be disturbed. I told her that sometimes, when I went for a short walk or just down the street to a store, I didn't take my phone with me and so couldn't answer her calls.

"Well don't do that," she said. "Take it with you *all* the time. What if it's an emergency and I need to talk to you?"

"What do you mean, an 'emergency'?"

"How should I know? It could be anything. What if I fall or something, or get into a car accident?"

"Well, in that case you should be calling for an ambulance, not me."

"Oh, thanks!"

"You know what I mean."

"Just keep it with you. Just stick it in your pocket. It's not a big deal and I might need to talk to you."

One week I saw Jessica on the weekend and Nicole on the two nights afterwards—and missed out on two potentially interesting and instructive funerals. Those I did manage to catch were local and resulted in reviews so far beneath my standards that I abandoned them as impossible fragments. It's hard to wax poetic about a fine receptions, or to denounce, with a vigor equal to the enormity of the offense, a family member who throws the attendees into distress by fainting away for grief, when two people whom you care about are exerting their influence on you in separate and antagonistic ways.

Continuous worry over lost time for my work, and increasingly little sleep, was taking a toll on my health. My blood pressure was starting to rise owing to stress which was present even when I wasn't aware of it. I had a blood pressure monitor at home and occasionally took my reading. It had always been a very healthy 115/73, but it had crept up to 123/82. The thought that I was on my way to hypertension, with all its possibly disastrous consequences, was like a tonic slap across the face. There's nothing like a health scare to make one rethink one's priorities. In my case there were no two ways about it: I needed to be alone for a while.

I told Jessica and Nicole that I wouldn't be available for the next couple of weeks. Their reactions were strangely similar in that they were both suspicious of what I would be doing, or rather whom I would be seeing.

"Are you going somewhere?" Jessica asked.

"I'm not going to do anything. I'm staying

home."

"What for?"

"I told you: I just need some time off."

"Time off? From me?"

"No, not from you in particular. Just from things in general." And because I had to give her an excuse she might understand, I said: "I'm tired. I've been working a lot and I just want to relax by myself for a while."

"Well, excuse *me!* I didn't know being with me was such a chore!"

"It has nothing to do with you, Jessica," I said, in what was strictly speaking a fib, but which as a response to the way *she* meant it was not.

We talked for another five minutes in pretty much the same vein, she trying to make me feel guilty, I holding my ground, resolved to get what I wanted and needed; and getting it.

Nicole was equally if not more sarcastic, only she immediately jumped to the conclusion that I needed the time because I would be spending it with Jessica. She implied so much by her comment, saying, "I'll *bet* you need time! For *who?*"

I laughed at that, since she was implying the very *last* thing I wanted to do. The immediacy of my derisive response convinced her more than words could that she was wrong. But that, if anything, only confused her the more. If I wasn't going to be seeing Jessica, then what was I going to be doing?

"I'm going to rest," I said.

"*Rest?* That's all you *do* is rest!"

"Very funny. I happen to have a job I go to."

"So what? I do too. Everyone does."

I would have liked to tell her that, yes, she and

everyone else had jobs to go to, but afterwards they went home and ate and sat on the couch and stared at a television till they went to sleep. They didn't struggle to overcome their exhaustion to work at another job. Instead I repeated my need for rest.

"Geeze," she said, "I didn't know I was such a slave driver."

Oddly enough, for the first couple of days of those two weeks I really *did* do nothing; did exactly what most people do: came home after work, ate, and watched television. But this was merely the battery recharging itself. On the third day, fully refreshed, I was eager to get back to work. While in my office at school I canceled a few appointments with students and spent the whole morning looking up obituaries. I composed a list of twenty funerals for possible review, and pared those down to five, all of which were within twenty minutes' driving distance of my home.

I went to one every other day. On the whole they were all pretty bad, and all for the usual reasons: drab venues, budget accoutrements, misbehaving relatives, uninteresting priests or pastors, eulogies which went on way to long, and receptions which didn't compensate anyone for the trouble of attending. I sighed and sighed through all of them. Two of them were owing to the pandemic, two of them to terminal illnesses, and one of them to suicide. This last was interesting from a sociological point of view. It was for a middle-aged woman who had overdosed on sleeping pills when she learned that the three multimillionaire executives she worked for, and who (according to her daughter) "worked her to exhaustion every day," had given her a yearly bonus of $300. The poor creature had never imagined that people could repeatedly praise her to skies for all her hard work and dedication, and then, when it came time for them to show it in a real, a monetary way, which was so easily affordable to them, fling her instead a donative whose smallness reflected their actual contempt. But she must have been a very silly or stupid woman not to have known, especially after thirty years in the corporate world, that it is the last place from which anyone should expect appreciation, much less financial reward, for dedicated service—a point which I mentioned in the review.

At one of the receptions I happened to meet a tall redhead with green eyes (oh my goodness!), long legs, and a body to die for. We exchanged a few words and she seemed attracted to me. But remembering Jessica and Nicole, I soon excused myself and escaped to the other side of the room where I had to strain every nerve to seem interested in a conversation between two imbeciles discussing their favorite baseball teams.

During these two weeks Jessica and Nicole called me every day, usually in the evening. Sometimes one of them called while I was on the phone with the other. She would always ask me later whom I had been talking to. I would tell Jessica I had been speaking to a member of my family, or someone from work about a school matter, or even with a telemarketer who had been hard to hang up on. To Nicole I could admit the truth, which, however, she didn't like to hear. One evening when I was on the phone with Jessica for almost an hour, Nicole tried to call me three times, and when she finally got through and I told her I had been speaking to Jessica:

"How annoying she must be! What does she talk so much for? God! It sounds like she's harassing you. Maybe you should call the cops." —A ridiculous statement in light of the fact that she called me just as much.

Those were a glorious two weeks for me. Not only had I somewhat regained my old productive rhythm, but I was also able to take stock of my situation with Jessica and Nicole. It seemed to me that I had been worrying too much about it. I no longer felt any great pressure to break up with Jessica because I finally admitted to myself that I would never be able to do so. It wasn't in my character to hurt someone who loved me. I admitted to myself, once and for all, that I was just too good to do such a thing. On the other hand I knew that continuing with both her and Nicole was ultimately impossible. Eventually something had to give. Eventually Jessica was going to find out about Nicole, or Nicole was not going to tolerate my seeing Jessica.

Of those ultimate outcomes, it seemed that Nicole's intolerance of the situation would manifest itself first, not only because she was impatiently expecting it to change in her favor, but also because she was the kind of person who liked to be control of her circumstances. When she wasn't, the whole focus of her thought and energy was on how to get control of them, and till then she was irritable. Consequently her once easy-going, fun-loving, free-spirited notion about "dating" transmogrified into its severe opposite, and a disappointed expectation of exclusivity undermined her usual lightheartedness. She no longer asked me if I had "spoken" to Jessica: she expected me to have done so. "Well?" she would ask me—the first words out of her mouth when we met face-to-face; and she looked at me with the kind of portentous authority which, in a former age, a dreadful judge of a court of assize must have deposed a prisoner he was determined to execute. And when, shifting my eyes away from hers and burbling out an excuse about why I hadn't yet done what she had expected, she would look on me with piercing eyes, tight-lips, and folded arms, barely restraining an impulse to castigate me.

One morning she stood at the open closet in my bedroom and pulled out a hangar on which hung one of Jessica's articles of clothing. Then she pulled out another, and then another, and held them all at once and asked:

"What is all this stuff?"

She knew as well I did that they were Jessica's clothes, and I told her so much.

"So what are they doing here?"

"She put them in there a *long* time ago," I said, stressing the "long" so as to make sure Nicole understood they were not the result of some recent stay.

"She's out of her mind!  Look at all the stuff she has in here!"—and pulled outward more hangars full of clothing.  She looked about her and said, "I need bags!"

"Bags?"

"Yeah, *bags*.  Do you have any bags?"

"What kind of bags?"

"Any bags. *Big* bags."

I told her there were garbage bags in one of the

cabinets over the kitchen counter.

"Perfect!"

She went into the kitchen and came back in a few minutes with four or five folded plastic garbage bags. She fluttered open the first one and started taking down Jessica's things, stuffing them willy-nilly into the bag.

"Hey, what are you doing?"

"I'm bagging up her stuff so that the next time she comes over she can take it all back home."

"But you can't do that! You can't just shove them into the bag like that! You're going to ruin them."

"This is all *garbage*," she said, not stopping for a second, not even paying any attention to me, but continuing to grab one article of clothing after another, pulling it off a hanger, and shoving it into the bag. Within a couple of minutes she had cleared out that section of the closet, looking suddenly cavernous and filled only with wire hangers hanging there like triangular skeletons. Nicole took the stuffed bags out of the room and threw them into a corner of the living room.

"Next time she comes," she said, "you tell her to take her junk back home! *Got* it?"

She was so energetic, so determined, her movements so impulsive, her attitude so pugnacious, that I shrank from doing or saying anything to counter her behavior. If I had uttered a peep she would have said something vicious. A little later in the day, however, when she again was her old calm self, I told her that her bad attitude had surprised me in a disagreeable way because it was contrary to the principles of dating which she herself had enlightened me about.  She bristled under the criticism and announced:

"We are *not* dating anymore!"

"We're not?"  It was news to me.

"No we are not.  We're in a relationship."

It seemed to me she was making a distinction without a difference, and only because the distinction suited her.  I reminded her that we had only been going out with each other for five weeks.

"Oh, yeah?  So what are you doing, counting the days?"

"No, I'm just saying ..."

"Well five weeks is a long time.  It's on the way to two months.  It's not like we just went out for dinner a few times.  Listen," she said, becoming more earnest, "you and me are together now.  We're good together.  We're *compatible*.  Do you know how hard that is to find?—someone who's compatible?  I don't think you want to blow something like that.  So I think it's about time you do what you have to do.  Tell Jessica *goodbye*.  Got it?  You told me you were going to end it with her a long time ago."

"I'm going to."

*"When?"*

"When it's the right time.  You just can't blurt out something like that."

"Why not?  *I* would, in a second!"

"Well I'm not you.  You have to consider other people's feelings."

"What about *my* feelings!"

She had a point there.

"Listen," she said, her tone of voice serious, her expression dire, "I'm going to tell you something:  I'm not doing this anymore.  Make up your mind.  Me or her. Period!"

Really, I needed another two weeks off. I needed a couple of weeks, a couple of years, off from everybody, from everything. I fantasized about winning the lottery for hundreds of millions of dollars, and giving up my land-based life and buying a yacht, one with sails, and hiring a captain and perhaps a few crew members to sail it for me, whereupon I would point it toward the Atlantic and give the command "Weigh anchor!"—the sails crowding, the boat standing seaward, league after league leaving Connecticut, and two persons in particular, far behind me! —And all this even though the idea of a shipboard life strikes me as claustrophobic and dangerous: like being, as Samuel Johnson says, in prison, only with the possibility of drowning.

When Nicole left my place later that day, I took out all Jessica's clothes from the garbage bags and hung them back up. Some of them were badly wrinkled and I could only hope they would smooth out as they hung. Even as I did this the futility of my effort occurred to me. Sooner or later they *would* have to go. My allowing them to remain in my home only misled Jessica as to my ultimate intentions toward her, and made those intentions harder to effect.

When I look back on those days I can see that the real cause of my troubles was my own goodness. I was too good, too good, too good! I couldn't bear the thought of hurting anyone's feelings, and the result was that I hurt everyone's. I should have told Jessica, or told Nicole, that I was not going to be able to see her anymore. But whichever one lost me as a boyfriend would have been devastated, and

I couldn't bear the thought of putting anyone through that kind of horrible deprivation. Ultimately therefore doing the right, the kind, the noble thing by them came down to maintaining what to me was an exasperating status quo.

But there was a limit to my resilience. Every day I felt my nerves being stretched a little more. The sense of dereliction of duty to my critical work weighed increasingly heavily on me. I knew how fast the minutes and hours added up to days, and these to weeks and months: and how you no sooner snapped your fingers, and another year had passed. This sense of the passage of time highlighted the choice of whether I would be a good guy or a good critic. There was no question that of the two of them the latter was far more important. The world had plenty of relationships, of all kinds;—complicated, abusive, beautiful and poetic: but all of the best of them put together didn't make a single funeral easier to bear. The world didn't need another relationship; it needed a funeral critic. And who was there to be that aside from me? And even if there *were* someone else, this person, not having my sensibility, would do (there was no question of this in my mind) inferior work in a matter which had to be done as rightly as possible. And so my relationship with Jessica and Nicole came down to this moral choice: selfishly try to make two people, including myself, "happy," or fulfill a duty which would better the lives of millions of people whom I would never know?

# VIII
# FROM WORST TO WORST

Jessica had not often mentioned her parents to me, but when she had done so it was always enthusiastically. She had a good and close relationship with them. They lived only a few miles away from her and she saw them fairly often. One day she told me she was inviting them for dinner and wanted me to be present. I wasn't any more enthusiastic about meeting them than I had been about meeting anyone else she knew, and for the same reason: I didn't want to have to make the hours-long effort at politeness. But I didn't object. They were her parents, after all, and she was certainly entitled to have them for dinner.

As never before she was particular about how I should look for the evening. She asked me to "wear something nice." I complied with her request to the extent of ironing a white shirt and polishing my shoes. When I arrived at her place she looked me over and wasn't impressed with my choice of clothes.

"You're wearing those old pants again?" she asked, looking me up and down.

"What's wrong with them?"

"They're not nice!" She shook her head at them. She seemed disappointed. Then she shrugged and sighed and said with a faint smile, "Well, never mind, it's okay."

In the minutes leading up to the time of her parents' arrival she tugged at my shirt to take out some slack and adjusted my collar, saying, "There, that's a little better."

I have never mentioned Jessica's last name for the obvious reason of wanting to protect her identity, but it was German in origin and had an odd sound similar to that of "Tootz," which I note only for the sake of referring to her parents, Ralph and Charlene Tootz, who arrived that evening at seven. They came bearing a bottle of expensive red wine and a white, string-tied box of bakery goodies. They were both casually but well-dressed and had taken pains to look their best. They were typical for their time of early old age: both a little stout, both a little worn, both possessing but half the personal comeliness of their younger years. Mrs. Tootz was just under medium height, with short, dyed, light-brown hair and even features; she had probably been nice-looking in her youth. She was outgoing and cheerful. She took my hand enthusiastically when Jessica introduced me to her, smiling, or rather beaming upon me, as she said, "It's *so* nice to meet you!" Her husband was a large, bulky fellow with a reddish face and thinning gray hair. He also expressed pleasure at our introduction, though without his wife's enthusiasm, taking my hand with a firm simple grip and saying only, "Hello there." Though they were the same age Mrs. Tootz looked older than her husband, though in this matter appearances can be deceiving as to health or longevity since it's usually the husband who kicks the bucket first.

We sat in the living room before dinner. Jessica

made us drinks. Mrs. Tootz accepted a small glass of wine. Mr. Tootz preferred just ginger ale. When she wasn't serving her parents, Jessica sat close beside me on the couch. She was in the best spirits, apparently loving her parents much and glad to see them again.

The Tootzes naturally wanted to learn more about me. I freely told them all about my work as a guidance counselor. They seemed to like the idea that I had been doing it a long time; they liked the idea of that kind of "stability." As for themselves, Mrs. Tootz had worked various jobs from telephone company employee to dentist's assistant to a real estate agent; not because she had had to, mind you, but just to "get out of the house." Her husband was the real breadwinner. Till a few years back he had owned a successful limousine company for twenty-five years. He had made good money, invested some of it in rental properties and various dividend-paying stocks, and was, though retired, doing well. Mrs. Tootz was keen on my not mistaking her husband's former business as some penny-ante operation with just a few old cars let out to hire. She assured me it had been a *big* company.

"He had *fifty* limousines," she said. "Always the best, newest ones. And he dealt with some of the *biggest* people. Top executives, doctors, lawyers, politicians—they all used his company. Didn't they, dear?" she asked, as though coaxing him to back up her claims.

Mr. Tootz was indifferent to emphasizing the size or importance of his former business, either because it was in the past or because he thought his wife was making it out to be more than it was, and said only, "Some of them were."

That was only the first of many instances in which Mrs. Tootz was quick to impress upon me that in her, in her husband, and in her daughter, I was dealing with no ordinary class or quality of people. While we sat in the living room, and later as we sat at the dinner table, she used every opportunity to talk up her daughter. After she had exhausted the subjects of Jessica's goodness and sweetness, she emphasized her education. Jessica had indeed gone to college and gotten a degree in business: but she was also "top in her class!" as Mrs. Tootz assured me. "She always came home with the highest marks! I told her, I said, 'Apply for a scholarship, go for your PhD—go to Harvard, go to Yale—you can do it! She could have been a big professor, easily. But she didn't want to do it, so what could I do?" she asked, looking at me helplessly.

There were other members of her family she held up to me as shining examples of excellence. One of her brothers was a doctor, a cardiologist; the other owned "one of the biggest" home renovation companies in the state. She had nephews who were working for "big banks," nieces who were married to "top executives" of this or that company. It became increasingly clear to me where Jessica had come up with her wisecrack about my being the head of General Motors. Mrs. Tootz was also keen on informing me that she was well-traveled. She had gone everywhere. She and her husband had visited every country in Europe, many of those in the Far East, always staying at the "best" hotels....

Poor deluded woman: she had imbibed—hook, line, and sinker—the typical American hogwash of what constituted respectability, blind utterly to the only real measure of it: creativity and talent. She had no idea how her affectation of sophistication was the ultimate display of vulgarity. Only her own kindness and good intentions enabled one to overlook her foolishness and think well of her.

By the way, I realize that in referring to her nationality I sound as though I myself am not an American, which I am and am proud to be. But you can be born into a nationality and yet feel estranged from it, just as you can feel at odds with the religion, or even with the era, into which you were born; in which case you are bound to be objective about it; and if you are objective you cannot help seeing that not everything is or can be as good as you might hope. So far as I could see Mrs. Tootz embodied the worst characteristics of her nationality, if not rather the age in which she lived—the childish adulation of tinsel, the ignorant disdain toward those whose patient labor and rare gifts, recompensed so often with indifference or worse, nevertheless resulted in an increase in civilization and the gratitude of the best of later generations. Her attitude might have been overlooked in the young, whose immaturity and short acquaintance with the world excuses so many of their foolish notions; but it is always unacceptable and shameful in a person of her age, who has lived long enough to know better.

I had come to Jessica's parents as a blank slate, waiting and watching for them to make their revelatory marks on it. Mrs. Tootz had begun scratching away at once, simply, honestly, and without a thought that her strokes and wriggles denoted a less than impressive character. Her husband on the other hand was more cautious. He had taken up the chalk too—but so far he only held it in his hand and (one had the sense) would apply it only after wiser consideration. He had not said much so far, only smiling a great deal and looking on Jessica, his wife, and me with a kind of pleased if bland contentment.

Conversation took various turns, from the Jessica's good cooking, to politics, to home prices in the area, to the weather projections for the coming winter, to the jobs I had had in my younger years. Mr. Tootz chimed in and spoke a little of the jobs he had had. It was no wonder that he should have come to own a limousine company because he had driven for a living when he was young. He had early on gotten his commercial license and had driven tractor-trailers cross country, but after a few years had quit that too-nomadic life for something closer to home. Then he had driven a truck for the post office, and after that had driven a cab for a few years. Why, there was even a year when he had driven a hearse—

My ears pricked up. I even sat up a little straighter. "You drove a hearse?" I asked.

He nodded and almost laughed and said, "Sure did. For a year."

"Must have been interesting," I said, and prodded him on to talk about it: "What was that like?"

His wife had to be a party pooper and interject, "Dear, I don't think we want to talk about *that*, do we? It's hardly a nice subject over dinner"—and she shook her head and looked at me with a sympathizing frown as though she were apologizing for her husband.

"Yeah, Dad, please: we don't want to hear about

*that!"* Jessica—Party Pooper #2—chimed in.

"But I think it's a fascinating subject," I said, and encouraged Mr. Tootz to continue by saying, "There aren't too many people who have done that. You say you did it for a year?"

He nodded, yes.

"What—you just applied for the position?"

He nodded yes again. He was suddenly mum on account of his wife's mild comeuppance. But I needed him to talk, for it occurred to me that hearses were never mentioned in my reviews, and he might offer me some information which might be turned to account for an entertaining article on the subject.

"So what happened?" I asked. "You just walked into a place and applied for the job? Just like that?"

"Well, like I said, I was already driving cabs for about a year. But I got fed up with it—I didn't like dealing with the public. People can be so difficult! They would eat in the back seat and leave their messes, or at night when they got out of nightclubs they would be drunk and throw up, or they skipped out on the fares ... I couldn't take it anymore. So I applied for the hearse job. At least the customers kept quiet and never made a mess!"

He laughed. I laughed too: not because it was such a funny witticism, but to show his wife and Jessica that I didn't find the topic at all off-putting.

But again Mrs. Tootz intervened. "Ralph, please," she said, almost between her teeth, her smile tight, her voice a little tense and, again, reprimanding.

"But he wants to know!" her husband very reasonably said.

"Oh, absolutely!" I said.  And in order to prevent Mrs. Tootz from discouraging her husband to talk, I threw a sop to her self-respect by complimenting her husband, saying, "It seems to me that someone who's driven a hearse has to be a very special, a very rare kind of person.  I don't think just anyone can do it, at least not for long.  Were you ever creeped out?" I asked him.

"By my passengers?  Nahhh, why should I be? Even if they could do something to me, they wouldn't. As a matter of fact—between you and me?—I always thought they rather *liked* my driving them around."

"Daddyyyyy!" Jessica said, tilting her head and looking at her father incredulously.

"Your husband's an amazing man!" I said to Mrs. Tootz, who again had been about to object to the conversation.  "Most people would have exactly the opposite attitude.  But if everyone felt that way, where would we all be?  He did a service to society.  I'm impressed."  And turning my attention back to Mr. Tootz: : "So you say you *liked* the job?"

"Sure, it was a good job.  Maybe I wasn't 'creeped out,' as you call it, because I always felt like I was helping people."

"Which you certainly were!" I said, nodding in agreement and looking impressed.

"I mean if I didn't do it," he continued, "who was going to do it?  *Somebody* has to. And don't ask me why—maybe it was just out of respect—but I was a lot more careful driving *them* around than the live people who used to come into my cab.  I made sure to take the curves really easy and to avoid potholes so that they wouldn't be bouncing around."

"Oh, Ralph, dear, *please*," his wife murmured.

"Wha-uuhhht?" he asked her.

"That was really considerate of him," I interjected, trying—yet again!—to shut up his wife. "Just think how many other hearse drivers wouldn't think twice about how rough the ride was? Especially young guys! How old were you then?"

"Oh, about twenty-six, twenty-seven."

"A young guy, then," I said. "Most guys that age would get behind the wheel of one of those babies and take it for spin, see what it can do: start speeding, and taking fast turns, and flying over bumps! Let's face it, we all did that kind of stuff when we were young."

"Well, there's where I have to disagree with you," Mr. Tootz said. "A hearse isn't exactly the kind of vehicle you want to 'take for a spin.' First of all, they don't have the zip for that: they're just standard limousines that have been customized, and they just have regular car engines. I guess back in the day they had V-8's, but even so they were just the standard versions. And then there's the cortege. You have to drive slowly because you've got a lot of cars following you—speeding away with the casket wouldn't exactly win you any friends."

"That's true," I said.

"The one I drove," Mr. Tootz continued, and for the first time that evening he seemed to be genuinely interested in the conversation, "was a modified '72 Cadillac. That was a great year for those cars! Are you interested in cars at all?"

"Not really. I mean I like to look at newest models, the way everyone does. But I don't really know much about them."

"Well, the '72 Cadillacs were *amazing*. Had a beautiful, streamlined look. Big as houses, by to-day's standards, and heavy as tanks, the way a lot of luxury cars were back then—that's why they rode so smooth. Anyway, mine was a modified '72 Caddie. The interior was absolutely stunning: all sky-blue, with a bench seat as comfortable as a couch and lots of room to stretch your legs. The dashboard had a huge speedometer and was loaded with controls. The coach section—I remember it now—had a dark blue shag carpeting and white velvet pleated cur-tains covering the windows. Those curtains were better than the ones I had in my apartment! Had a good stereo system, too—an 8-track. I had a stash of tapes in the glove compartment and used to play all the bands I liked—Cream, Hendrix, Zeppelin, the Stones. Loved it! Sometimes I felt a little guilty, rocking out to all that cool music and then looking out the sideview mirror and seeing behind me a long line of cars filled with really sad people; but hey"— he shrugged—"my job was just to get the client there, and listening to music always helped me con-centrate on the road. still does, though now I'd rather listen to Sinatra or Perry Como or something. Anyway, to answer your question if anything strange ever happened to me," he continued, though I didn't remember asking him any such thing, and it was probably just his way of continuing to talk about that younger, more interesting time of his life, "the answer is definitely yes. On one occasion—"

"Dear, do we have to hear this?" his wife inter-rupted, rolling her eyes.

"We absolutely do!" I said; and this time added, "Mrs. Tootz, *please!* " And to her husband: "Do go on! This is so interesting!"

"Well ... on one occasion," Mr. Tootz continued, "I made a routine pickup and was supposed to drive to a cemetery that was far away from the funeral home, and I mean far—like twenty miles. It was in the winter, about five o'clock or so, and it was already dark outside when I made the pickup. So we load up the client and I start off. And it begins to snow. Hard. Visibility is terrible: can't see more than a hundred feet in front of me. I keep looking in the side-view mirror to make sure the cortege is still behind me, and sometimes I can't see them so I have to stop till the lead car comes up close behind me. So there I am, driving along, driving and driving, turning here and turning there, and after ten miles or so the snow lets off a little and I can again see in my side-view mirror all the cars behind. So I get to the cemetery and someone there directs me to the gravesite and I drive to it. The pallbearers take out the casket and place it over the grave. The priest is already there and he's just waiting for the people to park their cars and come up to the grave, which they do. But then someone in the family asks him who he is. He tells them—I forgot his name now—and then they ask him what happened to Father So-and-so, who had given the eulogy and was supposed to lead the prayer. The priest looked confused. He didn't know the priest they were talking about. Everybody was confused at first. Then somebody mentioned that the casket wasn't the same, and one by one they all noticed the same thing. At the same time the priest realized that he didn't know any of the family. For a few minutes everyone was confused. They couldn't understand what had happened. Well, what had really happened was that they had followed the wrong hearse—mine!"

"No!" I said.

"Yes!"

"But how is that possible?"

"We figured out later it must have happened when I went around a traffic circle. There must have two processions that had reached it at the same time, and the driver of the hearse leading that one must have gotten as far ahead of his processions I did of mine, so that by the time we were opposite each other the people behind us followed the hearse in front of them."

"That's incredible!"

"What are the odds, right?—has to be millions to one. I tell that story to people and they don't believe me. I should have gotten signed affidavits or something to back me up. Anyway, as you can imagine, the families weren't too thrilled. The one at the cemetery I pulled into blamed me. Me! Can you imagine? What did I do? I just did my job—I went to the place I was supposed to go. I told them, I said, 'Look, if you're going blame anyone, blame the person who was following me and who you were following!' That turned out to be a brother of the deceased, so they weren't going to blame him and make him feel worse than he already did. Well, they got all got back into their cars and followed someone who knew the way to the cemetery where their relative was being buried. We had to wait around for an hour before the right mourners arrived. It just goes to show you," Mr. Tootz concluded, shaking his head, "things can happen that you'd never believetill they do."

Later that evening, after her parents had gone and while I was helping Jessica clean the table, she said:

"I'm sorry about my Dad telling you about that hearse story. But you were the one who asked."

"I don't see what there is to be sorry about. It's an amazing story. Did you know about that?"

She nodded yes. "He must have told it a hundred times."

"And it's true?"

"So far as I know it is." Then she asked, "Did you like them?"

"Your parents? Sure. They're very nice people."

"They liked you too," she said, beaming with pleasure to think so, and grateful for my having made a good impression on them. "Especially my father. He usually doesn't open up like that but you really got him going."

"He seems like a nice guy."

"He really is. He's the best. And my mother too."

I had no reason to doubt Mr. Tootz's veracity, but the story of the mis-followed hearses was so astonishing that it seemed it must have made the news at the time, if only in some local newspaper. When I got home I searched the Internet for reports about it, or even for anything similar to it, but my hours of research came up empty-handed. Then again perhaps this was to be expected, since those who had been part of the incident would naturally have thought it disrespectful to the families of the deceased to bruit it about too publicly.

During my stay at Jessica's that Saturday night

I knew better than to keep my phone on lest Nicole call me. Sure enough she did and left a message on my answering service, asking to call her back and taking another potshot at Jessica whom she referred to as "that witch." Of course whenever I saw her, as I did that week, I never mentioned Jessica and discouraged her inquiries in that way by answering monosyllabically and at once turning to a different subject. But I was still so fascinated by Mr. Tootz's hearse story that I couldn't help repeating it to Nicole, who dismissed it with, "Yeah, right."

"You don't believe it?"

"Of course not."

"Why? The weather was bad and people couldn't see where they were going. And it was a traffic circle."

She shook her head again and asked, "Where'd you hear that nonsense?"

I told her I had read the story "somewhere" on the Internet.

"So you believe everything you read on the Internet? C'mon."

A little later that day she got out of me that I had seen Jessica over the weekend. Her only concern was whether or not I had told her I was breaking up with her. When I admitted that I hadn't, she said:

"What is *wrong* with you?"

"Nicole, I couldn't. The right moment never came up. I couldn't just blurt it out."

"Sure you could—if you *wanted* to!" She turned away from me, this time not only impatient but positively angry with me. Then, no doubt bethinking herself that acting out her emotions could not make me more sympathetic toward her, she calmed down and asked in a neutral tone of voice:

"So what did you two do all weekend?"

"First of all, it wasn't all weekend, it was just Saturday. She had her parents over for dinner."

"She *what?*"

"We had dinner with her parents. They came over."

"Did you *ask* to have dinner with her parents?"

"Why would I ask that?"

She looked at me with amused incredulity, as though she couldn't believe I didn't see what she did. "Did it ever occur to you *why* she had her parents over for dinner?" she asked.

I could only offer what seemed to me the most logical response: "Because she likes her parents and wanted to see them?"

Nicole smiled at me pitifully before saying, "You know, for a smart guy you're pretty dumb. No, she did *not* have parents over for dinner just because she likes them. She could have seen them any time. She had them over to dinner to meet you. It's the introduction—don't you get it? She's expecting you're going to be part of the family. She's expecting you to marry her."

"That's ridiculous. I'm not proposing to anybody."

"You don't have to. *She* will."

—Which struck me as even more ridiculous so that I dismissed Nicole's prognostication with a scoffing wave of my hand. I couldn't even imagine Jessica being so foolish as to do such a thing.

And then I *could* imagine it, and when I did it terrified me: not because the thought of marriage was so disagreeable to me—on the contrary it seemed to me a lovely institution—but because I couldn't imagine being married to *her*. Even after spending a couple of days with her I couldn't wait to be by myself again. Her company was enjoyable, but only, like that of Nicole's, in small doses, as interludes of companionship balancing out an otherwise enjoyably solitary and hard-working life. That she should ask to marry me, or should let me know, in however roundabout a way, that she wanted me to ask her, made me eager to ensure she would never put me into the position of inflicting on her a humiliating rejection. Thus the next time I spoke to her I maneuvered the conversation to the subject of marriage, bringing it up in such a way which left her no doubt about how I felt about it, saying, "Isn't it great not to be married? It's so liberating. I get to do what I want, and you get to do what you want. There's nobody to answer to and nobody to question you. You have to admit it's the best thing to be!"

She answered, "Sure."

But there was a significant, somehow dismayed pause after she said that, and for the rest of the conversation she wasn't her usual loquacious self. When I got off the phone with her, I breathed a sigh of relief and silently thanked Nicole for her insight, feeling as though I had dodged a bullet.

The only problem was that Nicole was shooting a few of her own. She might not have had marriage on her mind but after my disclosure about meeting Jessica's parents she became a lot more possessive of me. She told me that we weren't seeing each other nearly enough. She said it wasn't fair to her, or to me, that we were seeing each other only once or twice a week. What kind of relationship was that?

She demanded more of my time. As we didn't live too far from each other, she wanted me to go to her place, or wanted to come to mine, every other day. I told her that I would love to have her but just wasn't up to it because I was too tired after work and just wanted to rest.

"So you can't rest when I'm around?" she challenged.

"Not as well," I replied, honestly.

In fact I needed more time to accommodate the greatly increased number of funerals taking place due to the worsening pandemic. People were dropping off like flies. Ambulances could be heard in my neighborhood four, six, eight, ten times a day, their sirens blaring as they sped down streets on their way to people whom the disease had hit hard. The funeral industry was having a field day. More than ten times the usual number of people were being taken to the satanic cleaners, getting tumbled round and round in intensified sorrow, then fed through mangles of grief till their last bit of misery, and in some cases their last bit of cash, was wrung out of them. It had to be recorded—it had to be brought to light! In a disgraceful turn of events, receptions all but fell by the wayside. This omission was supposedly to reduce the transmission of the disease, but I suspect it had a lot more to do with cheapskates wanting to save money. Fortunately there will always be people who believe in doing the right thing no matter what, and receptions continued to be held. They were not as comfortable as formerly because everyone was required to wear a mask; but there was also a positive side, namely, fewer people attended them and so you didn't have to worry about the good dishes running out before you had a chance to fill up on them. Indeed at one reception the hosts encouraged their guests to take the desserts home with them and I managed to snag a whole tray of the most delicious sfogliatelle.

Then I got a still larger break. At the end of August I learned that schools would not be reopening in September or indeed "till further notice." The news made me jump for joy. I couldn't have been happier than the most school-hating child—probably more so since I would not only not have to work but would keep getting paid thanks to the wonderful teacher's union. There would not only be plenty of funerals to choose from but I would also have a lot more time to review them. I foresaw a delightfully prolific period in front of me in which I might expand my website, gain more subscribers, and increasingly influence the industry.

What I did not anticipate were the increased demands which would be made on me by Jessica and Nicole. The pandemic began having a negative effect on the economy; businesses began closing down, furloughing or laying off workers; and Jessica and Nicole were two of the innumerable casualties. They had been prudent enough over the previous years to save up nest eggs which, combined with unemployment benefits, ensured they would not have to worry about money any time soon. (Thank goodness! For I was in no position to help them financially.) But now they had nothing to do all day but think about how they had nothing to do all day, and looked to me to alleviate their boredom. Each of them spoke enthusiastically to me about all the things we could now "do together."    Jessica wanted to visit the South for a couple of weeks and talked of driving through the North and South Carolina, Georgia, and Mississippi.    Nicole talked about renting a cabin somewhere in the Adirondacks—for a month!

My reaction to their propositions was a calm, patient, smiling, "Well, we'll see." But inwardly I was appalled.  To me days or weeks of inane idleness was a horribly boring waste of time:  to be deprived so long of the excitement of my work would have been unbearable.  Instead I planned to not see either one of them again for a few weeks in September so that I might take in as many funerals as possible.  I broke the news to each of them straightforwardly, saying again that I needed time "to do things."

"Like what?" Jessica asked.

"Things I have to do around the house ... I have to fix up the basement ..."

"You do that any time you want, can't you? You're not working now.  Do it at night or something."

"I have to take advantage of the time while I have it," I said.

"But you already took two weeks off.  Why didn't you do it then?"

"That was different—that was just to ... rest. Now I need some time to get some work done around the house."

"I don't believe you," she said, outright.

"Then don't believe me.  You don't have to.  I'm just telling you ..."

I spoke emphatically, confrontationally; trying to start an argument which might escalate into a fight to be used as a pretext leading to our separation. At first she seemed to take the bait, asking, or rather exclaiming, "You know something ...!" But she didn't follow through on her anger, either because she didn't want to stir up any strife between us or because she reconsidered that my demand, while irritating, was not something worth getting angry over.

Nicole was no less resistant, no less accusatory. She reminded me that we lived only fifteen minutes apart so that no matter how busy I was we could surely spend *some* time together each day. As for my intention to fix up things around the house:

"I'll come over and help you. You'll get it done quicker."

"That's all right. I can do it myself. I don't want to be distracted."

"Oh, really! So now I'm a 'distraction'?"

"I didn't mean it *that* way, Nicole. You know what I mean. Besides, we can't be together *all* the time. It's good to spend time apart. It's like what Kahlil Gibran says about marriage: it's stronger when two people stand apart, as the pillars of a temple stand apart, and because an oak and a cypress can't grow in each other's shadow."

"Who said that?" Nicole asked.

"Kahlil Gibran."

"Yeah, well, I wouldn't listen to him. He sounds like a nut."

In the end I had to compromise with both of them, agreeing to see each of them on a weekly basis, and taking consolation in my still having more time for my work because no longer having to go to my job at the school.

Quite apart from the stresses in my personal life,

it was an odd time for me as a reviewer. The pandemic was getting worse by the week. In my area tens of thousands of people had contracted the disease, and a small percentage of them had died from it. At the back of my mind was always the worry of my increased likelihood to contract the disease by attending funerals. Jessica and Nicole also raised my anxiety by warning me about "seeing people."

"You'd better stay home and not go anywhere," Nicole told me. "It's dangerous out there!"

And Jessica: "Only go out to buy food or get some exercise, and get right back home—understand? And whenever you touch something outside, make sure you wash your hands. 'Cause if *you* get it, *I'm* gonna get it, and I don't want to get it!"

Their paranoia was understandable: no longer having to work, nor having anything to keep themselves occupied all day but watching television, they absorbed the almost non-stop news reports which emphasized the increasing death rate and showed people who had been hit hard by the disease gasping for breath as they lay in hospital beds. The reports rarely mentioned that these were the extreme cases and that most people would experience only mild flu-like symptoms. Nor should this surprise anyone. In the United States the news is a business, and there's nothing better guaranteed to keep bored people attentive to a television screen, and consequently watching commercials, than a steady stream of exciting hair-raising horror.

Fortunately I did not watch much television and had a characteristic disinclination to hear bad news, shying away from it as one might from a nerve-shattering screech. And now that my job at the school had been temporarily suspended, I was never bored but found constant excitement and challenge in my critical work.

The next funeral I attended was for one Barbara O'Donnell, who had passed away at 88 from a blood infection. It promised to be a satisfying event because she was the great-granddaughter of Johann Lifschols, a freight company magnate from the 1950s. The company had been out of business for thirty years, but her address was in a fashionable part of Danbury—her home (an aerial picture of which could be seen online) rested on six acres of lovely real estate. It could be assumed that she had been the beneficiary of the "old money" made by her great grandfather, which she might have increased through wise investments.

Schlitzer & Schmidt Funeral Home was perhaps the worst-named I had ever come across  Quite apart from it sounding like a beer factory, it was hard to pronounce. Just try saying it fast five times! It was a fairly large establishment. It was also very clean, the furnishings of good quality, though conventional styling. The O'Donnel funeral was held in the biggest of its visitation rooms, which was blandly neutral in its color scheme of white, beige, and light blue. There was no music and the mood was somber and depressing.

The guests were mostly dressed in black, and family members in the front row were grieving freely. I offered my condolences to them telling them I had been an acquaintance of their dearly departed, then went up to her to get a better look. The casket was an indifferent, mass-produced, run-of-the-mill box. A tiny label at the bottom of one of the side panels had the manufacturer's name, Rowand Company, which later research informed me had gone out of business two years before; thus, this was old stock. On either side of the bier rose two floral arrangements, a few blossoms in which looked somewhat wilted. My guess was that they had been recycled from previous services. Barbara herself was dressed in a plain, pastel-yellow outfit—not a gown or dress, mind you, but some sort of pantsuit, which looked loudly out of place on a woman of her age and certainly for her final presentation. She was frowning as though in disappointment at the remissness of those whom she had trusted to make her presentable.

I sighed and returned to my seat, thinking the funeral was a wash. I could only hope that the reception would be good and make up for the shortcomings of the service. "Don't be so quick to judge," I told myself. "You never know. Things could get more interesting."

—Oh my friends be careful what you wish for!

In the ensuing fifteen minutes I whispered my observations into the digital recorder in my breast pocket. Out of the corner of my eye I could see when a few more guests entered the visitation room. They would continue on to the front, to the family and the casket. One of them however suddenly stopped at the end of my row, and I turned to see that it was—Nicole?

My mouth opened a little and I stared. At first I thought it was only someone who looked like her, but in the next second it was obvious that the similarity was too close, that it was she. She stepped into the aisle, passed before me, and sat on my right-hand side, doing so with a slight and (for me) unnerving smile as though she had been expected. A few surreal seconds passed in which we sat side-by-side in silence.

"Nicole, what are you doing here?" I finally whispered.

She seemed too distracted to answer me. She was surprised to find herself at a funeral and looked about with uncomfortable curiosity. Then she saw that I was still looking at her, awaiting an answer, which she whispered back:

"I came to see you."

"Came to *see* me?" I stared at her in mute amazement.

How on earth had she found me *here?* I wondered if she didn't have some magical, psychic ability by which she had tracked me down. The few seconds that this thought lasted made me supremely uncomfortable till common sense discredited it and forced me to search for a more likely cause. Then I remembered how I had begun noting funeral schedules on a "reminder" app on my phone, its icon in plain sight on the home screen. That was it, of course—the only possible explanation: she had snooped on my phone. But when? It was always about my person, in my shirt or pants' pocket. The only times I put it away from me were when I showered or slept. She must have taken it up during one of those times, having remembered or written down the password to get into it;—the little sneak! And having seen the name, date, address, and time of the funeral, she must have thought it denoted a rendezvous with another woman.

The funeral director must have wondered at her

appearance because she was not dressed formally or in mourning clothes but in an everyday outfit consisting of a blue and pink cotton blouse, a white and pink scarf around her neck, jeans and sneakers, and casually carried her handbag over her shoulder and her jingling keys in her hands. When she was directed to the visitation room she had stood uncertainly at the threshold, dismayed to find herself before a scene of mourning, but nevertheless scanned the people sitting in the rows of chairs and recognized me.

"How did you know I was here?" I whispered.

I wanted her to incriminate herself—I wanted to hear her confess that she done something blamable behind my back. It would be a suitable basis for a little anger and resentment of my own. She knew this as well as I did, so she didn't answer, and so I answered for her: "You went through my phone!"

Rather than admit it she shook her head a little, noncommittally, as though to say that even if she had done so, it was nothing to get upset about, hardly anything even to talk about. But I wasn't going to let her get away with it so easily.

"That wasn't very nice!" I whispered through clenched teeth.

"Well, what do you want me to do?" she whispered back emphatically.

"What do you mean, 'What do I want you do to'! What are you talking about? You're not supposed to go into other peoples' things! I never went into *your* things!"

"You *made* me do it!"

"I *made* ...!"

A few people several rows up turned around at

our too-loud voices.  I was so angry that I could have shouted at her but contained myself and sat there stiff as a board and staring straight ahead, only shaking my head a few times.  Nicole saw my silent fury, and if she didn't see it, she felt it.  It must have emanated off me in waves, cowing her into silence.  We watched for the next five minutes as a few people stepped forward to the casket to pay their respects to the deceased.  Then, in a lower whisper, she asked:

"Where is Barbara?"

"Barbara?"

"Yes, Barbara!  Where is she!"

Suddenly I realized that she meant the deceased, whom she must have thought was another woman I was seeing.  I slumped a little into my seat at the thought of her ridiculous suspicion, then nodded to the front of the room, and said out of the corner of my mouth, "She's right *there!*"

Nicole must have felt very foolish just then for having imagined yet another woman in life.  In a quiet and rather sheepish whisper she asked, "Who is she?"

"I don't know," I whispered back.

"What do you mean you don't know?"

From the corner of my eye I could see her looking at me curiously.

"It's someone's funeral.  Please be quiet."

But asking Nicole to be quiet was like asking angry pit bull to stop snarling.

"You don't know her?" she whispered.

"I do know her.  Kind of.  Shhhh...."

She shook her head at me as though to say she didn't understand and wasn't going to accept the ex-

planation of 'kind of.' I was going to inform her, in
the same way that I often introduced myself to family members, that Barbara had been a distant
friend of mine when, again out of the corner of my
eye, I saw someone else who had just come up to
my row and was standing at the edge of it, looking
in my direction. It was Jessica.

Or was it? Maybe it was just someone who
looked like her. Maybe it was her twin—maybe it
was her doppelganger—maybe it was an hallucination! But the hallucination, after looking at me,
then looking at Nicole, stepped into the row and
took a seat on at my left-hand side. She didn't say
a word.

"What the heck are *you* doing here?" I asked
her. I was still struggling to process Nicole's presence, let alone Jessica's. It was extraordinary that
one of them had shown up: but *both* of them?

Nicole leaned forward to look at Jessica, and
asked me, "Who is *she?*"

Jessica likewise leaned forward to look at Nicole,
asking, "Who are *you?*"

"Be quiet!" I whispered.

What struck me most forcefully at that moment
was that Jessica could only have found out about
my presence here in the same way Nicole had: by
somehow gaining access to my phone. So they were
*both* snoopers! Obviously! The audacity of their
mistrust took my breath away. How could they
treat me like that after how good I had been to
them? It was some seconds before I could ask Jessica the same question I had asked Nicole, whisper-
ing:

"How did you know I was here?"

She too was not about to admit her sneaky behavior; she knew it would make her look bad. Instead she looked past me to Nicole and asked me in a sneering whisper, "Is that the other woman you've been seeing?"

She didn't use the word "woman," but another word, which also starts with "w," and which I refuse to attribute to her in persistent print out of respect for her better self. Her question surprised me however not so much for her unwonted use of bad language so much as showing that she had along suspected me of seeing someone else. Before I could say anything, Nicole whispered in my ear:

"Is that Jessica? Oh, God, she's *horrible!* What is she doing here? Did you invite her?"

Jessica was only a head away from Nicole and heard her whispered remarks almost as well as I did. She leaned forward again and told Nicole:

"Yeah, I'm *her!* Get a good look because you're not going to be seeing either one of us again!"

By way of response Nicole took up my hand, held it, and pulled it toward her, into her lap, as though to show Jessica the real state of the affairs.

Jessica responded by taking my other hand, grabbing it just as tightly, and pulling it toward herself.

They were angry and they were strong. They pulled hard, each in opposite directions, and it hurt. I tried to disengage myself from both of them, but it was like trying to pull your hands out of a hydraulic ringer.

"Cut it out!" I said, trying to pull free. "This is not the time!"

"Tell her to go!" Jessica whispered.

Nicole heard this, learned forward, and said past

me to Jessica, "I ain't going nowhere. Get lost!"

They had both whispered a little too loudly. Again people a few rows ahead turned around again to see what the commotion was about. When they did so I assumed a pleasant, subdued smile and nodded toward them in a friendly way as though to assure them everything here was in order and there was nothing to be concerned about. When they had turned back around I whispered emphatically to both Jessica and Nicole:

"Be *quiet!* This is a *funeral!*"

And with some struggle I managed to get my hands back to myself and folded them on my lap.

It must have finally sunk into them that this was not the time or place for unseemly behavior. They grew quieter, looked about them, and began to feel the solemnity of the moment. A new guest entered the room, walked up to the family sitting in the front row and offered them his condolences, then went to the casket and stood before it with a bowed head. Nicole and Jessica watched him as silently as children watch a magic trick. But their rapt attention was only momentary. As soon as they had come to terms with the unexpectedness of the venue, their thoughts, their emotions, came back to me and to each other. Jessica whispered:

"I need to talk to you—now!"

Nicole, who of course heard this, bent forward and told Jessica, "He doesn't need to talk to *you.*"

Jessica grabbed the sleeve of my jacket and pulled it toward herself, then started to get up with me in tow, saying, "Cmon!"

She would get loud—she would make a scene—if I refused to follow her. I got up to do so, and, as might have been expected, Nicole followed me and Jessica out of the visitation room.

The funeral director happened to be there, in the lobby of the funeral parlor. He was standing idly about, waiting for the service to end. He looked at me and Nicole and Jessica in that pleasant, somewhat eager way which people in business have when they expect a customer might need their "assistance." Perhaps he thought we were leaving early, in which case he was prepared to see us politely off. But he was disabused the moment Nicole opened her mouth to Jessica:

"Listen, this is the way it is:  he doesn't want to be with you anymore!  Get lost!"

"Who the hell are *you?*" Jessica shot back, and looked to me, and asked, "Is this Barbara?"

"My name is *Nicole*," Nicole said.

"Nicole?  Then where is Barbara?" Jessica asked me.

"You moron," Nicole said.  "Barbara's in *there*"— nodding toward the visitation room.  "It's her funeral."

"Who is she to you?" Jessica asked me.

"She's nothing to me," I said.

"What do you mean she's 'nothing' to you?"

"Yeah," Nicole said, "what do you mean?"

"She was just an acquaintance of mine from years ago," I said.

"Oh yeah?" Nicole asked.  "What *kind* of acquaintance?"

"A neighbor of mine, okay?"

"I don't believe that for a minute!" Jessica said.

"Neither do I," Nicole said.

"Well then you both need to go in there and get a

good look at her! She's old enough to be my grand-mother!"

The funeral director, who had been standing nearby listening to this, took a step forward and said:

"Excuse me, but could you please take this out-side? This really isn't the place—"

"Shut up!" Nicole told him.

"So who is *this?*" Jessica asked, shifting her eyes to Nicole and scowling with disgust as though some-one had just shoved a piece of rotten cheese under her nose.

"I'm his girlfriend," Nicole said. "Get a good look."

"You're going out with her?" Jessica asked me.

"Jessica, it's not what it seems—"

"What do you mean, it's not what it seems?" Nicole asked, stepping in front of me and looking at me angrily. "It's *exactly* what it seems!"

"Are you involved with her?" Jessica asked me, her eyes pleading.

"Jessica, we were just … dating—"

"'Dating'!" Nicole exclaimed angrily, and stomped her foot.

"Sir, ladies, please," the funeral director inter-jected again, "you should take this outside—"

"Shut your pie hole!" Nicole told him, and to Jes-sica, "We've been seeing each other for four month-s"—which was an exaggeration. "And he doesn't want to see you anymore!"—which was not quite an exaggeration? "He's been trying to break up with you but he keeps holding back because he doesn't want to hurt your feelings, but now that you know, you know, so just forget about it and get lost!"

I put my hands to my face and shook my head as though I could make the moment disappear. I didn't like the angry forcefulness of Nicole's attitude toward Jessica and beneath my breath mumbled, "Nicole ..."

Jessica seemed to ignore what Nicole had said. She concentrated on me, her expression uncertain and hopeful and fearful all that once. "Is that right?" she asked. "Have you been going out with her?"

"Jessica ... it's not how it seems. I would have to explain it you—"

"You don't need to explain anything, sweetie," Nicole interrupted. "I'll do it for you." To Jessica: "I'm his girlfriend. He's with me. He doesn't want to be with you. That's the way it is. Got it? Now go—go!"—and with a few, quick, angry flicks of her hand she waved Jessica away as though the gesture could send her flying into space.

But as though Nicole didn't exist, as though she were less than a shadow and couldn't think or speak or make a sound, Jessica ignored her and kept her eyes on me, unwilling to hear the answer from any-one but myself.

I looked to the funeral director as though giving him the opportunity to say or do something which would divert us all from this terrible confrontation, but he seemed to have become interested in the drama playing out before him and looked to me as earnestly as Jessica did, waiting for my answer.

The only answer I could fall back on was the one which Nicole had offered me from the first. In an appeasing, becalming tone of voice I told Jessica again that Nicole and I were "just dating."

Jessica looked at me with an expression more wounded than angry, more disillusioned than determined. All of her suspicions about what I had been doing on my own time, and all her fears about another failed relationship, had coalesced in her mind into the certainty that she had been mistaken about our future together  All three of us (four, if one included the funeral director, whose eyes shifted from me to Nicole to Jessica as though he were an interested party of long standing) stood there in silence for about ten seconds before Jessica, who, like the lone-surviving soldier who realizes he cannot possibly resist the forces ranged against him and so lays down his arms, suddenly and quietly surrendered, saying only, as she looked at me with all the regret of having given up on a beautiful dream, "Alright ... alright." She walked out of the funeral parlor.

"Good riddance to bad rubbish," Nicole said.

"Nicole," I said, shaking my head and looking at her reprovingly for having taken any satisfaction in another person's heartbreak.

I felt an impulse to run after Jessica, to stop her, to reach her before she got into her car and drove away, to wrap my arms around her, to tell her how sorry I was and promise I would never, ever do anything to hurt her again ... but I realized that it would only have resulted in extending a relationship which, even if it could have been revived, was bound to end sooner or later. Besides, I would only have chased after her because I felt sorry for her; and while our capacity for pity is an accurate measure of our goodness, it is never suitable as a basis on which to build a romantic relationship, which requires a support sturdy enough to uphold the weighty element of self-interest.

For several long moments the three of us (again

I am including the funeral director, since he was still there, as silent and as expectant as ever) stood there in relieved silence: a calm, quiet, static, somehow exhausted sense of having endured something unpleasant.   That it was the end of my relationship with Jessica seemed pretty certain, and if Nicole didn't gloat it was only because she saw that the confrontation had been difficult for me.   The funeral director also saw this and for a few moments said nothing, but then he ventured with a solemn and authoritative voice:

"Sir, this is not the place.  *Please* ... out of respect for the family ..."

I left with Nicole, and once we were outside she, still seeing my discontent with the way things had happened between me and Jessica, and not wanting to antagonize me, assumed an appeasing manner and told me it was all "for the best," that at least now we could "get on with our lives." Her words didn't upset me because I could see the matter through her eyes as well as through Jessica's.   She turned to look at the funeral parlor we had just stepped out of it, and her brows knit together a little as a curious thought struck her, and she asked, "Where did you know that woman from, whose funeral this is?"

"Just an acquaintance from years ago. It's not worth talking about."

She didn't pursue the subject, seeing I was in no mood to talk about that or anything else.   A little uncertainly she said, "Alright ... well ... I'll call you later."

I didn't even realize how much I had been traumatized till after I was once again in the quiet of my home: my appetite was gone, my heart was beating fast, and my hands were shaking. I suspected my blood pressure had risen and I wasted no time taking it. Just as I suspected—130/85! I could scarcely sit or stand still, but paced a lot, breathed heavily, sighed, and put my hands to my head, wondering as in a daze how things had come to such a crisis.

The next several days were not any better. It happened that Jessica called me and reprimanded me for having carried on an affair with another woman. For nearly fifteen minutes I had to listen in silence as she told me everything wrong with me, then hung up. She called me the day after to give me another nasty earful. Despite her castigations and grievances she talked as though we were still together. Nicole on the other hand told me how lucky I was to have gotten rid of Jessica, who had been "bringing me down." I stopped answering their calls. They started texting me in the same vein, and I texted back that after all that had happened I thought it might be better not to communicate with each other for a while. To my mind "for a while" meant forever. They had put me under a lot of stress, and my sensitive nature needed quiet and calm. I blocked their calls and texts.

I have to hand it to both of them: they knew a good thing when they had it. They weren't about to let go of me so easily. Not able to get in touch with me by telephone they came to see me. Nicole was the first to do so—she came the day after I had blocked her calls. At the sight of her pulling into my driveway my stomach tied up a little into knots. There was no way I couldn't open the door when she knocked because my car was parked just outside and it was obvious I was home. We didn't have much of a conversation. She was unlike her usual self in that she was peculiarly condemnatory. Apparently she had had some sort of epiphany about our relationship and saw its toxic aspects. She blamed me for having put her into a "degrading" situation by continuing to see Jessica. My answer was that the situation had not exactly been pleasant for me either, that it had exposed me to a lot of stress which, for all I knew, might have caused me permanent physical damage.

"What the hell are you talking about?" she asked.

I mentioned my elevated blood pressure.

"Oh, gimme a break!" she scoffed.

And then she said she had reached her limit. She was putting her foot down. She demanded that I never again see or talk to Jessica. Unless I could give her such a guarantee she was ending our relationship. Period! The End!

She didn't realize what a perfect opportunity she had given me to extricate myself from difficulties which—till that second—had seemed to me inextricable. She had just opened a door to the clear, bright, carefree place I had been unsuccessfully trying to reach. I didn't hesitate to step, to leap, across the threshold by saying, "I can't make any promises."

She knew what I meant—what I intended. Her expression was at once hard and uncertain and disappointed. For the first time she seemed to be at a loss for words. She nodded, almost affirmatively, and then stared at me in silence for a few seconds before frowning and saying, "I'll talk to you later"— and walked out the door.

Jessica visited me a few days afterwards. She came just after five o'clock in the afternoon. When she knocked on my door I wasn't expecting her—I thought it might be a delivery. When I saw her we stood for a few seconds in silence, looking at each other. She showed no emotion.

"I came to get my things," she said.

I opened the door for her and she stepped inside. She walked past me into the living room, and I followed her. She went into the bedroom and opened the closet and began taking out her clothes and draping them one by one over her arm till they formed a pile. She asked for her hairdryer and I brought it to her and put it atop the clothes over her arm. I offered to help her get anything else of hers but she didn't answer me—ignored me as though I didn't exist.

As she went about collecting her things, I almost hoped she wouldn't say anything: would only "do what she had to do," and leave in silence, however contemptuous or hateful. Perhaps that was her intention when she came to my place. But too many grievances consumed her, churned within her, too much hurt and anger were twisting her guts, and she couldn't hold her tongue. She turned to me suddenly and started by saying, "You know something?"—and it all came out, the whole long angry laundry list of her disappointments with me as a boyfriend. She catalogued all my faults. She told me how rotten I was. She told me how unsuitable I was for any kind of relationship. She said she had never expected it of me—never, never! I had seemed to be so good, so nice! But it had been an act, a big lie, and she didn't know how she could ever trust anyone again. And the worst of it all was that she had really cared about me, as she had never cared for anyone in her life. Did I know that? Did I know what I had done to her?

I listened to her in silence, my head bowed. I only sighed.

She went on and on. Once she had gotten started it seemed it was hard for her stop. It occurred to me that there I was again, being way too nice for my own good, and so I started defending myself, refuting the points she was making against me, and summing up the real state of affairs by assuring her that she couldn't have had relationship with a nicer guy. To which she only said:

"You're totally out of your mind. You know that, don't you?"

When she left I followed her, though from a distance as though getting too close might be dangerous, for who knew but that she might, at the last moment, turn around and physically lash out at me? But before she could walk outside I said:

"Jessica, I'm sorry about everything. I know it's all my fault. I apologize. But no matter what you think, it didn't come from a bad place, and I didn't like any of it. In fact I've become sick because of it."

She turned to look at me. "Sick, you? How?"

I told her about my high blood pressure reading.

"You know what?" she said, calmly. "I hope it goes through the roof and your head explodes."

"That's not very nice."

"Why should it be?" she asked, and paused—not so much because she expected an answer from me as because it occurred to her to say something else: "I really feel sorry for you. One day you're going to regret everything."

To have said something in return would only have antagonized her, so I let her remark go unanswered. But I thought what a different opinion she would have had of me if she had ever read one of my reviews. She would have seen then that however questionable my life might have been in some areas (who's perfect, after all?), these were more than made up for by the extraordinary nature of my critical work. The odds of her ever again meeting anyone capable of such things were the same as the odds of her flying to the moon. Thus after she left I found myself not half so wounded by her last words, understanding that they had arisen out of ignorance of the best part of myself. No, I *wasn't* the Head of General Motors: but I had just finished "Cruising to Eternity," an informative, thought-provoking, and in some places really poetic article about hearses inspired by the recollections of her own father, Mr. Tootz. Though it had been on my website for only two days, it had already been read by hundreds of people who were delighted to learn how hearses were made and the options they offered—and appreciated the warning about potential confusion arising from traffic circles.

And so Nicole had "won" in her rivalry with Jessica. One would have thought that now that she had me all to herself she had had everything she could possibly want. Now it was she and I who spent weekends together and during the week she would call me every day—she had made me unblock her phone number. If I were at home I always spoke to her, but of course at funerals I shut off my phone. At first she left messages; then she didn't.

A few days passed when I didn't hear from her, and I called her to ask if she wanted to go to dinner over the weekend. There was something different, something distant, in her voice when she told me she would be unavailable, that she was tired and wanted to stay home. Of course that didn't bother me at all, since it meant I would have more time to work on a review.

"I understand completely!" I told her. "Not a problem. Rest up—enjoy yourself."

"Don't worry, I will," she said.

I thought her response was a bit odd, a bit too obliging, especially since she had always been so eager to see me. That there was something amiss became evident the next time I saw her. She came to my place and, unusually, didn't kiss me in greeting; indeed rather pulled away from me a little as I hugged her. Assuming a distant and artificially cheerful demeanor, she asked me to sit down with her because she wanted to "talk" to me, then forged ahead with the conversation she must have gone over in her head a dozen times in the last week. She told me she had met someone new—someone she liked—someone she had already gone out with, and that she was sorry but she wouldn't be able to see me anymore.

"You're kidding me," I said.

"I'm sorry. I didn't expect it to happen. I wasn't looking for it. It just … happened. But I wanted to be honest with you."

I didn't know what to say—I was so absolutely thrilled. I sat looking about me as though I were incapacitated in the face of an overwhelming emotional disaster; in fact I was telling, commanding myself not to betray, either by word or expression, how happy she had just made me. In an earlier place I mentioned how, before meeting Jessica and Nicole, my life had seemed to me a golden age of freedom; now it seemed as though the dawn of another such age had just arisen, with a light more golden and effulgent than ever.

"Nicole, this is so hard for me to believe," I said, with just the right amount of gasp and sigh which might be expected from the first shock of a broken heart.

"All I can say is I'm sorry."

"Who is it?"

"No one you know. Someone I wasn't expecting to meet. We just went out once ... you know, on a date."

I nodded, putting a hand to my mouth and assuming an air of sad thoughtfulness. Of course I wasn't sad, but I *was* thoughtful: already I was calculating how many funerals I might attend in the coming week. Still, I felt it incumbent on me to continue my show of surprise and regret, and I said:

"After all we've been though ..."

She lowered her eyes, tensed her lips, and said only, "I know ... I'm sorry."

Poor woman: she was doing the right, the honorable thing;—in just the way she had once told me I should do it to Jessica. One had to give her credit for the strength and integrity of her convictions. This raised her immensely in my estimation, and just then I felt a small pang of regret at losing her.

When she left my house a few minutes later, I poured myself a drink. Then I turned on the stereo, played some disco music, and for the first time in a long time, and emphatically, *danced*. I don't recall at this time what the dance was—it was probably just freestyle—but my exuberance in this way lasted a good ten minutes so that by the end of it I was winded. Winded, but how joyful, how grateful! My new, fresh lease on life (as it seemed to me) was too good a thing not to be exuberant about. The next thing I did was to get on my computer and start looking up obituaries.

By the way, while looking over a few unfinished reviews I happened to come across the one for the funeral at which I had met Nicole. It was mostly done—7,000 words worth—and needed only my examination of the headstone to make it complete; which I finally got around to doing, one very brisk November day. It was mediocre at best, and the funeral received ▮▮▮▯▯.

# IX
## CRITICAL EVOLUTION

Having been traumatized by my experience with Jessica and Nicole, I was no longer interested in meeting women, at least for a while. When I saw an attractive woman at a funeral my initial eagerness to meet her was tempered, then repressed, by the fear of the kinds of complications which had made my life so difficult for the last several months. I had also learned my lesson about getting involved with more than one person at a time.

I also came to reassess the kinds of funerals worthy of review. Too many of them had been bad and all for the same bad reasons. The funeral parlors were stuffy and oppressive, the accoutrements of the service were predictably mediocre, and the demeanor of the black-clad guests was offensively woeful. Worst of all were the receptions. They were mostly arranged by cut-rate caterers or restaurants whose food, however well presented on shiny plates set on linen-covered tables decorated with candles or flower arrangements, was quick, starchy, canned, reheated, and, in a word, cheap. Really, how many more cold pasta salads could I eat? And as for adult beverages, only the bottom-shelf variety was offered—just the kind of hastily-distilled rotgut to give you a banging headache the next day. All of this was owing to the middle-class families involved. The fact is, and has always been, that good things, beautiful things, things of quality, usually cost a lot of money. In these expensive times there is no way that a lovely and inspiring funeral and a fine reception can be afforded by those who aren't wealthy or haven't had the foresight to save up for the event. And even if the money were there, the needed sensibility would most likely *not* be. Lower- and middle-class people spend so much time earning a livelihood, their heads are so filled from morning till night with getting the next paycheck and paying the next bill, that they haven't the time consider the social and emotional implications of the funerals lying in their future. No wonder that when the bomb drops, and they must plan a service, they are like deer caught in the headlights: stunned—standing or sitting with eyes glazed over before a funeral director, nodding mechanically in acceptance of his "suggestions," which roll over them like Juggernaut.

Thus I shifted my focus to the funerals of the affluent. The kind of work the deceased had done, whether or not he came from a wealthy family, the area where he lived, any pictures of his house or property—these were the criteria which helped me to decide whether I would attend the service. I was able to make pretty accurate deductions on rather limited public information. If someone had moved in high circles, if he had belonged to an exclusive social club, if he had owned a large business, and especially if this was international, then it was likely that he had left behind enough cash, and enough of a reputation to protect, that his family would have no reason to stint in sending him off.

And yet as we all know wealth is no guarantee of good taste; it is especially no guarantee of munificence. Some very rich people are as stingy as the day is long. They hold on to every dollar till it wears holes in their pockets. In the name of practicality, or out of crude indifference to what happens to them after they die, some people worth millions have stipulated in their wills that their funerals be of the simplest, cheapest, quickest kind, with no more than a plain stone slab for their headstone. Now, nearly every instance of this can be attributed to mental illness. Either the person in question became senile and lost all sense of propriety, or a lifetime of stinginess so hardened his heart that he became indifferent even to how the manner of his disposal would affect the reputation of his family or offend the sensibilities of his friends. Whatever the reason for such wishes, they should always be ignored, and usually they are.

Unfortunately it sometimes happens that the family is more concerned about holding on to an inherited fortune than honoring the memory of the person who accumulated it for them. Aware that the cash cow has died, they become careful about "unnecessary" spending. The funeral of Dr. Herman Fleece was a case in point.

He was an internist who died at the age of 69. He practiced medicine till the last year of his life and had amassed an immense fortune through the fraud and extortion that is now synonymous with the medical profession in the United States. He had also made very profitable investments in the stock market. He had a huge house ten miles outside the city limits of Stamford, sitting on thirty

acres of beautiful property.  He had three children,
who had never worked a day in their lives:  his oldest daughter spent her time riding horses in "compe-
titions," his second oldest daughter was a
"coordinator" for celebrity charity events, and his
youngest child, a man in his thirties, was an "artist"
who lived in an expensive New York City loft, taking, during the day, silly black and white photos
with a plastic camera, and spending his nights in
trendy bars and cafes hobnobbing with people as absurd as himself.  The reader will excuse the sneer
in my voice on mentioning these do-nothings, but I
can never think of them, or those like them, without
the bitter reflection on how much more good work I
might have done if my circumstances had been
equally easy.

Dr. Fleece's wife of thirty-one years had been
very pretty in her youth, the trophy wife of a rich
doctor.  One is always amazed at wealthy unattractive men like Dr. Fleece who think that beautiful
women are interested in them for themselves.  It is a
strange delusion, which results either from a flaw in
their intelligence or, still less excusably, an indifference to their own humiliation.  At any rate, Mrs.
Fleece's husband no sooner died than she showed her
true colors, for she gave him the cheapest funeral
possible.  The casket was made of oak, to be sure,
but unworked and plain.  The flowers were few and
sparse; the arrangements composed mostly of inexpensive Baby's breath and carnations.  No effort had
been made to humanize the starkness of the funeral
parlor; it was too brightly lit, oppressively silent, and
cramped given the large attendance of over fifty persons.  The seating had no armrests and the uphol-

stery was so worn and thin that after a while one uncomfortably felt the underlying wood or metal.

During the service Mrs. Fleece wore the impenetrably dark sunglasses mourners sometimes wear to give them a sense of privacy in their grief. But in her case they were used to obscure eyes which would have betrayed a dry indifference. She did not hold a tissue or a handkerchief because there were no tears to dab at. As for the three do-nothing incompetents who were the Fleece children, they were not so much aggrieved as stunned. They sat in the front row with pale, unblinking, often open-mouthed expressions as though they had suddenly been transported into a bizarre world where bad things happened. They were not used to bad things happening; they were not used to things not going their way. In the face of the sometimes hard realities of the world they stood as confused and astonished as deer caught in the headlights.

The priest's eulogy was one of the biggest faux pas of the funeral. Over the years Dr. Fleece had donated to his church and the politic priest was undoubtedly looking forward either to a bequest in the will or to continuing donations from the widow. For forty-five minutes he spoke glowingly of Dr. Fleece as though he had been a saint who had routinely sacrificed his interests to heal the sick—a far cry from what he had really been: a physician who had turned away countless patients because they couldn't afford his outrageously high fees, who had overcharged insurance companies, and who had defrauded the Medicare system. (I learned all this at the reception afterwards from a guest who was seated next to me and who, after two screwdrivers,

spilled the beans.  He also told me that the govern-
ment had instituted a lawsuit against the doctor several months before his death, and which undoubtedly
contributed to the stroke that killed him.)

This was one of the few times I went to the cemetery to witness the burial, and again only because I
didn't yet know where the reception was to be held.
The line of cars following the hearse stretched for
several hundred feet and was as slow as molasses.
Even I was tempted to beep my horn.  By the time I
parked my car and reached the open grave the
priest—the same one who had given the eulogy—was
already ending his prayers and was blessing the coffin suspended over the open earth.  Mrs. Fleece and
the children were gathered round.  The latter were
sad-faced and *not* dry-eyed—one could tell so much
for the glistening streams visible below their sunglasses.  But *she* stood there like a statue, probably
only a little crestfallen at the thought that an accustomed phase of her life had ended. The priest dismissed the gathering before the casket was lowered
into the ground.

Despite the inferior service and its appointments,
I had high hopes for the reception.  I looked forward
to it the more because I was particularly hungry
that afternoon.  It was held in a Polish restaurant,
and it was a disappointment from start to finish.
The main course included a meat dish, mushroom
soup, and pierogies.  The first was too fatty, the second too salty, and the dough of the third was excessive and undercooked.  The borscht soup was tepid
and insufficiently seasoned, and my order of "Spring
Salad"—for which I had to wait a whole twenty minutes—had no olives, no tomatoes, no onions, no

mushrooms, and was nothing more than a bowl of wet lettuce with a few wisps of shredded carrot. What kind of salad is that?

I found myself seated at a table with six other people who had known the deceased personally and one of whom was drinking a little too freely. It was he who gave me the above-mentioned lowdown on Dr. Fleece's real character and business practices, doing so in a rather apprehensive whisper as though he were a whistle-blower, which in a sense he was.

Mrs. Fleece wandered among the guests, thanking them for coming and accepting condolences. She held a napkin which she frequently brought to her Saharan eyes. When she reached my table the men stood up. She thanked me, as she did everyone, for coming.

"It was an honor for me to attend, Mrs. Fleece," I said.

Was it hypocritical for me to say this even though the funeral disappointed and was on track for receiving a low rating? Perhaps; but one has to be polite.

She looked at me a little more critically and said, "I'm sorry but I forgot your name." And when I gave her a false one: "And ... how did you know my husband?"

Clearly, now that the distraction of the funeral was behind her, she had become a little suspicious about my presence, and this had to be nipped in the bud.

"I was a patient of his many years ago," I said. "Actually he saved my life. I was having abdominal pain for months and your husband discovered that I had a tumor in my intestines. It was as big as a grapefruit."

"Oh my!"

"Yes, it was pretty bad," I said, with the half-sad, half-terrified expression one might be supposed to assume at such a diagnosis. "I had to undergo immediate surgery. It was a six-hour operation. I actually died on the operating table: my heart stopped. Thankfully there was a defibrillator on hand and the surgeon was able to revive me. Anyway, I got better under your husband's care. When I noticed his name in the obituaries I was shocked and sorry. It's not every day that someone who has saved your life passes away. He was not only a brilliant doctor but also, and foremost, a good human being, a man of conscience, a true humanitarian and a benefactor of society, and his passing is a tragedy for the whole world."

—Sure, it was laying it on a bit thick, and for a minute I thought I might have gone a little too far with that bit about my having died and come back to life. But her suspicions had melted away beneath the warm gush of my praise. In fact a genuine tear formed in her left eye, though it only barely glistened there.

"That's *so* kind of you," she said. "Of all the people my poor husband must have helped over the years, you would think a lot more would have come by to pay their respects. I appreciate your coming. Thank you."

She moved along and I sat back down to finish a disappointing meal. I stayed at the reception only long enough to appease my ravenous appetite after a long afternoon.

Well, what was there to say about this funeral?

It was a medley of missed opportunities. Too many corners were cut. There was nothing creative in the presentation. The casket was mediocre. The atmosphere was oppressively silent. The behavior of the family *seemed* to be nobly subdued, but this was only because of an unseemly lack of sentiment; and self-control is only admirable when strong emotions have been overcome, just it is not bravery but recklessness where no fear has been surmounted. The eulogy delivered by the minister was an intellectual insult and therefore a moral misfeasance. Granted that there had been nothing honorable about the deceased, that ultimately he had been a thief wielding a stethoscope, a hoodlum in scrubs; still, one would have expected the family, in light of their wealth, to send him off in the better style everyone had a right to expect. There was also some question about the wholesomeness of the food which had been served because by the time I got home that evening my stomach wasn't feeling so well. I think there was something wrong with those pierogies.

A month afterwards I returned to the cemetery. One might have hoped that in the weeks succeeding the funeral his widow would have come to miss her husband a little, and would have wanted to do the right thing by his memory in providing a good headstone. Not a chance. That tightwad wasn't letting go of a single dollar unless she absolutely had to. She was probably more conscious than ever that the printing press had shut down and she had to be careful about how she spent money. She put over his grave a small, square, unadorned piece of granite. It had to be the cheapest model available. Nor were any flowers placed before it, which seemed to indicate that it had not yet been visited; and probably never would be, at least not by *her*.

In the end the Fleece funeral wound up with a rating of ⚰⚰⚰⚰⚰. If they had been a family of lesser means, they would have gained another half coffin out of consideration for the *intention* to provide a pleasant reception, since it can never be cheap to feed some sixty persons even at a bad restaurant.

But let us turn our attention to something more uplifting: the funeral for Harold Marcus Hoffstein. It was one of the best funerals I ever attended and was to have significant consequences for my future.

Just to show you how fate works, how a word here, a glance there, how a "chance" incident can change the course of our lives, it happened that one day I went to my office in school to pick up a few stationery supplies for home. As it happened, there was another person in the building: Mr. Furmanski, teacher of "earth sciences" (whatever that is), who had also stopped into his office. We chatted for a while, both of us expressing our delight that school would be out for the foreseeable future. He told me he was planning to take his family that weekend to Oyster Bay, New York, and enthusiastically mentioned all the things there were to do and see there: fishing, eating at great restaurants, staying in small hotels in lovely neighborhoods, and so forth. He hoped one day to live there himself, he said, except that he doubted he would ever be able to do it "on his salary."

"Is it so expensive to live there?" I asked him.

"Oh, I'm sure it is! A lot of rich people live there. You should see the houses. They're huge."

I remembered his comment the next day when,

having a few minutes to myself, I got on the Internet to look up obituaries. I went to online news sites for Oyster Bay, and found The *Oyster Bay Journal*. The "Obituaries" was a category among a dropdown menu running at the top of the page.

The first one listed showed the large color picture of a man in his sixties with a ruddy face, pale blue eyes, brown hair streaked with gray, and nearly all-white sideburns. He looked distinguished. He was wearing a jacket and tie—the photograph was formal. The accompanying text ran as follows:

"Mr. Howard M. Hoffstein, CEO of Hoffstein & Sons, died peacefully at his home in Oyster Bay, Long Island at the age of 87. He was associated with Harvard University, the North Shore Sailing League, and was an avid art collector. A private memorial service will be held at 1 P.M. on Saturday, October 24, at his home."

Though I was able, by this time in my career, to read between the usually few lines of an obituary to determine whether or not it was worth reviewing, the Fleece funeral had shown me that my ability was not infallible, and that sometimes what promised to be an excellent service could turn out to be a dud. A little gun shy from my latest disappointment, I did not immediately decide to review the Hoffstein funeral till I could learn a bit more about the deceased, and came up with the following information:

Howard Marcus Hoffstein was born in Philadelphia, Pa., Feb. 25, 1933. He graduated from Harvard Business School in 1957 and went work for Procter & Gamble, working his way up to Vice President in only five years. In 1964 he left Proctor & Gamble to join his family business, which provided bulk supplies to the restaurant industry. He changed its name to Hoffstein & Sons in 1971, since by that time he had married and had children. Under his leadership the company grew dramatically and by the late '70s was among the largest foodstuff distributors on the East Coast. By 1987 it was the largest in the country, having gained a reputation for providing quality products and good service for reasonable prices. In his spare time Mr. Hoffstein liked sailing his yacht, *Vanessa*, named after his wife of forty-nine years. An avid traveler, he collected art from around the world and became an expert in 19th Century Turkish ceramics. He was a consultant to the Harvard Business School, a member of the Long Island Business Association, and was a resource of the New York State Council on the Arts to which he made occasional donations. His home on Long Island was often the scene of fashionable political and social events. He was survived by his wife, his son Eliot M. Hoffstein, his daughter, Lisa M. Gill, several grandchildren, and numerous nephews and nieces.

What was there not to like in such a resume? Everything about the deceased bespoke affluence, high connections, and at least a recognition of refinement. True, I was somewhat skeptical of his reputation as an "avid art collector," since this often refers to someone who has more money than he knows what to do with and spends huge amounts on things which, if sold at a flea market, wouldn't fetch more than $127. But at least it indicated a *desire* to seem cultivated: and one has to have the desire before one can have the result.

Another point in his favor was that he had lived into his late eighties. Surely he had attended dozens of funerals in his time, had come to know good ones from bad ones, and had become conscientious about the manner of his own.

The service took place on one of those bright, crisp autumn days of the sort that raises and energizes the spirits and seems a harbinger of the good things to come. With a perfectly yellow sun shining through a cloudless blue sky, with the windows of my car down and the brisk fresh wind blowing about me, I drove south along fast thruways with the radio turned up high to a station playing pop oldies to many of which I sang along. I was, as usual, surprised at how good my voice was.

After reaching Oyster Bay it took me another fifteen minutes to find the Hoffstein property, which was located on the eastern side of town. A narrow road ran alongside his fifty-acre estate and a still narrower road led into it. This was ordinarily closed off with a gate, which on this day however was wide open in expectation of guests.

The road continued on for about hundred yards through wooded property before giving out to a clearing at the end of which stood the Hoffstein house—a mansion of some twenty-four rooms. Ten acres of lawn surrounded it, and beyond this some fifty acres of land spread out in lawns, gardens, and, farther out, pristine, wooded land. A long, wide, semicircular driveway reached to its colonnaded facade. Here a couple of valets were present to take and park guests' cars. These were overwhelmingly luxury models so that when I drove up in my modest compact the valet who came up to me to take my keys looked at me with wry smile.

But if my car didn't make the appropriate impression, I'm sure my person did. In keeping with my new resolution to review only upper-class funerals, I had bought some new and expensive clothes. No, they weren't tailored—I wasn't prepared to spend *that* much—but they came from a men's clothing store reputable for quality, and a knowledgeable salesman helped me make the selections of two jackets, four pairs of slacks, six white shirts, and five silk ties. And so I appeared comfortably in place at the Hoffstein funeral amid the well-to-do attendees who included family, friends, eminent business people, and a few local politicians. When anyone looked at me it was with one of those pleasant nods and smiles with which strangers acknowledge one another at events to which they've all been invited.

The funeral was well-planned, ensuring that no guest should experience any embarrassment or uncertainty about where to go or what to do. As soon as one stepped out of one's car and walked toward the house there were ushers on either side of the double front doors to greet one with a smile and direct one across the gleaming, high-ceiling foyer to the open doors of another room. Here a pre-funeral cocktail hour was under way.

Kudos to that person who came up with this innovation, which I have advocated ever since. For what could be better to get people in the right mood for a funeral? A few drinks and some good food and conversation cannot but assuage any apprehension some people might feel at such a time. No one had to make an effort to order a drink: young men and women in livery took orders and their service was prompt. They also plied hors d'oeuvres, expensive morsels among which were foie gras and caviar. I could not in good conscience partake of those cruel foods but I did help myself to several (ten, to be exact) servings of baked brie, which were in the form of small crusty pastries two inches across and which melted in the mouth, and several (let's say another ten) servings of truffle butter gougères. As all of us drank, ate, and talked, a jazz pianist played tinkling music in the background.

All of the attendees that I talked to were delightful people. Even when they weren't, strictly speaking, good-looking, they were so well-dressed, so polite, so well-educated and well-mannered that their good breeding shone through and made them attractive. Several of them asked who I was and how I knew the deceased. None of them doubted my story of having done business with Mr. Hoffstein when I had—oh, many years ago now—owned a restaurant in New York City. But I daresay that even if they had found out I was crashing the event they would have winked hard at my presence.

There was no announcement that the cocktail hour had ended; instead a tinkling bell sounded and the next thing we knew there was a general movement into another room. At the entrance to it a few of the liveried servers stood to relieve the guests of any drinks they might still be holding, and which they placed on nearby, linen-covered tables; always, as they did so, saying with a smile, "Thank you, sir," or "Thank you, ma'am."

One would never have suspected, to look at the outside of the house in all its modern newness, nor from the foyer and the room in which cocktails had been served, both of which were also modern in most respects, that there existed, just beyond the doors through which the guests now passed, a space which seemed more properly to belong to a castle in Moorish Spain, or in the kingly edifice of a Moroccan grandee.  Perhaps it was the whim of Mr. Hoffstein, who had seen something like it in one of his world travels.  Its architecture, or at least its design, was Moorish.  The floor was covered in zellige-style tiles of black, white, russet, and pink, and geometrical patterns ornamented the tiles of its high ceiling. Most striking of all, an arched colonnade which ran around the room a few feet away from the walls like the peristyle of a medieval courtyard.  Three skylights usually allowed the full light of day to stream into the great room, but on this occasion their linen shades had been drawn, softening the illumination to a softer orangish hue.  One stepped into this vast, ornate place and almost held one's breath at the unexpected splendor of it all.

It was here that his funeral was to take place. The great room was filled with couches of different kinds.  They had probably been taken from elsewhere in the house and moved here.  They were arranged in a semi-circular pattern and faced the front of the room where the casket stood.

*Was* it a casket?  At first I wasn't sure.  It looked rather like some large, albeit generally rectangular, sculpture meant to complement the exotic architecture.  That it *was* the casket became apparent when one saw the survivors of the Hoffstein family sitting before it in the front row.  They had not been present during the cocktail hour but had remained here, no doubt emotionally preparing themselves for the service. There was Mrs. Hoffstein, a woman in her seventies, and her two sons and daughter, all in their forties. Organ music was playing—the musician and his instrument were located behind one of the columns at the front of the room—but the music was not of a dark, heavy kind, but was lighter, more hopeful, and stirred the emotions of love and longing: selections from Ravel and Barber and Debussy—airs melodious, contemplative, and sweetly sad.

For the next half hour guests approached the family, offered condolences, and stepped up to the casket whose head panel was not attached by hinges and had been taken off for the viewing. They stood before it longer than people usually do but it was not Mr. Hoffstein who held their attention; it was his large, beautiful, almost fantastic receptacle. Their heads moved back and forth as they looked all along its length in admiration. A few of them even stepped to one side or another to get a better look at a particular detail. When they returned to their seats their expressions were not sad or regretful so much as thoughtful.

I myself was eager to approach it. Really, if there had been no one around I would have run up the aisle. But first I offered my condolences to the family. Their restrained and dignified demeanor impressed me. For just then, when their hearts were breaking, not one of them slouched or shed a tear. Their world had crumbled around them, and all the privilege money had given them suddenly meant so little now that they, the children, were orphaned by half, and she, the widow, felt the terrible sting of abandonment which would darken the rest of her days;—yet just then, when they all knew their lives would never be the same, never be as good, as it had been because gone forever was the man who had shared their joys, and so increased them, and sympathized with their disappointments, and so lightened them;—it was just then that they showed their nobility by bearing up magnificently. The widow, the sons, the daughter took my offered hand and quietly thanked me for coming; not knowing who I was and only grateful that yet another person had come to pay his respects to a loved one who had deserved all the respect in the world.

I turned away from them with fresh impatience to examine the casket. Each step I took toward it disclosed more clearly the quality of its construction and the abundance and finesse of its ornamentation. A carved pattern of vines and leaves ran along its bottom: tendrils running above, below, and sometimes backtracking on themselves amid ivy-like leaves turned this way and that, their triangular lobes intricate with veining. Just above this was a bas-relief of forestry, mostly of boles and branches: an underpart of a canopy ascending and blending into a depiction of clouds, these forming a cornice or top molding. The massive corners were made of fluted zebra wood. The top panels were ornamented with small but detailed wooden sculptures of cherubs lying on puffy clouds. On the bottom panels, which were in place, one of these creatures was lying on his stomach, his wings folded on his back with one chubby leg crossed over the other at the calf. His hair was thick and curly, each lock distinct from every other. He held up his head in one hand and looked out with a relaxed, dreamy, perhaps slightly confused expression as though to say, "What's all the fuss about?"

Mr. Hoffstein looked every one of his 87 years, and was not nearly so distinguished as he had looked in his obituary photograph. He had probably been a "nice-looking" man in his youth but with the passing decades had become a little rounder, a little less defined, a little grayer, till in his old age he had become a generic "old man," just the sort of character a casting director might choose as an extra to play a retired gentleman playing chess in a park. His expression was blandly indifferent as though he hadn't (and, let's face it, he *hadn't*) the smallest care in the world. It was hard to conceive that such a face had ever burned with anger, or been flushed with pleasure, or hardened into a mask of severe concentration on business affairs, though like everyone else he had experienced a gamut of emotions. —Which led me to think again that mortuary cosmetologists should not always try to make their clients appear "at peace" but instead recreate, for a last, all-important time, some characteristic expression. Surely that would make them appear more "like themselves." From all accounts Mr. Hoffstein had been a serious and skeptical man, so it might have been appropriate if one of his eyebrows had been ever so slightly lifted as though he had just heard something doubtful.

There came a point at which Mrs. Hoffstein and her children approached the casket. As they got up to do so they glanced at one another with sad misgiving. Here was a prearranged, a formal exercise which either had been suggested to them or which they had agreed upon among themselves. They did it bravely, holding hands in common commiseration as though to give one another strength. They stood before their dearly departed with bowed heads and while the organ music still played. At one point the widow reached out and placed a trembling hand on the casket, and the children did the same. It was very touching. A few people around me pulled out handkerchiefs and dabbed at their eyes. I think something of a tear formed in one of my own eyes— though it *could* have been my allergies, since this funeral took place before the first frost of the season and the pollen levels were still high. After a few minutes Mrs. Hoffstein and her children returned to their seats, their heads bowed but still containing themselves in an honorable silence.

A eulogy was given by Edward Hoffstein, the deceased's oldest son. He spoke of his father with reverent but not extravagant praise, and his voice was clear and composed. Only with his last few words did his voice crack a little.

Then a minister spoke. He led a brief prayer, then offered his own eulogy, emphasizing Mr. Hoffstein's kindness and how he would live on in the hearts he had touched. Though he mentioned God he didn't utter a word about an afterlife, angels, resurrections, and so forth; leaving out all that hocuspocus perhaps at the family's or at Mr. Hoffstein's testamentary request.

The burial took place in a small cemetery not many miles from the Hoffstein residence. I attended it because at the pre-service cocktail hour I had met so many charming people, and talked so amicably with them, that my absence would have been more than ordinarily noted. The cemetery was no more than five or six acres in extent and was full of ornate headstones from the 19th century, a time when families understood the importance of making them as fine as financially possible. Here the minister said another short prayer. My attention however was focused on the casket which hung suspended above the open earth beneath it. To think that it would be buried alarmed me. It should have been, it was worthy to have been, aboveground forever and put in some visible or even public place to be appreciated by living eyes; and instead it would be covered up and rot away. One could almost see this concern for the waste of the thing in the face of the other guests. Fortunately we did not have to witness the actual interment.

The reception was given at a banqueting hall in Oyster Bay. The space was large, bright, and sparkling clean. Mrs. Hoffstein had spared no expense on the event. Some twenty tables were set wide apart from one another and in a circular pattern around a large open area. They were set in white-linen, with flowered centerpieces and fine tableware. Four main courses were offered, one of which, most thoughtfully, was vegetarian and sounded so good as almost to tempt me away from the rib-eye and lobster platter. (I *wish* the menu had mentioned that the lobster was presented still in the shell, for when my platter was set before me poor boiled thing was set upright, its boiled milky-white eyes staring up at me as though to ask, "Really, how could you?") The wine list—as might have been expected—was impressive. Some of the finest offerings from the Hoffsteins' private collection were made available.  On a tablemate's recommendation I ordered a French Sauvignon Blanc whose name I have forgotten but whose vintage was 2012 and which was an excellent accompaniment to my meal.

During dinner my tablemates regaled me with interesting, good-humored conversation.  They all spoke highly of the late Mr. Hoffstein.  A couple of times during the meal we raised our glasses in a toast to him, and the same thing happened at every other table.  On the whole however the conversation was characterized by the kinds of miscellaneous subjects usually arising among people who have come together in polite fellowship.  What with the good food and drink, the elegant appointments of the dining hall, and the atmosphere of solemn good cheer, it was easy to forget that one was at a funeral—which is the highest compliment which can be paid to one.

For me the only awkward moment came on account of a slight misunderstanding with Mr. Hoffstein's granddaughter, Emma.  I had seen her before at the cocktail hour and during the service.  How could I not have?  She was twenty-two years old and very pretty, with strawberry blonde hair, blue eyes, a fair complexion, and a great body.  She wore a tight, dark, low-cut gray dress and tastefully restrained jewelry with rubies or garnets.  At one point toward the end of the reception she came to our table to speak to someone she knew and, after a few minutes, pulled up a chair and sat beside me.  We began talking to each other.  She told me a lot about herself:  where she lived, what kind of music she liked, where she had gone to school, and the kind of job she hoped to get.  She mentioned she was single and was "dating" but that it was hard to find a "good guy." Was I so wrong to interpret this to mean she that considered me that good guy? I had forsworn having any other relationships for a while but she was so attractive that it seemed to me I might make an exception in her case. Wanting her to know I was as interested in her as she seemed to be in me, I reached out for her leg under the table and gave it a squeeze, expecting her to put her hand on mine. Instead she turned to me with a furious expression and said, "*Excuuuuse* me?"

It was embarrassing. Apparently I had misinterpreted her. I fumbled out an excuse about looking for my keys.

After dinner the jazz pianist was replaced with a four-piece ensemble consisting of drums, keyboards, and two guitars. Mrs. Hoffstein announced that her beloved husband would not have wanted anyone to be sad, not even at his funeral, and had made her promise him that his guests would have a good time. Well, then, what could ensure a better time than a little dancing? She encouraged everyone to do it out of affection for her husband. Who could resist such an appeal? The music started with an up-tempo beat. At first only a few young people got up from their tables and took advantage of this proposal; and some of the older folks looked dismayed by this *too* unfunereal proceeding; but even they, after a while, got into the good spirit of the thing. At my table one of the women looked onto the dance floor with almost wistful longing, then would turn to her husband with inquiring eyes, all but prodding him to ask her to dance, but he frowned a refusal, either because he thought it was inappropriate or because he was one of those men who think dancing detracted from his dignity. He was a bore and a killjoy. I ventured to say to her:

"Would you like to accompany me?"

Her husband glanced at me and frowned again. He would have preferred his wife remain at the table. But he gave way before her hopeful expression, saying, "Go ahead."

"Yes, let's!" she said to me.

Gentleman that I am, I hastened to her chair, pulled it out for her with a smile, and gave her my arm.

I did the Watusi, the swim, and the mashed potato. I even took a few steps of the moonwalk. My partner evidently didn't expect me to be such a good dancer because at one point she stood still and watched me with a wondering smile. She probably didn't like the idea that I was getting all the attention because she took my arm and said, "Thanks, I've had enough—let's go back"—and led me back to our seats.

It was just as well because by then the Viennese tables were being rolled out into the dining room. They were loaded with the most luscious sweets and pastries. I was among the first to go up to them with my plate and load it up with delicious morsels. There were mini napoleons with real egg-cream filling, chocolate cake so dense with flavor it was almost black, apple, peach, and raspberry tarts with buttery crusts which melted in the mouth, golden strudels, crisp baklava, cream horns dusted with a coca-infused powdered sugar, and other pastries. I washed it all down with two cups of strong aromatic coffee.

The reception came to an end at about eight o'clock. Mrs. Hoffstein and her children stood at the exit bidding goodbye to their guests and thanking them for coming. When I reached and expressed again my condolences, she looked at me curiously, apologized for not recognizing me, and asked me how I had known her husband. I repeated my story about having owned a restaurant in New York City and having done business with him, and, before she could ask any questions, extolled her late husband, saying:

"There wasn't a finer man in the world, Mrs. Hoffstein, and tonight you've honored his memory in a way that he would have been very proud of."

She accepted this compliment with a soft nod and glistening eyes. "Thank you," she said, with a little gasp.

The Hoffstein funeral put me into a great mood. As usual I had taken copious notes: throughout the event the recorder in my breast pocket had been running, picking up my murmured observations and, best of all, the ambient sounds and music, which would go a long way toward refreshing my memory of the event. I wrote most of the review that weekend, for it came to me easily and quickly. Four weeks later Mr. Hoffstein's headstone was ready for my examination, and it did not disappoint. It was made of white marble and stood four feet tall and three feet wide. Its decorative engraving consisted of gates opening toward a floating crucifix in the distance and from behind which shot forth stylized rays of light. Between the open gates was a representation of flooring composed of tiles, some dark, some light, seen in perspective and which provided the sense of depth, of entering into another, distant, bright region. This image consumed the upper half of the headstone. Beneath it was the name "HOFFSTEIN" in capital letters, and beneath this his dates of birth and death. At the very bottom rang the succinct and touching words, "In Our Hearts Forever."

The Hoffstein funeral was so good in so many ways that it might have served as a model. To this day I can never look back on it without a sense of satisfaction. It earned a very rare ▮▮▮▮.

It was my highest rating up to that time. But why did I withhold that half coffin that would have given it the perfect score? Because "a man's reach should exceed his grasp, or what's a heaven for?"— because in holding out some ideal of perfection never yet achieved those who have come closest to it are likely to maintain their own high standards, while those who have yet to try may be inspired to greater effort with the thought of first reaching the ultimate goal. In this way there is a general and continual upward trend in quality. In this way every generation gets a little better overall. Who knows? Perhaps there may come a day when funerals which would have earned only a one-, two-, or three-coffin rating will be a thing of the past; when even the most thoughtless families, the most venal funeral directors, will no more tolerate a shabby service than they would jump off a bridge. We have a long way to go before we get there, but the only way to get there is by setting the highest standard.

A week later I attended another funeral which proved to be equally satisfying and would also have important consequences for myself. It was for one

Patrick Van Dorn, a real estate developer from Bridgeport who had specialized in building luxury condominiums. His fortune was estimated to be some hundred million dollars. His family's Connecticut estate spread over forty acres, much of it pastureland on which he indulged his love of horses, prize animals which he bought, rode, and bred. His wife was also a horse aficionado; indeed he had met her at a polo match during which they had both been spectators.

Mr. Van Dorn had learned the farrier's craft so he could shoe his own horses. While working on a back hoof of one of them, "Daffodil," who happened to be his favorite, he had ignored the precept of always standing off to the side, and had instead stood right directly behind her. It was a fatal mistake. Either because she had become frightened or because he had caused her pain Daffodil kicked him full force in the face, killing him instantly.

She also left the imprint of a horseshoe on his face. It was so deeply impressed there that even two days after the accident it was plainly visible. In addition to her grief over the loss of her husband his widow was anxious about his funeral, thinking that there was no way she could have a viewing with that tragic mark so visible. She had the good fortune however to have contacted a first-rate undertaker, Mr. Toby Maxwell, of Crystal Springs Funeral Home, in New Haven. He assured her that he would be able to make her husband presentable.

As stated on its website, Crystal Springs has a "long, proud history of serving southern Connecticut since 1911." It is two stories tall, with a white clapboard exterior, light-blue shutters, and a long porch quaintly decorated with potted flowers and a porch swing. A hundred years before it had been an inn; now it was the gracious point of bon voyage for citizens of the surrounding communities. Unlike so many funeral homes of long standing, its interior is renovated every five years so as to ensure it has a fresh contemporary feel. The décor is mostly neutral with white trims around the windows and doors, and bolder dashes of sky blue or peppermint green color at strategic points—such as in the upholstery of the furniture or in the bases of lamps.

About seventy people were already there when I arrived. They constituted a well-dressed, attractive group, the men tall and confident with rosy faces, the women looking good for their various ages—and more than a few of the younger ones having great legs. The atmosphere in the anteroom of the funeral parlor was reverential but not gloomy; people spoke with one another in polite low voices. At my entrance several people turned to me with welcoming smiles. No doubt they were trying to place me, to remember who I might be and whether they had ever met me before; and when they couldn't they naturally assumed I was familiar to someone else.

The visitation room was appointed with light blue carpeting and padded beige chairs. Over its tall windows pinkish translucent drapes had been pulled, softening the daylight coming in from outside. At the front of the room lay the casket, an attractive metal model with a matte copper finish and pewter-colored fittings and trims. On either side of it and behind it stood fluted columns upholding arrangements of pastel-colored flowers. To the right of the rightmost column was a picture of the deceased in happier living days, proudly standing beside several of his prize horses, each labeled with its name;—among which Daffodil was conspicuously absent.

Mr. Van Dorn himself made a first-rate appearance. He had always been a fashionable fellow, enamored of fine clothes, and this penchant of his was honored by his family, who dressed him in a lovely Brooks Brothers suit consisting of a dark blue linen jacket, a light pink shirt, and a plaid ascot. Three corners of a white handkerchief peeped up from the jacket pocket, and along edge of the foremost corner the initials PVD were embroidered in silver-colored thread. His expression was decidedly content if not pleased.

Most interesting of all was the absence of any sign of the face-shattering wound which had caused his demise. I moved a few inches from side to side, shifting the angle of my gaze to try to see some evidence of the reconstructive work that had been done on him. Perhaps with a magnifying glass it might have been detectable, but it certainly wasn't with the naked eye. Clearly here was the work of a mortuary cosmetologist who knew his business! After standing there a full five minutes—much longer than anyone else—I turned away from the casket and went to offer my condolences to the family.

The widow was a good, brave, socially-conscious soul who had graciously done her crying in private. She sat with impressively stoic sadness, only the darkness around her eyes hinting at the emotional trauma she had endured over the last few days. I reached for her hand, which she offered me, and bent down slightly to her and expressed sympathy for her loss, adding that her husband had been a wonderful man. She did not ask me who I was or what relation I bore to him. She had too much class for that. It was her oldest son who was the busy-body. He was in his late thirties and sat beside his mother. He regarded me curiously when I shook his hand and said how sorry I was for his loss. Rather than thanking me, he asked: "And what is your name, sir?"

I gave a false one: "Rudy Rollers."

"Rudy Rollers," he repeated, apparently accepting it with a nod. But then asked, "How did you know my father?"

"Oh, I met him many years ago. We were just casual acquaintances."

The son nodded slightly; but there was still some-thing skeptical about the way he looked at me; and he was still holding my hand, as though to hold on to me. "That's funny," he said, "because my father didn't have many friends or acquaintances. When was this that you knew him?"

"Oh, years ago—decades." I had to pull my hand away. "You were just a young child back then. Per-haps your mother remembers me," I said, turning to her with a hopeful air.

Mrs. Van Dorn only shook her head, no, not re-membering anything of the kind.

Nevertheless the son nodded as though the meet-ing between his father and myself might very well have occurred when he was a boy. But there was no doubt that he was suspicious, for after I had re-turned to my seat, and just as I was murmuring a few notes into my recorder, I saw him turn around in his seat a few times to look at me.

I decided that it might be in my best interest to

leave. This disappointed me because, telling from the first-class appointments of the service, the reception promised to be good. The opportunity for my exit came when the minister showed up. Just as he stepped to the front of the room to lead a prayer or deliver a eulogy, I got up and slipped away.

Mr. Maxwell, the funeral director, was standing idly in the lobby as he waited for the service to end. He had just seen the minister enter the room and wondered why I hadn't remained to hear him. He must have thought I needed or wanted something because he asked me:

"Is everything alright, sir?"

"Yes, fine. I just couldn't stay any longer. By the way, were you the one who prepared Mr. Van Dorn for the viewing?"

He regarded the question as odd, perhaps as a prelude to a criticism, and said uncertainly, "Nooo. Why do you ask?"

"I understand he was kicked in the face by a horse. There's hardly any sign of it. Whoever worked on him did an impressive job."

He looked at me curiously, skeptically, and asked, "Are you a funeral director?"

"No, but I've attended a lot of funerals in my time, so I know good work when I see it. He was worked on by ... ?"

"Our cosmetologist."

"He wouldn't happen to be here, would he? I'd like to offer my compliments."

The funeral director exclaimed under his breath, "Really!"—and it was hard to tell whether he were glad or wary of my appreciation for his employee's expertise. Certainly no one had ever asked him for such an introduction. He looked about him to make sure his presence wasn't needed—it wasn't, everyone was in the next room, listening to the minister who even now was speaking—and he said, "Yes, he's downstairs. If you want to meet him, I'll introduce you."

"Please!"

The basement of the funeral home was spacious, and almost as well appointed, as the first floor. Here the business of the company was conducted: besides the preparation rooms for clients, there were storerooms, a bathroom, and several offices, one for the funeral director himself, one for his assistant, and one for the resident cosmetologist. His door was closed when we came to it and the funeral director knocked on it lightly. From inside came a perky, "Come in!"

I hadn't expected him to be so young—he couldn't have been more than twenty-six or -seven. Most noticeable about him was his hair: it was so brightly red and thick that it almost didn't look real. A real carrot top! Freckle-faced, smiling, energetic in his movements, cheerfully nonchalant, he greeted his boss and me with a simple, "Hi there!" He listened to his boss tell him there was "someone who wanted to meet him," and I introduced myself and shook his hand. His name was Charlie.

"He likes your work," the funeral director said, not without a wry tone in his voice at the unusual nature of the introduction.

"Yes, I was upstairs," I said, "and saw Mr. Van Dorn. You did a great job on him."

"Oh, thanks," Charlie said.

"I didn't see the least evidence of a wound, though there must have been a noticeable one considering how he died."

The funeral director and I stepped into Charlie's office. It was small, cluttered, and taped to the wall behind his desk were a few color printouts of paintings by pointillist masters along with a few others of a more abstract design and which I didn't recognize;—which meant they were probably his. Suspecting that he was not only an artist in his vocation but also in the more conventional sense, I nodded toward the printouts and said:

"Are those yours?"

"Some of them, yes. These two, and this one," he said, pointing them out.

"Very nice. Oil paintings, or ... ?"

"Yes, oil."

"Ah, very nice. They show a lot of talent."

In fact it was hard to tell how much talent they showed because they were just photographs of artwork which in person might have made a much different impression. But that wasn't the point. The point was that young Charlie was an artist whose talent was exhibited in his day job. So that he might be more willing to give me some insights into his cosmetological work, I complimented him again on his paintings and without skipping a beat asked him what he had done to make Mr. Van Dorn look so good. He took the bait, saying:

"Well, it wasn't easy, I can tell you that! He was a real mess when they brought him in. Quite apart from his facial injury he had also lost one of his eyeballs—must've popped out when the horse kicked him. They found it but we couldn't use it because the horse stepped on it. That wasn't such a big deal because I just put a wad of cotton in the socket, and his eyes were going to be closed anyway. But the horseshoe really left an impression! You could see it in his forehead and the left side of his face, in part because some of the skull was crushed beneath. In the I had to iron it out."

"Iron it out?"

"I tried everything and nothing was working, so I got the idea to use a patch of very thin parchment and mold it along the area with an iron. I put the iron on a low setting—'Permanent Press, Light Steam'—and just kept passing it over the area, barely touching it. It took a few minutes, but it worked. The parchment softened up and molded right onto the skin, then I shellacked over it and used some makeup to blend it in with the surrounding skin."

"Ingenious!" I said.

Charlie basked in the compliment, looking proud.

The funeral director, who had been standing beside me the whole time, asked me again, "Are you *sure* you're not in the funeral business?"

Again, I told him I wasn't, that I just had a passing interest in it.

"How so?" he pressed.

I am always reluctant to disclose my status as a professional critic to someone in the industry. I don't want to seem to be promoting myself, and such a disclosure puts people on their guard and makes them less candid. To the funeral director's question I replied that I was merely someone who could appreciate good work, no matter in what line, and added:

"I doubt if Charlie could have been a good cosmetologist if he wasn't also a good painter—which
he clearly is."   And turning back to Charlie: "You
say you set the iron for Permanent Press?"

"... and Light Steam, that's right," he said. "But
even after the shellac a seam was still visible where
the parchment met the skin.   I used a very fine-
grade sandpaper–P1000 grit—and worked close so
make sure the edge got really thin.  Then I did a
kind of micro-fill between the seam and the skin,
using a very fine brush and a maulstick to steady
my hand.   But the real trick was to get the flesh
tones just right.  That's usually the hardest part.  I
use my palette for that. Here it is, right here."

—He moved aside a layer of business-related papers and food wrappers on his desk and uncovered
an artist's palette in the traditional curved shape.
It was made of plastic and splotched with the stains
of various pigments.  He took it up, saying:

"I always use this.  I always have to experiment
with colors to get them just right.   In Mr. Van
Dorn's case I used the cosmetic equivalents of tita-
nium white, cadmium red, burnt sienna and raw
umber.  His skin tint is on the light side of the red
spectrum, and somehow the cadmium red just
wasn't cutting it, so I used a naphthol red instead—
has more of a pink undertone—and that seemed to
do the trick.  I mixed my colors in funeral parlor itself—I always do that because you want to mix by
the same light in which the service will be held.
That's something a lot of painters—I mean, cosmetologists—don't understand, and that's why a lot of
their work looks chalky or unnatural."

"That makes sense," I said.  "Please tell me

more!"

"Well, the other thing is to keep in mind is the lining color of the casket and the clothes the client will be wearing. In Mr. Van Dorn's case that turned out to be really important because his family went with a light blue sports jacket, so I had to tone down the redness in his makeup with a little blue-gray. It's very subtle but it makes all the difference. And fortunately the casket lining was white, so that helped provide a neutral background to work with. But these days casket bedding is coming in some pretty crazy colors, like purple and teal and mustard yellow, and they can really throw off your eye. That's why I prefer to work on the client after he's fully dressed and in the casket, this way I can take all that stuff into consideration."

"Fascinating," I said. "You certainly know your business. I also noticed that he seems to be smiling a little."

"Oh, yes, thanks. I always do that—*juuuust* a tad," he said, holding up a forefinger and thumb only a quarter of an inch apart as though to show the subtlety of the effect he is after. "It makes the client seem ... you know ... happy. The family always feels a lot better to see them like that."

The funeral director looked at his watch and said, "I really have to be going back upstairs"—which was hint enough that my time with his cosmetologist had come to an end. I shook Carrot Top's hand, thanked him for his time, and followed my host.

The minister had finished his eulogy and people were in the process of leaving the funeral parlor for their cars to follow the hearse to the cemetery. Obviously I wasn't going to do that since I would have run into the young Van Dorn again.

A few months later I visited Mr. Van Dorn's grave to see his headstone. It was a little too conventional for my taste, but it was large and sturdy and had some interesting scrollwork on the top. The immediately surrounding area, however, reflected badly on it, for the cemetery was old and a few of the nearby headstones were worn away to mere thin slabs tilting forward or backward, their engravings worn away or mere shadows of themselves.

In consideration of the fine funeral, the noble behavior of the family, the good work done the deceased, and what was undoubtedly a sumptuous reception, the Van Dorn affair earned a respectable rating of ⚰⚰⚰⚰. If the headstone had been a little nicer and not devalued by its shabby surroundings the whole affair might have earned another half coffin.

My strategy of attending only funerals of the affluent turned out to be a wise career move. I was never again bitterly disappointed in their services. Even when there were a few things wrong, there was never *everything* wrong; and usually refined tastes combined with the means of indulging them ensured that even when something wasn't entirely first-rate, it didn't fall too far below very good. The Hoffstein and Van Dorn funerals were followed by those for Grant Porter (⚰⚰⚰⚰), Bess Worthington (⚰⚰⚰⚰), Samuel Hearn (⚰⚰⚰⚰), and Maurice Wyatt, whose funeral earned a lesser rating (⚰⚰⚰⚰) only because the otherwise enjoyable reception was thrown into a hubbub when during dessert one of the older guests suffered an asthma attack, threw his table into a hubbub, and had to be hauled away in an ambulance.

The tone of my reviews became much more positive; went from blaming what was wrong to commending what was right. Readers who contacted me about this new direction in my work found it no less instructive and entertaining than it had been. And why not? One can learn just as much from good examples as from bad.

But after three months or so I began to fear that I was losing the "common touch"—might be getting too far removed from the lower- and middle-class mentality which it had been the special object of my reform. It's easy to give a good funeral when you have plenty of money, but it's a different story when you're on a tight budget. But when I recalled the harrowing nature of the typical funeral, I decided that losing the "common touch" was not such a great loss after all. Besides, I was getting older and no longer had the stamina, the stomachic strength, to witness more middle-class funerals! I had done fifty reviews about such emotional disasters, and covered and castigated every degraded point about them. What else was there to say? You don't have to roll around in the muck more than once to know how filthy it is.

# X
# INNOVATIONS

A critic must always beware of becoming jaded. One has seen so many movies, read so many books, seen so many plays, or (as in my case) attended so many funerals, that it becomes harder to be enthusiastic about even good ones. One begins to fear the loss of passion for one's work. Whenever this happens to me I realize it's time to take a break. The batteries, as it were, have to be recharged—the slate has to be wiped clean the better to receive new impressions. But workaholic that I am, a couple of days of doing nothing instills into me a terrible sense of waste and an urgent sense to be doing again.

It happened that during this time, when I could not attend another funeral in the right, receptive state of mind, I received via my website an email from a casket manufacturer who inquired about the possibility of placing an advertisement with me. He had sent along several PDF brochures of his company's products, which were interesting in a good and fresh way. I agreed to host a few ads from him for a small fee.

Soon a dozen manufacturers appealed to me for advertising space. Some of them I had to refuse as politely as possible, saying only that for the time being my "advertising list" was full, because I could

tell even from the pictures and the suggested retail
prices that their offerings were cheap and nasty, and
I refuse to promote the kind of inferior products I
have always railed against.    On the other hand,
some of the requests opened my eyes to the wonderful creativity on the part of some, usually new and
as yet small, manufacturers.  Their caskets use traditional materials and adhere to the classic oblong
design but are customized in such a way as to highlight the personality or interests of the deceased, and
so bring a special, personalized touch to the service.
Here are a few examples, along with their promo-
tional copy:

*The    Patriot*  (American    Casket    Company,
Springfield, IL.)  "Designed to celebrate the freedom
and liberty that has made America great! *The Patriot*
is constructed of Virginia oak and maple assembled
with precision dovetail joints.   High gloss lacquers
bring out the wood's natural beauty.  In an homage to
the War of Independence the front panel is inlaid with
brass ornaments in the shapes of muskets, canon, fifes
and drums, while the end panels are etched with the
American monuments of Mr. Rushmore on one side,
and the Capitol Dome on the other.   A pewter bald
eagle, with wings outstretched, lies across the top
panel. The shirred satin interior is red, white, and blue,
and the satin pillow is ornamented with a circle of
thirteen stars to reflect the original Colonies.  Truly a
unique and lovely casket to highlight and honor the
American spirit!"

*The Traveler 2000*.  (Supreme Caskets, Provo,
UT).   "For the person who lived the globe-trotting
lifestyle the world beckons once again in this exciting
tribute to world travel. Every part of The Traveler 2000
has been sourced from overseas suppliers whose

countries are renowned for a particular product. From the vast forests of Canada and Russia come the fine poplar, larch, and pine which make up the primary construction; from the exotic climes of Africa come the rare and costly ebony and snakewood of the trims; from specialized foundries of Japan come the meticulously-cast brass fittings; from the historic mills of the Middle East come the bedding made from the woolen and hemp fabrics colored with natural, vibrant, long-lasting dyes; and—perhaps most important of all—from the United States comes the design which combines these elements into an exciting whole. It is the perfect tribute to anyone who was, or wanted to be, a world citizen."

*The Seven Seas* (Boston Casket, Boston, MA) "For people who have worked on the sea, lived near it or simply loved it, this sea-themed casket is made of 18 gauge steel finished with a glimmering Ocean Blue enamel. Shell-shaped handles and a chased littoral design along the base molding continue the oceanic theme. The upholstery is imprinted with coral reefs and colorful tropical fish, and the lining of the head panel displays a golden treasure gleaming out of a magical deep-sea cave. Your loved one will rest among the romance and glory of the Seven Seas!"

*Viva Las Vegas!* (Rocky Mountain Caskets, Provo, UT). "The end of life need not be the end of the exciting and glamorous world of gambling! Memorialize forever those thrilling nights when grapes and oranges spun, bells rung, lights flashed, and the fabulous jackpot seemed just within reach. Constructed of aluminum and steel, the casket comes in three finishes: standard Slot Machine Silver, glossy Blackjack Black, and—for those who lived with true gaming panache—premium Jackpot Cherry. The interior is finished with a Winners' Circle™ velvet-covered mattress, and our unique Roll-of-the-Dice™

pillow with its 'Lucky Seven' dot pattern. Ensure that your loved one will rest eternally among the gaming atmosphere which gave his life the excitement and meaning he could find nowhere else."

> *The Majestic I* (and *II*) (Joie de Vivre Industries, New Orleans, LA). "For the plus-size man or woman, this casket celebrates a lifetime of culinary excitement. Built to extra-wide proportions, it can accommodate loved ones up to 500lbs. (*The Majestic II* can accommodate loved ones up to 700lbs. For still larger sizes, please see our Il Grande line, which can be custom built for loved ones up to 1100lbs and have slotted bases for use with a forklift.) Our SureHeft® extension handle system allows for up to twelve pallbearers on each side. Extra-strong bracing (made with the same high-tech carbon fiber material used by the aeronautics industry) strengthens the bottom of the casket so there is no chance of a malfunction when the unit is lifted. The upholstery is made of high-density plastic foam guaranteed not to shift or deform for two years. The lining is made of a new, soft, yet strong nylon-cotton material available in several scrumptious: Chocolate Brown, Cheesecake Yellow, Red Velvet Cake Red, and Mint Ice Cream Green. Contact the manufacturer for other options or special requests."

—Who can look over this list and not be impressed by it? Note, too, that these are all *American* companies. That is not by accident. Such originality could only have come out of a country, out of a people, with a history of individual independence, of freedom of thought, of taking chances; of, in short, the kind of free-market capitalism which sees a need and fulfills it. The country that gave the world the telephone, the light bulb, the transistor, the microprocessor—and dozens, hundreds of other inventions which have advanced the quality of life the world over—is now offering caskets built to reflect the predilections of the deceased. Granted that some people have expressed skepticism at these innovations: for instance, some Europeans. The French, for instance, have published articles deriding these caskets as further examples of "crass American commercialism." Well, commercial they may be, but so what? Don't people have a right to make a living? And the last time I checked the Frenchies weren't exactly giving their stuff away. As for "crass," that is hardly the right word to describe something which helps grieving families by providing a tangible way of honoring and remembering their loved ones. And you may be sure that foreigners, for all their grousing, will sooner or later adopt this American style just as they do in so many other things, and for the same reason: because it satisfies a human need or desire.

As interesting as all these personalized caskets are, none of them struck me as wonderful as the one I had seen at the Hoffstein funeral. It had left a great and lasting impression on me. Even several weeks after the funeral I often thought about it. Where had it come from? Who had made it?

I called every funeral home in Oyster Bay to ask if they had provided it to the Hoffsteins. None of them had. Then I tried calling places in the surrounding areas. After my twentieth call I hit upon the right place in the nearby town of East Norwich. The funeral director, who probably regarded me as a potential customer, was happy to give me information, saying:

"Yes, I remember it very well. I believe it was Mrs. Hoffstein who picked it out. It was very nice."

"Stunning!" I said. "I couldn't take my eyes off it."

He told me it came from a company called Progressive Industries, in Hope, Arkansas, which specialized in "high-end" products. He would not disclose the price of the Hoffstein casket, only saying that it was expensive and shrewdly adding that the company did not sell directly to the public but only through "authorized dealers," of which he was one.

"Do you have any more?" I asked.

"No, I just had that one. But I do have a catalogue here. If you're interested you could come by and we could go through it together."

I told him that I would have to think about it and thanked him for talking with me. No sooner had the call ended than I looked up Progressive Industries online and contacted them for a catalogue of my own.

It came in the mail a week later: a 32-page, 11" x 8" publication filled with glossy pictures of the most stunning caskets imaginable. Most of them looked like grand, somehow royal chests embellished with carvings of leaves or animals or architectural details. There were only six models, two in each category: an "Empire" line, which took its design cues of arches and Corinthian capitals from Imperial Roman, a "Cathedral" line, which used the slender, winding, graceful traceries of the Gothic age, and the "Renaissance" line, similar to the "Cathedral" with the exception that the decorations were busier and bolder. Every casket had a magnified "blowout" photo of some decorative detail to highlight its intricate craftsmanship. I could not help but notice how the copy accompanying these photos echoed opinions expressed in my reviews. For instance it emphasized the importance of creating an atmosphere which will "contradict and overcome negative emotions," of "providing a focal point which will elevate the service into something truly special," of "enabling the family to take pride in the moment," and so forth.

I called the phone number in the catalogue and asked to speak to someone who could give me more information about the company, and was put through to the owner and CEO, Mr. Dante Mc-Cough.

I was pleased and flattered to learn he knew "all about" me and my work. He was a regular reader of Betterfunerals.com, a "big fan." I told him about the Hoffstein funeral, mentioning also the name of the funeral home which had provided his casket, and he not only remembered the sale, which had taken place two months earlier, but even remembered the model of the casket.

"That was the *Paradiso Mark II*," Mr. McCough told me. "It used to be part of our mid-range line. They were very nice and a great value. But since then we've moved on and are only producing for a still higher end of the upscale market. They're in the catalogue we sent you."

"Yes, they all look great! I've been drooling over them for the last two days."

"Thanks. We had a professional photographer come in to take the pictures. Took him a whole day."

For the first fifteen minutes we discussed his products, their manufacture and design, and how he had started his company, but then our conversation drifted to other areas. We found ourselves agreeing on a lot of things. We had a great rapport and al-

most before I knew it he had invited me to Hope, Arkansas, for a tour of his factory, hinting that it
might be a subject for me to write about.  He even
went so far as to say he would pay for my flight and
hotel.  No doubt he was looking for the free publicity
my website offered—by this time it was pretty well-
known in the industry—but  that was understandable and in return he would be giving me material
my readers would be interested in.

I took the trip a week later. I got to Bradley International at 7:00 PM on a Friday night, and
landed in Hope about four and half hours later.
Then it was right to the hotel for a good night's
sleep.  The next afternoon I met the man who, it is
no exaggeration to say, is revolutionizing an important part of the funeral industry.

Dante McCough is a Texan born and raised and
rather stereotypical of his heritage; is tall, lean, angular, tough;—not the kind one would want to get
into a physical confrontation with.  His accent is
Texas-thick; his speech direct, perhaps even at times
a little gruff.  He is not above cracking a lascivious
joke.  He is one of those people who does not think
before he speaks and therefore occasionally says
things that can be taken the wrong way, though they
seldom are because there is also an essential inno-
cence about him: he so clearly means well.

When I called him from my hotel he invited me
to lunch with him before taking me to his factory.
He picked me up a little before noon in his Cadillac
and we drove out first to his home where he introduced me to his wife, Patty, who had made us burg-
ers and fries accompanied by salad and a delicious
homemade coleslaw.  As we sat down to our meal

one of the first things I asked him was, "So, how long have you been in the casket business?"

He flinched at my question, or rather at my language, and said, "I notice that you use that word in your reviews, but don't you think that's a little old-fashioned?"

"How so?"

"Well, I know everyone uses it, but really—I think it's time for that to change. It has too many negative connotations. I prefer to use the term 'memorial enclosure.'"

I smiled at his creative use of language. He used that term in his brochure. Out of deference to him as my host, I nodded as though in approval.

"Because ideally," he went on, "we'd like to take all references to death and dying out of the memorial industry. They have no place in it—not really. All that doom and gloom—as you often refer to it— that's the enemy, that's the thing we've got to get rid of. And that's the philosophy behind our company: we make products to be enjoyed, that bring pleasure into people's lives, and just when they need it most. I like to think that when people see a Progressive Industries memorial enclosure, no matter how devastated they may be over losing someone, they can't help feeling nice and warm inside. Frankly, I'm determined to do all I can to take death out of dying, and put some life into it."

I nodded in agreement.

"And didn't you write somewhere that people need to start getting serious about dying?—that they need to start growing up and become adults, and not try to sweep it under the rug?"

"I'm sure I've expressed that idea several times."

"Well, it's a damn good one! Dying is like eating and sleeping—sooner or later everyone has to do it. And if everyone has to do it, then it's high time we started making the best of it. A depressing funeral is a sign someone didn't want to face reality. It's a sign of immaturity, or maybe just plain stupidity— take your pick. Anyway, it's certainly a bad reflection on you and rude to your guests. I'm aiming for the day when anyone who gives a shabby or depressing funeral will be regarded as low-class—real trash!"

It was refreshing and heartening to see how much influence my work had had on this man, who was putting its principles into practice.

He related in greater detail how he had founded his company. He had started out as a carpenter working on home construction sites, responsible for the wooden framing and so forth. From there had advanced to building cabinetry, decks, fireplace mantels, and other more complicated items. Then he became interested in furniture-making, which he was passionate about and from which he sought to make a living. But he discovered that to make a living from this labor-intensive work he would have to charge prices few were willing to pay when they could get something factory-made for a third the price. Then the event occurred which would change his life: the death of his beloved dog, Peanut, a nine-year-old Pomeranian who was hard of hearing and had been sniffing about the railroad tracks near her then house when a freight train ran over her. "As you can imagine," he said, "there wasn't much left of her—just a paw and a tail, The train took the rest of her away. It was heartbreaking!" He had intended to bury her remains in a plain cardboard box, but affection for the animal impelled him to do honor to her memory with something more elaborate; and two days later he had created a lovely little casket with inlays of various woods and designs carved into its sides. When his wife saw it she said, "I hope one day *I* have one that nice!" That gave him the idea that there was a market for something more artful and attractive than the everyday casket.

He began building one for his wife. Hadn't she said that she wanted one for herself? Of course he knew, as he worked on it, that she hadn't been so literal as really to want to be presented with her own casket, no matter how well-made and attractive, and that she might regard it as a roundabout expression of an impatience for her demise. But he also knew the purity of his own intentions and Patty's common sense. After two months of working on it in his spare time, it was finished, and very pretty it was, intricate with designs made of variously-colored woods and accented with shiny brass fittings. How he managed to keep it a secret from his wife while working on it, he didn't say. She probably never had much of an interest in his woodworking projects and so never visited the shed where he worked on them. He presented it to her as an anniversary gift.

"You should have seen her expression when I pulled the cover off it," he said.

As he spoke his wife managed a tight smile as though even now she wasn't whether she should be angry or pleased. Certainly at the time she was *not* pleased.

"Tell him what I told you," she said, turning from him to me.

"She said I'd be the first one to go into it," Mr. McCough admitted, blushing a little.

"There I was," she said, "expecting a nice piece of jewelry or maybe a new car, and instead he gives me a coffin. Thanks a lot!"

"A memorial enclosure," Mr. McCough corrected her.

*"Whatever,"* she said.

"She was pissed off at me for a while after that," Mr. McCough said. "It took her a whole month till she finally came round and saw that it wasn't such a bad gift after all."

"No, dear," she contradicted, "it wasn't that I didn't think it was a bad gift—it *was* a bad gift." And to me: "He's just lucky that I'm a practical person. I figured I was gonna need it one day, so I might as well have it." And to him: "Tell him what I made you do."

"I had to make one for myself," he admitted.

"You're damn right," she said. "If I'm gonna have my memorial enclosure ready, he'd better have his ready, too, because for sure he's going to need it before I will!"

"I'd love to see them," I said.

"They're not here anymore," Mr. McCough told me. "Patty didn't want them around, so I keep them at the warehouse."

We continued talking about his business and the industry in general. He expressed his dismay over alternatives to proper burial, such as cremation, which he despised as much as I did, and mentioned, with even more distaste, the newer alternative of "water cremation."

"Water cremation?" I asked.

"Ah so you don't know about that?  Well, let me tell you something, if you thought regular cremation was bad, this is a lot worse!"

He explained that water cremation, or, as it was more properly called, "alkaline hydrolysis," was the latest degrading version of disposing of people in an "environmentally friendly" way.  The deceased was put into a stainless-steel capsule and immersed in caustic chemicals which dissolved him in four or five hours.  The process required about sixty gallons of water and unlike its fiery counterpart, created no noxious fumes so that no carbon was emitted into the atmosphere, thus helping to reduce global warming.  All that remained was a heap of friable bones so pure white that they look as though they were made of plaster, and which could be ground into a powder as fine as confectioners' sugar and which was pure calcium phosphate.

"Isn't that nice to know?" Mr. McCough sneered. "Pure calcium phosphate?  It's touted as a 'natural' compound.  It even has nutritive qualities: in the diet it helps builds strong bones and teeth.  Very good!  It won't be long before they find a way to recycle it, maybe to fortify breakfast cereals!"

"Harrowing!" I said.

The subject of water cremation inevitably brought up the "Green Movement," as it relates to burial practices, and, as might have been expected, my host could hardly wait to decry it.  He had given a lot of thought to it and traced its origin back to conventional religious training.  Christianity, Judaism, Islam, and every other religion he could think of, stressed the littleness of man before God.

"And that is always wrong, wrong, wrong!" he said, vehemently. "For when you believe that man is as 'nothing' before the Almighty, when you put him in the same relative position to a god as an insect might be to a man—then what intrinsic value does he have?   Why should there be any objection to stepping on him, crushing him, as you would a cockroach?   But I reject this.   I say that Man is God's equal.   I go even further and say that Man is greater than God.   Yes, *greater!*   For without man, where would God be?   No object without a subject, as the philosophers tell us; consequently, a being, a concept, without a mind to contemplate it, is a logical impossibility.   Thus Man deserves enormous credit as the upholder of the godhead.   And this is why his funeral should be as magnificent, as glorious, as celebratory as possible, a homage to his importance in the universe.   On the other hand the 'Green Movement' is disgraceful precisely because it would pack us up and away like so many faucets to be crated up for shipping, or potatoes to be tossed into a sack. Disgraceful and disgusting! Appropriate for scoundrels, for violent criminals and the like, but intolerable for people who strove to live good and decent lives.   They should go out of the world with dignity, in splendor, like kings and queens, their memorial enclosures as grand as golden chariots."

"Well said, Mr. McCough!" I exclaimed.

"Now, now, dear," his wife said, "don't get yourself worked up again."   She glanced at me with a somewhat apologetic smile as though to excuse her husband's vehemence.

"It just pisses me off, that's all," he said, fidgeting

a little in his seat. He settled down and content-edly continued eating his lunch, but that he contin-ued to think about the issue was apparent when, after about fifteen seconds, he resumed:

"It's not just in this country that people are go-ing crazy. It's happening all over the world. Did you know that in Japan they have electronic ceme-teries?"

He explained that on account of the expensive-ness of real estate in that overcrowded island na-tion, even a narrow burial plot has become unaffordable to many Japanese, who have come up with the idea of the "electronic cemetery." It is lo-cated in a building which from outside looks like any of those around it—it fits inconspicuously into its neighborhood. Its basement descends many floors below ground and contains hundreds of rows of storage racks on which are lined up urns in the shape of golden eggs. A clawed mechanism, not un-like those which one finds in arcade game ma-chines, travels back and forth on tracks over these aligned eggs. It is computer-controlled. Relatives come to pay their respects by entering a room out-fitted with the traditional red and gold ornamenta-tion of a temple, but there is also a screen on which they can poke out the identification number of their deceased. This sets the robot claw in the basement to stop over their loved-one's egg, snatch it up, and transport it, via a complex of conveyor belts and lifts, to a softly-lit alcove in the visiting room. The door to the alcove opens, and the golden egg glows there magically while a little Buddhist bell poignantly rings. Visitors' heads bow, their hands come together, and they offer prayers. But no sooner do they end their devotions and leave the room than the little alcove goes dark, its door closes, and the dirty work behind the scenes begins again: the robot claw comes down from above, grabs up the egg, and with computer-controlled, electro-mechanical precision, it is returned to its spot on the subterranean shelf.

"Can you imagine?" Mr. McCough asked, sneering with disgust. "You live your whole life, you work, you raise a family, you go through so much—and you wind up inside an egg in a basement! And what if nobody ever comes to see you? You just stay there, in your egg, in the dark, lying on a shelf and gathering dust with a thousand other 'eggs'!"

"The place must look like a hatchery in a monster movie," I remarked.

"Oh, that's good! That's very good! Yes, that's exactly what it must look like. It hasn't come to this country yet, but just you wait—it's only a matter of time before some nut here tries to start the same nonsense! I don't have to tell you that even the traditional memorial enclosure is threatened with crazy ideas. Have you seen the wicker ones?"

"I can't say that I have."

"Well, look 'em up. There's plenty of pictures of 'em on the Internet. They're horrible! Put someone in one of those and you might as well send him off in a picnic basket! It's ridiculous!"

"It sounds it."

"And then the 'burial wraps.' Have you seen those?"

I shook my head, no.

"They're even worse! Basically they're just bed sheets, like the ones you sleep on each night, only maybe a little thicker. They have leather straps so you can tie them around the deceased, who winds up looking like a mental patient in a straitjacket."

"Horrible."

"But even that's not the worst of it. The company that's been making them out of cloth is now making them out of 'biodegradable plastic.' It has a reddish-brown color and it makes the deceased looks like a giant hot dog. How is anyone supposed to take a funeral like that seriously?"

"I certainly couldn't."

"Of course not! You'd pan it. You wouldn't even give it a one-coffin rating."

"Mr. McCough you are extraordinarily well-informed about the trends in the industry. Kudos to you."

He took the compliment graciously, saying modestly, "Well, I am in the business, after all."

After lunch he drove me to his factory ten miles away. It consisted of two buildings, one larger, the factory proper, where his products were made, and a smaller one where they were packed for shipment and stored.

First we toured the factory. Much of it is automated: computerized saws and routers do most of the cutting and shaping of the raw materials. These basic pieces are afterwards handed off to workers who refine their surfaces or shapes, which are in turn brought to the artisans in a space walled off from the noisy machinery and who either individually or as a team create the details of the final enclosure, each one of which is therefore unique. The designs are sketched out and sent to Mr. McCough for approval. Then, with precision tools, the artisans, sometimes wearing magnifying lenses, gouge and chip, and sand and plane, their designs into wonderful existence. During my visit I watched one of the workers putting finishing touches on a representation of ivy leaves folding in and out among one another.

After its exterior is finished the casket is transferred to the upholster, a woman who has worked in the textile industry and consults with Mr. McCough on fabrics to be used. Her priorities are quality of the material, visual appeal, and comfort. She and an assistant can complete the most complicated upholstery, with all its pleats and crimps, in about four hours. Quality control includes her lying in each casket for at least ten minutes to ensure it is completely comfortable, for, as she says, "If I wouldn't want to spend ten minutes in it, I don't see why anyone would want to stay in it forever." Another dedicated worker!

I noticed that all Mr. McCough's products were made of wood and asked him about it. He explained:

"A few reasons. Wood is easy to work with, for one thing. And it has natural beauty. We've also come up with proprietary stains and polishing methods, and we have specially-made tools for all that. But most importantly, it *breathes*. Metallic memorial enclosures don't breathe. Their manufacturers claim they can be 'hermetically sealed' and advertise that as a benefit, as something that will help preserve the deceased. Well let me tell you right now that's a lot of hogwash. In fact it's a dirty lie! Metal memorial enclosures are no better at preserving the deceased than wooden ones, and the hermetically-sealed kind are the worst of all because they seal in aerobic bacteria—the kind that don't require oxygen, and produce putrefaction rather than decay. Do you know what that means? It means that rather than gradually and gracefully becoming a part of the earth, a part of the cycle of life, a nutrient for the trees and grass, so that one does, in a sense, live again as a leaf or a flower—instead of that you just lie there growing more and more rotten, getting softer and blacker, till within two or three months you're just a blob of stinking bubbling putrescence! The pressure that builds up in such an enclosure is immense, and if you were stupid enough to open it you'd be blown away by the disgusting explosion. No matter how sturdy the seals are they eventually give way. It might take decades, perhaps even fifty or sixty years, but eventually they fail, and in the meantime you're just lying there, stewing in the obscenity of your own gelatinous stench. Oufa! Who would want that for their loved ones? I'm sure most people would never choose that if they were made aware of it. It's something you might want to mention in one of your reviews."

I couldn't help smiling at the asperity of his opinions; clearly he had given a lot of thought to the subject. It was inspiring to see an entrepreneur, in business to make money, also inspired by a larger ideal, which informed the design and construction of his products. But they were prohibitively expensive, and when I mentioned that he might make a few unimportant compromises in order to make them more affordable, he replied;

"Even if I cut a few corners I couldn't make anything good for under $6,000. But believe me, it wouldn't matter. I tried that. It doesn't work. The average person isn't interested in buying anything nearly that expensive. They're content with the cheap stuff from mainstream manufacturers. That's why I decided to go upscale, to cater to people who had the means to afford and appreciate the finer things in life. In a way I feel bad about it because it shuts out so many people from a better funeral, but like I say, most people are too concerned about costs, and between you and me, let's face it, they don't have the slightest notion of what a good funeral is. They just want to get it over with as fast as possible."

His strategy of producing only for the uppermost end of the market was working: his sales were doing well in such places as Malibu, Palm Beach, and Long Island's North Shore. He mentioned that several "high-profile" people had been among his customers, but declined to name names out of respect for their privacy, though he assured me they were some of the most well-known people in the worlds of entertainment, finance, and politics. Some of his purchasers had been so enamored of his products that they could not bear to see them buried but used a plainer, drabber, less-expensive casket for the actual interment.

"That's what gave me the idea," he said, "for our upcoming 'Ultra Excelsior' line of display enclosures."

" 'Display enclosures'?"

"That's right: they're only for display—only for the funeral, but they don't get buried. It's going to be sold with a companion enclosure—something a lot simpler but still tasteful for the actual interment. Want to see what I'm talking about?"

"I can hardly wait!"

He conducted me out of the finishing floor to another part of the factory. We came to a door, which he opened, politely extending a hand for me to enter first. It was a large room filled with the first memorial enclosures of his upcoming "Ultra Excelsior" line.

What struck me first about them was their size: they were almost twice the size of a regular casket. Nine feet long and four feet wide and high, each one looked big enough to accommodate two, perhaps even three normal-sized bodies. They were made of oak, maple, or poplar whose grains had been matched as closely as possible so as to give the impression that the whole had been constructed out of a single piece. Exotic woods were used as inlaid trims. They came in contemporary and traditional designs, the former taking its cues from Art Deco and having intricate zigzags, starburst shapes, and soft curvatures. They all stood on four feet at their corners: some in the shape of lion's paws, others tapering down with Shaker simplicity into ends of shiny brass or silver-plated stainless steel, and one ending in large balls of ruby-colored crystal. Polished to a high gloss, varnished and sanded several times over, their surfaces were as smooth and reflective as mirrors. Each was unique, for each, in its decorative phase, was the work of an individual artist.

There was one that stood out from this remarkable group. Like the others it was large, but its design derived from classical Greek architecture and culture. Four Doric columns rose at its corners; the end panels were decorated with triglyphs and metopes, these last ornamented with medallions showing noble profiles of mythic gods; and the public-facing side displayed a bas-relief of a feast or festival with robed men and women standing or sitting in graceful poses, some of them with outstretched hands in mutual greeting, others with cups raised to their lips, still others bearing wine-filled amphoras. The figures had been meticulously executed, their limbs and faces ideally beautiful, the flow of their robes marvelously realistic. One stood in awe at the large amount of time and talent it must have taken to create them. There was only one word to describe it, and it was the word I allowed myself to utter:

"Magnificent!"

"Thanks. We think so too. This one's the top of the Ultra Excelsior line. We call it *The Royal Athenian*."

"It must have taken a long time to make it."

"Four months," Mr. McCough said, proudly.

"Who sculpted these?" I asked, and couldn't resist the temptation to reach out and touch several of the figures.

"Oh, that's my boy, Mark," McCough said, pride in his expression and affection in his voice. "Don't get me wrong: not my son. Just works for me."

"He's very, very good."

"The best!" McCough said.

He told me how he had searched "high and low" for someone who could do this level of work. Then he saw a few of Mark's sculptures at an art show, and tracked him down. "Guess where this kid was living? In a trailer outside of Houston. A cheap, broken-down trailer with a leaky roof. He had been sculpting all his life but couldn't make a dime from it. Anyway, I offered him the job and gave him carte blanche. He still isn't making a lot of money with me—can't afford to pay him what he's worthtill the line takes off. But it will take off—it's already taking off; and then I'll be able to compensate him more fairly for his work. In fact he'll be getting a percentage on each sale of the Excelsior line he works on. In the meantime he's happy as a lark just to make a living at what he loves to do. And you can see that he loves his work: stuff this good comes out of joy, not drudgery."

I could only wonder at what The Royal Athenian was going to cost and asked about its price in a roundabout way by saying:

"Something like this must be tremendously expensive."

"Yes it is. It retails for $100,000."

"No!"

"Yes!"

"But who could afford that?"

"Some people can—someone already has: this one's sold. I'm sure he bought it for an investment. You have to remember something: this doesn't get buried. It's a *display* enclosure. It's something bought once and used over and over again, for generations. The whole family can use it: mothers, fathers, aunts, uncles, kids, grandkids—everybody! And that's quite aside from its artistic value. You could put this into a museum and people would gather round to gawk at it and take pictures. I've read your reviews long enough to know that you believe funerals ought to be a lot more than a scene of misery and mourning, that one ought to get real spiritual and emotional lift out of it; well, what do you think's going to happen if you put something like this in a funeral parlor? How many people do you think are going to be crying and 'carrying on,' as you like to call it, when they have this in front of them? I'll tell you how many: none! They're going to be too busy staring at it, admiring it. And you know how, during a viewing, people feel obliged to go up and look at the deceased even though they don't want to? Well, stick the old geezer in something like this and you'll see how fast everybody comes running up for a closer look. And they won't have to force themselves to stand there, either. No sirree. They'll stand there for five, ten minutes at a time—they won't be able to tear themselves away. But when they *do* tear themselves away it'll be with a sense of having seen something special, of feeling good about it."

As he had been speaking I bent down to get a better look at one of the details at a corner and noticed a cord descending from the back and leading to an electrical outlet in the wall. I straightened up, asking uncertainly, "Does this have to be plugged in?"

"Ah, so you noticed! Well, it doesn't *have* to be: but it does if you want all its features. There's a lot of technology built into this thing. Watch this." He turned to *The Royal Athenian* and said in a moderately loud voice, "Head panel—Up 30%!" As if by magic the head panel of the enclosure rose, slowly, and stopped about a third of the way up. "Foot panel—Up 100%!" And sure enough at the sound of his voice the foot panel slowly rose till it stood up at a ninety-degree angle.

"Voice-activated controls," he said to my mar-

veling self.    Returning his attention to the enclosure, he commanded: "Lights: 247 dash 221 dash
48!"

—And a series of LED lights, hidden beneath
the rims of both the head and foot panel lit up with
a soft yellow glow, and when he said, "Lights: 121
dash 48 dash 247!"—the lights changed to a soft
purple.   He called out various sets of number, and
each time the lighting changed to a different color."

"What are those numbers?" I asked.

"RGB values," he said, explaining that they were
universal color codes.

"Amazing!"

"We're not finished yet.  Follow me."

He walked around to the back side of the enclosure and gently pushed inward at one of the decorative rectangular panels there, which proved to be a
separate hinged part.   It moved inward slightly
then sprang outward to reveal a metal faceplate
with several labeled dials and buttons.  He said:

"*The Royal Athenian* is a very sophisticated
piece of technology; it's computer-controlled and wi-
fi enabled.  That means that every setting you can
make to it manually you can also make over the Internet, via your home computer or smartphone with
our patented 'Celestial' app.  For instance, let's say
something comes up—something unexpected—and
you have to call off the funeral for a day or two.  Or
let's say there's a really large family and the funeral has to be extended two or three days.  Ordinarily the deceased would have to go in for a whole
new round of cosmetic refreshment but with the
Athenian you just close the lids, like so"—he
pressed a button, and the top panels of the enclo-

sure closed—"then turn on the 'Eterna-Cool' setting, like so." He pressed a button and a soft whir could be heard emanating from the base of the enclosure. "And there you go!—the built-in refrigeration unit turns on, maintaining a temperature of 35° Fahrenheit and keeping your loved one looking fresh for up to a week at a time."

"You're kidding me!"

"No, sir, I am not! This thing takes an active role in keeping the occupant looking fresh. Here's how we see it: when a funeral is done right—when it's really something uplifting, something that makes you feel good about yourself and the world—why should it be limited to just a few hours or a single day? It should last a lot longer: a few days, maybe even a whole week."

"Does it do anything else?" I asked, turning my attention back to *The Royal Athenian*.

"Well, these," he said, pointing out a few more buttons and dials, "are for the video. You didn't notice it—you weren't supposed to—but there are two tiny cameras, one of them among the figures of the front side panel, and the other is built into the head panel, on the inside, facing the occupant. Each of these is capable of taking high-definition video. You can record the whole service, or, if you happen to be away and just want to check on your loved one to see how he's doing, you can use the app to switch views to the interior camera. There are also two hidden microphones, one at each end of the enclosure, so you can have stereo sound."

"Remarkable. And all controlled by an app?"

"That's right: for your smartphone or your home computer. It goes over the Internet. You just punch in your code and voila—you have full access to all the features. And we intend to add a lot more new features. We're working with a software company in Taiwan that handles all that. The software and firmware updates will be available on our website."

At one point he excused himself to take a phone call and I chatted with a few of his employees who happened to be milling about. They hardly made more than a living wage yet they all professed contentment with their jobs. You could almost see it in their smiling or contented faces. This was especially true among those responsible for decorating the enclosures, for they took pride in their artistic contribution and regularly tried to impress and outdo one another. Called upon to exercise what was best in them—their intelligence, their creativity—they were enthusiastic about their work and found it endlessly fulfilling. One fellow told me that he usually got so "caught up" in his job of producing decorative moldings that he lost track of time, that the day whizzed by and it was time to go home before he knew it. He often wanted to work overtime, though this was not permitted on account of certain labor laws which would have mandated Mr. Mc-Cough pay higher hourly wages. What a difference between such workers and their sour, glum, resentful counterparts in almost every other industry! It just went to prove that the only real success in life is joy in one's work. An endless and indolent leisure seems an ideal to most people only because it is better than the alienating labor which has turned their lives into a hateful torture. But to work at something one loves, and which demands the best, most creative part of one's faculties;—to

awaken each day impatient to do again what brings
one pleasure, and makes the lives of others more interesting or easier:—what could be a greater blessing? All the workers here hoped this was the last
job they ever had, and many of them said they
planned to be buried in a company-made enclosure,
perhaps one of their own making.

When Mr. McCough returned to me I offered him
my phone and asked him if he wouldn't mind taking
a few photos of me beside *The Royal Athenian*.

"Be happy to!" he said.

He snapped away a few shots: of me, smiling
with my left hand resting proudly on the foot panel;
—of me, smiling and leaning in toward the open
head panel, giving a thumbs up sign;—of me, not
smiling and standing at the foot of the enclosure, my
hands clasped before my waist. I buttonholed one of
his employees to take a few shots of us standing together before the *The Royal Athenian*. In these photos you can see the pleasure in both our faces. Mr.
McCough gave me permission to use them on my
website.

My trip to Arkansas and Progressive Industries
was an inspiring testament to American inventive-
ness and the entrepreneurial spirit. Mr. McCough
had risked his own capital and hard work to make a
product for which he saw a need, and now he not
only fulfills that need but also is changing an industry for the better. He is even having a positive influence on the nature of work itself by enabling people
to exploit their better talents. The social benefits of
this cannot be overestimated.

I was no sooner on the plane back home the next
morning than I began writing my article about his

company and products. I also decided that I would purchase for myself a memorial enclosure from his company—not *The Royal Athenian*, which at my age I wouldn't have enough time to save up for, but some other less-expensive model which would nevertheless make a good showing. Mr. McCough said he would give me a discount.

# XI
## MORE INNOVATIONS

It is said that Napoleon, when he met Goethe, turned to his entourage and exclaimed admiringly, *"Voilà un homme!"*—"There's a man!" The same might be said of Dale ("Dilly") Diller, the funeral director of Spring Gardens Memorial Home in Bristol, Connecticut. He is someone who always understood that his industry had been stuck in pessimistic drabness and needed a new, fresh direction. As much as I would like to take credit for his refreshing perspective on funerals, the fact is that his was the result of no outside influence but came instead from his own distinctive personality.

I knew nothing about him when I entered his establishment to review the funeral of Jacob Williams, who had died in a motorcycle accident. According to the obituary the poor young fellow had died twenty-four days earlier—though that was apparently a misprint. I had chosen to attend it because his family owned a chain of grocery stores throughout that part of the state, and had the means to provide a good service. The moment I stepped into the funeral parlor I knew I was in for a treat. It was bright, airy, and invigorating. Sunlight flooded through the tall narrow windows. The furniture was contemporary, upholstered in an off-white fabric, and had sleek lines and polished chromium-plated metal, glass, and translucent, almost luminous acrylics. A rug with a design of sharp blue, light green, and yellow-gray patterns covered the center of the floor of polished bleached birch. A few abstract paintings, all original oils, hung on the wall. Even the doors leading to several visitation rooms were interestingly attractive: white with pastel purple trims and pewter knobs and hinges.

But it was the visitation room which surprised me—and left me unsure of what to think about it. It was unusually large and dim. The ceiling was black, which gave a sense of great space overhead, and the floor sloped gently downward to the front of the room, where a platform, led up to by three steps on either side, formed what can only be called a stage. The seating was padded and theater-style, consisting of twenty rows bolted to the floor, each row consisting of fifteen seats across with seven on each side and an aisle down the center, and each comfortably distant from the one behind and before it so as to allow one to stretch out or cross one's legs. The walls were dark beige and interrupted in three places by pleated drapes about six feet wide and extending from ceiling to floor. They not only broke up the monotony of the walls but also hid the loudspeakers connected to the audio system, for a dais and microphone was often placed on the platform for the use by ministers or eulogists.

There were already some fifty persons gathered, sitting silently and looking toward the stage where the casket rested on a bier draped in white cloth onto which shone tiny purple and blue spotlights located at floor level. Soft music was playing and sounded very good: it was crystal clear, as soft as the air itself, yet its bass lines were deep and rich, the decay of the notes, even at this low volume, perceptible.

I took a seat in the middle of the room. I noticed that the front row was unoccupied—the family was not present. This odd fact was not lost on others, who whispered their confusion over ittill —whisper by whisper—we all found they would arrive when the "service began." In another ten minutes it did. The lights of the room dimmed. The tiny purple spotlights which had illuminated the bier shifted in color, going from a soft pink to a dark peach, then shifting again from a light blue to a velvety cyan. At the same time the music became a little louder and onto the wall behind the casket a series of images were cast of the deceased in his younger, to his middle-aged, to his older days. It was now that the family entered the room from the back They walked down the aisle and climbed the short stairs to the stage, spreading out before and around the casket and looked on their dearly departed. What an odd yet refreshingly affecting spectacle was formed by them before the casket! Colored lights still twinkled upon them and the bier, and the volume of the music rose. It was all unexpected and different from anything I had ever seen.

In a few minutes the family took their seats in the front row while the lighting shifted from one soft color to another. Someone arose to deliver a eulogy. She was not a minister or any religious official; somehow one saw this at once in her young and pretty person, in her casual and poised address as she strode to the front of the room and mounted the platform. A spotlight shone on her and for a few seconds she stood looking out at the guests whom she surely couldn't see for the darkness before her. She seemed used to this—to being seen without seeing.   She stood silently for several seconds as though to ensure she had everyone's attention, then began speaking in a high, clear voice about the life and character of the deceased.  She spoke of his charming quirks as a child, of the promise of his youth, of his love for his family, of his dreams for the future, of the kindness which had made everyone like him.  She related things he had done which had been silly or foolish but which, far from denigrating his character, elevated it to the fallibly and loveably human.  She quoted things he had liked to say, repeating them as though she had herself heard them.  At one point she came out from behind the podium, took a few steps forward (the spotlight on her always), and spoke yet more directly to the guests, this time becoming more emotional, but never faltering in her speech, never searching for a right word or a better phrase.

Was it a eulogy, or a eulogizing monologue? Only after she had finished did one realize that she could not have spoken it all impromptu.  It had been too clean—too measured—too well done.  People in grief didn't and couldn't talk like that; they certainly weren't so self-possessed.  My hunch turned out to be correct.  She was not a family member but a drama student who had been hired to perform the eulogy which the funeral director himself had written, or rather rewritten based on texts submitted by the family.  He had convinced them, as he did most of his clients, that the occasion was too sacred to risk awkward compositions and an unpracticed presentation.

Everything about the funeral was unusual, surprising, and stimulating. The appearance of the deceased was no exception, though not for the obvious reason—unless one knew why it *was* obvious. He seemed to be like any other young man who had met a regrettably untimely end. But as I stood before him I remembered that according to his obituary the date of his demise had been several weeks in the past. Yet he looked as though he had died only the day before. Somewhere, somehow, there was a discrepancy, and I wrote it off to a mistake in the obituary. It would not have been the first time a date was misprinted, though it seemed to me this was a gross example of it.

After the service, the funeral director stood at the front door and said goodbye to those who were accompanying the casket to the cemetery. I waited till I was the last one so that I might speak with him in private. He smiled politely when I reached him and said, "Goodbye, thank you for coming," and maintained his obliging manner even when I didn't move on but stopped and said:

"That was an interesting funeral, sir."

He nodded as though in thanks, yet also with uncertainty, not sure whether my remark was entirely positive. I wanted to leave no question in his mind about this, and continued:

"The lighting effects were remarkable. I've never seen that at a funeral. Very innovative. And the way the family came into the room, in single file, then spread out across the front of the casket ... and the young lady who gave the eulogy ... all quite unique."

"Thank you, thank you," he said. He glanced outside and saw the last of the guests getting into their cars. "Aren't you going with them?" he asked.

"You know what, Mr. ... I'm sorry, I don't know your name?"

"Diller. Dale Diller."

"Mr. Diller. Mr. Diller, the fact is I wasn't really very close to the deceased and ... well, I'd rather talk to you about the interesting service I just saw."

His smile faded somewhat as he asked, "Are you a funeral director?" He was suddenly suspicious. His first thought (as he later informed me) was that I was an operative for another funeral home and sent here on a mission of corporate espionage.

"Not at all. I'm just a curious layman."

"A curious layman," he repeated; and looked at me skeptically. "I've been in the business for twenty years and I've never come across a 'curious layman' before. You must be involved with the industry somehow."

As mentioned earlier I am disinclined to reveal myself to funeral directors, but this one was as sharp as a razor and able to sniff out untruths and deflections the way a bloodhound picks up a scent. It also occurred to me that in this one instance it might be a benefit to reveal myself because my credentials might secure his confidence. I told him that as a matter of fact, and if he absolutely must know, I *did*—"sort of"—have a connection to the industry.

"And what connection might that be?" he pressed.

I mentioned my website, Betterfunerals.com.

"No!" he blurted out, and his eyes and mouth

flew open.

It was hard to say if he was angry or enthusiastic, though in another second he made it clear it was the latter by saying:

"Are you *really?* I go to it all the time! I can't believe it! You wouldn't happen to be ... you're not *the* funeral critic, are you?" And when I couldn't bring myself to lie to the man's face, and my silence equaled assent, he breathed, "Well, well, sir, this *is* an honor!"—and he put out hand, took mine, and shook it heartily.

—Really, he was as giddy as a schoolgirl meeting her pop star idol. He shook my hand for the next half a minute, singing my praises: what an inspiration I was to him, how my reviews had encouraged him to pursue his "vision," how weightily periodic, yet delightfully flexible, he found my writing style. In short, it was an honor for him to meet me and (this with a hint of anxiety in his voice) he wondered if I had found anything wrong with the service?

There were a few minor things, which, however, I didn't want to mention, thinking he would take them too hard, so I shook my head, no, and told him how I thought it was pretty good on the whole and just wanted to know more about him. Perhaps we could sit and talk for a while?

"I'd be delighted!" he told me. "Let's go into my office."

I followed him there. It was on the ground floor, at the end of a hallway. As he entered it, he asked:

"Would you like something to drink? Coffee, or perhaps a soda or something?"

"A soda would be fine."

There was a small refrigerator in the corner of

the room, and from it he took out two colas, one for me and one for him. He handed me mine, saying, "There you go! Would you like a glass?"

"Not necessary."

As he took a seat in the big plush chair behind his desk, he bade me have a seat in the armchair before it. He looked at me again with a wide, appreciative smile, and said:

"This really is an honor."

"You're too kind."

"No, no, I mean really—really it is! I think what you're doing for the industry is great. I have other undertaker friends and they all think the same thing."

"It's very gratifying."

"So you did like my service?"—a tad apprehensively.

"Oh, absolutely. Very good. Refreshing. I like the sensibility behind it. There was something ... *showy* about it—in a good way.""

He smiled with relief and gratitude. I asked him to tell me more about himself. How long had he been in the business? How had he come about offering his unique kind of service, and how had he thought of it?

He told me he had never intended to become a funeral director. What young person ever does? That was the last thing on his mind when, at twenty-three years old, he moved from Memphis, Tennessee, to New York City to pursue an acting career. Like so many actors he had to struggle for recognition—even to make a living. Throughout his twenties and into his early thirties he never got beyond acting in off-off-Broadway plays. Frustration with his stagnating career on the East Coast prompted him to move to the West, hoping he would have more and better opportunities in Los Angeles, where he spent the next six years with no better luck. He moved back to the East Coast where lived for a few months with a relative in Danbury, Connecticut. Desperate for work, he took the first job he could find: an assistant to a funeral director. He told himself he would only do it for a few months before finding something more amenable to his character.

But as the weeks and months went by he became accustomed to his job, especially because the pay was good. He also started having ideas about how to make the services more interesting. These he presented to his employer, who was, however, stuck in his ways and scoffed at the innovations proposed by his protégé; who consequently did what a lot of scoffed-at protégés do:—he went off to implement his ideas on his own. He became a funeral director and opened his own establishment.

His unique and (he confessed) dramatic presentation of a funeral service was influenced not only from his early experiences as an actor but also and more importantly from his conviction that much of life is theater. For with the exception of toddlers and the feeble-minded, people presented to the world an image of themselves somewhat, and sometimes very much, different from the reality. No one would get through a day without a confrontation if he acted just as he pleased and said just as he thought. We often smiled patiently when were annoyed, spoke pleasantries while harboring unkind thoughts, and remained calmly obliging in the midst our annoyed

impatience. Only the masks and falsehoods of politeness made civil society possible, and not the
finest, award-winning performances of stage or
screen could vie for the perfection with which people
every day acted out parts inconsistent with their
real characters. Having, through the course of our
lives, completed so many performances, should not
there be something special about the close of our
last scene? Should it not make the biggest and best
impression possible? Even those who had lived the
most obscure, unsuccessful, unhappy lives: didn't
they deserve to be, at least once and however belat-
edly, the stars of the show?

Taking that lifelong effort into consideration, it
had seemed to "Dilly" (that was his nickname,
which after a few minutes he insisted I call him)—it
had seemed to him that a funeral should highlight
the theatrical aspect which made up so large a part
of our existence. Guests should know that they
were more than mourners—they were *spectators* at
the last exit of a player on the stage of the world,
and that it should therefore be as grand, or at least
as magical, as possible. All three of Dilly's visitation rooms reflected his interesting perspective.
They took their design and architectural cues from
the theater. Thus the darkened ceilings, which
added an air of spaciousness and mystery, and
served the utilitarian purpose of obscuring any
lighting fixtures attached to it. Thus the floors
which sloped gently downward toward the front of
the room to a raised area upon which spotlights
could shine.

I mentioned the misprint in Mr. Williams's obituary, to which Dilly leaned back a little and said:

"What misprint?"

"Well, the obituary said he died last month."

"He did."

"How can that be?" I asked. "He looked so good. Was he refrigerated?"

Dilly shook his head and said, "Nope."

"I don't understand."

"I'm using something new—I mean, for clients like Mr. Williams, who can't make their appearance in a timely fashion. It's a formaldehyde alternative. They've been using it for years in Russia. I forget what the actual, chemical name is ... something like buta- .. moxyl- ... nitrate-something. But Mold-Away™ is the trademark name. It was originally developed to prevent rye ergotism, but it does a first-rate job in people too."

"Really! I've never heard of it before, and I know plenty of funeral directors. You'd think a lot of them would be using it."

"They probably *have* heard about it," Dilly replied, "but just can't get their hands on it. It's not available here yet. It's patented and a lot of the American chemical companies don't want to pay the licensing fees to make it. Some people also say it's too toxic and bad for the environment—might cause problems by leeching into the water table. Personally, I don't think it's any more toxic than a lot of the stuff we use, and as you can see it does a first-rate job. But it does have its drawbacks. The main one is that it's highly inflammable, and very temper-ature-sensitive. When it's used on crops it's diluted, so you don't have to worry about that, but for em-balming you have to use its concentrated form, and then it can start to burn at only 120° or so. I would never use it in summer. Sure, we have air conditioning, but what if there's a power-outage and it got really hot in here? I don't want to be responsible for someone's loved one bursting into flames."

Unfortunately we couldn't talk as long as I would have liked to: there was a reception to get to and Dilly told me it was being held in a local restaurant with a reputation for good food. We took leave of each other, not without exchanging emails and my assuring him (upon his inquiry) that I would be happy to receive any information about proposed upgrades to his establishment.

The reception was held at a swanky Italian place called *Il Modo*, about five miles away from the funeral parlor. The food was tasty. I had a lovely eggplant parmigiana smothered in a delicious, garlic and basil marinara sauce, a mushroom risotto done to perfection (not gloppy at all, but with the grains of rice firm and somehow toasted), a side dish of broccoli rabe with white beans, and a small plate of stuffed artichokes. For dessert I chose cannoli filled with chocolate egg cream, a slice of rum cake, a slice of cheesecake, a slice of carrot cake (with a whipped vanilla icing which was fabulous), and a couple of puffy cheesy-lemony sfogliatelle, all washed down with a couple of cups of cappuccino. To make the event still more enjoyable the family conducted themselves with gracious reserve, and there was a pretty girl across the room with whom I exchanged a flirtatious glance or two, though I shied away from introducing myself to her.

The headstone was something of a disappointment because it had a picture of a motorcycle etched into it in deference to the deceased's love of motorcycling.  Surely this was inappropriate, considering how he had died.  But it would have been inappropriate in *any* case.  How many times does it have to be said?  Headstones should not be marred by the whims of pictorial personalization!  What could be more appalling than a cemetery where every other headstone had picture of the deceased's hobby or interest?  Motorcycles here, cars there, woodshop tools in another place, RC airplanes on yet another—the list is as endless as it would be vulgar.  No, a headstone is supposed to be an ideal testament to the deceased, the solid bulwark resisting and rising above the fashions of the day.  Mr. William's headstone was a mark against his funeral, but on the whole it was good enough to earn ❚❚❚▖◌.

Given Dillie's background and consequent satisfyingly theatrical approach to funerals, it should come as no surprise that actors increasingly make up his clientele.  He wrote to me about a recent client who struggled to make a name for herself in acting and who had expressed the wish that at her funeral any grief would be expressed in *applause*.  As Dillie wrote me:

"It turned out to be a capital idea.  When the curtain was raised on her casket she received a standing ovation!  I can't begin to tell you how right, how uplifting and touching it was!  There wasn't a dry eye in the house, yet the moment was not so much sad as it was proud and joyous—as though the poor woman had finally gotten her due.  It seems too that the very act of clapping, of such a communal expression of approval, has a positive influence.  I am going to make it customary for all services of my fellow actors."

He emails me fairly frequently about changes he is making to his services and his plans for the future, perhaps in order to sound me out on my opinion. So far they have all met with my approval and encouragement. I am sure he would not mind my sharing part of one of his emails to me:

> .... To my mind (and to yours, I trust) nothing is more important than *atmosphere*. It decides the character of the funeral and the reactions of the family and guests. As you yourself saw for Mr. William's funeral, I use lighting and color to promote certain emotional states; in particular, to evoke in the audience an attentive peacefulness. And as you so often and rightly point out, music should also be heard during a service. I agree with you that live music is always best, but many of my clients either do not wish to have it or cannot afford it, so ours is mostly recorded. But the presentation more than makes up for medium, since we have a very good surround-sound system powered by high-current Krell monoblock amplifiers powering huge JBL horn-loaded loudspeakers strategically placed behind the draped walls. You have already heard it, so you know how good it is. I wish that I had remembered, while you were here, to give you a demonstration of the system. Believe me, when I crank that baby up to even moderate levels, the effect is truly spine-tingling!
>
> The family is expected to cooperate with our vision of the enhanced service. Two things especially are required of them: first, that they shall not draw attention to themselves by unseemly behavior (e.g., loud crying or sniffling) and thus upstage the deceased, and, second, that they shall enter the visitation room and dispose themselves around the casket in specific manner. Sometimes they balk at these suggestions, especially if they are still in shock over the passing of their loved one. They cannot understand why I would be directing their behavior

and even every movement at a time when all they want to do is sit there and cry their eyes out like so many dripping bumps on a log. It can take up to an hour to convince them that this would be disrespectful to their dearly departed, who most assuredly would not have wanted them to be so sad, and neither would have wanted people who were kind enough to show up and pay their last respects to experience undue stress. In short, I have to remind them that the whole point of the funeral is to honor their loved in the most *positive* way possible, since this is precisely what he or she would have wanted.

If we are expecting a large crowd, I hire a few young people from a nearby dramatic arts school as 'Ceremony Associates.' They greet the guests and lead them to their seats. They are attractive and talented, and have plenty of experience in standing before an audience and speaking lines. Depending on their skill level, I use them to deliver eulogies—and you saw for yourself how good they can be. They are encouraged to infuse their performance with a dignified pathos but never sadness. I always tell them (as you would) that our objective is to make the lives of the survivors and guests less, not more, miserable. You might be interested to know that the young lady who delivered the eulogy the day you were here has landed a supporting role in a big-budget movie to be released out next year, so her career is really taking off. Her name is Maggie Biscoff—a name to watch out for!

When you came to Mr. Williams's funeral the casket was already exposed; now, however, all caskets are behind curtains as the guests arrive. This adds another element of curiosity and anticipation to the service. Only after all the guests are seated does the funeral start. The house lights darken and a musical overture begins, starting out very low but rising to a moderate level. Conversations cease as everyone becomes aware that something is about to happen. I try to draw out the suspense as long as possible. It depends on the crowd. But it's usually never more than ten minutes because then people start getting restless. But it's just then, when everyone's impatient for something to happen, that the lighting and music change again, and the curtain rises to reveal the casket. Needless to say, this galvanizes everyone's attention. It brings an added measure of wonder and respect to the ceremony.

After the eulogy the immediate family takes part in a "viewing procession." As you saw at Mr. William's funeral they start off at the back of the room and proceed, with measured steps and to the sound of stately music, to the casket. Once they reach it they spread out on either side of it and stand there for several minutes. At this point changing and dramatic lights are cast on them, endowing them with a touch of dramatic mystery. I always remind them that it is especially now, when they stand before their audience, that they must, absolutely must, control themselves and refrain from any displays of grief lest it ruin the noble tableau we are trying to create. And would you believe it? To date, not one of them, even the most emotional among them, has broken down on me. They know they are in the spotlight. They know this is the most important role of their lives, and they've got to play it well. And they do.

They may remain where they are, or return to their seats, when the minister arrives. I always encourage him to wear most splendid regalia of his faith—whatever robes, staffs, miters, or jewelry is a part of it, and the more magnificent better. If they are simple pastors or ministers, who ordinarily wear secular clothes, I encourage them to dress as well as possible and add interesting or unexpected accessories to their outfits, such as hats, unusual glasses, rings, gold bracelets, and so forth; anything which will add an interesting dash to their appearance. They often resist this suggestion. They don't see what it has to do with a funeral. Again I have to argue. How tiresome it gets! But I always remind myself that I am working on behalf of a distraught family, of people who need my help, and so I don't let up in making the point that anything which distracts the family from their grief is necessarily a good thing. The ministers, if they are reasonable, if they aren't dogma-hardened petrifacts, find it hard to discount that kind of reasoning and eventually come round to my way of thinking.

Believe me when I tell you that guests who come to my funerals are always surprised. They can't believe what they're seeing and sit there with open mouths. Do some of them think it's inappropriate? No doubt yes, at first. But they soon realize that the assault against their spirits, which they had anticipated and steeled themselves against, did not happen; that instead they are fascinated, astonished, sometimes confused—but never saddened or stressed. Amid such lovely music, such interesting changes in color, such choreographed movement, negativity has little place. Indeed they realize that for the first time they are at a funeral they can actually *enjoy*.

By next year I hope to take my services to the next level and realize an exciting concept which I call 'Funeral in the Round.' This will require a new, much larger visitation room, which will be circular and feature in the center a round platform on which the bier, casket, floral arrangements, and any musicians hired for the service will be placed. Curtains surrounding the platform will hide it till the service begins, whereupon they will be drawn up. The platform will be able to rotate, and the bier will be outfitted with a mechanism by which to raise the casket at a 45° angle so that, as it turns, everyone can get a good look at its occupant.

But that is not all! I am taking the lighting to the next level. The high, black-painted ceiling will be crammed with the latest computer-controlled systems capable of limitless color combinations and patterns., Image multiplexers, pinpoint spotlights, gel filters, gobo patterns, and so forth will be used to create exciting effects on the circular platform as well as on the attendees themselves. Video projectors will flash onto the walls various photographs or videos taken from the happiest moments of deceased's life. These mesmerizing lights and images, accompanied by synchronized music calculated to enhance wistful and pleasant (but never gloomy!) sentiments, will make Funeral in the Round a truly stimulating audio-visual experience. I am even looking into holography as an option. Just think how wonderful it would be if we could make the deceased himself appear and address his family and friends!

One has to hand it to Dilly—he is a true innovator, a real artist, as well as an entrepreneur with a keen understanding of the marketplace. Having gained a following among people in the performing arts, he intends to capitalize on this success and open another funeral parlor in Hollywood and advertise himself as "Undertaker to the Stars." His dramatic interpretation of a funeral is bound to generate a lot of business from people in the entertainment world. Who knows but that one day his services may even be broadcast as television specials, complete with celebrity-filled audiences and special appearances by famous singers, dancers, or actors, who will grace the stage with cameo performances? I can foresee him as the Master of Ceremonies overseeing the glittering, star-studded event. Such broadcasts would surely have a positive influence on reshaping the public mind about funerals, since children would grow up with a whole new paradigm of how inspiring, indeed how much pure fun, they can be.

I also asked Dilly to give me more information

on MoldAway™ and he referred me to his Russian exporter, from whom I learned that it was not a Russian product but—yet again!—the result of American research and ingenuity. Only the laboratory where it was made was in Russia. The patent itself was owned by Keefe Chemicals Co., headquartered in Secaucus, New Jersey. I contacted the company and asked for more information, and was put through to a sales representative who quoted me figures of quantity and price—he was looking to make a sale. I explained to him that I wasn't interested in buying but in reporting on it. Knowing that as a salesman his motive was profit, I told him about my website, making it sound much more popular and influential than it is, saying that it was ready by "the whole industry" and it would be great advertisement to his product. He took my name and number, saying he would pass them along to the "right" people.

The right people, or rather the right person, turned out to be the chemical engineer, Dr. [PhD] Earl Muffin, who had created MoldAway™. We talked for a half hour and he was happy to tell me about why and how it had come about. Keefe Chemicals specialized in detergents, disinfectants, and produced one of several formaldehyde solutions used by funeral industry. But sales for this last item had been declining over the years due to competition from third-world countries where labor was cheap and safety standards low. He had been charged with finding something which was better as well as cheaper than anything which could be imported.

"The idea came to me," Dr. Muffin related, "while I was helping the wife with some housework. She wanted me to clean the refrigerator, which I did, and

I happened to find at the back of the bottom shelf an unopened bottle of salad dressing. It had been lying hidden there for over a year—it was six months past its expiration date. Well, being the thrifty sort, and curious to see if it was still edible, I put some of it on a salad I made myself for lunch. And wouldn't you know it! It was fine! Tasty as ever. I think it ranch—no, no, it was blue cheese! Anyway, as I was eating my salad it occurred to me that if we already have compounds that can keep a bottle of salad dressing preserved for over a year, surely we can improve on them and come up with something that can keep a dead person looking good for at least a month, and just as inexpensively. I studied the molecular structure of various antibacterials and dedicated myself to enhancing their preservative properties. There was a lot of trial and error involved. We must have gone through four hundred chickens."

"Chickens?" I interrupted.

"We tested our compounds on fresh chickens bought from the supermarket. You know: roasters, ready for the oven. We'd inject 'em and coat them with the latest version of the compound and leave them out on one of the lab tables at room temperature to see how they'd hold up. Most of the time they only lasted a day or two before they started to turn color and stink. We also had a big mishap in our tests when one of my assistants, who was hard of hearing, mistook my instructions for 14ml of nitroethylene and put in nitroglycerin. When I was injecting the solution into the chicken the syringe exploded and nearly blew my hand off! Anyway, after about four months, and endless variations and revisions, we came up with something which worked wonders. I remember how we injected it into a chicken on a Friday night with the expectation that when we came into the lab on Monday morning we'd find it as decayed and discolored as its predecessors. Instead it was perfect! It looked so nice and yellow, was so soft and plump, that really, I thought some-one was playing games and had replaced our test roster with a fresh one. But no—not at all. It was the same one. So we let it sit there. And each day it stayed the same. A whole week passed, and it looked great. Two weeks passed, and it still looked great. Three weeks—still great! Only midway into the fourth week it started to flatten out and stink a little—but just a little. It far exceeded our expecta-tions. We also tested it on pork, beef, and lamb, on which it worked equally well: so of course there was no question that it would work on people too."

"Doctor, that's fascinating!"

"What do you think of the registered trade name, 'MoldAway'? Like it?"

"It's certainly catchy."

"We had a contest in the lab to see who could come up with the best name, and one of the assis-tants came up with that one. She won a clock radio. Now don't get me wrong," he continued, "it's not a perfect product. It has its downsides. It's as toxic as formaldehyde per unit, though much less so *in prac-tice* on account of the lesser amount of it that has to be used. It's also inflammable at a rather low high temperature, though this is much higher than will ever be encountered in normal situations."

"And yet it's not available in the United States?"

"It *is* available: it just has to be ordered from

overseas distributors."

"Why is that?"

"Because there's a lot of corruption in our country. Keefe Chemicals is a small company; we don't have clout to go against the big boys who are turning out formaldehyde by the ton and want to ensure there's a market for it. I'm sure the EPA was bought off. They said they couldn't confirm the 'safety' of MoldAway™ for mortuary purposes, so they banned its sale in the United States. We worked around this by submitting it again as an agricultural product. We had discovered that in a diluted form it could kill and prevent fungal infection of cereal plants, though it had to be used early in growth cycle to ensure that it left no residue in the harvested product. Well, they wouldn't approve that either, and for the same reason: 'concern for safety.' But note that while they banned the *sale*, they didn't ban the *use*. That's how we got around it. We licensed it to overseas labs. So technically speaking, you can use in the United States, you just can't buy it here."

I requested that he send me any test documentation he might have about the product and a list of his overseas distributors, saying I would post the information on Betterfunerals.com. He did so, and two weeks later I wrote the article describing how an old bottle of salad dressing inspired an important innovation for the funeral industry. I gave it the title "From Eternal 'Ranch' to Eternal Rest," even though, to be precise, the dressing wasn't ranch but blue cheese; but surely I will be permitted some creative license here?

One thing, as they say, always leads to another,

and while writing "From Eternal 'Ranch' to Eternal Rest" (isn't that a nifty title?) I discovered that seven out of the ten overseas distributors were Russian. While researching them I happened upon a company, also Russian, whose name translates into "Diamond Light Casings," and which seeks to dispense with caskets altogether and to present the deceased in a fundamentally new and potentially beautiful way.

The founder and CEO of this company is Mr. Andrei Kusnetsov. After exchanging an email with him, we spoke on the telephone and he told me in his broken English about his company. He had worked for years as a salesman for a Russian food importer. He had been very successful—was one of the top salesmen in his region. He had attended the funeral of an aunt—a degrading affair which had utterly depressed him—and was brooding about it while sitting at his desk staring at a "trophy" he had recently been awarded in recognition of having exceeded sales goals. It was one of those clear acrylic business trophies containing a three-dimensional version of his company's logo with his name, in golden letters and also three-dimensional, beneath it. These otherwise indifferent-looking items appeared wonderfully attractive in the crystal-clear casing. Recalling the bad impression his aunt had made at her viewing, he could not help thinking how much better *she* would have looked if similarly contained. And it occurred to him—why not? Why *not* give people the benefit of this polished, refractive, diamond-like material? Thus "Diamond Light Casings" was born. As Mr. Kusnetsov explained to me in his broken, halting English (the following is therefore something of a paraphrase):

"The process is similar to that which is used in the creation of business trophies but there are several important differences. The main obstacle we had to overcome was preserving the integrity of the subject while the acrylic was cured under heated pressure. We did this through recomposing the acrylic itself, so that it has a much lower curing point, and properly preparing the client. I can't tell you exactly how we do that—it's a trade secret—but I can tell you that it is a combination of chemical treatments and temperature control. After curing, which ensures any gas bubbles clouding the material rise to the surface, the casing is sanded and polished to a high gloss. The result is breathtaking! If light-diffracting facets are added, it's like seeing your loved one in the middle of a gigantic diamond. I'll be happy to send you some pictures."

—Which he did; and which were indeed breathtaking. Rather than set on a bier, the deceased in the Diamond Light Casing is set upon gold- or silver-colored prongs in much the same way a gemstone is set into a ring. When a soft blue or amber light is shone up into and suffuses the acrylic, it glows with color and result is magical, entrancing. I could not help thinking of Dilly Diller when I saw these pictures: here was something he could certainly put to good effect! I copied the address of the website and emailed it to him, and the same day he wrote back to me with, "Outstanding! Thanks for the info! Will definitely look into it!"

We can learn a lot from people like Dilly Diller, Dr. Muffin, and Mr. Kusnetsov. We can learn, first of all, that the great advances in a given field are not necessarily the result of years-long, single-minded dedication. Sometimes they are merely the happy coincidence of capacity (character) and circumstance (chance). Of those two factors I am inclined to think the former is more important, since circumstances may be fairly constant or repeat themselves yet never be taken advantage of for lack of someone with insight into their possibilities for exploitation. As in history, so in the funeral or any other industry, the influence of an individual personality should not be underestimated. Western societies have tended increasingly to dismiss this notion. Even in America, where individuality and thinking on one's own was traditionally encouraged, and has unquestionably resulted in great technological advancements, there has been a shift to encouraging people to be inventive or work out problems in a more general, more "inclusive," way, which is usually summed up in the word (always uttered with an air of reverence) "teamwork." Now let me assure everyone that teamwork never did nor ever will come up with anything extraordinary. Even in a "team" which makes some significant breakthrough, you may be sure there was one person in particular who was responsible for it. The notion of the effectiveness of the "team" is really a monstrous adoption from the corporate world, which has been romanticized out of all proportion to what it is, namely, a place where fourth- and fifth-rate intellects are busy from morning till night in sixth- and seventh-rate endeavors. Such people have a penchant for calling together "teams" in which their ideas are heard, pondered, discussed, modified, and generally treated seriously by creatures as empty-headed as themselves, and in sessions ending with literal or figurative pats on the back all round, this the equivalent of throwing dust into one another's eyes in an attempt to blind themselves to their common foolishness.

# XII
## A DOSE OF REALITY

Here is the peril of work which is too gratifying: it induces a state of constant low-level euphoria which distorts one's sense of the passage of time. Caught up in the blur of busy contentment, the months and years pass less noticed than they otherwise would. And then something happens which brings home to you how much things really *have* changed. It may be that one sees a friend or relative for the first time in years, and is surprised to discover they have become parents, or grandparents. Or one hears a favorite song, which was one of the delights of one's youth, only to realize it came out twenty or thirty years ago. But the worst case is when someone we know dies. One day I learned this about my cousin's wife. Bill and I had been fairly close when we were young, though we had drifted apart as people do in growing up. We had spoken now and then on the telephone, he calling me out of the blue every five or six months to say hello. And so when he called me again I thought it would just be a pleasant brief checking in to see how I was doing. Instead, his voice cracked as he spoke, then he cried into the telephone, telling me that his wife had died, and in the most horrible way.

He and Corinna lived in New Hampshire and every autumn took a trip to Maine to go crossbow hunting. While out in the field they lost track of each other and Bill, hearing a rustling in the brush ahead, thought it was a deer or a bear, and fired: but in fact it was Corinna. She had momentarily taken off the bright orange cap which hunters wear as a safety precaution and was bending over to shake a pebble out of her boot when he, thinking she was a bear behind the brush, shot her. He was horrified to discover what had happened: there she was on the ground, the bolt through her neck; bleeding, her limbs flailing, her eyes wild, desperate as she choked on her own blood;—just like so many of the animals he had shot in the past. The funeral was planned for two days after his phone call.

I was surprised that he wanted me to go. Over the preceding few years two of my uncles and one of my aunts had died, and their children, my cousins, had neither called nor written to me to tell me about when the funerals would take place. In fact my family had pretty much stopped expecting my presence at funerals after finding out I reviewed them professionally. (I had made the mistake of confiding the name of my website to a second cousin, and the blabbermouth had pretty much broadcast it to his known universe.) Did *Bill* know about my critical work? I believe he did but I don't think this factored into his decision. Either he had never read my reviews or took it for granted that I could never be so indiscreet as to criticize the funeral of a relative—about which he was right.

In the end I went. Why? First because, as I say, I was surprised at receiving the notice at all. And second because it roused up in me a nostalgic sense of family feeling.  Bill breaking down on the telephone also affected me greatly.

Everyone looked so different, so much older, from the way I remembered them.  Aunts, uncles, cousins, second cousins—they had all become much older, grayer, heavier, slower; just as I undoubtedly was to them.  Half the exuberance of greetings exchanged at such times is in part an effort to hide one's surprise at the transformation which has taken place in people one has not seen for a long time.  Yet one finds that after all they are essentially the same. They have the same twinkle in the eye—the same tilt of the head—the same inflection in the voice; they smile and nod and move just as we remember them; so that however much their hair has thinned or their movements slowed, our surprise at the changes in them is counterbalanced with the comforting assurance that they are the same people we have always known.

Of them all Bill looked the worst.  He was the thin, pale, nervous wreck of his former confident and cheerful self.  He had been beating himself up with guilt since the accident. His wife's family had been beating him up still more.  With the crudest, most offensive words they could muster, they had blamed him for his wife's death.  They had openly called him a murderer.  By the time of the funeral they had stopped speaking to him but they never turned their eyes in his direction without expressions of disgust and condemnation.

Corinna's mother was a chunky woman of fifty-seven years old and sat in front row of the visitation room.  Every article of her clothing was completely black except for a horrid brown handkerchief she repeatedly dabbed her eyes with. She would be silent for several minutes at a time, then suddenly throw out her hands and shriek something in Greek— making everyone jump and causing her sons and daughters to gather round her, patting her, stroking her, trying to calm her down by effusive assurances of their love and understanding. Her outbursts triggered a chain reaction of weeping.

Really, it was too much!—totally unbecoming to those who indulged in it, and stressful to the guests who had taken time out of their lives to pay their respects. After all, it wasn't as though Corinna had died the day before. Almost a week had passed since the accident. The worst of the shock should have been over by now. It is likely that Mamma had mostly cried herself out and it was the tawdry nature of the funeral which had renewed the worst of her grief and caused her uncontrollable outbursts.

For instance, Corinna's casket was a cheap Asian import. It was all black: even the hinges, even the handles. Vinyl veneer covered its fiberboard construction, and crudely overlapped itself at the edges. The metal fittings were not cast but stamped, and nailed in rather than more securely screwed. A few staples were visible at the edges of the bedding whose scant padding consisted (one could almost see it through the thin material) of excelsior. Talk about poor workmanship!

Corinna herself was looking pretty bad. A thick satin collar surrounded her neck, probably to hide her mortal wound. She had never been a pretty woman, but she had been charming, cheerful, patient, and devoted: her inner beauty had shone out of her living face and manner, and had made her attractive. Now that her spirit had gone, her physical self had to make whatever impression it could on its own merits, of which there weren't many. Thus she needed all the help she could get, but the cosmetologist had not done her any favors. Her makeup was grossly overdone: the rouge too red and delineated, the lipstick too thick, and a blue eyeshadow extending too far out on either side of the eyes to which long artificial lashes had been applied. Her teased out hair stuck out like an unraveled steel wool pad and looked as though she had received an electric shock. She wore some kind of silky or satiny gown which might have come straight out of a vampire movie. Altogether it made for a harrowing impression.

When I took Mamma's hand to offer her my condolences, she nodded a few times with her head bowed and gulped, "Thank you for coming." Suddenly she pulled me toward herself and started crying violently, her whole frame shaking and leaning toward me for support. It was unexpected, shocking, and rude. For a moment I was flustered. I tried to calm her down, saying gently, "I know, I know ..." and "I'm so sorry, so sorry ..." and "I understand ..."—all the while trying to pull away, but she had clamped down on me with the grip of a dragon. My nerves got the best of me and I yanked my hand away with an imperious, "I'm sorry!"—and rushed back to my seat. One can imagine how irritated I was.

The only high point of the service was the Greek Orthodox priest who led the prayers and delivered the eulogy. He came some twenty minutes after the service had started and made a grand entrance. It would have been a lot grander if his entrance had been accompanied by music, by some sort of orchestrated, processional march, but he did pretty well without it. A loud and perhaps purposeful bustle behind the closed door announced his arrival, and when everyone in the room turned toward it the door swung open to reveal Reverend Father Osteopopolous.

He was old, at least seventy, maybe eighty, with a long white beard and decked out in the Byzantine splendor of the vestments of his office. His *phelonion*, or covering robe, was made of blue velvet embroidered in silver- or gold-colored thread sewn into intricate crosses and patterns of leaves and vines. Beneath this an *epitrachelion*, or stole which wrapped around his neck, descended past his knees, its sides trimmed in gold-colored fabric, embellished with flower-patterns amid more crosses, and ending in golden tassels. His *kalimavkion*, or flat-topped priest's hat, was not the usual black but dark blue and also embellished with Christian iconography. Last but not least he grasped in his right hand a crozier as tall as he was, lifting and lowering it as he made his way down the aisle with an air of authority. The guests rose in respectful greeting. His expression was severe as he glanced to his left and right, and only softened a little when he reached Corinna's family in the front row. He took their hands and offered them his condolences. Everyone in the room sat down and watched him step up to the casket.

He stood there with his back to us, his head bowed and his hands before him for a few seconds in what seemed to be silent prayer. Then, still holding his crozier, he raised his hands, stretched out his arms, and in Greek obtested heaven in Corinna's behalf, his ornate robes spreading out on either side of him. After he had done this two times he turned around to the family and the guests and stood there silently, almost demurely, his hands close in to his chest as though in the meekest humility, then he slowly raised his arms—the sides of his robes expanding like the glittering wings of some fabulous bird—and when they had extended to their fullest extent he assumed a disapproving expression and exclaimed:

"Θεός!" Theos!—God!

—The word exploded into the room. It was so sudden, so loud, that if it didn't make one jump (and a few people in the front row did), it certainly made one lean back as though against an assault. It was the opening shot of a sermon by turns loudly condemnatory, earnestly imploratory, and sadly contemplative: rising to a galvanizing loudness one moment, only to subside into an almost apologetic murmur the next. But the high sharp moments were always sudden—so many verbal thunderbolts coming out of the blue. A few times he held out his crozier toward us as though its polished cap would shoot forth a stream of destructive lighting. What with his flowing vestments, his long beard, his severe expression, his often loud and warning voice, he looked and sounded like some Old Testament prophet come back to life to denounce threats of destruction on an erring world. I couldn't understand a word he said (it was all Greek to me), but he seemed to be threatening any of his auditors who doubted the truth of their religion, and to be assuring them that this was not the end of Corinna but her new and better beginning. His dictatorial manner seemed at odds with such a hopeful message, but perhaps he had calculated that a softer presentation would not have enough point to penetrate a distracting grief. At any rate he engrossed everyone's attention; poor Corinna had quite receded into the background. Even Mamma had momentarily stopped her crying and sniffling and sat up a little straighter to watch him attentively.

Did he *believe* what he was saying? A man so old, with a long experience of world, who knew what was and wasn't possible, and who, like any other modern, had the benefit of centuries of scientific discovery and speculation behind him—did he *believe* in his brand of hocus-pocus? It was hard to say. It depended on one's outlook on the human condition. From an optimistic point of view he accepted the legitimacy of his faith based on the metaphysical concepts underlying it, but which he knew to be too abstract for a majority whose understandings were not quite so subtle or refined: *they* required purely worldly events and characters, along with (and as contradictory as it might sound) a huge dollop of fantasy thrown in, and would in any event have no interest in a religion which did not assure them that their disappointments in this world would be compensated by rewards in the next. From a pessimistic point of view, on the other hand, he was a charlatan, a man who knew he was pulling the wool over peoples' eyes, but who could have a good conscience about it because, after all, that was what they wanted, and were better off for it than otherwise. Besides, it enabled him to make a living—and even a priest needs to eat.

Reverend Father Osteopopolous belabored us with warnings, adjurations, and promises of paradise for forty minutes. He might assume a kindly tone as he spoke of salvation, only in the next moment to shout out the terrible things awaiting those who did not do rightly. By the time he ended his ministrations he had pretty much worn us all out.

While preparations were making for closing and removing the casket for the burial, I approached the funeral director and introduced myself. I asked him about the casket, saying I had never seen one "quite like it." The equivocation didn't throw him off: he knew I was referring to its low quality. After telling me the brand name ("Happy Dove," made—does this surprise anyone?—in China), he tried to exonerate himself from any involvement in its use by saying:

"Unfortunately the family were not in a position for better options."

"I see. That's often the case."

"I just hope there aren't any accidents this time," he said. "The last time we used a Happy Dove casket the bottom fell out as we were lifting it for interment. And the gravesite was on a small hill, so the body actually rolled down the incline."

"No!"

"Yes."

I shook my head, speechless. But you could see he knew it was a chance he would not have suggested taking. Then I mentioned Corinna herself, saying that I thought her makeup had been applied in a "most interesting" way.

Again, he knew what I was getting at. His cheeks flushed a little as he blew out a sigh, then said with some embarrassment:

"Too much, right? That's Candy's fault. My cosmetologist. I keep telling her she's overdoing it but she doesn't get it. She can't get out of her nightclub mentality."

"What does that mean?"

"She was an exotic dancer before she came here. She thinks all that stuff looks good."

Fortunately the bottom didn't fall out of the casket when it was transported to the cemetery and Corinna was laid to rest uneventfully. I did not attend the burial, having been so depleted by the depressing service that I actually needed some time to recruit my spirits. I waited at the church for the reception, which was to be given in its social hall, and at which Bill was understandably absent.

The food was good and plentiful. The maternal side of the family had done exactly what I always suggest poor families do when they cannot afford a well-catered reception: provide their own food. Consequently they had laid out a spread of tasty homemade Greek dishes: moussaka, spanakopita, pastitsio, bowls of tzatziki with lovely rounds of slightly-charred pita breads, small bowls filled with green, red, and black olives, skewered souvlaki, various hot and cold condiments, and, on another table, for sweets, trays of baklava and the fresh, creamy, custardy galaktoboureko. There were wines aplenty, both red and white, both dry and sweet, and soft drinks. It was all nicely presented on two long tables covered in white linen and decorated with centerpieces of bowls of flowers in the center of which a single candle flickered charmingly. Unfortunately the lighting was too bright to create a soothing ambience and the seating was inadequate because some of the chairs were ranged against a wall, which always makes those who sit at them feel uncomfortably exposed.

But the biggest and most unforgivable fly in the ointment was Corinna's mother, who simply would *not* be quiet and let people enjoy their meal. I had just put into my mouth a delectable piece of spanakopita when out of nowhere came an explosive "Nooooo!"—which almost made me jump out of my skin. The next thing I knew Mamma was throwing out her arms, looking about in wild-eyed distress, and holding her throat as though she had swallowed a fork. Like a nuclear trigger her behavior caused a chain-reaction among her children who also started carrying on. How was anyone supposed to relax and eat with all this commotion going on? And what kind of host goes through the trouble of cooking a lot of good food and then makes it nearly impossible for anyone to enjoy it? Even the most sympathetic guests were getting a little tired of these repeated outbreaks, especially if they had been about to rip into the moussaka or the souvlaki. They would freeze, their forks held mid-air, and turn with guilty yet irritated expressions to watch the mother's disturbing antics. Some of them took to filling their plates and discreetly leaving the room to go into a corridor outside.

I did not review my cousin's funeral out of respect to my family and—I confess—out of embarrassment. How could I not have been embarrassed when it comprised almost every atrocity of bad taste? People would naturally tell me, or think of me: If your own family doesn't take you seriously—if even *they*

don't follow your advice—how can you expect anyone else to do so? The answer to that is easy and
credible enough, namely, that consanguinity is no
guarantee of shared values. One's relatives are like
everyone else, just regular people who don't think
twice about accepting the same disgusting conven-
tions my work is trying to improve. But if
Corinna's funeral had *not* been that of a relative, I
could not have given it more than ❚❚❑❑❑;—and that
only for the spark of showmanship provided by the
Reverend Father Osteopopolous.

Days after Corinna's funeral I was agitated and
a little depressed. This had nothing to do with grief
over her death, since I had not been close to her,
nor could it have been on account of the way she
had died, though that was tragic enough. It was
because (I realized after some consideration) her funeral had been *so* bad despite her relationship, however distant, to me. What a pickle I would have
been in if another funeral critic had reviewed
Corinna's service and reception, and mentioned me
as a relative at that horrid affair! It would have
been a slander hard for me to live down because it
could not have been credibly denied.

Moreover this death in the family reminded me
again of my own mortality. By the time your aunts
or uncles, and certainly some of your cousins, have
died, you are old enough, mature enough, to understand that they weren't *so* much different in age
from yourself, and that therefore it is unreasonable
in you to expect to live much longer than they did.
Thus they become the warning standard of measurement of the extent of your own life. Granted
that Corinna's death had been unnatural, a bizarre

accident; but accidents and sudden illnesses happened all the time. I was still healthy, vigorous, and
extremely handsome, but "something" could happen:
an air conditioner could drop out of a building and
fall on my head, or I could be cut down with a stroke
or heart attack.  You just never knew where you
would—or wouldn't—be the next day, nor even the
next thirty seconds.

Nearly always having been aware of this, I have
made arrangements for my own funeral.  I have
done this the more thoroughly because I have no
children who might have been relied on to make the
arrangements for me.  And even if I had children, I
would know better than to leave it up to them.  How
many times have I seen sons and daughters cheap
out on their parents!  Even when they were loving,
dutiful, and had the means and desire to do the
right thing, they simply didn't have the taste, the
breadth of mind, or the nobility of spirit to ensure a
good service but rather took the thoughtless conventional route, and committed every desecration of
darkness, and malignity of misery, of which vulgarity
and ignorance is capable.

Fortunately I come from a generation which was
raised to believe in self-sufficiency.  Having nearly
always known that a good funeral is expensive, I
have saved up for my own over the last twenty years
by living as frugally as possible.  I have never gone
on a vacation, never bought more new clothes than
were necessary to remain decent, and never gone to
bars or restaurants.  I have eaten the least expensive foods and bought only enough fresh fruits and
vegetables to maintain my health.  I have even for-
gone coffee or tea, drinking only plain water that

comes out of the tap. Every possible dollar, say rather every nickel and dime, has been carefully and methodically squirreled away into the bank. And the result? The accumulation of a small fortune which will enable me to give myself the kind of funeral I deserve.

Before anyone accuses me of having foolishly given up immediate and definite joys for a future benefit I will not be aware of, let me say this: I am *already* aware of it. It has been, and will be for as long as I am alive, a daily, ongoing pleasure for me to know that my funeral will be top-notch, just the kind of thing that would have earned a rating of at least ▮▮▮▮.

# XIII
## INTIMATIONS OF IMMORTALITY

In planning for my own funeral I have met with three talented funeral directors. Why three? Out of an abundance of caution, in the unlikely event that two of them keel over before I do. My first choice however is Mr. Walter Slate of Morning Bright Memorial Home in Bridgeport, Connecticut. I have attended several funerals at his establishment and they were all excellent, earning ratings of at least four coffins. He not only brings a certain *joie de vivre* to his funerals but is also a nice guy who gives his customers value for their money; and as he is twenty years younger than myself, he should certainly outlive me. When I contacted him about possibly providing my funeral he was pleasantly surprised and flattered, for he is a fan of my critical work. We made an appointment to discuss the matter one weekend and worked out some rough preliminaries, such as which room in his establishment would be used (the biggest), the kind of seating that would be available (padded armchairs throughout), the kinds of floral arrangement (oversized sprays), and so forth. We agreed that indirect lighting would be used and in the warm, sub-2500 kelvin range. Borrowing an idea from Dilly Diller, I proposed throwing up against the wall behind the casket a golden light in a fan-

shaped pattern so as to look like the spreading
rays of a sunrise, and Mr. Slate assented enthusiastically.

"What about guests?" he asked.    "Any idea
whom you'd like to invite?"

That was something of a sticking point.    The
fact is that I don't know many people, and the few I
have known over the years would probably be
happy to see me gone. I provided him with a list of
a few family members who might, or might not,
drop by.  He was skeptical of the low number and
reminded me that a good funeral required something of a crowd.  For a few minutes we sat racking
our brains trying to figure out whom else to invite.
Then his face brightened and he said:

"I have an idea! Why don't we make it an open
service for the industry?"

"How so?"

"Easy!  A lot of my people in the business know
who you are.  I'm sure they'd love to go to your funeral!"

"That's not a bad idea."

"And you know how we undertakers are: at
heart we're all gossips and busybodies: we just love
finding out what other guy is up to. Sure," he said,
nodding reassuringly at me, "if we have an open invitation they'll be lining up around the block to get
in here and see how well you've done."

"You mean how well *you've* done," I corrected
him.

He nodded, somewhat modestly, and said, "Well,
we're working together.   But yes, we could get
enough guests easily enough.  Now, will this be an
open-casket viewing?"

"That depends on how I look."

"Oh, I'm sure you'll look fine. You look pretty good for your age—no reason why you shouldn'ttill the end. And you know my cosmetologist is first-rate. But do you want us to go for the younger you, or the natural, looking-your-age you?"

"Definitely the latter."

"Any idea what you'd like to wear?"

"Formal attire, please."

"A suit?"

"A tux."

"Splendid! Any particular style?"

"Yes. White tie, tails."

"*Very* nice!" He almost clasped his hands together in enthusiasm.

"But no top hat," I told him. "That would be pushing it."

"Well, I don't think we could get the top hat in anyway, could we?"

"With the casket I've chosen, you probably could."

"Oh? What casket is that?"

I told him all about Progressive Industries and their products. By this time I had decided to buy a mid-range model in the "Renaissance" line in a custom light oak finish with gold-plated fittings. He listened with interest, though I detected a little disappointment that he would not be selling the casket to me.

Then we came to the matter of a minister or a religious service. As I belonged to no traditional religion because I couldn't believe in God as Grandpop in the Sky (Mr. Slate tittered at the phrase), I proposed doing without one and suggested music—a pianist who might play background music, in particular some soft beautiful melodies from Ravel, Debussy, and Rachmaninov, or some dreamy jazz standards. Mr. Slate agreed that this would be a nice touch. This still left the question of eulogy.

"I'm going to write my own," I told him. "After all, nobody knows me better than I do and I want to make sure it's well-written. Perhaps you could speak it for me?"

"I'd be honored," he said, adding that once he had it he would be happy to go over with me the tone he should take.

"Now, assuming we get a good crowd," I said, moving on to other matters, "I'd like to extend the funeral for as long as possible, maybe a whole week."

For the first time he looked at me with some concern. "What do you mean?"

"I mean there's never too much of a good thing, right? So if we draw a good crowd and people are really enjoying themselves, why not make it a week-long event?"

He looked confused. "I don't see how we could. I don't see we'd be able to ..."—he paused to consider how to phrase delicately his concern, the nature of which was clear to me, so I relieved him of the discomfort of broaching it by saying:

"Have you heard of a product called MoldAway?"

He shook his head, no. For the next few minutes I told him about the product, my firsthand experience with its marvelous preservative properties, and its implications for my funeral. The more he heard, the more enthusiastic he became. One of the refreshing things about discussing such matters with professionals like Mr. Slate is that they're al-

ways eager to learn about advances in their industry. He jotted down the name of the product, saying
he would look into it immediately after our meeting,
and that if it was as effective as I made it out to be
he would happily use it on me.

But then there was the economic question of how,
if the funeral proved to be a success and was extended for a week, we would handle the reception, or
rather receptions, afterwards. A new one every day
would be prohibitively expensive. But if only one reception were given, presumably on the last day of
the funeral, a lot of unscrupulous people might show
up only then to take advantage of a good meal. I
had to admit he was right about that because no one
knew better than I did how people turn into vultures
when they find out there's free food. But it was he
who came up with the solution.

"We can do this," he said. "During the week—
you know, the first four or five days—we just have
light refreshments after the service: just hors d'oeuvres and drinks. I know a caterer who would be
good for that—not expensive, either. We can compile
a list of people we would like to have for the main
reception to be held on the last day."

"Any idea where it would be?"

"We have a few options there, but the first one
that comes to mind is Markham Terrace. Ever been
there? No? It's very nice. They have a 'Grand Ball-
room' that's huge, with a gigantic crystal chandelier
hanging from a high domed ceiling, large round tables that can seat ten people at a time, and a raised
stage for live music. They host a lot of weddings
and bar-mitzvahs. I don't think they've ever hosted
a funeral reception but that shouldn't be a problem.

The thing is, they're always busy so you have to book way in advance, sometimes up to a year, so we could get it if you have a good idea when you're going to leave us. If you ever come down with something serious, and the doctor is able to tell you how long you have, and its far enough in the future, well, just let me know and I'll try to reserve the place."

"And if we don't have the time?"

"We have other options. I know of several banquet halls that are very nice and we wouldn't need more than a few days' notice. I take it you're looking for something formal, like a sit-down dinner?"

"Absolutely."

"Music?"

"Of course."

"Any particular type?"

"During the meal, something light—you know, something soft and low so people can talk comfortably. But maybe after the meal we could have something more lively."

"Do we want dancing?" Mr. Slate asked.

That was a questionable point. My whole professional life has been a crusade against the kind of dour and depressing atmosphere that makes so many funerals impossible to tolerate for more than five minutes; logically and ideally speaking, then, the reception for my funeral ought to be as joyous as possible, and nothing makes people happier after a few drinks than hearing music with a great beat and getting on the dance floor. I also recalled how, at the Hoffstein funeral, dancing had lifted everyone's spirits. The problem in my case was that it might be taken advantage of for mean purposes.

Having become fairly well-known in the funeral industry, I had plenty of fans but I also had my share of enemies—people who had been the subjects of harsh criticism in my reviews. It was easy to see how they would express their glee at my passing by a too-enthusiastic funky chicken. Why should I give those bums that satisfaction?

"No, let's not have dancing," I said. "But I would like some light jazz, and a singer too: someone with a good voice to sing some nice standards. Just some good entertainment—know what I mean?"

At the end of our meeting I let Mr. Slate know that I was going to contact two more funeral directors because, after all, neither of us knew what the future held and—who knew?—it was possible that he might die before I did. He commended me on my prudence but said he was sure I would die first because he was in perfect health and was a lot younger than I was. We walked together out of his office and at front door to his building we shook hands, and he said enthusiastically:

"I promise you it'll be the best funeral ever! I can even see it getting into the news! Which come to think of it might not be a bad idea. What do you say we send out invitations to news organizations?—invite a few reporters?"

That was a possibility, I told him, but hinted that we probably shouldn't expect much interest from that quarter: the mainstream media had never received my work kindly.

In the next few weeks I contacted two other funeral directors and went over possible plans with them. They were no less helpful than Mr. Slate. They both agreed to the general ideas I laid out, and both understood that whether or not they got the job depended partly on which of them outlived me. Mr. Halt of Serenity Funeral Home was especially understanding in this regard because he was seventy-seven years old, not feeling well, and admitted that he might not have the pleasure of seeing me die before he did.

The particulars of my funeral service and the reception having largely been taken care of, I turned my attention to finding a burial plot. I knew all the local cemeteries, having spent a lot of time in them, and none of them was acceptable to me because each was old and crowded—all the good plots had already been taken. As in buying a house, as in opening a business, so in choosing a burial plot, location is everything; and the major factor in finding a good one is the age of the cemetery. Owing to the practice of burying people from the "center outward," beginning from that place which, on account of its idyllic character, made the area seem suitable for a cemetery to begin with, prime locations become unavailable over time and new tenants must settle for less-desirable locationstill after twenty or thirty years all that's left is some remote corner or a weedy area behind a groundkeeper's toolshed. And after all my hard work, after all I had done for the industry, I was not about to let myself be degraded in that way!

My research led me to Serenity Meadows Memorial Park, one of the few new cemeteries in my home state. I happened to find out about it before it opened, hastened to contact the management company for a tour, and bought a plot located in the highest of its three major eminences. The plot is twenty-by-twenty feet, so I don't have to worry that after I'm gone undesirables might move into my neighborhood and bring down the property value with their tawdry headstones. The sales contract however did present a sticking point. A "limitations" clause in the fine print stated that the management company would not be required to "honor and maintain" any plot more than 99 years;—which was unacceptable to me. I said I required a minimum of 200.

The woman who worked for the management company and had escorted me on a tour of the grounds was not sure how to react to my cavil. At first she said there was nothing she could do about it, that the contract "was what it was," and was in keeping with industry standards "for our area." With some amusement in her voice she added, "Why would anyone need more than that?"

—The poor creature hadn't a clue. Ignoring her attempt to humor and reconcile me to the contract, I asked her if there was any way we could amend that clause in my case and extend it by another hundred years.

"Another hundred?" she asked, incredulously. "But we don't even know if our company is going to be around that long!"

"Most likely it won't be. But whatever organizations succeed yours will probably honor the contract, or at least we can hope they will."

She shook her head, doubtfully. I began to feel rising between us a conflict of wills which I couldn't win because she held all the trump cards, and so to avoid this I said understandingly:

"I know you don't have the authority to change the contract, and maybe it can't be changed, but is there anyone else in the company I might speak to about it?"

Again she shook her head uncertainly; she would have preferred to assure me she had the final word in the matter, but she knew I knew she didn't, and answered, "Well ... if you want to try ..."—and she gave me the name and phone number of her boss, the president of the management company.

I called him the next day and he too said there was nothing that could be done. I suggested that all he needed to do was scratch out "99" and write over it "200"—a process that would take all of three seconds.

Again he refused. I seemed to be at an impasse. The difference was that he, unlike his employee, could help me surmount it.

Contracts written for or by companies always have about them an aura of irrefragable legal authority even though they may be based on nothing more immutable than the preference or convenience of those who wrote them. But ultimately the motivation behind them is profit, and so in order to change them one needs to offer a motivation greater than the one for which they were written. In short, I had to resort to bribery. It had to be done subtly. One can never say outrightly, "Do this for me and I'll give you that"—at least not to people who think they are honest. Corruption is most effective when disguised as compensation for legitimate services rendered.

"I understand completely," I said. "I know you're busy, and to change a contract would take time. It might also require other legalities I'm unaware of. But I'm willing to compensate you for your time.  I could write you personally a check for, say ... $1000?"

There was a pause on the other end of the line; a few deep breaths; a lot of thinking going on.  Then, "We really can't change any contracts."

"Obviously it would take more of your time than I thought," I said.  "I would be willing to go as high as ... $2000?"

Another pause, this time longer; then, "Well ... I guess I could help you out ..."

I thanked him profusely and sent him the check.

Why did I insist on 200 years?  Why not longer? Because it wasn't necessary.  The monument I intended to raise on the site would, by that time, be regarded as a protected landmark.

As I have often written in my reviews, the quality of a headstone is very important.  Though I sometimes like to think my critical work will endure, that my reputation as a social reformer will live on, I know this is not likely to happen. When I go, so will go the only means by which my message has been able to reach people, namely, through my website. When it is no longer paid for it will be shut down, deleted with the press of a button by some bean counter at my ISP.  Though I have made hard copies of all my reviews, the likelihood of their publication will be small to nonexistent.  On the other, more hopeful hand, my tombstone, if it is solid and grand enough, will be apparent to living eyes for centuries. And I had long decided that mine would be as large and solid as possible within the considerable means which a lifetime of working and saving had enabled me to amass.

After some research for a headstone vendor, I settled on Mohindra & Meyers—a Hindu-Hebrew concern, "Purveyors of fine monuments," located in Lancaster, Pennsylvania. They were not just another mass-market outlet for pre-cut headstones of the vulgar squat rectangular kind; no, they created custom products, nearly always large and decorated with tasteful restraint. After looking over their offerings online, I called them about buying a monument for myself. I was put through to one of principals, Mr. Mohindra himself. After expressing surprise at my request (this was the first time, he told me, anyone had ever called to buy a monument for himself), he happily made an appointment for us to meet the following weekend.

Anyone who sees Mr. Mohindra for the first time has to be a little uncertain of what he's seeing. For he looks like a character out of central casting in the days when national stereotypes were the order of the day in Hollywood. He is 53 years old, of medium height, portly, and a Sikh. A very thick, very black handlebar mustache embellishes and stick out on either side of his dark, round, wide face. On the day I met him he wore a business suit, to be sure, but also—remarkably—a turban. Nor was it just any turban. It was large and fluffy and white, and made the more outlandish by the addition of sparkling rhinestones along its rim, and a red gemstone at its peaked center on his forehead. He wore three rings on his right hand: one of agate (index finger), one of onyx (ring finger), and one of turquoise (pinkie); all oval, all large, all adding to his imposing presence. He needed only to have worn a white flowing robe to have fit the image of some antique rajah. There he was, in Lancaster,

Pennsylvania; a transplant from the opposite side of the world, speaking English with a thick Indian accent and cheerfully offering me his assistance.

We sat in his office, he behind his desk and I beside it. "So, let me show you what we have," he said, and produced a huge three-ring binder filled with laminated color photographs of his company's offerings. Most of them were already familiar to me from his company's website. Nevertheless he flipped through the pages one by one and talked up the excellence of the designs, all of which were more or less conventional and based on religious themes or natural objects. There were headstones in the shape of diamonds or triangles or parallelograms, their surfaces matte or sheen, incised with crucifixes, Stars of David, or Islamic crescents. There were kneeling angels holding out their hands as though pleading for mercy, or standing with heads bowed as they sorrowfully clutched at their hearts. Some designs—clearly aimed at a Chinese clientele—had upward-swooping edges like the roofs of a pagoda. still others had ornamental elements reflecting the interest of the deceased: for instance, a guitar or piano if he had been a musician, or a stethoscope if he had been a doctor, and there were about a dozen in the extra-wide variety for spouses who wished to lie side-by-side.

There were over a hundred designs in that thick binder. I silently looked on as he flipped through one laminated page after another. When he had reached the last one, he asked:

"Do you see anything you like?"

"Well," I replied, "no one can say that you don't have a large selection. But I have to tell you—and please don't think I'm bragging about this—I have a lot of experience with headstones."

"Oh?"

"You can't imagine how many I've seen in my day. Hundreds—thousands. Maybe even tens of thousands."

"Really?"

"Your headstones are very good, very interesting. But in all honesty, Mr. Mohindra, I can't say that any of them would make the impression that I'm aiming for."

"And what kind of impression would that be?"

"Frankly? The envy of the cemetery."

He leaned back a little and with a faint smile looked at me uncertainly, as though trying to figure out whether I had just tried to be humorous. In another moment however he understood how serious I was when I continued:

"I've already bought my plot at a place called Serenity Meadows Memorial Park—nice name, don't you think?—and it's in a prime location, in one highest points of the landscape there. Naturally whatever gets put there will be visible from a long way off, so I want to make sure it's worth seeing. I want it to be very big and very tall. I want it to be something which will leave a lasting impression."

He took a deep breath and shook his head a little—the rhinestones of his turban sparkled—in wonder at how much thought I had put into the matter, and uttered a single word:

"Wow."

"Yes. You see how seriously I take all this."

"I think I do," he said, nodding affirmatively, the rhinestones sparkling away.

"So I have to have something really special,

something you've probably never made before."

"I see. That's ... a pretty tall order."

"Literally."

He looked down on the binder full of headstone photographs, tapping on it with the fingers of his right hand; thinking, thinking; and finally said:

"Well, you're right: you won't find anything like that here. What you want is something custom-made."

"I would think so."

"And you want it to be large."

"Very."

"Interesting.... Let me think ..."—and so he did, sitting there, slightly nodding to himself as he considered whatever it was he was considering, till he finally turned his dark eyes to me and said, "I might be able to help you." He got up from behind his desk and stepped around it. There was something hopeful or knowing in his eyes and smile as he said, "Follow me, please."

We left his office and the building in which it was located and walked some hundred feet away to his company's warehouse, a large, steel-sided structure which contained the raw blocks of granite from which the headstones were cut. As we entered it through a steel sliding door which was partly open, he explained to me that his partner, Mr. Meyers, was responsible for buying the company's raw materials. Twice a year he journeyed to Canadian quarries looking for the best granite at the best prices, and he always came back with a "great haul," the latest of which had been delivered only four weeks earlier. It was there, in the warehouse, lying on dozens of pallets covered in dusty tarpaulins. Many were stacked atop one another and rose into great hulking entities twenty feet tall and weighing dozens of tons. We walked to the far side of the building where most of the wall consisted of a sliding door, now shut, but which, when open, was wide enough to accommodate the passage of forklifts which unloaded tractor trailers. Here, to one side, on the cement floor, and again covered in tarpaulin, lay a bulk some twenty-five feet long and three or four feet in depth and width. Mr. Mohindra went to one end of the it, took up the tarpaulin, and, holding it tightly, dragged it away.

Really, if someone, or some higher power, had been able to plumb my most secret and cherished hopes and presented them to me in their fullest realization, I could not have been more delighted than by the stone thus revealed. Even with its roughened edges, even with the gouge-marks visible from the machines which had quarried it, or from the power tools used by workmen to reduce it to its general shape, its irregular scarred surface displayed lovely striations of pink and white in which crystalline veins glinted like streaks of diamond. I knew that it was meant to be mine—mine in some absolute, mystical way. For consider the impossible odds by which it and I had come together! It had lain in the heart of a mountain for countless eons, for a stretch of time so unimaginably long that the face of the planet had changed, that species of animals had come and gone, that empires had arisen and declined, that mankind itself had evolved from out of half-brutal creatures;—and through all that time and change the stone had remained constant, silent, hidden away till the moment when the might

of great machines had exposed it, wrenching it free
from the mountain's grip, transporting it to a distant
place, that one place out of thousands where I had
gone and happened to find it. For almost a minute I
walked back and forth before it, tears almost coming
to my eyes, so entirely was it the one thing needful:
the matrix containing the perfect polished thing
meant to bear my name for the next several hundred
years. I turned to Mr. Mohindra and said, "I'll take
it."

"What's that?"

"I'll take it."

"What do you mean? You're only looking for one
headstone, aren't you? This is for several."

"No, sir, I am not looking for just a headstone. I
am looking for a *monument*—something bigger and
more imposing than a headstone. And this is it. I'd
like it to be made into an obelisk."

"An ob—"—he didn't finish the word; he was
speechless for a few seconds. Then, "But ... the
whole thing? It's twenty-two feet long."

"Too bad it's not thirty-two."

"But..." He shook his head, and his rhinestones
sparkled furiously. He put a hand to his mouth,
thoughtfully, his eyes shifting a few times between
me and the stone. "Let's go back into the office and
talk about this," he said.

He was silent and contemplative on our way back
to his office. He seemed to disapprove of my choice
of the stone. Once we had again sat down however
he indicated that his "concern" was whether or not
his company could manipulate so big a piece of granite. They had made obelisks before, but only short
ones, no more than three or four feet high. But this

was a very different matter. He mentioned again the difficulties of working with something so large and heavy, and continued:

"The labor would be very expensive too. We're talking about a lot of work here. It's got to be carefully chiseled into the rough shape and then more carefully pared down to finer surfaces. That takes time. And then you can't just stick something that tall and heavy into the earth because in time it would sink or topple over;—it would require a base, a pedestal, and that'll add to the cost. I don't know right now how much it would cost—I'd need some time to work that out—but if I had to give an estimate I'd say we're talking somewhere around ...." As though he couldn't even bring himself to utter the price, he took his pen from his pocket, jotted down a figure on a pad, and turned this around for me to see.

It was enormous. Even I hadn't figured it would cost that much. I wondered if he had come up with a wildly inflated figure for the sake of dissuading me from the purchase, either because, as he had said, the stone was meant for several headstones and he could make more money from it that way, or because his company did not have the expertise to create something so big. But my heart was set on that stone, on the splendid thing it could and must become. Besides, hadn't I worked for it, sacrificed for it, for a lifetime?

As a businessman Mr. Mohindra would naturally be looking to maximize his profits, and if he saw that his enormous estimate hadn't dissuaded me he might have been inclined to raise the price. Therefore I stared at his figure with an open mouth as though I were taken far aback; shifted uncomfortably in my chair; glanced up at him half despairingly, half incredulously; then looked at him disappointedly and said:

"Mr. Mohindra, I wasn't born with a silver spoon in my mouth. I'm a working man, like you. That is *a lot* of money."

"I am sorry," he said, in his thick accent rolling his "r"s. "It is just an estimate. Perhaps ... it wouldn't cost *quite* so much. But I don't see how it could very much less. It is so big—it would take so much time—so much work—you have to understand what's involved ..."

After mowing disapprovingly, even resentfully, and fidgeting a bit more, I shook my head a few times, no, no, no, as though it were quite impossible for me to afford something so expensive. I shifted my eyes down thoughtfully and looked at the floor as though listening to my better self trying to dissuade me from the purchase. Finally, breathing deeply, sighing once or twice with pursed lips, I turned my attention back to Mr. Mohindra with a resigned air and said:

"Meeting your price would represent a big sacrifice I'm not sure I can afford. Can't you do *any* better?"

"I don't know ..."—he was staring down at the figure he had written, shaking his head slowly, doubtfully.

"All right, listen," I said. "I recognize that it's a large stone and might require more than the usual amount of labor. But I do feel it's the right thing for me. If you can keep the price pretty much to your estimate, we can call it a deal."

He hesitated a moment as though he realized he had committed himself to something he was unsure he could provide. "Well, I must say," he responded, "this is unusual. But at least you understand that good things cost money."

"I never thought otherwise."

He let out a breath of relief and said, "That's good to hear. You have no idea how many people come into this showroom and want everything cheap cheap cheap! It gets depressing sometimes. Do you know I actually had someone come in here and tell me he didn't want to spend more than three hundred dollars? Three hundred dollars! I told him he'd have to go somewhere else—maybe a tile store. Mohindra & Meyers doesn't carry junk! We take pride in what we do. That's why a customer like you is so refreshing."

We continued discussing particulars. I insisted that the obelisk be cut into not four but into eight sides, all of them highly polished.

"That's going to add to the cost," Mr. Mohindra said.

"Yes, but not much more," I replied, coolly, rather insistently, hinting that if he tried to price gouge the deal would be off.

We discussed several more points. The obelisk was to rest on a tapering pedestal five feet tall, which in turn would rest on a slab of marble one foot tall and five by five feet long and wide. These two additional components would raise the height of the monument to some thirty feet. I agreed that they would only raise the price "nominally." One face of the pedestal would be engraved, in enduringly deep letters, my name and birth and death dates, and just beneath this would be my epitaph.

"Which is?" Mr. Mohindra asked.

"I haven't written it yet. I have to think about it a little more. I'll send it to you as soon as I compose it."

Before leaving his office I wrote him a check in down payment. Again he was a little surprised at the facility with which I presented him with what, though a small percentage of the overall cost, was still an unusually large sum. He wrote me a receipt and promised to send me a sketch of the monument to be made and pictures of the progress on it once the cutting began.

Perhaps the reader doesn't understand my insistence on my obelisk's specification?—for instance, its polished, multi-faceted design? It's very simple: its surfaces are bound to reflect sunlight in all directions and so look from afar like some kind of high-powered spotlight or beacon, drawing all eyes toward it. Thus while all about me corpses lie indifferent beneath their dull puny headstones, my monument will shine resplendent, a towering point of attraction for the curious.

—All of this took place over a year ago and since then my monument has been created, paid for, and—put in place. Yes, it is already standing at Serenity Meadows on my plot. The president of the cemetery's management company had to be convinced through another personal donation to allow me to carry out this "pre-placement," but I was determined to be able to enjoy it while I could. I've visited it several times, have taken at least a hundred pictures of it, and it makes a good showing from all sectors of the cemetery. I shown these pictures to family and friends and their reaction is always the same: wide eyes and open mouths. Are they envious, astonished, incredulous? Probably a little of all three.

I also composed my epitaph, which is prominently inscribed on the base in lettering engraved deeply enough to be perfectly legible even after the gilding has dissolved:

> Here lies a man who knew
> Always the right thing to do
> So when he dropped dead
> Even his enemies said
> He had a good funeral too.

—Which, I think, is rather smart.

www.ingramcontent.com/pod-product-compliance
Lightning Source LLC
Chambersburg PA
CBHW070634180626
46817CB00006B/2115